Dear Benjamin

Dear Benjamin

Ω1

written by
ID

translated by
HJ

illustrations by
Ereyz

BLOVED PUBLISHING

DEAR BENJAMIN, VOLUME 1

CONTENT ADVISORY:

DEAR BENJAMIN IS RATED MATURE FOR LANGUAGE, SEXUAL CONTENT, INTENSE VIOLENCE, GRAPHIC SEXUAL CONTENT, STRONG LANGUAGE, HORROR, MATURE THEMES, BLOOD, VIOLENCE, NUDITY, SENSUALITY, AND ADULT ACTIVITIES. READER DISCRETION IS ADVISED.

ORIGINALLY PUBLISHED UNDER THE TITLE 디어 벤자민

FIRST PUBLISHED IN KOREA BY BOOKCUBE NETWORKS CO. LTD.

THIS ENGLISH EDITION IS PUBLISHED BY BLOVED PUBLISHING LLC IN 2025 BY ARRANGEMENT WITH BOOKCUBE NETWORKS CO. LTD. THROUGH RIGHTOL MEDIA (COPYRIGHT@RIGHTOL.COM).

COVER AND INTERIOR ART BY EREYZ

TRANSLATION: HJ

COVER AND INTERIOR DESIGN: ADDIS

COPY EDITOR: SOFIA

EDITOR-IN-CHIEF: ADDIS

PRINTED IN CANADA

FIRST PRINTING: MAY 2025

TABLE OF CONTENTS

What is Omegaverse?

While each omegaverse is different, the omegaverse is an alternate universe where people have a secondary biological gender in addition to the traditional male and female roles. This system has three main genders: alpha, beta, and omega. These terms are borrowed from animal behavior research, and each gender has distinct characteristics that influence their societal roles. All these characters are fully human and do not shift into animals!

The Three Genders:

Omegas: Omegas are the most vulnerable gender, capable of giving birth regardless of their primary biological sex. Male omegas can get pregnant, just like female omegas. Omegas experience monthly heats, during which they become extremely fertile and release pheromones that attract alphas. Due to their perceived weakness and low fertility rates, omegas are often marginalized in society.

Alphas: Alphas are the dominant gender in society, often seen as leaders. They have a knot at the base of their penis, which inflates during intercourse with an omega, ensuring a secure "dam" to increase the chance of pregnancy. Alphas can mark their mates through a bite on the neck, creating a lifelong bond.

Betas: Betas are the most "normal" and populous gender, making up around 70% of the population. They don't experience heats or ruts, and they don't have the heightened pheromones that alphas and omegas possess. While they can still form relationships with other genders, they don't participate in the more animalistic aspects of Omegaverse dynamics.

Recessive alphas and omegas: Recessive alphas and omegas spend most of their lives believing they are betas until they eventually present as an alpha or omega. Due to their recessive traits, their pheromones are usually weaker, and their heat cycles or ruts are often uncontrollable even with suppressants—or they may not experience them at all.

Key Terms:

Pheromones: Unique odors emitted by only alphas and omegas that can be perceived by each other.

Heat Cycle and Ruts: Omegas go into heat, a monthly cycle of intense fertility, while alphas experience ruts—periods of heightened sexual desire often triggered by an omega's heat. These cycles play a significant role in mating and reproduction.

Suppressants: Omegas use suppressants to manage their heats, delaying or stopping the cycle. Overusing suppressants can lead to health problems and issues with the Omega's inner spirit. Some versions of Omegaverse also include rut suppressants for Alphas.

Mark: This is a bite on the neck's scent glands that marks an omega as an alpha's mate. Once marked, an omega cannot bond with another alpha. The bond formed by this mark connects the pair physiologically and sometimes spiritually or emotionally.

Scent Glands and Scenting: Scent glands on the neck and wrists release pheromones that convey a person's secondary gender. Scenting is used to mark territory, calm others, or attract mates. Scenting can also be done to objects or people as a sign of affection or protection.

Slick: Omegas produce copious amounts of a sexual fluid called "slick" when they go into heat to make breeding easier. Male omegas often have self-lubricating anuses.

Prologue

Huff! Huff! Huff!

Ragged breaths formed into wisps of white in the cold night air. A man tore through the darkness, sweat dripping down his jaw as his soaked shirt clung tightly to his heaving chest. He didn't stop running. He *could not*.

Bang! Ba-bang!

Explosions echoed in the distance, booming one after another like earth-shattering thunder. It was hell on earth, but his ears barely registered the noise. What mattered now was the state of his body.

Fuck! Of all days!

Profanities spilled haphazardly from his chapped lips, his breath hitching with desperation. His body was feverish, hotter than he'd ever felt in his twenty-seven years of life, but he kept running. Darkness threatened to swallow him as he veered toward a solitary building in the distance.

An old, rundown warehouse.

It was situated some distance away from the noise. He knew it wasn't safe but it was his only option.

Crack!

He kicked open the door, relieved that it held together despite its dilapidated state. He slipped inside and quickly shut the door behind him, his eyes darting around, scanning his surroundings.

Thankfully, the warehouse was empty. Considering the chaos outside, it seemed unlikely anyone else would hide here.

Another explosion echoed in the distance, yet the man felt an unsettling detachment from everything. Remaining on high alert, he moved cautiously through the shadowy warehouse, eyes scanning every corner with unwavering vigilance.

The space was cluttered with piles of hay, old farm equipment, and a jumble of forgotten junk. It was far from ideal, but it seemed safe for now. He quickly crouched among the haystacks, positioning himself beneath a cracked window through which a thin beam of moonlight spilled.

Much like the door, the window was old and battered; its glass, clouded with grime and scarred by a jagged crack, seemed ready to shatter at the faintest tremor. Still, it was an escape route if things went south, and he relied on the dim light to inspect the pills he'd pulled from his pocket.

In his trembling hand lay a mix of pills—suppressants. The dim light blurred the pills into indistinct shapes, making it impossible to tell their color or form—they were nothing more than smudged shadows resting in his palm. But it didn't matter; he didn't have time to sort them out. Desperation clawed at him as he tossed all the pills into his mouth, swallowing them in one go. The uncontrollable heat surging through his body distorted his vision and clouded his judgment. Breathless, he waited, praying for relief.

But it didn't come.

If anything, his fever was worsening, like an unrelenting fire consuming his veins.

"Shit!" he cursed under his breath.

The suppressants weren't working—none of them. He'd brought a variety as a precaution, but all proved utterly ineffective. Panic ignited as his breaths quickened, each inhale fueling the fire within him, like a furnace roaring with every desperate gasp.

He had spent his entire life believing he was a beta. But when he came of age at nineteen, everything changed. He unexpectedly presented as a recessive omega—a revelation that shattered his world. It was unthinkable, a secret he couldn't let anyone discover.

Thankfully, his recessive status gave him a fragile sense of security.

Though he presented as an omega, his pheromones were faint, barely more potent than when he was a beta. A single pill taken once a month had been enough to keep his omega status hidden. He had lived among alphas without their pheromones ever affecting him, and he had never experienced a heat cycle—until now.

If only it had stayed that way.

His first heat cycle was hitting him with full force, and it couldn't have come at a worse time. In a final, desperate attempt, he swallowed the last of his pills before curling into himself as the searing heat raged through him.

He couldn't believe this was happening. It was the worst-case scenario—a nightmare beyond anything he had ever imagined. It couldn't get any shittier than this. Grinding his teeth in frustration, he struggled against the relentless heat waves, but his body refused to obey.

The heat grew more unbearable with each passing moment. Sweat poured off him like rain, soaking his clothes. His vision blurred until everything around him became a hazy, indistinguishable fog. The pressure between his legs was unbearable—his cock was so hard it strained painfully against the front of his pants, the pressure so intense that the seams looked ready to give way. His underwear was already sopping wet with precum.

The man trembled, his breath ragged as he fought the overwhelming tide of heat consuming him. Panic clawed at his chest—if the alphas outside caught even a trace of his scent, it would be over. Desperation overtook him as he yanked down his pants, his mind clouded by primal need. His hand gripped himself tightly, the cold touch against his fevered flesh sending a shudder through his body. Broken gasps and curses escaped his lips, raw and unrestrained.

His moans echoed through the warehouse; his strokes became frantic, his breath escaping in hot, ragged gasps. The rhythmic slap of flesh against flesh filled the air, blending with the moans that escaped his throat, growing louder and more desperate with each passing moment. The two sounds seemed to merge in perfect sync.

Time slipped away as his mind dissolved into a murky haze, swirling with the intensity of a hurricane. He clamped his other hand over his mouth, stifling a loud moan as he climaxed, hot semen spilling over his palm and fingers. But the relief was momentary; the hunger within him surged with renewed ferocity, a relentless, insatiable tide that only grew more excruciating and unbearable.

This wasn't enough.

This feeling, this overwhelming need—it wasn't something he could satisfy with his hand.

The inside of his ass was slick, overflowing with watery fluid, becoming unbearably needy. He had never been with a man; he never even *thought* about being with another man before and had spent his entire life pretending to be a beta. But an omega was an omega, and his heat-ridden body craved more. The realization hit him like a ton of bricks, sinking in as his brow unfurled, forcing him to acknowledge it for the first time. It devastated him, but what was more devastating was how helpless he felt as his body heated up, turned on against his will.

Is this what a heat cycle feels like? Now he understood why omegas would throw themselves at alphas when they forgot to take their suppressants. The realization made him curse, but deep down, he couldn't escape the truth. Some part of him secretly longed for one of the alphas outside to catch his scent, track him down, and end this unbearable torment.

His body felt like a cruel joke, betraying him at every turn. If this went on, he feared he might throw open the door and crawl into the chaos himself. He had to do something—anything—before it got that far. Despite the anger and resentment simmering inside, he reached back, his hand trembling as it moved toward his ass.

Shuddering, his thoughts scattered and unfocused, he spread his cheeks. It was his first time using his body this way to satisfy his desires, and he groaned with effort as he awkwardly eased a finger inside. Tight as it was, the slickness eased the discomfort, making the intrusion bearable. Yet, no matter how deeply he prodded or how many fingers he used, it was never enough.

His frustration boiled over, a hot breath escaping his lips as his flushed face pressed against the rough floor. Quiet, desperate whimpers slipped from him as his trembling fingers worked feverishly. Yet, the searing ache only intensified, an insatiable fire consuming him and dragging him perilously close to the edge of madness.

"Someone…help…" he begged, his voice trembling, his tear-filled eyes pleading for mercy.

As if answering his desperate plea, a flicker of movement caught his eye—a shadow shifting just beyond the edges of his vision. A voice broke through the haze, rich with amusement and mockery, "Wow, this is great. You're really turning me on."

The omega's eyes snapped open in shock.

Was it a ghost? No—it couldn't be.

The omega froze, his skin turning deathly pale as if doused in icy water, his fingers still buried deep inside himself. He hadn't even had the chance to withdraw them before the gravity of his situation came crashing down, rendering him motionless and exposed.

Even though his senses struggled to catch up, he was sure there had been no sign of anyone else when he entered the warehouse.

Unbeknownst to him, the large warehouse had a second story—not a full level, but a shadowy balcony tucked away in the darkness. He hadn't noticed it before, but now someone stood there, leaning casually over the railing, watching him with unsettling calm.

"Go on. I want to see more." The voice was relaxed, laced with a casual amusement that clashed sharply with the gravity of the moment.

Then, a powerful wave of alpha pheromones hit the omega, leaving his body trembling uncontrollably. The sudden presence of the alpha, combined with the suffocating pheromones, shoved him to the brink of panic.

"An alpha?"

"You're only just figuring that out?" The figure smirked, his tone mocking. "Even with your pheromones suppressed, how could an omega in heat not notice an alpha? Are you even a proper omega?"

The alpha chuckled at the absurdity of the situation, his amusement cutting through the tension like a knife. The omega found no humor in the situation. He was overwhelmed by an onslaught of alpha pheromones so intense and all-encompassing that it eclipsed anything he had ever encountered. The sheer potency left him gasping for air.

His usual regimen of suppressants had rendered his pheromones nearly nonexistent, shielding him from the effects of alpha pheromones. On the rare occasions he did catch a hint of them, it was never enough to overwhelm him or make him lose control.

But this—this was different. The alpha's scent was so powerful it clouded his vision, pressing down on him with an almost physical, suffocating weight. He had never encountered an alpha like this before.

What was it about *this* man?

The strength of the pheromones gnawed at his senses, smothering him and leaving him utterly paralyzed.

The omega curled his trembling body into a tight ball. Whatever faint stirrings of desire he'd felt earlier were nothing compared to the tidal wave of lust that surged through him now. It was terrifying. His fingers shook uncontrollably, his stomach clenched, and heat surged through his body as if he were being consumed by fire.

"Go on. Or shall I make you?" The alpha's voice sliced through the haze, each word accompanied by a surge of pheromones that grew even more potent, wrapping around the omega like an unrelenting, invisible shroud.

Overwhelmed, he writhed on the ground, unable to withstand the pressure.

"N-No more…" he begged, his voice trembling. The flood of pheromones consumed him completely. His untouched cock throbbed, precum sliding down in betraying evidence of his body's surrender. His eyes rolled back as unbearable waves of ecstasy overtook him. Slick gushed down his thighs, soaking his trembling form in his own fluids. The overwhelming sensations wracked his body, driving uncontrollable, sobbing moans from his lips.

"Quite a reaction. Not bad."

The omega gasped desperately for air, his chest heaving as he fought for control.

"Who knew I'd find an omega in heat in a place like this?" the alpha mused, his voice dripping with amusement. He leaned casually against the balcony railing, his piercing gaze fixed on the trembling, writhing figure below. Then, with a heavy thud, he leaped from the balcony. He landed with unnerving grace despite the impact, a cloud of dust rising around him as he straightened.

The omega barely managed to lift his bleary eyes. The room was too dark to make out the alpha's face, but he could see his boots—polished to an immaculate sheen, untouched by the dust that had begun to settle around them.

The alpha sauntered closer, his eyes never leaving the omega sprawled helplessly on the ground. Dropping to one knee, he tilted his head, his piercing gaze sharp and unrelenting. "What do you think? This is no place for an omega in heat, right?"

As faint moonlight filtered into the warehouse, it illuminated the alpha's face, casting a soft glow over golden locks that seemed to shimmer in the dark. For a fleeting moment, the omega's heat-fueled haze faltered. His wide, glassy eyes froze in recognition, his lips parting in silent shock.

"Oh? That look on your face—it's almost like you know me."

The omega groaned weakly as the heavy pheromones surged again, overwhelming him anew. Whatever clarity he'd gained from recognizing the alpha's face vanished instantly, replaced by uncontrollable need. Despite having come twice, his cock stiffened once more, betraying him yet again.

The alpha's hand reached out, his grip firm as he lifted the omega's chin, forcing their gazes to meet.

"But I don't recognize your face at all. How unfair," the alpha murmured, his thumb brushing over the omega's dirty cheek. A faint frown tugged at his lips as he realized the grime wouldn't come off. With a look of mild distaste, he wiped his soiled thumb on his pants.

"Never mind about your face," he whispered, leaning closer until their breaths mingled. "Do you want me to fuck you?"

The words were daring, deceptively sweet—a promise laced with dominance, spoken so softly it felt intimate.

The omega swallowed dryly, the sound audible in the heavy silence. His trembling body flared with need, the fire inside him impossible to extinguish. He couldn't afford to refuse—anyone who could soothe the unbearable ache was welcome, even this alpha.

He nodded, his desperation evident in the slight, frantic motion.

In an instant, the alpha yanked the omega's pants and briefs down from where they had bunched around his knees. He let his hand glide over the omega's thick thighs, his touch deliberate and slow. When his fingers made contact with the omega's round, dripping ass, he gave it a firm squeeze, eliciting a sharp gasp.

"Too bad. I prefer to play rough—like a beast."

"That's…fine…" The omega swallowed the rest of the words, *Just fuck me,* forcing them back down. But the alpha's lazy, knowing chuckle made it clear he already understood.

"Of course, you're in heat. It's strange, though—how faint your pheromones are for an omega in this state. But somehow, that only makes me want you more."

Desperation overtook him. Trembling hands reached out, clutching at the fabric of the alpha's pants. "Please, h-hurry…do something…"

The alpha's dark gaze sharpened, a predatory intensity gleaming in his eyes. "Turn around and spread your ass."

The command hit with the full force of his dominance. It wasn't just his tone; it was the raw power of his nature and the authority he exuded so effortlessly. The omega clenched his teeth as he complied, shame and anticipation warring within him. Turning around, he raised his ass, his trembling body quaking under the weight of the alpha's presence. Any lingering humiliation was drowned out by the burning, all-consuming need that overtook him.

The omega's vision blurred as the massive girth stretched him.

"Hold on tight. Or you might end up in pieces," the alpha warned.

The omega's mouth fell open, his breath coming in ragged, warm gasps as saliva trickled down his chin. He was on the verge of losing his mind, uncontrollable sobs wracking his body as he pressed his forehead against the grimy ground, completely overwhelmed.

Despite having never been with a man, his body seemed to respond as if it were made for this. His ass, soft and yielding, took the alpha's enormous cock with surprising ease. The alpha, too, was driven by relentless need, his cock thrusting in and out, his own climaxes adding to the chaos. He lost count of how many times he had come, his body overwhelmed by the sensations.

In no time, his lower half turned into an even bigger mess.

The wet slaps of flesh meeting flesh filled the space with a lewd rhythm. The man could barely remember the chaos outside;

the alpha's deep thrusts stretched and filled him, every movement pushing him further into ecstatic delirium. Even his moans sounded desperate.

"More…Deeper…" The man pleaded, his voice trembling as he shook his hips, wanting *more* in his ass. Each time the alpha paused, he wiggled his hips, the need coursing through him unbearable. He grasped his leaking cock, stroking it furiously as he begged for more with every ragged breath.

"Amazing. I've heard an omega in heat is irresistible, but I never imagined it was this intense," the alpha remarked. "You're making me lose control."

The omega could only moan and sob in response.

The alpha's relentless thrusts were driving both of them to the edge. His lust-filled gaze sent shivers through the man's entire body, heightening his arousal. With each powerful thrust, the omega's body shook violently, his toes curling in pleasure, guttural sounds escaping from his open mouth. It still wasn't enough. The alpha's unyielding pace pushed the man further into a frenzy, compelling him to beg for more.

I'm crazy, the omega thought vacantly, his hand tangled in the alpha's golden hair. The alpha's mouth was relentless on his already swollen nipple, and he clenched around the alpha's cock as if he were desperate to devour it.

"You…Where did you learn to wriggle and grind on my cock like that?" The alpha's frown was accompanied by the teasing roll of his tongue over a sensitive nipple. The omega wasn't inexperienced, but this alpha was his first, and admitting it was pointless.

"Stop talking…just fuck me…" The omega's breath was ragged, his voice desperate.

The alpha's low laugh reverberated through the room as he tightened his grip on the man's firm thighs. "Don't move. Just stay here."

Gasps and moans filled the air. "More, more…"

"I'll fuck you as much as you want, whenever you want," the alpha promised, showing no sign of fatigue despite hours of relentless thrusting without pause. The man's mind had become a haze of satisfaction, his remaining senses solely focused on the pleasure coursing through him.

Each greedy shake of his hips created a lewd, fleshy sound, and his cock sprayed out semen uncontrollably. Even without the alpha touching his cock, he continued to spill. His naked body was slick with sweat and fluids, the floor beneath him soaked. The man shook his head, sobbing at the intensity of it all.

"You're out of your mind. Is it that good?"

"Good, it's good, so…" he let out a guttural groan, "Don't stop, more—" His groaning whimper cut off his pleas.

The alpha laughed, a dark sound of satisfaction as he looked down at the man's delirious, ruined state. He gripped the man's thighs more tightly, spreading them further, his movements taking on a frightening intensity as he pounded into him with a primal fervor. The man's clouded eyes drank in the sight, his hips twisting at a sudden upward thrust.

"Fuck, why is it so good?" The alpha's voice was rough, mingled with the sounds of his harsh bites on the nape of the man's neck, leaving red marks behind. True to his warning, the alpha ravaged the man like a beast. His savage approach was just as evident in the lewd noises of his relentless thrusting.

"Ah, seriously, I'm going insane!" The alpha, teeth gritted, wrenched the man's waist, a crease forming on his smooth forehead. The man below instinctively knew the alpha was about to come and lifted his legs, wrapping them around the alpha's waist and contracting his inner walls to squeeze his cock.

Even in his haze, the omega didn't realize he was squeezing, but the alpha responded with a guttural moan, his control breaking. And then, deep inside him, a scorching wetness gushed forth.

His moan was harsh, taking his very breath with it. The sensation of semen flooding his stomach was stark—his lower belly tightened, and a thrill shot through his entire body. The man groaned breathlessly and instinctively hugged the alpha's back.

The alpha had already come inside him numerous times without pulling out, but the red-hot sensitivity of his inner walls made this release feel almost chilling. Tremors wracked his body, and he buried his face in the alpha's shoulder, gasping out heated breaths.

Then, the base of the alpha's cock, still embedded within him, began to swell. The alpha, who had been nibbling at the man's nape, swore softly, his voice laced with surprise, "Shit!"

Both men were momentarily stunned by the unexpected development.

Knotting…?

The alpha's cock, already stretched to its limit inside him, began to swell even further, causing a sharp cry of pain to escape the omega's mouth. The intense pressure made his inner walls feel like they might tear apart. He couldn't hide the agony on his face and clung desperately to the alpha.

Knotting was a phenomenon exclusive to alphas. Like canines, the base of their cocks swelled to prevent the semen from leaking out. He had heard about it but never imagined he would experience it firsthand. His breaths came in short, ragged bursts as he stared at the alpha.

"Don't blame me too much. It's your fault for exciting me too much." The alpha chuckled awkwardly, noting the omega's pained expression. Though his attempt at reassurance was hollow, he added, "This is a first for me, too."

Just how long did he have to stay like this? When would this knotting thing end? The man's limbs trembled as the intense pleasure gave way to an overwhelming pain. Cold sweat trickled down his face. He struggled to form harsh words, unable to voice his frustration.

"Bear with it a little longer. This wasn't in my plans; I'm just as surprised as you are."

Tears streamed from his wide-open eyes, and his face became blotchy and red. The alpha, breathing heavily, lifted his hand to wipe the man's wet face. As he cleaned away the sweat and tears, a flash of curiosity crossed his eyes at the sight of the man's pale skin.

"Now that we're like this, I want to see your face even more," the alpha said, his voice tinged with regret as he continued to caress the man's wet face. But the man was beyond hearing him. Overwhelmed by the searing pain in his stomach and anus, he could only whimper.

His mind couldn't process the whirlwind of sensations and emotions. He gritted his teeth and eventually blacked out.

Chapter 1

As the clock neared ten, the street outside the window was dark and quiet. Isaac glanced around his tidied shop, preparing to leave. Downtown San Diego's stores usually closed at nine on weekdays and an hour earlier on weekends. After office hours, the bustling daytime crowds vanished, leaving the area empty and silent.

Tonight was an exception. Isaac had kept his shop open due to a backlog of orders. Normally, he would have closed at nine sharp and gone home, but he needed the extra time to finish his work—rushing was never his style.

He grabbed his bag and made a final check on the flower baskets and potted plants scheduled for delivery the following day. But before he could leave, the doorbell jingled louder than usual. Isaac looked up as three large men pushed their way inside.

"We're closed for the day," Isaac's voice was swallowed by their raucous conversation. Their entrance was so noisy it drowned out Isaac's soft protest.

"See?" The leader of the group chuckled. "What did I say? I told you there had to be a place still open, didn't I?"

Isaac tried again, "We're closed," but his words were again lost in the din. The men continued their loud conversation, ignoring Isaac's attempts to shut them out.

"Hell! There's a place still open this late?"

"Impossible."

"Impossible, my ass. Come on, how much was it? Pay up." The man at the head of the group confidently extended his hand to his hulking companions, cheerfully pocketing the money they provided. His slightly flushed face and the thick scent of alcohol made it clear he was drunk.

A drunkard. How troublesome. Isaac put his bag back down and scratched his cheek. He watched as the man collected a hundred-dollar bill from each of his hulking companions and stuffed the money into his own pocket.

"Well, now that I've got some cash in my pocket, why don't I buy a bouquet to give a pretty miss?" the drunkard said with a smile, making his way over to the counter where Isaac was standing.

Under the bright lights, the drunkard's face came into full view. His messy yet glossy blond hair, deep Prussian blue eyes, sharp nose, and plump, shapely lips painted the picture of someone who could easily be mistaken for a Hollywood star. Not only was he strikingly attractive, but he also towered over his companions. His firm, broad shoulders and bulging muscles were evident even through the casual, rolled-up sleeves of his shirt. Everything about him exuded an air of extraordinary presence.

"A bouquet—"

"I'm sorry, but we're closed for the day." Isaac glanced at the drunkard's handsome face before firmly stating his hours. The drunkard tilted his head, clearly confused.

One of the men, who had been scowling ever since losing his hundred-dollar bill, stepped between the drunkard and Isaac, his voice rising in anger, "You think you're funny, huh? What do ya take us for? We're customers! What's this about being closed when yer lights are on, and yer doors are open? Huh? You want to see this place get wrecked?"

Really, how troublesome. Isaac sighed, already sensing trouble when they walked in. Being harassed by this burly man wanting a bouquet was just the last straw.

"Jack."

To Isaac's surprise, the overly attractive drunkard placed a hand on the man threatening him and gently pushed him back. The hulking man snapped his mouth shut. The drunkard then turned to Isaac, offering a radiant, mesmerizing smile—one that oddly reminded him of his flowers.

"See here, florist. How about this? Double for the bouquet. Since there's something called overtime."

Issac was dumbfounded.

"Go make a bouquet worth a hundred, and I'll pay you double that." The drunkard slapped two hundred dollars on the counter, which he had just collected from the men. Behind him, the men sighed in unison, like a background woodwind.

Isaac stared at the crumpled bills on the counter, his annoyance simmering just beneath the surface. If this was how it had to be, so be it.

"Please," he said, his tone clipped but polite, "choose the flowers you want."

The drunkard's smile widened at Isaac's reluctant response, "I'll leave it up to you."

"Is it for a date?"

"Yeah. A cute miss with curly brown hair." The drunkard waved a hand when he saw Isaac reaching for the roses. "Ah, but I despise red roses, so pick something else."

Isaac's hand froze mid-air but quickly recovered. After carefully selecting an assortment of lilies, lisianthuses, carnations, and a few other flowers, he turned to the worktable, his arms full of vibrant blooms.

The drunkard, observing Isaac's selection, moved to a chair near the door and plopped down. The burly man, Jack, who had earlier growled at Isaac, followed him and sat down quietly. Isaac kept an eye on them as he continued trimming the flower stems in silence.

Isaac had dealt with all sorts of unusual situations before, even before he took over the flower shop. A drunkard barging in late at night was hardly a big deal.

While pruning the flowers and trying to ignore his unwelcome guests, the drunkard's voice cut through the silence, "Are you always this stoic?"

Isaac turned his gaze toward him, puzzled by the question. His expression conveyed that he didn't understand its relevance.

"This is a customer service job," the drunkard continued. "Shouldn't you be more pleasant and make small talk with your customers? You lack business acumen."

The drunkard propped his arm on the armrest, resting his chin on his hand, and stared intently at Isaac. His rich blue eyes, deep as ocean trenches, were unsettling and made one instinctively wary.

"I see. I'm afraid I'm not very good with words," Isaac said, averting his eyes as he pulled out a piece of pink and pale purple wrapping paper.

He was about to focus on wrapping the bouquet when the drunkard spoke again, "How are you going to attract customers like that?"

"Maybe he's just really good with flowers," Jack muttered before Isaac could reply,

"Shut up," the drunkard snapped.

Whatever they were on about, Isaac chose not to engage. Wrapping was always the trickiest part. The wrapping paper crackled loudly as he worked, but the process was slow, especially when he was in a rush to get these men out of his shop. He finished the bouquet off with lace and a pink ribbon.

"It's done."

Isaac set the large bouquet on the counter. "Do you need a card?" he asked mechanically. Most customers added a card with a short message. Different kinds of cards were on display, but the drunkard shook his head.

"What am I supposed to do with this?" The drunkard scoffed, taking the bouquet in one hand. He examined it critically, turning it this way and that.

"The flowers are pretty," he said before dropping the hand holding the bouquet and looking at Isaac. His face was unimpressed. "The wrapping is dreadful."

"Are you dissatisfied?"

"What a funny florist you are," the drunkard continued. "How do you expect to make a living running your business like this? You can't even hold a conversation or wrap flowers nicely."

The harsh criticism didn't bother Isaac much; he knew his bouquet-wrapping skills were lacking. Issac considered offering a refund. He regretted the time he'd wasted trying to appease the rude men who had barged in past closing. But he understood the risk—if things didn't go their way, they could easily cause trouble or damage. Reluctantly, he decided to play along.

"Would you like a refund?" Isaac asked, not bothering to explain his bouquet skills. A refund seemed better; making another bouquet would be a bigger hassle.

The two one-hundred-dollar bills still rested on the counter. The drunkard's fingers brushed over them lightly, and for a moment, Isaac thought he might take them back. But instead, the bills slid across the counter toward him. "Keep the money safe. What if some bad guy steals it? It'd be awful if you got robbed on top of all your business struggles."

"Thank you." Isaac was taken aback by the unexpected remark. The drunkard then turned on his heel and tossed the bouquet to Jack. Isaac watched in bewilderment. As the drunkard turned, his arm brushed against a card peeking out from a stack of notebooks on the counter. Naturally, the drunkard's gaze fell on it.

"Dear Benjamin." He read softly, his shapely lips curving into a smile. "Nice handwriting."

Isaac, who had been standing in a daze, snapped back to reality and quickly grabbed the card. The drunkard's gaze followed his movement. The card was small and cute, clearly not something Isaac would have chosen. The drunkard snickered, "A lover? What a tender form of address. Quite unlike you."

"That's none of your business," Isaac said, his placid voice taking on a sharp edge.

"Sure," the drunkard shrugged, but the hulking man behind him wasn't as casual. His glare bore into Isaac, and with a deliberate motion, he drew his finger across his throat in a silent, menacing warning. Isaac chose to ignore the threat and slid the card into a drawer.

"I'm curious now," the drunkard said, stepping back and placing his hands in his pockets. He tilted his head to the side. Before Isaac could ask what he was curious about, the drunkard leaned in and asked in a low voice, "Does Mr. Funny Florist wear the same stoic face during sex?"

The question was unexpected and bordered on sexual harassment. But Isaac's expression remained impassive, almost as if he hadn't heard the question.

"I'm curious to know what kind of sounds you make, what kind of face you make." The drunkard studied Isaac's unflinching face for a moment. When it became clear that no reaction or answer would be given, he shrugged and straightened up. His hand reached for a business card on the counter, plucking it up with casual interest. He turned it over in his fingers, examining it briefly, before his lips curled into a mischievous grin.

"Mr. Isaac the Florist. Thanks for your trouble this late at night." He flicked the business card between his fingers and turned to leave. The doorbell jingled loudly as he exited, just as it had when he first entered. The drunkard walked out, no longer showing any signs of intoxication. He melted into the darkness and disappeared.

Isaac stared at the spot where the drunkard had vanished as if he had been a mirage. Then, out of the corner of his eye, he noticed another hundred-dollar bill quietly placed on the counter. Isaac looked up, breaking free from his thoughts.

It was the third man—the one who had been silent throughout, except for when he lost the bet at the beginning. He looked the

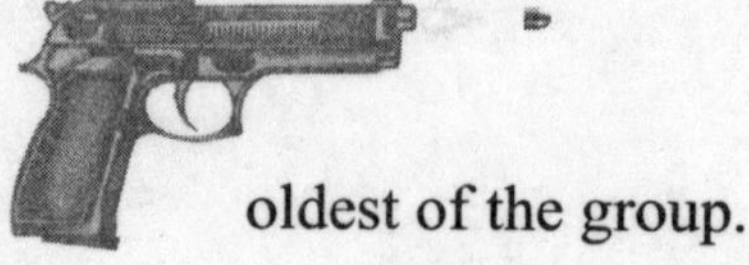

oldest of the group.

"A tip," the man said, his tone polite despite his intimidating appearance. "Thank you for the trouble."

Isaac's mouth hung half-open in bewilderment, but before he could utter a word, the man was gone. In the blink of an eye, the shop was empty.

Isaac glanced down at the bills. Three hundred dollars for a bouquet that was hardly worth a hundred. Was this right? He rubbed his neck in discomfort, then shrugged. It was his overtime pay, after all.

He was exhausted after the unexpected late-night ordeal. A glance at the clock revealed it was nearly eleven. He decided he'd better sleep as soon as he got home.

Chapter 2

The small shop was crammed with all kinds of flowers and plants. Unlike other flower shops, Isaac's was so packed that there was barely any room to walk on the flowerpot-laden floor.

In truth, Isaac preferred trees and potted plants to cut flowers. A cut flower was already dying, its beauty fleeting and bound to fade, no matter how nicely it was wrapped.

On the other hand, a potted plant represents life itself. Though it might end up in a small pot instead of a spacious garden, it was alive, growing tall and green under his care. The more he nurtured it, the more verdant its leaves became and the more vibrant its blossoms. He liked that.

Therefore, he tended to recommend potted plants over bouquets for gifts—like the boat orchid. Of course, it depended on the occasion and the recipient.

"Hey, Mr. Isaac, the Florist."

Isaac froze mid-motion as he moved plants back inside from their sunbathing spot. His eyes fell on spotless luxury boots that stopped beside him. He looked up from the immaculate footwear, following the long, denim-clad legs to a solid chest stretched beneath a gray sweater. Finally, he met a handsome face. A complicated expression crossed his face before smoothing into neutral.

To be greeted this way…he hadn't expected such familiarity. Never mind that. Was this man supposed to be strolling around San Diego like this? Isaac lowered the plant he'd been carrying and straightened his posture, doubts clouding his thoughts. "You've come again."

The man's smile widened, clearly pleased with Isaac's

grudging acknowledgment. His gold-spun hair fell casually over his forehead, fluttering in the breeze—a beautiful sight. "You remember?"

Issac paused before replying, "You're very good-looking."

"Wow! Is that a compliment, Mr. Florist?"

The man exaggerated his delight, raising his arms as if celebrating. Whether his enthusiasm was genuine, Isaac couldn't tell. He dusted off his apron and led the man into the shop. The man followed willingly.

Jack wasn't present today. Only the silent man who had left a tip was present.

"What is it that you're looking for today?" Isaac asked as he began to move around the counter.

Click. The metallic sound of a gun being cocked sent an unpleasant chill to his temple. Isaac resisted the urge to reach for it, instead shifting his gaze toward the man. He looked as charming as ever, his sunny smile in place—even as he pressed the cold muzzle of a Glock to Isaac's temple.

"You know me, don't you?"

Despite being asked with a smile, the question had an unmistakable edge. Isaac swallowed dryly and kept his gaze straight ahead, taking in the crowded mess of flowers and plants that filled the shop.

"If you are the famous Felix Felice, I've seen you in the newspaper." Isaac's response was plain and straightforward; there was no room for excuses in this situation. Felix's eyes widened in surprise, then he burst out laughing.

"You really knew? I wasn't sure." Felix's disappointment was palpable as he exaggeratedly shrugged and removed the gun from Isaac's temple. The silent man behind him stepped forward, extending his hand. Clicking his tongue, Felix slapped a hundred-dollar bill into the man's palm. "I never win against Tony in these bets."

"It's because you severely lack awareness."

"My level of awareness is just fine. It's yours that's too high."

Tony shot the grumbling Felix a withering look before shaking his head and tucking the bill into his wallet. Isaac swallowed back a sigh, bewildered by their antics.

What was going on? Holding someone at gunpoint, gambling...

Was this really Felix Felice? While his strikingly beautiful features matched the rumors, his behavior was far from what Isaac had expected. He wasn't the kind of person to be walking around carelessly on a busy street.

Felix Felice, a notorious arms dealer, was known for his ruthless and dangerous nature. An Italian-American in his mid-thirties, he had amassed enormous wealth and power through black-market weapon manufacturing and sales. As a man with the grit and means to succeed in this deadly line of work, he was ruthless and dangerous, on par with the mafia. Rumor had it that his grandfather was an executive in the infamous Italian mafia, Cosa Nostra, though this remained unconfirmed.

With multiple groups, including the FBI and CIA, pursuing him, Isaac couldn't understand how he was able to walk around so openly. Had there been some kind of agreement? Felix had been hiding for the past four years, making his current behavior all the more confusing.

As Isaac was lost in thought, Felix lifted his chin with long fingers, guiding his gaze upward to meet those piercing, deep blue eyes. A playful glint danced in them as Felix smirked. "Anyway, I wonder what the newspaper said about me?"

It wasn't like Isaac had anything to hide. "Four years ago, your secret base on a small island in South America was uncovered. The CIA led an investigation but found nothing. You were arrested but ultimately acquitted." Isaac laid it out plainly. Felix cocked his head.

"You know a lot about me. The CIA went through shit because

of me. Well, I went through a lot of shit because of that, too." Felix snickered as if he were chatting about petty gossip, but Isaac couldn't help but notice that the playful glint had disappeared from his eyes.

His hold on Isaac's chin tightened, causing a dull ache. "And is that all?"

Issac remained silent.

"Is that all you know about me?"

For a moment, Isaac lost himself in thought, gazing into Felix's blue eyes. He also knew that Felix Felice, the notorious arms dealer, was a rare hyper-dominant alpha—a man whose natural charisma, competence, and striking looks made him a constant subject of gossip, often hailed as the playboy of the century. However, Isaac saw no need to mention this to him.

"That is all."

Felix smiled with narrowed eyes. "You recognized me from just a news article?"

"As I said, you're very good-looking." Felix's face was far too distinctive for someone in his dangerous line of work, though he seemed blissfully unaware of this inconvenient truth. Felix hummed thoughtfully, studying Isaac with lingering suspicion.

"So, you knew who I was from the start and still played innocent?" Felix's thumb brushed against Isaac's chin, just below his bottom lip. Isaac desperately wanted to pull away from the provocative touch, but the memory of the earlier gunpoint threat kept him frozen in place, so he stayed still.

"A customer is a customer," Isaac replied. "It's not as if I can do anything about it."

"What a strange guy. You have some guts." Felix laughed. "How can you be so churlish?"

"That's just my personality."

Felix's smiling face tensed strangely, "Have we met

somewhere?"

"A week ago, you came in here late at night and purchased a bouquet," Isaac deadpanned.

Felix's deep gaze seemed to pierce through him.

"That's right," he muttered before sharply turning around.

Isaac rubbed his sore chin after being released from his iron grip.

"Make me another bouquet today," Felix said casually, placing his order without even looking at Isaac.

Isaac was still rooted in place. "That's all you're asking for?"

"Yeah, so?" His simple answer, along with his sidelong glance, was so innocent it left Isaac dumbfounded. As though he sensed his confusion, Felix continued in a leisurely tone. "My friend over there, Tony, was talking big, saying he was sure you knew me. He's usually very good at picking up on things I miss, you know?"

Issac didn't reply.

"So, I questioned you."

Was Felix demanding to know if Isaac recognized him just for a bet? Holding him at gunpoint to get an answer felt absurd. The more Isaac thought about it, the more ridiculous it seemed. But getting upset with Felix Felice, a man whose notoriety far surpassed that of an average mafia member, would do him no good.

"If my approach was too harsh, I apologize. It's rare for ordinary people to recognize me, so I was surprised."

"Did you think I was FBI or CIA?"

"Or some other sort," Felix added nonchalantly. His dark eyes swept over Isaac from head to toe. "For a florist, you're awfully bad at making bouquets. Suspiciously so."

Isaac met the rude gaze and sighed before asking, "And that was the conclusion you came to? Do you think I disguised myself as a florist to track you down?"

"I don't know," Felix said with a dismissive shrug. His nonchalant tone and carefree demeanor made it clear he wasn't taking the situation seriously. "For now, you just seem like an odd florist who can't make a decent bouquet to save his life. Or maybe I'm just hoping you're not tangled up in this mess."

"It's true. I'm just an ordinary florist who has trouble gift-wrapping flowers."

"We'll see about that."

"We'll see." Isaac had no choice but to repeat his words and be done with it.

Felix leaned on the counter, his grin widening, his eyes curving to help form a million-dollar smile. It was striking, but it only made Isaac more uneasy. In truth, Felix didn't genuinely suspect that Isaac had deliberately approached him—most people lacked the courage to do so. Felix had been the one to intrude on the small shop, and he knew Isaac was just an ordinary citizen. He was simply enjoying the opportunity to tease him.

"You'd better hope you're an ordinary florist."

"I am, so I can't really hope for more."

Felix's eyebrows creased. He glared at Isaac before ordering, "Just make the damn bouquet."

Isaac felt a rush of tiredness and dragged a hand over his face. "Didn't you say you dislike my wrapping?"

"A guy who claims he's just an ordinary florist but can't even make a proper bouquet? Well, I might as well make him practice."

Issac didn't know what to say.

"Oh, and pick flowers with more class this time. It's for a date." Felix propped an arm on the counter and rested his chin on his hand, adopting the guise of an ordinary customer. With no other options, Isaac trudged over to the flower baskets.

"The counter is a mess. What's all this junk?" Felix muttered, his chin resting on his propped hand. The counter was cluttered with notes and cards scattered about. Felix's eyes scanned the mess and settled on a specific spot.

"Dear Benjamin." The words slipped from his lips with a lazy drawl. The words were the same as before—the same opening line.

Isaac dropped the flowers he was holding and hurried behind the counter to snatch the card away. Once again, he quickly stashed it in a drawer.

"Who is it that you're always writing to so sweetly?"

Issac ignored him.

"Are you in some kind of long-distance relationship?" Felix's grin widened, his curiosity evident as he continued to watch Isaac. "Then why would you write in a card instead of a letter?"

Isaac, refusing to engage, turned his back and resumed selecting flowers. Felix's gaze remained fixed on him, undeterred.

"'Benjamin.' Is he really your lover?"

"Would you prefer pink or beige?"

"It's definitely a man's name, but you're a beta. Are you gay?"

"Beige and yellow may be suitable if you want something classy and elegant."

"Surely you're not an omega, right?"

In the endless back-and-forth of mismatched questions and answers, Isaac's hand trembled ever so slightly among the flowers, a motion so subtle it was nearly invisible.

"Because omegas grind my gears," Felix said softly, a dark edge in his voice, his mesmerizing smile unwavering.

"Fortunately, the calla lilies are beautiful and fresh today. I'll make them the centerpiece of your bouquet," Isaac said calmly, meeting Felix's gaze. Thankfully, Felix didn't press further with his borderline harassing questions. The shop fell into a tense silence as Isaac worked.

Felix remained silent throughout Isaac's time at the work

table. When the bouquet was finally ready, Felix's criticism came swiftly. "The wrapping is still terrible," he said, pulling a couple hundred-dollar bills from his wallet. "This is why I keep doubting you. I'd almost prefer carrying the flowers unwrapped."

"That's too much money. If you're unhappy with the wrapping, I'll give it to you free of charge."

Felix ignored Isaac's protest and slapped the bills onto the counter. "I ordered the bouquet. No matter how bad the wrapping is, I still need to pay you for the flowers and your effort. Do you think I'd stiff you over a measly bouquet? And, as I said, it's for practice."

Issac could only stare at Felix.

"This will cover whatever the flowers cost; the rest is your tip. Do with it what you will." Felix grumbled in displeasure, his lips protruding, as he turned on his heel and left with the bouquet. There were no farewells. Tony remained silent and followed him out the door.

The shop fell into perfect silence. Isaac let his tense shoulders relax, feeling as if he might have been caught in a daydream. But the two hundred-dollar bills on the counter confirmed it was all too real.

Felix Felice had been like a stone thrown into the calm waters of his life, creating a disruptive splash that disturbed his peace. It was an unwelcome intrusion. As he scrubbed at his weary face, Isaac silently wished he would never have to see Felix again.

Chapter 3

Dear Benjamin,

The beginning of the card was always the same. The next part, however, always proved difficult. Isaac sat with his pen poised, thoughts swirling in his mind, only to set it down whenever something interrupted him. On and off, like this, it could take an entire day to finish one card; some days, he couldn't complete even a single one. No matter how hard he tried, expressing his feelings on paper felt impossible.

Whenever he wrote the name "Benjamin," warmth and joy surged through him. His heart raced, and he had to take deep breaths to calm down, losing track of time as he pondered what to write next.

"I miss him," Isaac murmured, burying his face in his hands. His mind drifted to the person he loved most in the world, yet the card remained blank.

"Who do you miss so much? Could you be thinking about me?" A playful baritone broke the silence.

Startled, Isaac straightened up from where he leaned against the counter and turned to see a man standing before him—with blinding blond hair and an unsettling presence. There had been no sound, no hint of movement, no warning, yet he was suddenly there. It sent a chill down Isaac's spine that someone of such an impressive build could approach so quietly.

How did this happen? No matter how preoccupied he'd been, the doorbell hadn't even rang. He glanced around and noticed the door was wide open.

Ah, he sighed in dismay. He often left the door open in the afternoons, fearing people would assume the shop was closed if it was shut. He'd forgotten.

With a disgruntled look, Isaac pressed a hand to his throbbing temple. Felix Felice became a regular, showing up every two or three days. As usual, Felix stood by the counter, hands in his pockets, eyes fixated on the cluttered surface.

Isaac quickly slid the colorful card he'd been writing into a drawer, hiding it from view.

"How can I help you?" he asked, feigning indifference, though he couldn't quite meet Felix's eyes. Was it because he'd been thinking of Benjamin? Restlessness churned in his stomach.

To hide his unease, Isaac glanced at Tony, who had followed Felix inside. The older man, seemingly in his forties, lounged on a chair, engrossed in his phone. His relaxed demeanor was deceptive—Isaac knew Tony was always on high alert as Felix's bodyguard.

"The cards you keep in there, do you ever finish them and send them off?" Felix's sudden question pulled Isaac's attention back to him.

Isaac met Felix's piercing gaze with the remark, "Of course I do."

"Really? 'Dear Benjamin' was all I saw. Nothing else. Just made me curious." Felix shrugged as if it were no big deal. Isaac, of course, wasn't about to explain himself, and Felix didn't push further. He never did. Felix knew to expect his stoic response.

It had been two weeks since Isaac had prayed never to see the dangerous arms dealer again. Yet here Felix was, strolling around Downtown San Diego like an average citizen, dropping by his shop with unnerving regularity.

Every time, Felix would purchase a bouquet—at a ridiculous price—and then complain about the wrapping. Yet he kept coming back, insisting on ordering another, claiming Isaac needed the practice.

It was a nonsensical demand, but Isaac didn't argue. If Felix wanted to waste his money, that was his business. All Isaac had to do was make the bouquet and get paid.

"What kind of bouquet would you like today?" Isaac asked, keeping his tone neutral. He couldn't even count how many times that same question had made its way past his lips. Felix, his new regular customer, made him feel old every time they met.

With his hands in his pockets, Felix leaned against the counter and scowled down at him—one of his regular crabby looks. "Do you miss that Benjamin of yours so much that it makes you sick to talk about it?"

Isaac knew he should ignore the question and focus on asking Felix what kind of bouquet he wanted. Yet, Felix's continuous probing into his personal life was starting to wear on him.

"Yes, I miss him," Isaac replied promptly.

An unexpected flicker crossed Felix's face. He hadn't anticipated such a direct answer; Isaac usually sidestepped these questions.,

"Is that so?" Felix murmured with a sigh.

"So, what would you like today?" Isaac asked for the third time, still without a response. The following silence felt strange—Felix usually had no problem spewing words.

"What's your preference?" Felix asked suddenly, catching Isaac off guard.

"What?" Isaac blinked.

"In flowers. What's your preference?"

Isaac hesitated. "I prefer a plant over a bouquet."

"A plant?"

"Yes," Isaac answered simply.

"Really? Let's see..." Felix let out a thoughtful hum. "How about this one? Bright, pretty...Does it suit your taste?"

He pointed to a deep pink boat orchid. The flowers were in

full bloom, graceful yet bold, embodying their meaning in the language of flowers—beauty and temptation. The combination seemed to fit Isaac's idea of Felix perfectly.

"Yes, I do like it."

"Then wrap it up."

Isaac silently wrapped the potted plant in paper and ribbon. Felix watched him in uncharacteristic silence. After paying nearly double the price, Felix lifted the plant, and Isaac wondered if he'd finally be leaving.

"Take it," Felix said, holding the plant toward him. Isaac stared at him, bewildered. "Take it. You said you like it."

"Why are you giving it to me?" Isaac asked, thoroughly confused.

Felix set the plant down on the counter with a thud, his usual radiant smile in place. "Why else? I'm interested in you, and I am trying to seduce you."

Ah. How fitting that Felix had chosen the perfect plant to accompany such a statement.

Beauty.

Temptation.

The words echoed in Isaac's mind as he scratched his cheek awkwardly. He hadn't expected Felix to say something like this.

"Why me?"

"I don't know. I keep thinking about you, but I don't know why either." Issac was silent while Felix continued, "That's why I keep coming back—paying a premium for those awful bouquets." He clicked his tongue before finishing, "You're a bit slow on the uptake."

Isaac stared at the man who, in a single breath, managed to insult him and then attempt to seduce him. How did Felix even manage to date anyone with such an overbearing personality?

Isaac shook his head slightly. But this was Felix Felice, the notorious arms dealer. With his face, power, wealth, and notoriety, who would dare deny him? Like it or not, most people would have accepted his offer.

"I'm flattered, but I'll have to decline," Isaac said without hesitation—likely the first rejection Felix had ever encountered. One of Felix's eyebrows shot up as if he hadn't heard right. Seeing his disbelief, Isaac felt a heavy weight settle in his chest.

"Why? Because of that Benjamin guy?" Felix burst out before Isaac could respond. The expression on his face darkened, and his eyes grew more violent by the second.

"Yes." Isaac met his gaze, swallowing dryly.

"It's a long-distance relationship, isn't it? I'm not telling you to stop seeing him. Just see me on the side while I'm in town."

"I don't do affairs."

"Then cut Benjamin off."

"No."

Felix's eyebrow shot up again at the resolute answer. His fists clenched and unclenched, the veins in his arms protruding. Clearly, the rejection had infuriated him, and he seemed to be holding himself back with considerable effort.

Felix's voice dripped with irritation, his smile caustic, "Do you know you're the first person to reject me?"

Isaac almost wanted to laugh. If someone told Felix that not even third-rate novels used lines like that anymore, it would probably wound his ego.

"I figured as much."

Isaac had assumed Felix wasn't used to hearing "no," but to listen to him declare, "You're the first" so openly? Seeing Felix now, Isaac realized the man had a childish streak. It was like peering into the mind of a rude, arrogant, and cunning man—but strangely, Isaac didn't find it entirely off-putting.

"And yet you refuse?" Felix tilted his head, lips pursed in a pout that made him look like a petulant child.

"Sorry."

"Think about it again. You'll regret turning me down. I can make you scream louder than anyone else."

For a moment, Isaac studied the overly confident man, chest puffed up in such a juvenile way that he almost looked…cute. A faint smile curved Isaac's lips for the first time since meeting Felix.

Felix's eyes softened in response, a strange shift in his usually sharp demeanor. "Anyway, a gift is a gift, so take care of the orchid."

"I don't—"

"I'll give you time to think. But next time, I expect a proper answer. I'm more persistent than you think." With those words, Felix spun around and stormed out as if he could no longer stand to stay.

Isaac closed his mouth, watching Felix's retreating form disappear out the door. Tony, sitting quietly and trying to remain unnoticed, approached the counter.

"If you leave a tip again, I don't want it." Isaac didn't want to take any more of their money.

"If I were you, I'd run as far as possible," Tony shook his head. "But even if you did, I'd bet money you'd be caught in no time. Still, shouldn't you at least try?"

Issac was dumbfounded.

"I'll tell you this—the boss has a deep aversion to men who look like you. Yet, he still ends up sleeping with them. Do you understand what I'm saying?"

Tony's low tone sent a chill down Isaac's spine. The meaning was clear—Felix hated men like him, yet would still fuck them until they could no longer walk. What a vicious temperament.

With that warning, Tony ignored Isaac's refusal of a tip and left a hundred-dollar bill on the counter. As Tony exited the shop,

Isaac felt a pounding ache behind his temples. Like before, when they had both descended on him without warning, Isaac buried his face in his hands and closed his eyes.

Everything had gone wrong from the moment Felix accidentally stepped into his shop. Isaac should have packed his bags that very day and disappeared. It was his mistake. He knew too much about the man to ignore the danger. No matter how much he belatedly regretted it, it was irreversible; it was too late. Regret weighed heavily on his chest as he closed his tired eyes, wishing he could turn back time.

Chapter 4

Felix sat in the back seat of a sleek sedan, grinding his teeth in frustration. Never in his life had he faced rejection. The situation was so outrageous that he could barely stand it. Whether men or women, they always came willingly when he extended a hand. Even without trying, they'd do whatever they could to catch his eye, hoping for a brief fling. All he ever had to do was choose.

"He can only make shitty bouquets, and he turns me down?" Felix fumed, the image of Isaac's stony face burning in his mind. Yet, despite Isaac's typically expressionless demeanor, a faint smile had spread across his face, like a delicate watercolor coming to life. Felix had been coming and going to the store for weeks, but this was the first time he'd seen him smile.

Fuck. Such a tempting, pretty smile.

The memory of Isaac's first smile made all the blood rush to Felix's lower half. *Fucking hell.* He held his head and sighed deeply, trying to regain control.

Sitting in the driver's seat, Jack glanced back grimly and pulled a Beretta from his waist. In a casual tone, he asked, "Want me to take care of him?"

"And what exactly are you planning to do with that?" Felix's head shot up, his fingers freezing mid-motion as he massaged his temples.

Jack didn't turn around, too focused on checking his gun. He shrugged. "He messed with you, boss. He's gotta go—"

"Shut the fuck up."

A rolled-up newspaper smacked the back of Jack's head before he could finish the sentence. Startled, he rubbed his head and glanced back, only to meet Felix's bared teeth and ferocious snarl.

Felix's eyes gleamed with murderous intent, his expression deadly. "What the fuck did you just say?"

Jack felt a shiver run down his spine. He gulped, bracing himself. Crossing paths with a wild animal would've been less terrifying than facing Felix's fury.

Visibly shaken by Felix's aura, Jack quickly returned to the steering wheel, gripping it with both hands. But Felix's seething gaze remained fixed on the back of his head as he cursed up a storm.

"Shut up! Can't even read the fucking room."

"Wow. Hearing that from you, boss, I feel like I've lived out my life on this earth."

"I said, shut up."

The car fell into a tense silence, the sound of Felix grinding his teeth the only thing breaking it. This time, Jack wisely kept his mouth shut and focused on driving. The sedan left the city center and merged onto the freeway. Inside, the atmosphere was deathly quiet—no one dared to speak.

It wasn't until they pulled up in front of the mansion that Felix, who had been glaring murderously out the window the entire ride, finally spoke. "Bring him to me."

Jack and Tony exchanged puzzled glances at Felix's abrupt command. Jack asked with a surly tone, "Bring who, all of a sudden?"

"Who else but the main character in the florist's letters?" Felix's blue eyes gleamed with a madman's intensity. "Benjamin. Whoever he is. Find that bastard and bring him to me."

As the order was growled out, his subordinates' faces stiffened. *What kind of nonsense was this?*

"Boss, kidnapping is a bit…"

"If you wanna stick it in the damn florist, then just tell us to bring the damn florist. Why are you telling us to bring the guy he's sending letters to?"

The two argued back simultaneously.

But Felix remained firm.

"Shut up and bring him to me." He repeated the command and got out of the car without a second glance. His walk towards the mansion was more violent than ever, his mood darkening with every step. Jack and Tony, now alone in the car, exchanged weary sighs.

Four years ago, back in Felix's prime, he was consumed by his plans to build a massive weapons warehouse and development center on a remote island in South America. He was at the peak of his arrogance, fueled by the confidence that came from never experiencing failure. As a hyper-dominant alpha, Felix was untouchable, or so he thought.

Suppose someone were to ask if he was better now—not really. He was still a young mafia boss and businessman with an inflated ego, utterly unbothered and unafraid of anything.

But reality never sits well with such hubris.

Even when selling weapons legally, Felix found high tariffs and restrictions frustrating. To bypass these obstacles, he leveraged the influence of his grandfather, a high-ranking mafia executive, to expand his arms-dealing empire. The government turned a blind eye to his illegal activities in exchange for bribes and additional taxes.

Still, that wasn't enough for Felix. After buying a small island in South America, he started operating in a third country, where he built his warehouse and research center to develop his own weapons.

With the mafia backing him, Felix's business grew rapidly. The real problem came when the government, unhappy with losing a major revenue source, and the military, who had personal vendettas against Felix, decided to intervene. They aimed to shut down his base, citing illegal modifications and distribution of weapons.

However, Felix was always a step ahead. There's always someone who runs over those who walk, and someone who flies over those who run. He obtained intelligence about the raid and cleverly used a decoy—purchasing another island that was nearly identical to the first. When the special forces raided the fake location, they found nothing. It was a massive embarrassment for the government and the military, who had resented Felix for years.

But even Felix didn't escape unscathed. It wasn't as if they had scheduled an appointment and conducted a warehouse inspection like they were doing a tax audit. The decoy structures and weapons were destroyed or confiscated, and there were significant casualties during the late-night raid. After that, his business faced relentless interference from an infuriated military government, forcing him to reach an uneasy compromise.

All those setbacks were irritating, but something entirely different bothered Felix the most.

"So, did you find him or not?" Felix's voice was sharp as he pushed himself up from the bed, his body slick with sweat. He swatted away the legs still wrapped around his waist, and the man lying beneath him collapsed back onto the bed, spent and motionless.

The man was a wreck. Black hair clung damply to his forehead and cheeks; sweat and semen slicked the insides of his thighs. He had passed out long ago, unable to endure Felix's relentless pace.

Felix ignored the unconscious figure sprawled on the bed and swung his legs over the side, standing up. He grabbed a towel and carelessly wiped himself off before glaring at Tony, who stood stiffly at attention in front of him. Tony's troubled expression deepened the longer Felix stared at him.

Though not as expressionless as a certain florist, Tony was

usually composed. Yet now, his face betrayed a hint of unease—a sign that something was bothering him. Felix, unfazed, discarded the towel, opened a bottle of water, and took a long swig, the liquid trickling down his chin.

"Um," Tony finally said, avoiding eye contact. "I think you should come and see for yourself."

"Seeing your expression," Felix wiped his chin, narrowing his eyes. "It must be something really good, huh?"

Tony remained silent, his expression tight.

"If it's something trivial, handle it yourself," Felix continued icily, striding toward the bathroom. His naked body gleamed under the dim light, muscles sculpted like polished marble. Tony's troubled gaze followed Felix's impeccable form as he made his way to the bathroom.

"I'll take a shower," Felix muttered as he shut the door behind him. "And dispose of that trash. I've lost my appetite."

Only then did Tony return his attention to the unconscious man on the bed.

The man looked the same as all the others—short black hair, a wiry yet solid build, small features, and dark eyes. Felix always lost control when confronted with that particular appearance.

It was even worse when the men were omegas with that kind of build. Felix wouldn't let go of them for days, tormenting them as if exacting some deep-seated revenge. Luckily, such omegas were rare; otherwise, there wouldn't be any left.

And yet, after thoroughly breaking them down, Felix would inevitably discard them, sickened by the very sight of them. This cycle repeated itself for four long years. While Felix's obsessive search had lessened, his preferences had never changed.

What kind of fuckery was this?

Tony shook his head, surveying the mess left behind on the bed. He opened the door and signaled to the men waiting just outside. They swiftly carried the naked, unconscious man away, and the maids moved in, restoring the room to pristine condition. By the time they were done, it was as if nothing had happened.

The sound of water in the bathroom stopped, and Tony could hear Felix moving about inside. There was no time to dwell on Felix's vile temperament. The real challenge was how to deal with what was coming next. Tony had been by Felix's side for a long time, but even he knew the days ahead would be some of the most difficult they'd ever faced.

He sighed deeply, steeling himself as the bathroom door opened, revealing Felix with a refreshed look on his face. Tony stepped forward, his movements heavy with the weight of what was to come.

Chapter 5

Around that time, Jack found himself lost in thought. The sleeping face before his eyes was oddly captivating, yet it stirred an unsettling sense of discomfort. It bore an uncanny resemblance to someone—someone very inconvenient.

"What do you think?" Jack asked, leaning back in his chair, his chin propped on his hand. He glanced at his subordinate, who was crouched beside him, studying the sleeping figure.

"Madonna," the subordinate replied without hesitation.

Jack's eyebrow arched in surprise. "Madonna?"

"Yeah, didn't ye know Madonna used to look like this? Blindingly blonde, pearly skin. Or Marilyn Monroe."

For a young guy, he sure knew a lot about old celebrities, Jack thought. But he couldn't deny it—the kid did have that kind of ethereal beauty. Shiny blonde hair, alabaster skin—it reminded Jack of someone specific, but he couldn't quite put his finger on it.

Just as the answer hovered on the edge of his mind, the door burst open. A group of men dressed in black filed in, led by that specific someone wearing a scowl dark enough to silence the room.

Jack promptly stood up and stepped back, making room for the man at the forefront. The beautiful man, who resembled Madonna or Marilyn Monroe at a glance, advanced and came to a halt in front of Jack. Felix's sharp, deep blue eyes locked onto the figure Jack had been watching—specifically, the child, who was still peacefully asleep, his breath moving his chest lightly, unaware of the tension in the room.

"What the hell is this?" Felix's voice rumbled low and dangerous as he narrowed his eyes.

"I brought him," Jack responded. "As you ordered."

Felix sounded incredulous. "When did I tell you to bring a kid?"

"Benjamin. You said to bring Benjamin. And it was really, really hard—"

"This is *that* Benjamin?" Felix growled, cutting off Jack's attempt to explain. His blue eyes darkened, and the veins in his neck bulged, signaling that he was seconds away from snapping.

"This is *that* Benjamin," Tony confirmed with a sigh, though Felix didn't bother to glance his way. His piercing gaze remained fixed on the sleeping child.

The boy had silver-blond hair, smooth white skin, rosy cheeks, and half-parted red lips. His gentle breathing and angelic appearance made him look like a cherub straight out of a painting.

"Fuck. Where did you get this squash of a kid?" Felix asked in disbelief, the kid far from an angel in Felix's eyes. "Explain to me how this brat is *the* Benjamin I ordered you to bring."

As Felix's teeth ground together in frustration, Tony let out another sigh, this one heavier, steeped in resignation. The explanation was straightforward yet unbelievable: after intercepting a few of the letters and cards Isaac had sent, they'd traced the recipient's address—and discovered it led to this child.

It turned out that Benjamin, a three-year-old boy, lived with his grandmother in La Jolla, north of San Diego. His parents were absent, and, for some reason, Isaac consistently sent letters and cards to this child.

"In any case, it was mighty difficult to sneak the kid out from preschool," Jack added with exaggerated drama. "The kid wouldn't stop crying, so we had to put him to sleep with Benadryl."

Felix's brow furrowed deeply. Kidnapping a child from preschool—no question, that was a crime. Of course, the order to capture and bring "Benjamin" was a crime, but this took things to another level.

By now, the boy's grandmother and Isaac had probably been

contacted—if Isaac was as attached to this child as it seemed, he would've been alerted already. Felix realized they might soon have an Amber Alert to deal with plastered across every neighborhood.

What a mess.

Who could have guessed that the subject of Isaac's heartfelt letters was a three-year-old child?

"So, you're saying Isaac is this kid's dad?"

"Nothing has been confirmed. We looked through his records, but there was nothing about him being his dad. We just suspect that they're related."

"Suspect?" Felix arched an eyebrow and gestured with his chin for him to go on.

Tony cleared his throat and continued, "Yes. The more you investigate it, the more suspicious it is. There's no sign of a family tie, but he gives continuous support."

"Support?"

"Yes."

Although irregular, Issac had been sending money for living expenses and child support. What was odd, however, was that neither Benjamin nor his grandmother had any connection to Isaac. Moreover, the payments were made under a completely different name and account; a clear attempt to conceal his identity.

Most people wouldn't have uncovered this information, which made it apparent that Isaac was trying to keep Benjamin's existence a secret. Felix's exceptional private intelligence team, which included a highly skilled hacker, was the only reason they managed to dig up this detail. It was clear that Isaac would be furious if he discovered they had learned this much.

"There's definitely some kind of backstory here," Tony said confidently. "Maybe the child was born out of wedlock, never registered, with the mother's side raising him while the florist only sends child support. But Isaac's extreme caution suggests it's not that simple."

Felix, who had been frowning while rubbing his chin, sighed in irritation. "It could be a sponsorship. You mentioned the kid doesn't have parents."

"He's too well-off for it to be a sponsorship," Tony replied.

"Right, you said he lives in La Jolla."

La Jolla was known for its affluence, even within San Diego—one of those picturesque seaside towns that exuded wealth. The opulence was evident just from looking at the houses and streets. The fact that Benjamin lived in such an expensive neighborhood indicated he wasn't a penniless orphan. So why was Isaac, who barely managed a small flower shop and struggled with his limited skills, sending money? Wasn't Isaac the one who needed support?

He couldn't make bouquets and was standoffish despite working in customer service—it was a wonder he could even pay his rent.

"If it were just sponsorship, Isaac wouldn't be so meticulous about security," Tony said.

"Hmm…"

"Given all this, it seems likely that the florist is either the child's father or a close relative, and there are likely complex circumstances involved."

Felix made a noise of frustration. The revelation that Isaac had a secret child was infuriating. The thought that those painstakingly written letters were meant for a three-year-old was absurd. He felt a mix of anger and disbelief—even if he'd been hit over the head in the middle of the street, he wouldn't have felt this way.

"Fuck! Who writes 'Dear Benjamin' to a damn kid?" Felix shouted, his temper flaring. At his outburst, everyone around him widened their eyes, raised a finger to their lips, and started making exaggerated shushing noises, as if rehearsed.

"Are you all insane? What's going on?" Felix demanded, glaring at them. The child, peacefully sleeping beside him, stirred and blinked his heavy eyes. Seeing this, the men in black turned pale and quickly recoiled, as if confronted by the most terrifying villain or ghost imaginable.

Simultaneously, their phones began to beep loudly. The cacophony of notifications in the confined space was overwhelming. Felix's eardrums felt like they were about to burst. He yanked out his phone, swiping at the screen as he tried to make sense of the chaos.

Sure enough, it was an Amber Alert. The notification displayed details about both the missing child and the vehicle involved. Meanwhile, the men around Felix looked pale and frantically tried to silence their phones. The alarm blared for a while before eventually subsiding on its own.

"Tony, is this your car's plate number?" Felix demanded.

"No," Tony replied.

"It's my car," Jack answered hesitantly,

Felix, grinding his teeth, clenched his fist and was about to knock him on the head when—

"Wahhh!" A shrill cry pierced through the silence. Felix's brow furrowed in frustration.

Tony turned his head as if he'd expected this. The others began to edge away while Jack rushed to the crying child and started making silly faces and gestures. "Who's a good baby? Who's a good baby? Why's the pretty baby crying? Peekaboo! Peekaboo! Do you want Uncle to give you a cookie? Milk?"

Has he actually gone insane? Felix stared, stunned, as Jack, resembling a hapless circus performer, flailed about in a desperate attempt to calm the child. Despite Jack's frantic efforts—his fretting, wheedling, and cajoling—the child's cries only grew louder. Tiny fists clenched and eyes tightly shut, the boy wailed with the intensity of a siren, each piercing note rattling Felix's already spinning head. The chaos was unbearable.

"This is why you should never wake a sleeping baby," Tony sighed deeply.

Felix, covering his ears, could no longer tolerate the noise. He stepped in front of the crying child, his intense frustration casting a dark shadow over his surroundings. Fearing that Felix might lash out with fists that had murdered men, Tony and Jack both paled and rushed to intervene.

"Shush." Felix loomed over the child, his voice icy and commanding. The chill in his tone made everyone flinch. Sensing the unusual tone, the child sniffled and looked up.

With his tear-streaked face and snotty nose, the child gazed up at Felix with wide, round eyes. The men around them gasped in unison. The child's scrunched-up face, in its effort to stop crying, mirrored Felix's features with startling accuracy.

With his shiny blond hair, distinctive facial features, and Prussian blue eyes, the child resembled Felix almost exactly. Even during the supposed "abduction," they had noted the resemblance.

Now, standing face to face, it was undeniable. The men were baffled.

Felix studied the child intently, narrowing his eyes. He remarked, his statement as puzzling as it was bold, "I don't see any resemblance to Isaac at all."

Are you kidding? Taken aback, Tony looked at Felix with a deadpan expression. Isaac's appearance—his slim yet solid physique, black hair, and black eyes—clearly matched Felix's sadistic preferences. However, Issac had no resemblance to the child. Was it really only after such a long stare that Felix had noticed this? Tony clicked his tongue, questioning the usefulness of Felix's observation. *What use did those eyes have other than being pretty?*

"Tony, who do you think this little squash resembles?" Felix asked, still focused on the whimpering child.

Tony hesitated, another complicated expression flickering across his face and opened his mouth with difficulty, struggling to find a response. "Doesn't…Doesn't he look like Marilyn Monroe? Or Madonna?"

"Huh?" Felix just stared at him. "Does that mean this kid's mom looks like Madonna or Marilyn Monroe?"

Tony's face grew somber as he realized Felix genuinely asked this question, even while staring straight at the child. The men around them shared the same bewildered expression.

That man and his notorious lack of awareness and tact were an ongoing problem. It was evident he had no idea the child resembled him. On the other hand, if he did notice, it was anyone's guess what kind of disaster might ensue.

Meanwhile, Tony's suspicions about Isaac only deepened. He began to wonder if Isaac was indeed taking care of an illegitimate child that Felix didn't know about. What was the connection between this child and Isaac? And what was the connection between the child and Felix? Tony had no answers.

The saying "the apple doesn't fall far from the tree" held true; children inevitably resemble their parents due to genetics. The child before them resembled Felix. Moreover, the child already exuded the distinct aura of an alpha—and not just any alpha, but a hyper-dominant one like Felix.

An alpha has a low chance of being born if both parents are betas, and only alphas can produce dominant alphas. Naturally, a dominant alpha is more likely to produce a dominant alpha, especially with an omega rather than a beta.

A hyper-dominant alpha could only be born from the pairing of an alpha and an omega, with the likelihood increasing if both parents were hyper-dominant. This revelation left everyone except Felix feeling lightheaded.

In other words, Isaac, a beta, couldn't possibly be the father of Benjamin, whose energy unmistakably marked him as a hyper-dominant alpha. If Felix—himself a hyper-dominant alpha—was the father, it would make sense. But then, who was the mother? Which omega had given birth to him?

Tony's thoughts spiraled back to the omegas Felix had been involved with over the years. Despite his well-known disdain for omegas, there had been a few. But Tony couldn't recall all of them. Could Benjamin truly be Felix's child? Or was the resemblance nothing more than a strange coincidence?

As Tony wrestled with these questions, Felix, seemingly unbothered by the child's unusual nature, merely frowned at him, his expression unreadable.

"Squash, is your name really Benjamin?" Felix asked in a menacing tone, looming over the sniffling three-year-old with his hands behind his back. He should have spoken more gently to the frightened child, who was suddenly in a strange place. Tony almost wanted to ask him what the fuck he was doing.

The clever child looked up at Felix and nodded. Perhaps seeing a bright, beautiful face among the men in black—one that resembled his own—brought him some comfort.

"How old are you?" Felix asked.

"Three!" The child declared proudly, awkwardly splaying his tiny, fern-like fingers. His confidence in stating his age drew soft murmurs of admiration from the onlookers and at the adorable sight.

"Where's your dad?" Felix continued.

"Daddy…Shop."

"Shop? What does your dad do?"

"Um, flowers! He has thiiis many flowers!" The child, now more animated after his dad was mentioned, spread his arms wide as if to show just how many flowers there were. His earlier tears seemed forgotten, replaced by a bright smile and cheerful voice.

The men in black, who had been tense moments ago, now stared in awe at the doll-like child who had stopped crying and was even answering questions with big bright eyes. Every time he spoke, they couldn't help but coo over his rosy cheeks and wide-eyed innocence. At this rate they would start clapping, but unlike them. Felix, however, remained unimpressed.

"Yeah? Is your dad's name Benjamin?"

"Daddy is daddy," the child answered confidently.

"Little squash doesn't even understand what I'm asking," Felix muttered with a shrug. Just as he prepared to ask about the boy's mother, the door suddenly burst open.

A man stumbled in, breathless and drenched in sweat. The once-relaxed atmosphere evaporated instantly as the men in black, who had been momentarily softened by the angelic child's presence, snapped to attention. They instantly drew their guns, aiming them at the unexpected intruder, the harsh sound of safeties clicking off filled the room.

Who would dare break into Felix's private residence? And *how*? Shock and confusion rendered the men speechless. A heavy silence settled over the room. Felix finally turned his gaze toward the door.

"Daddy!" The child, who had been seated as if under interrogation, bolted toward the man like lightning. He moved so fast that no one could stop him.

How could a child be so quick?

The men's mouths hung open as the boy leaped into the intruder's arms, wrapping his tiny limbs around the man's neck and bursting into tears. The woe of being alone in an unfamiliar place exploded upon seeing his dad—the same child who, just moments ago, was bravely answering questions.

"Benjamin!" Isaac's voice broke as he hugged the child tightly. Kneeling, he closed his eyes and let out a deep sigh of relief, murmuring, "Thank God."

His voice trembled as he comforted the boy, and the sound of sniffling echoed among the men, moved by the reunion. Anyone watching might have assumed they had bullied the child—though the mere act of kidnapping him was crime enough on its own.

"What is the meaning of this?" Felix demanded, rubbing his forehead with an awkward expression.

Isaac's sunken black eyes shot up, pinning Felix with a

murderous gaze. Felix flinched, momentarily frozen.

This wasn't the calm, composed man he knew.

In those fathomless eyes, there was deadly intent, and Isaac's face had turned cold as ice. He held the child so tightly that his muscles bulged, leaving no doubt about his intent to protect.

Even Felix, usually clueless, could see the fury burning in Isaac's eyes when he stormed in. Didn't even small animals fight back when someone threatened their young? That's exactly what Isaac looked like right now—a parent who had lost their child.

"What did I tell you?" Felix barked, taking a deep breath as his eyes swept the room before fixing on Isaac. "I told you not to do anything stupid! Why would you take an innocent child? Do you have any idea how terrifying kidnapping is? The kid's father was so scared, he came running in here!"

Silence fell over the room. The men exchanged uneasy glances, unsure of what to say. Felix had been the one to order the kidnapping, and now he was shifting the blame? They all felt sick to their stomachs, but no one dared to speak up.

With a sharp gesture, Felix ordered them out. His subordinates had no choice but to obey, filing out of the room with grim expressions, their bottom lips jutting out like sulking clams. The situation was a mess, but protesting would only make it worse.

Only Tony lingered, watching Felix with a mix of curiosity and surprise. The way Felix deflected Isaac's anger with a flimsy excuse was both dirty and quick. It was hard to believe this was the same man who usually lacked such awareness.

Slightly impressed despite being blamed for the kidnapping, Tony glanced at Isaac. The florist's eyes remained fixed on Felix, blazing with fury. Clearly, Felix didn't want Isaac to hate him, which explained his desperate attempt to distance himself from responsibility for Benjamin's abduction—something Felix wouldn't normally bother with.

Tony couldn't help but reevaluate Isaac with sparkling eyes.

Maybe it was the florist who was truly impressive.

"Why are you still here?" Felix snapped, cutting through Tony's thoughts.

Tony's new impression of Isaac didn't last long. He jerked his shoulders at the brusque tone of Felix's dismissal.

"Should I leave too?" Tony asked.

"I need to talk to Isaac. Wait outside."

"Understood." With a reluctant nod, Tony turned and left the room, the image of Isaac clutching Benjamin tightly still fresh in his mind. Felix, trying to appear composed while clearly anxious about Isaac's reaction, was a sight Tony had never seen before.

Who could have imagined Felix Felice, the infamous arms dealer, fretting over a florist? Anyone familiar with Felix would be stunned.

Tony cast one last glance at the scene—and at this never-before-seen side of Felix—before quietly stepping out. As he closed the door, a thought struck him: *How had that beta florist managed to get inside Felix's private residence unharmed?* Tony clicked his tongue, chalking it up to poor security, then bowed slightly to Felix, who wasn't even looking his way and left the room.

With Tony gone, an awkward silence settled in, broken only by the soft sniffles of the child in Isaac's arms.

The sound tugged at Felix's heart.

He scratched his cheek, unable to hide his discomfort. This wasn't how things were supposed to go. Who would have guessed that the person Isaac had been writing all those affectionate cards to with such a dreamy, love-struck face was a three-year-old boy?

Felix had assumed it was Isaac's lover and had planned to quietly call him in and persuade him to break things off with Isaac—that was a lie. Felix had intended to capture the man and *force* him to cut ties with Isaac. After Isaac had declared he wouldn't give up on Benjamin, having him had become a matter of pride. So Felix had devised an alternative plan; yet, somehow, everything had spiraled completely out of control.

Now, Felix hovered anxiously, biting his lip as he watched Isaac. This was entirely new—feeling so uncharacteristically on edge around someone like him.

"Isaac, I'm sorry," Felix finally said, letting out a deep sigh. "This is all my fault. It was my negligence. I take full responsibility."

If Tony or any of Felix's other associates had been there to witness this, they would have been floored.

The proud Felix Felice…apologizing? Unthinkable.

Felix was the kind of man who would rather die than admit fault, no matter what crime he'd committed. As an international arms dealer and mafia affiliate, he was notorious for his ruthlessness.

Yet here he was, swallowing his pride and apologizing, while Isaac refused to even look at him. And it was deserved. What parent could remain calm after someone endangered their child?

"Isaac," Felix called, his voice betraying his growing anxiety as he took a hesitant step forward. But Isaac, still gently patting Benjamin's back as the boy's sobs had finally begun to subside, stood up with the boy still cradled in his arms. Felix froze in place, his steps uneasy.

"Whatever your reasons, you went too far," Isaac said, his voice cold. "No matter who you are, there are lines you shouldn't cross. How could you kidnap a three-year-old child?"

All crimes are bad, but even the most hardened criminals draw the line at harming a child. No matter how much of a villain Felix was, he abhorred crimes against children. Yet here he was—having unknowingly kidnapped Isaac's child. His pride was wounded, and he knew he was in the wrong.

"I know. I wasn't aware, but I take full responsibility. That's why I'm apologizing," Felix said, dragging a hand over his chapped lips, his voice laced with regret.

"I hope this never happens again," Isaac replied coldly.

"Of course not."

"I'm leaving now. And please—don't ever come to my shop again."

Isaac's words were as emotionless as the northern winter wind. In a moment of panic, Felix grabbed his arm. Isaac turned to face him, a deep frown on his face. Even the child in Isaac's arms peeked at Felix with wide eyes. Felix looked at both of them and let out a helpless laugh like air escaping a balloon.

"You look alike," Felix remarked unexpectedly, his eyes filled with genuine wonder.

Issac paused before he answered, "Alike?"

"The kid. He looks a lot like you."

"Me?" Isaac tilted his head in surprise.

Felix hadn't expected such a reaction and smiled softly, "Yeah. The hair and eye colors are different, but his eyes and face shape are just like yours. It's fascinating."

Felix spoke in a low voice, then realized he was still holding Isaac's arm. Embarrassed, he quickly let go and stuffed his hand into his pocket, clearing his throat.

Isaac remained quiet, seemingly lost in thought, before finally sighing. "I've never heard anyone say Benjamin looks like me."

"Never? But you two look so much alike!"

Issac stared at him skeptically.

"Those people must have been blind with cataracts then," Felix said with a shrug, taking advantage of Isaac's slight hesitation to pull up a chair and sit across from him. Felix looked the most earnest he'd ever been, offering a seat. His dark Prussian blue eyes were as deep as the ocean's abyss. "Why don't you sit down? Benjamin has just stopped crying. Let's talk."

"No, thank you. I should go," Isaac replied, turning on his heel, clearly wanting nothing more to do with Felix.

But at that moment, the child in his arms reached out toward the table and shouted, “Cookie!”

Isaac stumbled in his tracks. He looked back to see milk and chocolate chip cookies on the table, where Felix casually tapped his fingers. They were snacks that Jack had prepared to calm the child, but they hadn’t been given to him in the chaos. Now, however, Benjamin had spotted them and was eagerly demanding one.

Without a word, Felix picked up a cookie and held it to Benjamin.

“Cookie!” the child repeated, grabbing the large cookie with his tiny fern-like hands.

“Let him have some. We have plenty,” Felix said, sliding the cookies forward as if trying to win the child over.

“He hasn’t had a proper meal yet. It’s not good for him to eat so many,” Isaac countered.

“Is that so?” Felix rubbed his chin, unsure of what to do. He debated whether to remove the bowl, but seeing the longing in the child’s eyes, he hesitated. What could he do when the dad was saying no?

Becoming sullen, Felix fidgeted with the cookie bowl. Finally, Isaac sighed and quietly sat down across from him, the child still in his arms. As soon as he did, Benjamin practically climbed onto the table, stretching his arms out toward the cookies. With one cookie already half-eaten in his hand, he was still eager for more.

Before Isaac could say no, Felix handed him another cookie. Only then did Benjamin look satisfied, sitting contentedly by his father’s side, clutching a cookie in each hand.

The sound of the child munching echoed loudly in the room. Isaac clucked his tongue, watching his son devour the treats gluttonously with a mixture of exasperation and amusement.

“Is he really your son? The resemblance is undeniable,” Felix murmured, cocking his head as he propped his chin on his hand.

Isaac simply replied, “Yes.”

"Where's his mother?"

"He doesn't have one."

"A single father, huh? Why did you separate? You dote on him so much. Why don't you live together? He's not even registered under your name."

"Did you look into that as well?" Isaac asked sharply, his expression darkening.

Felix, who usually wouldn't have cared about someone's mood, quickly noticed and waved his hand dismissively. "No, I didn't ask them to!" Felix said hastily, clearly flustered. "Tony just…found out a few things. In any case, you're upset. But I'm sorry for that, too."

Isaac's dark expression softened slightly. His wooden mask was the same as ever.

"Okay," he said quietly, but his mind was racing. His face may have remained calm, but the cold tips of his fingers betrayed his shock. An unexpected vulnerability had been exposed. He blinked slowly, trying to think clearly, but alarms were blaring in his mind.

What was he supposed to do now?

"How much have you found out?"

Felix shrugged at Isaac's question, indicating it wasn't much. Yet, it was clear that Isaac wouldn't speak until Felix explained in detail. Reluctantly, Felix recited the information Tony had given him earlier.

Isaac didn't react—no surprise, no anger. He simply remained silent, lost in thought, which only heightened Felix's curiosity.

"You're not going to tell me what's really going on?" Felix asked, pushing a sippy cup of milk toward the child, now covered in chocolate chip cookie crumbs. The cup, adorned with colorful illustrations, seemed almost out of place in the serious atmosphere.

Still clutching his cookies, the child grabbed the cup with both hands and took a sip. Felix watched in amusement, a small smile tugging at the corners of his mouth.

"What a greedy kid," Felix said softly. "You can put the cookies down, you know. No one's going to take them from you."

It was unclear if the child understood, but he kept a firm grip on both the cookies and the cup.

"There were many circumstances." Isaac's voice broke the quiet, emotionless and flat. Felix glanced up from the child. Isaac's face was as blank as ever, but something about his demeanor felt fragile, on the edge. Felix straightened, sensing the shift. It didn't sit right with him.

"Be clear," Felix said, his tone more serious. "Is it a family issue?"

"It's not."

"Then what?"

Isaac hesitated, torn between staying silent and revealing too much. Felix was a stranger—someone Isaac had no intention of confiding in. But after a moment of contemplation, Isaac let out a terse sigh and spoke, breaking the silence, "Truthfully, I'm being pursued."

It was an unexpected answer.

"Pursued?" Felix's expression shifted, caught off guard. "By whom? Why?"

"I can't tell you. That's why I didn't register Benjamin under my name—I wanted to protect him. We can't live together, but my mother is also unrelated to me on paper, so I asked her to take care of him."

Isaac's explanation was brief and detached as if he were discussing someone else's life, not his own. The dissonance made Felix frown.

He clicked his tongue before he answered, "So if whoever is after you finds out, you think you'll be able to keep Benjamin and your mother safe?"

Isaac didn't bother responding. The reality was obvious. He couldn't afford familial ties—couldn't leave a trail that could lead back to them. If his cover was blown, he needed to appear completely isolated. The hardest part was being separated from Benjamin, but given the uncertainty of his situation, there was no other choice.

But now Felix knew. He had discovered Benjamin was Isaac's son—and had even kidnapped him. If Felix could do it, others could too, and they might not be as lenient.

The thought sent a chill down Isaac's spine. He instinctively pulled Benjamin closer, holding him tightly. The child, engrossed in his milk and cookies, whined in protest like a puppy. Realizing he was squeezing too hard, Isaac loosened his grip, but the fear remained.

He couldn't let them take Benjamin. If they did, they wouldn't return him as easily as Felix had. There was no telling what they might do. Isaac's shoulders trembled with the thought.

To avoid detection, Isaac rarely visited. Once a week, at most. When he missed Benjamin too much, he watched from afar, unable to approach. No photographs, no traces. Each day, he wrote letters he could never send, pouring his longing into words that piled up, unsent. He'd told Felix he sent them when he asked, but in truth, most of them were left in a pile.

He moved frequently, every six months, sometimes more. His mother and Benjamin moved too, always nearby but never too close. It was better to have them nearby where he could look after them.

But moving was getting harder. Benjamin had just started preschool this year, and he'd be in kindergarten in two years. His mother, too, was aging, and the constant relocations were taking a toll on her.

Isaac wondered if it would be better to move on his own. He gave it serious thought, but then Felix had entered his life, showing an inexplicable interest in him. Tony had warned him to run, but where could he go? Felix's strange obsession had already reached Benjamin.

The situation was spiraling out of control. Isaac couldn't afford to make Felix his enemy. Part of him wanted to confide in Felix, to lay everything out—but could he trust him? How would Felix react if he knew the whole truth?

He'd admitted to being on the run, but now what? Isaac closed his eyes and pressed a gentle kiss to the top of Benjamin's head. The child's familiar scent—a mix of milk and baby powder—filled his senses, offering a moment of comfort.

"Daddy, don't do that," Benjamin giggled, wriggling as he shook his head in protest. Each movement made his soft hair brush against Isaac's cheek and nose, and despite everything, a smile tugged at Isaac's lips.

"I'll help," Felix's voice cut through the quiet.

Chapter 6

Isaac couldn't hide his confusion. What did Felix mean by helping? Help with what? How? He stared at Felix, unsure of how to respond.

"You're saying you want Benjamin and your mother to live peacefully in La Jolla, as they are now." Felix continued, his tone calm and deliberate, "Safely. And you want to watch over them without anyone knowing they're your family."

Isaac nodded slowly, still uncertain.

Felix's lips curled into a confident smile. "First, you should relocate the flower shop periodically. Even if it's just moving around within La Jolla, it'll make it harder for anyone to track you. I can help with finding locations if you want." He didn't wait for Isaac to respond. "Second, I'll assign private bodyguards to Benjamin and your mother. The best. They'll act as shadows, and if anything happens, they'll notify me immediately."

"What do you think?" Felix finished speaking with a touch of pride, but Isaac remained deep in thought, his reaction far less enthusiastic than Felix had hoped.

"Isaac," Felix called out, his patience waning. Finally, Isaac's dark, profound eyes met his.

"Why are you helping me?" Isaac asked, his expression filled with doubt. The Felix he knew didn't do favors. He was a man who took what he wanted, trampling over anything or anyone in his way.

Helping a stranger like him? It didn't add up. There had to be more to it—something he wasn't seeing. Countless questions and possibilities swirled through his mind.

Felix appeared to notice Isaac's doubts and started to clarify,

"First off, I wronged you." Isaac remained quiet, just listening. "And…I'm attracted to you." Felix's words were gentle, his tone smooth and heartfelt. Nevertheless, Isaac remained indifferent. Felix had previously admitted his feelings, so this revelation was hardly surprising.

Isaac had hoped there might be another reason behind Felix's offer, but his concerns appeared unfounded. Isaac's response was curt, and he returned to his thoughts. "I see."

Felix sighed, muttering, "You're no fun."

"It's not that I haven't considered bodyguards…" Isaac began slowly.

Felix's blue eyes brightened with curiosity, "But?"

"But ordinary bodyguards won't stand a chance against them." Isaac's statement was calm and matter-of-fact, but it made Felix frown.

"Who the hell is after you?" Felix demanded, his tone sharp and confrontational.

Isaac met his deep blue gaze, but instead of answering, he deflected. "If you really want to help…then there must be at least two bodyguards for my mother and Benjamin. Their priority should be to protect and evacuate them, and they should inform me immediately. Under no circumstances should they try to fight back."

"Gee, thanks for the confidence in my men," Felix said sarcastically, annoyed at the brisk terms. But Isaac pressed on.

"I would prefer the guards to be your men. They should stay discreet, but if they're forced to reveal themselves, it should be obvious they're under your protection. The enemy needs to know my family can't be touched."

"My protection."

"If the deal doesn't work out, don't worry about where I go," Isaac said, his voice steady.

"Deal?" Felix raised an eyebrow, surprised by Isaac's straightforward tone. But Isaac remained expressionless, meeting his gaze without flinching.

"Because you want something from me, too," Isaac continued. "You're not the type to show kindness for nothing. No one is. So, let's make it simple—a deal."

Felix smirked. "You're quite convincing."

Isaac said nothing, his silence heavy in the air.

"Something I want. You know what that is?"

"I have a guess."

Felix's eyes narrowed, pushing him to speak. Isaac swallowed, his throat dry, and glanced down at Benjamin.

Blissfully unaware, the child was munching on cookies he was usually not allowed to indulge in, focusing entirely on the rare treat. Isaac gently covered Benjamin's ears, shielding him from the conversation. Then, drawing a slow, deliberate breath, he spoke—his voice low and steady, even as his lips felt numb.

"My payment for your service is this…"

His eyes locked on Felix's, calm but resolute, blinking calmly. Felix's striking features remained etched in his vision.

"Once a week, you can make me your whore."

Chapter 7

"You'd think he's guarding his own kid." Tony rubbed his temples with his thumb, releasing a deep sigh.

"Isn't it his kid?" one of Felix's subordinates asked.

"They say he ain't."

"Ain't? Look at that face! How else could anyone have that fancy face? And with all the security, even a stray dog would think he's protecting his own flesh and blood."

Gossip buzzed around Tony, who let their chatter fade into the background as he thought quietly.

The more Tony thought about it, the clearer it became—Isaac was undeniably clever. By assigning Felix's men to guard Benjamin, whoever his opponent was, he was sending a clear message: the child was under Felix's protection, someone no one wanted to cross. Besides, Benjamin was practically a miniature Felix—anyone who didn't know better would assume they were father and son.

And if that were the case, who would dare touch the boy? Sure, Felix had plenty of enemies, and many wanted to extort weapons from him, but none were reckless enough to go after someone under his direct protection. Even the government wouldn't risk that kind of conflict. Anyone who threatened Felix's son would have to be prepared to gamble with their lives—and the lives of everyone they cared about.

If, of course, he was, in fact, Felix's son.

But Isaac had orchestrated this illusion, making it seem like Benjamin was indeed Felix's son. It was a calculated move, one that ensured no one would dare harm the child by placing Felix's men as his bodyguards.

Isaac was an enigma. The fact that he was being pursued by someone so dangerous that he needed these extreme measures, combined with the audacity to make bold demands despite knowing what kind of man Felix was—everything about him was strange.

And then there was the background check—clean as a whistle. His birthplace, education, employment—everything seemed ordinary. Too ordinary, in fact, to the point of feeling suspicious.

"Hey, does the boss have an older or younger sister?" one of the subordinates suddenly asked, snapping Tony out of his thoughts.

Tony glanced up, his gaze settling on the man who had spoken. "Don't you know? The boss is an only child."

Felix was born the only son of a wealthy family, with a grandfather in a prominent position within the Mafia. A rare hyper-dominant alpha, Felix was used to getting whatever he wanted. Spoiled from birth, he embodied pedigree and privilege.

"What about a cousin?" another subordinate chimed in.

"Hard to say. Maybe he has some distant relatives, but I wouldn't know. Why do you ask?"

"I just wanna figure out the kid's relationship with the boss. If he's not his son, maybe he's a relative."

"Enough jabbering," Tony said, raising a hand to silence them, his patience wearing thin. "Get back to your posts. I don't want to hear any more talk about the kid. Rumors like that can escalate into real problems."

The men snapped to attention at the stern reprimand, quickly silencing themselves. Tony wasn't one to speak often, but when he did, his word was law. As Felix's right-hand man and closest confidant, Tony held almost as much authority as the boss himself. Tony was second only to Felix in the organization's hierarchy.

Grumbling under their breath, the men reluctantly returned to their duties, chastened and subdued, like scolded dogs with their tails between their legs. Tony clucked his tongue while Jack, standing nearby, couldn't help but snicker.

"You know, when you give them that look, they practically piss themselves," Jack said, lighting a cigarette.

"That's the boss, not me," Tony replied, shaking his head.

"The boss, sure—but you're no pushover either," Jack retorted. "Still, what the fuck is up with the boss? Why's he going through all this trouble just to get into some guy's pants?"

Tony didn't respond, but Jack continued, "He'll just toss him aside after one night anyway. Why pretend to care?"

Tony shot Jack a glance as the other man grumbled. His gaze was strangely insulting as if he was either pitying him or finding him pathetic. "You're as clueless as the boss."

Jack stopped and jumped in indignation at Tony's merciless reproach, sputtering, "Hey, come on! What are you saying that for? Like hell anyone in the world is as clueless as the boss!"

Tony's gaze remained sharp, but he tutted. Play with him once and throw him away? Sure, Jack might have had a point—Felix's pattern was predictable: find a man who caught his eye, fuck them for a night, and move on without a second thought. But this time, something was different.

Tony had initially warned Isaac to run before Felix ruined him. But when Felix ordered them to bring Benjamin, Tony knew this wasn't just another fling. Felix could have easily taken Isaac, fucked him, and had his fill, yet he was going out of his way, instead of ordering them to capture his "lover" Benjamin. That wasn't like Felix at all. He had to do things the hard way.

Felix didn't want Isaac to hate him, so he shifted the blame—an unusual move for someone like him. It was almost impressive how much effort he put into this, especially for someone who rarely showed genuine care for others.

Looking back, Felix's behavior had been odd from the start. He made unnecessary visits to the shop, spent ridiculous amounts on gaudy bouquets, and even bought an orchid just because Issac liked it. That had shocked Tony as if he were hit over the head—Felix never did things like that.

"Something's off," Tony muttered under his breath.

Jack, puffing on his cigarette, glanced over, puzzled. Tony just shook his head. The idea that Felix might actually care for Isaac was unsettling. It seemed like a positive development on the surface, but it didn't make sense. Felix had never been thoughtful of anyone before. And then there was Benjamin—Felix's little lookalike.

Isaac insisted Benjamin was his child, but the more Tony thought about it, the less it added up. For starters, a hyper-dominant alpha couldn't be born from a beta. That alone raised red flags.

Tony knew he had to dig deeper. DNA tests on Benjamin, Felix, and Isaac would reveal the truth soon enough. Then it would be revealed who Benjamin's real father was.

Felix despised the idea of fathering a child carelessly. If a female beta or an omega claimed to be pregnant with his child, he would exude his murderous aura, and he would make it clear that he'd agree to a paternity test only after the birth—and if the results came back negative, the child would be left an orphan. Unsurprisingly, no one ever returned with a child. After all, they valued their lives.

But now, if Felix did have a bastard child out there—and if Isaac was somehow raising that child—then things could get very complicated.

Thinking of the worst-case scenario, Tony sighed, the sound terse and heavy. He could only hope Benjamin's resemblance to Felix was just a coincidence. Rubbing his throbbing temple, he turned away. Jack called after him, confused, still puffing on his cigarette. Tony didn't respond. He slid into the sedan, shutting the door on his thoughts.

"Just once a week, I can make you my whore?" Felix questioned.

"Yes," Isaac replied, deadpan.

"Wow, this deal is much worse for me than I thought."

"You were the one who offered to help first."

"Still—this feels like a scam." Felix leaned forward, chin propped on his hand. Though he complained about it being a scam, he was clearly amused. Isaac might have skewed the terms in his favor, but Felix still controlled the game. It was like he was the king on the chessboard, while Isaac played the role of a mere pawn.

Isaac swallowed, his throat dry and scratchy, each attempt feeling like sandpaper scraping against his throat. "That's why I told you—if the deal doesn't work, don't worry about where I go."

Felix's eyes darkened. "You already sound like you're planning to disappear."

With a knock on the table, Felix pushed back his chair, loud in the quiet room. As his footsteps approached, Isaac tensed, instinctively tightening his grip on Benjamin. The child stirred, letting out a soft whine.

"I get bored quickly," Felix's voice was low as he stopped behind Isaac, his hand resting lightly on Isaac's shoulder. "What will you do then?"

All of Isaac's focus narrowed to the weight of that hand, the heat of Felix's touch. His body stiffened, but his voice remained indifferent. "The same as always. You can back out anytime, but I've already paid my price. You'll have to protect me until I disappear. It won't take long."

"That's shrewd of you." Felix's fingers caressed the back of

Isaac's head, sliding beneath his slightly long hair. The fine hairs on Isaac's neck stood on end at the touch. Felix must have noticed his reaction because his fingers trailed lower, teasing along Isaac's spine.

Isaac fought to suppress a moan.

"Hey, did you know—" Issac didn't move. Felix's low voice, smooth and sensual, crooned in Isaac's ear, sending a tremor through his hips, "When it comes to business, I don't like to lose."

Isaac closed his eyes as Felix leaned in closer, mimicking what Isaac had done with Benjamin earlier. Felix pressed his lips to the top of Isaac's head and whispered, "Once a week, you'd better be ready."

Chapter 8

Isaac's hands gripped the sheets, trembling. A drop of sweat slid down his chin. He lay face down, his ass raised, as endless breathy moans escaped from his parted lips. He tried to bite them back, covering his mouth with his hand, but it was no use.

"Ah…Hah…"

Isaac's body was already a wreck. Felix was relentless, his hips driving into Isaac with a brutal rhythm, trying to claim him fully—stirring his insides ceaselessly. Every thrust sent a rush of heat through Isaac's body, and each time Felix buried his cock deeper, the cum filling Isaac's belly gushed out, dripping down his thighs. The sight only spurred Felix on.

On Sunday, at midnight, Felix knocked on Isaac's apartment door. After leaving Felix's place, Isaac had asked to meet, thinking he had time since the flower shop was closed on Mondays.

But he hadn't expected Felix to show up just as the clock struck twelve—right when he was about to fall asleep.

Isaac had been agonizing over his decision, wondering if striking such a ridiculous deal with Felix had been a mistake and should have just run instead.

As if sensing his doubt, Felix appeared on his doorstep without warning. Isaac froze at the sight. For a long moment, he could only blink, at a loss for words. It almost felt unreal that Felix Felice, the man he'd tried to avoid, was now standing like a statue before him.

Before Isaac could ask how Felix had found him, Felix grabbed the back of his neck and kissed him, fervent and impatient. The kiss was overwhelming—wet sounds filled the air as Felix's lips crushed against his. Issac was blindsided by Felix's kiss. His tongue explored Isaac's mouth with such hunger, that it felt like Felix was intent on devouring him whole. Felix pulled at him with such vicious greed that he felt like he was being robbed of his saliva and breath.

He gasped for air when the kiss broke, only to hear the door slam shut behind them. Felix had closed it and was already yanking at his clothes, rough and determined.

Isaac didn't resist. A deal was a deal. The moment the clock struck midnight, marking the arrival of Monday—the day he'd agreed to give himself to Felix. Whether he liked it or not, he had no choice but to surrender. All he could do was close his eyes and endure what would come.

Resigned, Isaac gripped Felix's shoulders as Felix undressed him, lips moving from his neck to his collarbone. In seconds, his light pajamas and briefs were stripped away, leaving him exposed. He'd been wearing a light pair of pajamas for bed, but Felix made it seem effortless. There was no time for Isaac to reflect on it.

Felix's lips were relentless as he guided Isaac toward the bed, his hands roaming Isaac's bare skin, carving his claim with every touch. Caught in a daze, Isaac soon found himself lying flat on his back.

"Fuck, I thought about it every day—how it would feel to take you, what kind of face you'd make under me." Felix hovered over him, his hands caging Isaac in, blue eyes dark with need.

Isaac, feeling the weight of that intense lust, swallowed hard. The second his throat bobbed, Felix's firm hands wrenched open one of his thighs, and Isaac knew there was no turning back.

"Did you take a shower?"

Isaac's face flushed at the blatant gaze Felix aimed at his lower half. He was thankful the light from the nightstand wasn't too bright, allowing him to hide his embarrassment, at least a little.

"Yes, I was getting ready for bed," Isaac mumbled, his tone low as he tried to mask his discomfort.

But Felix's following comment only deepened his embarrassment. "Your soap doesn't smell bad."

Isaac felt his face heat even more. He clamped his mouth shut and turned his gaze away, trying to ignore the rising tension. Meanwhile, Felix nonchalantly pulled a bottle of lube from his pocket, pouring a generous amount over Isaac's entrance. The coldness of it made Isaac's hips twitch involuntarily.

But the coldness was quickly replaced by something far more foreign—Felix's slick fingers, spreading the gel and rubbing it inside him. A stranger's touch in such an intimate place—it made his stomach flip. Instinctively, he grabbed the sheets and bit his lip, holding back any sound.

"Relax," Felix murmured, his voice low and soothing. As he spoke, a slick finger slid inside Isaac's body. Just one finger, but Isaac stiffened, unprepared for the intrusion as Felix pressed in deeper.

Felix's fingers were long and rough, and his knuckles prominent. They moved with deliberate rhythm, sliding in and out, rubbing against his sensitive inner walls—it was obscene. The number of fingers increased, stretching Isaac further, making it impossible for him to ignore the sensation. He couldn't tell how many were inside him, but it felt overwhelming like he was being pushed to his limit.

Without thinking, Isaac's hand shot out, gripping Felix's wrist. "Stop," he gasped, his voice shaky and desperate. But instead of stopping, Felix curled his fingers, grazing Isaac's most sensitive spot. Electricity sparked over his moist tissues, already sensitive from all the rubbing and churning. A shock of pleasure shot through him, making him arch off the bed.

"Ah, huh—" Isaac moaned uncontrollably, his body betraying him despite his efforts to remain composed.

Felix audibly ground his teeth, and then, suddenly, all his fingers withdrew at once. The abruptness made Isaac's body jerk again, leaving him breathless.

"Fuck!" Felix hissed, spitting out the curse as he gripped Isaac's thighs. His fingertips glistened with the lube. Isaac stared at them, barely conscious, his mind fogged with overwhelming sensation.

Then, without warning, Felix's cock breached his entrance, forcing its way inside. The sudden shock tore through Isaac, making his vision go white. It felt as if he were being split apart, a silent scream frozen on his lips, as his body was completely overwhelmed.

Now fully inside him, Felix growled low like a beast and began to thrust with reckless abandon. Each time his cock slammed into Isaac, his stomach clenched painfully, and he choked, struggling to catch his breath. His insides felt raw, battered by Felix's unrelenting force.

Relax? Easy for him to say when he was pounding into him with such brutality. Isaac gritted his teeth, helpless as his body twisted and tugged at the sheets beneath him. He felt like he was being split apart. Whether Felix knew it or not, there wasn't one iota of perseverance left in Isaac's movements. Felix continued to work him over frantically.

Normally talkative and capricious, Felix was now eerily focused, hammering his hips into Isaac with single-minded intensity.

"Huh…Ah—please, slow down…" Isaac begged, his voice trembling, tears pricking at the corners of his eyes. But Felix only increased the pace, his crazed expression terrifying him. The primal hunger in Felix's eyes was unrelenting, giving Isaac no reprieve.

Isaac cursed himself for proposing this once-a-week arrangement. If he'd known it would be like this, he wouldn't have made the deal at all. He would've run far away. His body shook uncontrollably, wracked with sobs as Felix drove him closer to breaking.

"Fucking hell, what is it with you?" Felix growled, his voice thick with mounting lust. He suddenly halted his thrusts and crushed his lips against Isaac's, kissing him with unrestrained hunger. It was as though he wanted to consume not just Isaac's lips, with shallow breaths barely passing through, devouring every breath he exhaled.

Felix bit and sucked on Isaac's lips until they were swollen and raw, greedily lapping up his saliva, dominating the inside of his mouth. Isaac could only surrender, parting his lips wider and allowing Felix to claim him fully. Their tongues tangled in a messy rhythm, wet, sloppy sounds filling the space between them.

Isaac, dazed and breathless, instinctively wrapped his arms around Felix's neck. Felix, while overwhelming him with kisses, let out a deep growl in response, his chest vibrating with the sound. Without warning, he plunged his cock deep inside Isaac again.

"Ah!" Isaac's hips jerked off the bed, the sudden sharpness making his entire body spasm. The burning stretch left him reeling, unable to gather his thoughts as Felix slid his arms beneath Isaac's knees, lifting his legs and folding him in half, taking full control.

Felix's cock pistoned in and out, each thrust driving brutally deep, from tip to base, again and again. With each stroke of his cock against his inner walls, the force of it sent Isaac's body sliding up the bed until his head hit the headboard. Felix, growling in frustration, gripped his hips tightly and yanked him back into position before resuming his frenzied pace.

Isaac's vision blurred from the relentless pounding. He bit his lip, enduring the fiery friction at his entrance as Felix went in and out, and at that moment, a tidal wave of heat surged within him, overwhelming his senses, and then, like molten lava, Felix's climax erupted, sending a searing rush through them both.

Felix paused, groaning low in his throat, his cock twitching deep inside. Isaac's breath hitched, and finally, he exhaled in shaky relief, realizing it was over. His limbs went limp, hands sliding off Felix's shoulders and falling onto the bed.

His chest heaved, damp with sweat, and he closed his eyes,

thinking he could finally rest. But he wasn't out of the woods just yet. Unfortunately, even after ejaculating, Felix showed no intention of pulling out. Instead, his cock twitched inside him, hardening again, filling him once more. Isaac went pale with alarm as he let out a gasp.

"Weren't you…finished?" Isaac's voice was raw, barely more than a rasp.

"Finished?" Felix let out a low scoff, as if he heard something ridiculous. "I haven't even started yet. Don't embarrass yourself by asking."

"At least let me rest! I—" Isaac couldn't finish his sentence.

Felix's cock drove into him with renewed force, slamming to the hilt and sending a shockwave through Isaac's entire body. His breath hitched, and a whimper caught in his throat. Isaac shivered, at a loss for what to do.

"Didn't you say I could make you my slut for the whole day?" Felix's voice dropped to a whisper as he brushed back the sweat-soaked strands of Isaac's hair.

"A-ah…Uh—"

"I haven't made you mine yet," Felix whispered, his voice dark with intent. Felix flipped him over, pinning him onto his stomach. Bent at one knee, a heavy hand gripped his ass, holding him in place before Felix took a breath and then drove back into him without hesitation.

Each brutal thrust pushed out the cum already inside him, wet, obscene sounds filling the room with every motion—*fwop, fwop, fwop.*

Isaac couldn't believe it was coming from his own body as he listened to the unfamiliar lewd noises and then closed his hazy eyes.

Of course, Felix was a bona fide hyper-dominant alpha, famous for his looks and brains, but his stamina was also unparalleled. Isaac sighed resignedly when he remembered this fact.

What had it been like back then…?

His thoughts drifted briefly to the past, to that hazy memory of his first and only time with someone—four years ago. The memory had been buried deep, but now, with Felix's body overpowering his, it was dragged to the surface, raw and vivid, making him feel like he was reliving that moment.

"Isaac." The past was about to overlap with the present when Felix called his name softly. Isaac lifted his eyes, torn from his thoughts.

Felix wrapped a large hand around Isaac's cock, using his other hand to hold up his ass. His cock had been limp, unresponsive amidst the overwhelming sensations, but now, Felix's firm touch stroking him made Isaac's hips jerk reflexively.

"H-Huh—what…?" Isaac looked behind him, eyes red. A man of his arrogance, taking another man's dick in his hand and stroking it? This was unexpected. He'd assumed he would simply take his pleasure and that would be the end of it.

"I'm losing my mind just from the taste of you," Felix murmured, "But now, I want to see you fall apart, crying from pleasure."

"Ah!" Isaac gasped sharply.

"Not like before, not from pain. I want to see you cry out in ecstasy," Felix nipped at Isaac's earlobe, his whisper sending a shiver down Isaac's spine. "Tell me—where do you like it? Do you want me to touch you? To make you come?"

"Tell me." His hand wrapped around Isaac's length, thumb brushing the sensitive tip—a jolt of heat shot through Isaac, making his toes curl.

Instead of answering, Isaac bit his lip, trying to stifle the moan threatening to escape. But Felix's skilled hand was relentless, and Isaac's cock throbbed under his touch.

He couldn't help it. Teased by his fingers, precum slicked the tip, betraying his desire.

"You like that? Here?" Felix asked, his lips trailing along Isaac's neck as he rocked his hips, the thick length of him still buried deep inside. The slow, teasing thrusts, paired with his hand, were impossible to resist.

"Ah…s-stop…" Isaac's voice trembled as he reached for Felix's wrist, trying to pull his ass away. His body tensed, hips shifting, but Felix's grip remained firm. The man wasn't letting go—not of his dick, not of his control. His giant cock hadn't been pulled out from his ass since he started fucking him.

But what overwhelmed Isaac wasn't just the pleasure from the hand stroking him—it was the way Felix's cock moved inside him, hitting every sensitive spot with perfect precision..

"Ah—ah—" Isaac's release came suddenly and with intensity, his body trembling as he spilled into Felix's palm. A broken moan tore from his throat awakening a long-forgotten sensation within him. His body instinctively tightened around Felix's cock. His forehead pressed into the rumpled sheets, helpless against the waves of rapture that took over.

Felix groaned, jaw tight, watching Isaac unravel beneath him. His hands gripped Isaac's hips, pulling him back to him, and the rough pace resumed. Isaac clutched the sheets tightly, bracing himself against the onslaught of powerful thrusts.

Every movement sent a deeper, more intense wave of pleasure coursing through him, his body responding instinctively as his hips shook involuntarily. He contracted his entrance out of the desire to suck in Felix's monstrous cock deeper and deeper, pulling Felix in, tightening around him. This body, which was instinctively chasing after pleasure, didn't feel like his own. It felt like he was becoming empty-headed, succumbing to the pleasure.

"Isaac, Isaac…you're blowing my mind. I'm going crazy. What is all this? You're not letting me go. Fuck, just look at you. Do you even know what your tight lewd little hole is doing?" Felix muttered full of fervor, staring at the way Isaac's hole clung to his cock, while Isaac lay face down, undulating his trembling hips to meet Felix's thrusts.

Isaac couldn't hear anything. He was spaced out, as if on drugs. Felix clicked his tongue, surprised at how quickly Isaac began to respond.

"You normally act like you're made of stone—what's with this face?" Felix groaned low and rocked his hips violently, unable to stop himself. "Not even a seasoned whore acts as needy as you. Fucking hell."

Isaac's body moved on instinct, every thrust igniting waves of pleasure that overtook him. His lips parted, breaths escaping in shallow gasps, and a trail of drool slid from the corner of his mouth.

"Ah…ah…Felix…more…right there—" The words spilled from his lips, barely coherent.

Felix cursed, driving into him with an intensity that bordered on savage, like a beast. Their nude bodies melded together, indistinguishable in the fevered rhythm of their movements, lost to the primal pull of desire. This time, Isaac didn't need Felix's touch to finish—just the sheer sensation of being fucked was enough to push him over the edge.

"Fuck! I'm fucking losing it," Felix growled, his voice rough with need.

Isaac's cries and moans of pleasure shifted, a breath ragged with despair slipping out. No matter how hard he fought it, no matter how many suppressants he took, how desperately he tried to mask his scent—he couldn't deny the truth. He wasn't a beta. He could only ever be an omega, helplessly responding to the alpha's cock buried deep inside his ass. He could only moan mindlessly, reacting to Felix's pheromones and seed.

It was almost laughable—this truth he had spent so long denying. But now, faced with it again, there was no hiding. His body shook like a whore, his face pressed into the ruined sheets.

He couldn't stop. His mind was severed from his body, as the overwhelming sensations overtook him. His pleasure-drenched mind had drifted far beyond the reach of rational thought. And this, ironically, was exactly what he had agreed to.

He had offered himself to Felix, knowing what it meant, and Felix wasn't about to hold back.

The night stretched on, with Felix's unyielding desire consuming him. Isaac tries to recall that night, as well as the faint memories after, but his thoughts blurred, disappearing. Issac's cries filled the night as Felix took control of him.

It was a long, endless night.

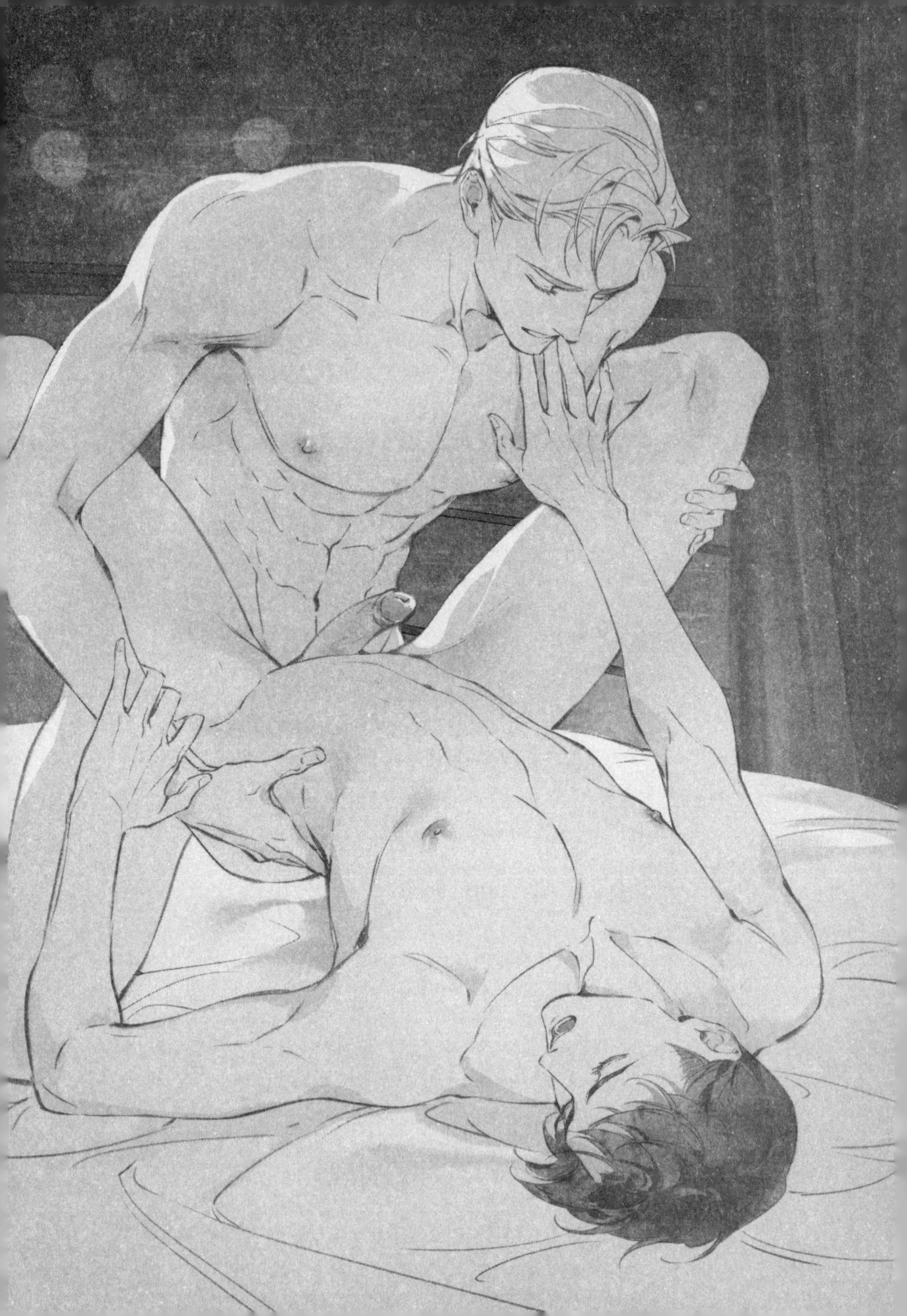

Chapter 9

Like most days in San Diego, today was clear and sunny. Fluffy white clouds drifted lazily across the sky, and the sun shone with a blinding brightness. Yet, despite the beautiful weather, Isaac was sore. Every movement brought a twinge of discomfort, his muscles aching from the past few days. He furrowed his brow as he shifted in his seat.

He still wasn't sure how he'd gotten through the last four days. After Felix had appeared on his doorstep Monday night, he'd barely made it to the shop the next day. Every joint hurt, his back refused to straighten properly, and the soreness between his legs made sitting a challenge. He'd debated closing early and heading home, but pride kept him there, fighting through the pain—at least until he gave in and left a couple of hours before closing.

The aftermath had been more intense than he'd expected. When he'd agreed to their once-a-week arrangement, he never imagined it would leave him this wrecked, struggling even to stand. He'd clearly underestimated the hyper-dominant alpha.

How was he supposed to keep going if every encounter left him like this? The thought made his heart sink. Isaac sighed, consoling himself that it was only once a week—thankfully, not twice.

Trying to shake off the negativity, Isaac settled into the chair behind the counter, staring absentmindedly at the clear sky. Lately, he'd spent more time like this, lost in thought rather than tending to the flowers. But the weather was too nice to ignore—the cool breeze, the warm sun, the kind of day that made San Diego feel perfect.

One of the city's biggest perks was its mild climate. People strolled around in T-shirts nearly all year round, while snow remained a distant, almost mythical notion. Except for the occasional heatwave in summer, the seasons blended into one long, pleasant stretch of warm days and cool evenings.

Spring, though, had a unique charm—the breeze softer, the sunshine gentler.

Isaac couldn't help but think how nice it would be to walk hand-in-hand with Benjamin through Balboa Park on a day like this, maybe have a picnic on the grass. He pictured Benjamin running around, laughing, playing with other kids, eating snacks in the sun. The reality that he couldn't do those carefree things with Benjamin weighed on him. He sighed deeply, feeling the familiar weight of frustration. It was nothing new, but he envied other people who could spend ordinary days with their children.

Isaac had so much he wanted to share with Benjamin, but the circumstances made it impossible for him to live the carefree, ordinary life he longed for. Would a day ever come when they could do those simple things together? The thought seemed like a distant, dreamlike hope, and Isaac smiled bitterly at the idea.

He slapped his knee hard, the sharp sound jolting him back to reality. He couldn't let himself spiral further into these dark thoughts. He'd be better off writing a card instead. Benjamin needed him to be strong, and wallowing in self-pity wouldn't help either of them.

Determined to shake it off, Isaac stood, ignoring the ache in his hips, and walked over to the card display by the counter. He picked out a Mickey Mouse card—Benjamin's current obsession. The sight of Mickey's cheerful grin brought a small smile to Isaac's face.

Dear Benjamin.

As usual, Isaac carefully wrote the same line on the card. His pen paused, pen in hand, mid-sentence, when he heard light footsteps—sneakers, not boots. Glancing up, he found an unexpected figure standing in front of him. Perhaps "unexpected" wasn't the right word. Felix was expected, but his attire was so startling that Isaac couldn't look away.

"What? You're just going to stare? No hello for your customers? How rude." The most arrogant man in the world—no contest—said as he walked toward the counter. Felix's smile was dazzling, his whole appearance striking enough to leave Isaac momentarily speechless, pen still in hand. He finally understood what people meant when they used the word "dazzling."

Felix typically favored dark, tailored suits, but today, he was wearing something completely different: a white polo shirt, ivory slacks, and light boat shoes, the kind with short laces on the front. A sweater, the exact shade of his striking blue eyes, was casually draped over his shoulders. He looked like he'd just stepped off a yacht straight out of a photoshoot.

Isaac couldn't stop staring, lost for words. After noticing the attention, Felix swept a hand through his glossy blond hair, locking his eyes with Isaac. Embarrassed, Isaac quickly looked away. Felix glanced down at the card Isaac had been writing.

"Writing to Benjamin again? Mickey Mouse this time?" Felix's voice was tinged with amusement. Isaac snapped out of his daze, sighed, and carefully closed the card before sliding it into the drawer, where a small stack of unsent letters lay untouched.

"Benjamin likes Mickey Mouse."

"Oh? You should take him to Disneyland."

Isaac couldn't respond to the gruff remark. Disneyland was just a couple of hours away, on the outskirts of L.A. They could go any time—if things were different. If the circumstances allowed it, like how they couldn't even make it to Balboa Park despite it being right next door.

The familiar weight of frustration crept up on him, tightening his throat.

"What's the point of writing letters if you can't even send them?" Felix tapped his fingers on the counter, muttering, almost to himself.

The sarcastic remark stung, but Isaac couldn't argue. He pressed his lips together in silence. Felix sighed, brushing his hair back in frustration.

"Isaac," he said, his voice firm. "There aren't any customers here. Close up and come out."

His tone left little room for debate, and the determined look in Felix's eyes made it clear he wasn't taking no for an answer. But Isaac hesitated, unsure how to respond.

Leave? It was barely one in the afternoon. Where was Felix expecting him to go at this hour, especially when he was supposed to run the shop? Isaac stared at him, confused, but Felix's brow creased, and he flicked his head toward the door—his silent command to come out.

"It's too early to close the store—" Isaac began, but Felix cut him off.

"From now on, I'll cover your sales—double, if that's what it takes. So get up."

Isaac's excuse crumbled under the weight of Felix's unwavering gaze, those piercing Prussian blue eyes making it clear arguing was pointless. Felix was dead set on dragging him out, no matter what. After a moment of hesitation, Isaac sighed and grabbed his crossbody bag.

"Where are we going?" he asked, locking the glass door behind him as the bell gave a faint chime. His tone was blunt, frustration bubbling up.

Felix, watching him, clicked his tongue.

"See? You usually act like you're carved out of stone," Felix muttered, half to himself.

Isaac didn't catch all of it, but as he pulled the shutters down, he glanced up to see Felix with his arms crossed, head cocked to the side.

"There's such a gap, isn't there? How does someone as poker-faced as you end up so seductive in bed? You were a bona fide temptress."

The low, languid whisper was too smooth and sweet, making him feel like he'd melt. Felix's eyes burned into him with such intensity that Isaac felt heat rising beneath his skin. His body, betraying him once again, simmered at the memory. He quickly looked away, straightening up.

"So, where are we going?" Isaac asked again, forcing a curt tone to keep himself grounded. If he wasn't careful, Felix's charm would sweep him away.

"You're no fun."

Isaac didn't respond.

"You'll see when we get there," Felix replied, his tone matching Isaac's curtness with equal brusqueness.

A sinking feeling settled in Isaac's chest, but there wasn't much he could do. Pushing down his doubts, he silently followed Felix out of the shop, bracing himself for whatever came next.

It was a quiet afternoon, and the weather was phenomenal. On a day like this, Isaac should have been at a picnic, enjoying the sunshine, not following a dangerous man to who knew where. What a waste of perfect weather.

His thoughts were starting to turn gloomy again.

Felix led the way to a sleek sedan parked on the mostly empty street. Isaac had been wondering about the whereabouts of Felix's usual entourage, Tony and Jack. His curiosity was answered when he spotted them standing silently by the car. One of them opened the door for Felix without a word.

Felix stood with one hand on the open car door and the other casually tucked into his pocket. His posture radiated arrogance as he gave Isaac a subtle nudge with his chin, signaling him to move.

"Get in," he said, in that typical, self-assured way of his, as if he were doing Isaac a favor.

Isaac knew better than to argue. Any protest would be pointless.

He flexed his sweaty palms, feeling his reluctance mount, but ultimately squeezed himself into the back seat. Felix followed, sliding in beside him.

Isaac hated being dragged along like this, but what choice did he have? When Felix said *let's go*, it wasn't a suggestion—it was a command. With a sigh, Isaac settled back as the sedan glided smoothly down the street.

They cut across Downtown San Diego, and before long, the sedan pulled up to a marina. San Diego was a coastal city, with the sea visible from almost anywhere, but the sight of so many yachts docked at the wharf still made Isaac's eyes widen.

"Are we going on a yacht?" he asked, suspicion creeping into his voice. Felix's outfit had been a red flag from the start, and now it all made sense.

"Yeah," Felix replied, flashing a smile. He seemed far too pleased with himself. On the other hand, Isaac felt his mood darken with every passing second.

Why was Felix like this? The thought of being alone with him made Isaac uneasy, but now, heading out to the open sea where no one else would be around? A knot of anxiety twisted in his stomach. Was Felix planning to throw him overboard?

"You're going to shrivel up if you keep shutting yourself in that tiny flower shop every day." Felix's comment left Isaac speechless. "You need sun and a little water to grow properly."

Felix's reasoning for dragging him onto a yacht was absurd, and it sapped what little energy Isaac had left. Still, no matter what Felix said, Isaac couldn't shake the uneasy feeling about what might happen out at sea.

"That's fine," Isaac replied dryly, "since I'm not a plant."

"What's fine? You're so pale sitting there—you look like you're on your last leg."

Isaac tried to argue, but as usual, his protests were useless. Felix tutted, leading the way with his hands casually stuffed into his pockets. "Just pretend you're a rich playboy with too much time and money on his hands. Taking a day off on a yacht, floating in the middle of the ocean, is the perfect way to relieve stress on a beautiful day."

"I get seasick."

"Then take a tablet. There's plenty on the yacht. Don't worry."

Oblivious to the doubts gnawing at Isaac, Felix kept marching toward the wharf. With Felix ahead and Jack and Tony flanking him from behind, Isaac felt more like a prisoner being escorted than a guest.

Isaac scratched his cheek, feeling uncomfortable, and absently raised his gaze. His eyes landed on Felix's back—broad and powerful, his blond hair fluttering in the ocean breeze, gleaming under the bright sun. With each step, his back muscles rippled beneath the fabric of his white polo shirt, highlighting a body that seemed almost sculpted. From head to toe, Felix was the epitome of masculine perfection. It wasn't just his looks, though—he had everything.

While Isaac admired Felix, they reached the deck. He quickly turned his gaze away. The blue waves glimmered under the blistering sunlight, the ocean stretching out in all its mesmerizing beauty. Despite his wariness of the sea, Isaac couldn't deny its allure.

He sighed out of habit, casting another glance at Felix, who was walking around the deck with ease. It struck him then—Felix and the ocean were alike. Both seemed calm and peaceful on the surface, but beneath, they held a terrifying power when stirred. Even Felix's enigmatic blue eyes were the same shade as the water.

Isaac stood at the stern, his attention torn between the sun-dappled waves and Felix. Then, the low hum of the motor sounded, and the yacht began to move. His shoulders tensed involuntarily as the boat surged toward open water. It started slow but quickly accelerated, making Isaac sway on his feet.

The salty air whipped across his face, carrying the unmistakable scent of the fishy ocean. It was far from refreshing, in fact, it only heightened his unease. Yet, Isaac maintained his composure, sat down, and looked around.

Given how swiftly they left the dock, the yacht must have been prepared to go as soon as they boarded. Even a private yacht usually requires time-consuming preparations.

As the shoreline faded into the distance, Isaac's stomach twisted with anxiety. They must be going to the middle of the ocean. His expression remained blank, but his nerves were fraying inside.

It wasn't until Felix finished speaking with his subordinates and the yacht had moved quite far from land that he finally approached Isaac, who was sitting placidly. Felix's dark sunglasses obscured his ocean-blue eyes, and Isaac almost felt disappointed; the thought was fleeting.

"Sorry I left you alone," Felix said, his smile easy and disarming. "Had a few things to sort out with the boys."

He stood with his back to the sun, that perfect smile plastered on his face. It was a smile designed to bewitch people. As if he hid his true nature and wore a picturesque smile, who could resist being bewitched by this blindingly beautiful man?

"It's fine," Isaac replied, trying to keep his tone aloof, though he couldn't help but admire Felix's radiant appearance.

Suddenly, the yacht picked up speed again, the motor roaring louder. Isaac swayed, a small sound escaping his lips.

"Is the damn captain in a hurry or something?"

Isaac didn't respond. His face paled, and before he could say anything, Felix leaned against Isaac's armrest, concern flickering in his voice.

"You okay?"

Isaac stared at his reflection in Felix's sunglasses, his hand covering his mouth. He tried to say, "Med—" but couldn't get the word out. A moment later, he vomited all over Felix's pristine, wrinkle-free pants. Felix's sunny smile faltered, clouding over as the moment soured. The only silver lining was that Isaac hadn't eaten much for lunch.

Chapter 10

Felix had showered and sat across from Isaac in another, even more casual outfit—a polo t-shirt and shorts. Isaac swept his eyes over Felix, from head to slippered toe, before sitting upright from his supine position on the sofa.

"Feeling better?" Felix asked.

"Thanks to you." Isaac's voice was flat as he sipped from the glass of water on the tea table. After taking several relievers, his motion sickness had finally subsided, but he still felt a lingering discomfort. He was forced to lie on the sofa instead of the deck until it passed; he was grateful it had passed. Still, Isaac couldn't help but have mixed feelings. He hadn't expected to vomit. Even though it had been a while since he'd been on a boat, he didn't think he'd get sick so quickly.

"I didn't think you'd just throw up on me like that with a straight face."

"I told you, I get seasick."

"Yeah, well, I didn't know it was that bad," Felix muttered as an excuse. The fact that he'd dragged someone prone to seasickness onto a yacht without warning seemed to weigh on him. His expression was tight and scrunched as he glanced at Isaac.

No matter how severely seasick Isaac was, he wouldn't have been surprised if throwing up on Felix Felice's pants had earned him a gunshot and a burial at sea. Instead, Felix seemed embarrassed. That alone told Isaac he was getting special treatment, a realization that sent an uncomfortable throb through his chest. Nothing good ever came from that.

"Why did you bring me out here?" Isaac asked, keeping his voice steady despite the subtle perturbed emotions in his gut. He couldn't afford to let his guard down over something as minor as this. Not with Felix. He always had to stay alert around him.

Isaac couldn't forget who he was dealing with—Felix Felice, a global arms dealer and mafia leader. The notorious Felix wouldn't have brought him out here without a reason. He'd casually told Isaac to enjoy the day like some idle playboy, but that couldn't be the whole story. Yet, Felix didn't seem in any rush to reveal his true intentions.

"We've got a party ready on deck," Felix said. "Feel like grabbing something to eat once you've settled down?"

Isaac shook his head. "Thank you, but I'm not up for it today."

"Hmm, well."

After vomiting like that, the last thing Isaac wanted was to put more food in his stomach. Felix frowned, clearly irritated that his plans had fallen apart.

Felix muttered, his brow creased in frustration, as if resigned to the situation, "Damn, I was hoping to bring this up in a better mood. What a waste."

Without turning around, he flicked his hand. Standing quietly behind him, Tony stepped forward and handed over an envelope. Felix pulled out the contents from the fancy envelope and laid them on the tea table in front of Isaac, the documents facing him.

"What is this?" Isaac asked.

"A contract." Felix's voice was flat, emotionless. The concern he'd shown earlier had vanished, replaced by a cold, businesslike demeanor. His sharp gaze made the air feel heavy, suffocating.

Nausea filled him as tension ran down Isaac's spine before he took the papers and perused them quietly. With each word, his expression grew more rigid.

"I want to make things official. If you go through it, you'll see I've included all your stipulations—exactly as you worded them."

Felix was the first to break the silence, leaning back with his elbow on the armrest, his chin resting on his hand. Isaac glanced up at him before returning to the contract. True to Felix's word, every stipulation Isaac had made was meticulously included. Not a single detail was off—except for one addition.

And that addition was the problem.

"I have to be with you during your ruts?" Isaac asked, staring at Felix in disbelief over the pages of the contract.

Felix shrugged casually. "Yeah."

"By myself?"

"Of course, by yourself. Why would I bring in someone else?" Felix responded, genuinely confused by Isaac's reaction.

A crease formed on Isaac's brow. He knew all too well what alphas' ruts were like, having witnessed them since he was young. A rut typically lasts three or four days. Alphas could take suppressants if they were busy or found it inconvenient, but when the conditions were right, they'd gather a group of betas and omegas and fucked them for days on end. One wasn't enough—they'd take three or four at a time, and even then, Isaac remembered, those involved were often left half-dead.

That was with regular or dominant alphas. But with a hyper-dominant alpha like Felix? Isaac didn't even want to imagine it, let alone be around for it.

He'd almost died the last time they were together, and that hadn't even been during Felix's rut. But to handle Felix alone during a rut? The idea was absurd.

"I have no plans to die in pieces," Isaac said coldly, snapping the contract down on the tea table. The memories of that night resurfaced, and the dull ache in his hips—barely healed—seemed to return.

"That won't happen," Felix replied smoothly. "All I'll do is make you lose your mind with pleasure."

Isaac narrowed his eyes, full of doubt. "Not likely."

"Don't you remember how much I made you scream last time?" Felix said these shameless things without a hint of embarrassment, even with Tony standing right behind them. But Isaac couldn't focus on Tony now. Felix watched him with a predatory gleam in his eyes, his chin propped up as if ready to devour him.

A shiver ran through Isaac's body.

"I won't tear you apart," Felix said, his gaze sharp as a blade but his voice smooth and sweet, like a crook tempting a child with candy. "So just sign."

Isaac's eyes narrowed even more, his expression full of disapproval.

Felix sighed, slapping his knee. "Isaac, I'll be honest."

Felix suddenly stood and moved to sit beside Isaac, casually draping an arm over the backrest. He turned to face him, and the deep ocean blue of his eyes seemed to trap Isaac, pulling him under their waves.

"I don't expect anything from you," Felix said quietly. "I'm a bit fickle," he continued. "After a night, I tend to lose interest. I've never kept a long-term partner."

Felix's gaze lingered on Isaac's lips as if he were imagining tasting them. The thought sent a cold shiver down Isaac's spine. His throat tightened, too dry to even swallow, let alone speak. "But ever since I first saw you, I was intrigued. I got curious to see what kind of face you'd make during sex. Even so, I thought that once I slept with you, I'd lose interest…but I didn't.

"Do you understand?" he whispered, his baritone voice sensual. Just by listening to it, Isaac's stomach clenched. It was worsened by the dusky alpha pheromones that hit his nose now that he was sitting so close. His breath was stolen.

"I can't stop thinking about you. It's driving me crazy," Felix admitted, his voice low. "It's not even my rut, and all I can think about is fucking you. This isn't normal."

Felix tilted his head, bringing his nose close to Isaac's neck as if inhaling his scent. His lips hovered just above Isaac's skin, barely a whisper away. The warm breath on his neck made Isaac's entire body tense. "You think you're in trouble because I want to fuck you all the time, not just once a week?"

"Even once a week is too much," Isaac muttered.

"Is it?"

Isaac sat rigidly, his back straight, his hand curled into a fist. Even though Felix wasn't touching him, the weight of his presence was suffocating. The thick alpha pheromones filled the air, overwhelming Isaac's senses. The scent was so overpowering that his vision began to blur.

He blinked, trying to stay conscious. He would've taken an extra suppressant if he had known this would happen. But Felix had dragged him out here without warning, leaving him unprepared.

"Well, that's too bad," Felix said smoothly. "For now, per the contract, it'll just be once a week. So, sign."

"I still cannot take responsibility for your rut."

"Isaac." He flinched at the warmth of Felix's lips brushing his ear, his name spoken in that deep voice. Isaac tried to steady his breath as he turned his gaze. Felix's blue eyes sparkled with amusement, a silent laugh playing in them. "Why do you think I brought you out here?"

Isaac didn't respond.

"If you don't sign, you're not leaving."

Hearing the obvious threat, Isaac nearly cursed aloud. *Why were his bad instincts always right?*

As Isaac's expression darkened, Felix simply shrugged, still wearing that infuriating smile. "I plan on spending my next rut with you. That's non-negotiable. But in return, ask for anything you want. I'll add it to the contract immediately."

"Immediately?"

"Didn't I mention we have a notary on board?" Felix said

casually.

You *didn't,* Isaac thought, but the words wouldn't come out. He could only sigh deeply, realizing just how neatly he'd fallen into Felix's trap.

"What happens if I don't stick to the terms?"

"Oh, that's on the last page," Felix replied.

Isaac quickly snatched the contract back and flipped to the last page. As Felix had said, the final article detailed the provisions regarding a breach of contract. Isaac's expression darkened further.

"In the event of a breach of contract, the contractor will engage in sexual intercourse with Felix Felice whenever and wherever he wants." Isaac couldn't contain his displeasure any longer; his stony facade cracked. "What is this? Please add a penalty fee instead."

"I have all the money in the world—why would I want anything else?" Felix's words were calm and self-assured, cutting off Isaac's retort. But Isaac felt his stomach knot. "Don't you get it? The only thing I want from you is that lewd body of yours. Besides, a breach of contract should have bigger stakes than the contract itself."

Wasn't this contract too vulgar? Even the breach clause sounded childish—undoubtedly Felix's handiwork. The entire deal had his fingerprints all over it, particularly that part.

Isaac pressed his temples, the memory of their first conversation about the deal flashing through his mind. Back then, just like now, Felix had smirked as he complained about how unfair it was, insisting he never took a loss. And now? He'd made sure he wouldn't.

Isaac's throat felt dry, but what could he say? He was the one who'd brought up the deal, knowing exactly what kind of man Felix was—a man who would bleed him dry.

"Isaac, what are you so worried about? I'm not even profiting from this."

"How are you not profiting?" Isaac shot back, eyes narrowing

in disbelief.

"Do you think I've ever handed someone a contract and said, 'Write whatever you want'?" Felix replied smoothly, confidence radiating off him. "I'm a businessman. I've never signed anything this unreasonable."

Isaac sighed.

"Besides," Felix continued, "who else can protect your precious Benjamin better than me? That alone makes sure you're not losing anything, right?"

Isaac said nothing.

"You don't think there's anything more important than your child's life, do you?" Felix's voice was like a knife, poking right at Isaac's vulnerability. The knowing look on his face made it clear he was fully aware of what he was doing. Isaac, though, as a parent, was stunned.

What could be more important than Benjamin? Any parent would do anything to keep their child safe. Not every parent, perhaps, but Isaac? Absolutely.

Yes, the idea of selling his body gnawed at him, but this was Felix Felice…

Isaac exhaled slowly, trying to organize his thoughts.

Felix's fingers trailed lightly across Isaac's nape. "Don't overthink it. It's just sex. And trust me," his voice dipped lower. "I'll make you scream even louder than last time. You might not be able to live without me. No—you definitely won't."

Without waiting for a response from Isaac, Felix continued, "Because I plan to make you mine."

Isaac turned his eyes to Felix, who whispered the words. The alpha's pheromones were thickening in the air again. Just from that, Isaac felt his cock stir, half-hard already. He bit his lip, trying to control himself.

It wasn't Felix's hyper-dominant nature that scared Isaac. He'd long since accepted the pull of Felix's pheromones, the way they made him swoon. What worried him was spending time with Felix during his rut. Would suppressants be enough? Isaac feared Felix's rut might trigger his own heat cycle.

He'd heard of omegas whose heats were triggered prematurely by an alpha's rut. It could work the other way, too—an alpha entering a rut from overstimulation after sex with an omega in heat.

Isaac's heat had been dormant since that night four years ago, but the fear still gnawed at him. Could he handle this dangerously captivating man, this hyper-dominant alpha, during his rut? Could he keep his sanity intact?

If Felix discovered he was an omega, what would he do? The thought unsettled Isaac deeply. He considered confessing the truth. If he did, the peaceful life he'd envisioned could shatter, but perhaps it was better to reveal it now than suffer the consequences later. He weighed the choice in his mind.

Felix broke the silence, his voice softer this time, as if sensing his turmoil. "Isaac, the first reason I want to spend my rut with you…is because your body is amazing."

Isaac snapped out of his thoughts and met Felix's dark gaze. Without breaking eye contact, Felix picked up the glass of water from the tea table—the very one Isaac had been drinking from just moments ago—and casually wet his lips.

"It's also because you're a beta," Felix murmured, setting the glass down with a soft thud.

Isaac's confession, which had been on the tip of his tongue, plummeted back down. What perfect timing. "Because I'm…a beta?"

"Yeah. I told you before I despise omegas, and I don't plan on having a kid anytime soon. But the problem with ruts is that if you're not careful, you can impregnate someone—especially an omega."

Isaac stayed silent while Felix continued, "So I never touch an omega while in rut. In that aspect, you're perfect. You're not an omega or a female beta, and your body is exactly my type."

Felix's voice was calm, almost matter-of-fact, while Isaac's mind went blank. If that was Felix's reason, then he'd already breached the contract. The right thing to do would've been to admit he was an omega before signing anything. But the words refused to come.

Isaac's gaze shifted to the contract and the empty glass on the table, anxiety creeping in. Suddenly, a fountain pen appeared before him, and without realizing it, he let out a faint hum.

"Sign." Felix had urged him to sign many times, but this time, it felt different. The look in Felix's eyes was dangerous; the pen held out in a way that made Isaac's pulse quicken with fear. If he still refused after all this coaxing, Felix might lose patience and do something drastic—like throw him overboard.

Swallowing dryly, Isaac took the pen with trembling fingers, his thoughts so scattered he felt queasy. He held Felix's gaze, then spoke with a voice barely above a whisper, "You said I could ask for anything."

"Yeah," Felix tilted his head, curious. "Has something come to mind?"

Isaac swallowed again. "Yes. I want to add one more thing."

"Tell me."

"Promise you will not, under any circumstances, harm me or my family. Put it as a clause in the contract and swear on it."

Felix, who had been raising his hand to call for the notary, froze. His brow furrowed in confusion. "Why would you think I'd harm you or your family?"

"Just in case. Let's say it's to prepare for all contingencies. Whatever happens, no matter the circumstance, no matter how angry you are with me, you can't touch me or my family."

Felix sighed. "That's..." he trailed off, muttering under his breath, "ridiculous."

He snapped his fingers, the sound cutting through the tense silence. Immediately, the notary stepped forward, Tony following close behind. Despite his complaints, Felix had the contract revised on the spot and signed it without hesitation before handing it to Isaac. Isaac accepted it with both hands, carefully reading through it again. Then, with a trembling hand, he signed.

The contract didn't specify that Isaac had to be a beta, so technically, there wasn't a breach. Besides, Isaac had no intention of secretly bearing Felix's child. But if it ever came out that he was an omega and Felix got angry…the clause that protected him from harm gave him some peace of mind.

Of course, Isaac knew that if Felix was truly enraged, he was the type of man to disregard any contract. But for now, Isaac felt satisfied with at least this tiny bit of protection.

"Hmm. Very good," Felix said, his voice filled with approval as he examined the signed document. He handed it over to the notary, who gave Isaac a copy of the contract in an envelope and explained the terms briefly. Isaac looked down at the pristine envelope with a swirl of mixed emotions.

"Now that the contract is signed…" Felix's voice came from beside him. Isaac finally lifted his eyes, trying to suppress the storm of thoughts in his head. He had been so preoccupied that he hadn't even noticed Tony and the notary leaving the room. The cabin's air felt thick and stifling.

Isaac's spine went rigid with apprehension as Felix's suggestive gaze lingered on him. The contract was signed, so why was Felix still like this?

"Unfortunately, I'll be away from San Diego next week for business."

"So?"

"So. I want to collect my contract price in advance—today."

The yacht trip out in the middle of the ocean wasn't just about signing the contract; Felix had orchestrated this moment, too. He gently grasped Isaac's chin, tilting his head upward. Their faces were so close that their lips were nearly touching. But before Felix could close the distance, Isaac lifted a hand and pressed it against Felix's mouth, stopping him in his tracks.

"I don't mind doing it in advance."

"Yeah, but?"

"But you need to take my personal life into consideration."

"Personal life?" Felix repeated, his tone making it seem like he had no idea Isaac even had one.

Isaac sighed. "Tomorrow, we're having Benjamin's birthday party. I want to attend…and I will."

"Birthday party?" Felix parroted the words, sounding incredulous. Isaac gave him a look, and Felix blinked, snapping back to his senses. With a frustrated click of his tongue, Felix pulled back, surprisingly giving up quicker than Isaac had expected.

But the way Felix ruffled his hair and pouted was like a child sulking after being denied a treat. Benjamin sometimes made that same face when he was caught sneaking too many chocolates and had to give them up. Seeing Felix wear the same expression made Isaac break into a snicker.

Felix stared at him sullenly. "The agreed day will be Monday. If you will not be available on Monday, let me know first."

Isaac softened his expression slightly. "As I said, tomorrow is Benjamin's birthday party. I need to be there by the afternoon, so if you want to do it now…don't be as rough as last time—"

Before Isaac could finish, Felix grabbed his neck and pulled him into a heated kiss. His grip was firm, almost possessive, and his lips pressed against Isaac's with a hunger that made Isaac's stomach flip. Alpha pheromones flooded the space, intoxicating and overwhelming. Isaac's eyes fluttered shut as he parted his lips, giving in to the kiss.

Their tongues met, tangling in a rough, relentless dance until

Isaac's felt sore. The kiss was wet, desperate, and possessive—Felix's lips sucked at his with such force it left them throbbing. His tongue explored every corner of Isaac's mouth, brushing against his teeth, claiming every inch. The intensity made Isaac dizzy, and a string of saliva slipped from the corner of his mouth.

"Uh, hmm—" Isaac gasped for air, instinctively wrapping his arms around Felix's broad shoulders. Only then did Felix pause, lifting his head. Isaac's chest heaved as he tried to catch his breath, his mind spinning from the kiss and the flood of alpha pheromones.

"Isaac, I'll do anything you ask…" Felix's thumb wiped away the saliva collected on Isaac's chin, and he growled low in his throat. Isaac cracked his eyes open, his vision hazy from the kiss, his body buzzing from Felix's presence. "Don't smile like that in front of others."

Felix traced Isaac's wet lips with his finger before leaning in to bite them lightly, a warning in his gesture. Isaac whimpered at the sharp sting.

Smile? Isaac's mind raced, still foggy from the kiss. Did he smile just now? He wasn't even sure what Felix meant.

Felix offered no further explanation, too focused on stripping Isaac with impatient hands. Isaac's shirt came off in a blur, followed by his pants and underwear, which were discarded swiftly.

Once Isaac was completely bare, Felix wasted no time shedding his clothes. His outerwear hit the floor, followed by the sound of his zipper being undone and his pants thudding to the floor. Even as Isaac lay back on the sofa, biting his lip nervously, his eyes couldn't leave Felix's lust-filled, muscular form.

"I'll make sure you get to Benjamin's birthday party by tomorrow afternoon," Felix promised, his voice thick with desire as he licked his lips and stroked his throbbing erection.

Isaac couldn't shake the feeling that he had fallen for another one of Felix's tricks. But there was no turning back now. Resigned to his fate, Isaac wrapped his arms around Felix's body as it moved toward him with predatory intent.

The sun, still glaring through the cabin's tiny window, illuminated the room, but the space was already suffused with a sensual heat as thick and stifling as the night.

Night had fallen.

Isaac had no idea how much time had passed. After all the convulsing, moaning, and sprawling, when he finally opened his eyes, it was already late—and he wasn't where he started. They had begun on the cabin sofa, but now he was stretched out on a large bed.

Groaning softly, Isaac tried to sit up, his body protesting with every movement. His ass, hips, and limbs ached all over. His wrists still tingled from where Felix had pinned them, and red handprints lingered on his thighs. His nipples, sore and sensitive, stung from the rough attention they'd received.

He'd barely recovered from the last time, and here he was again. He wondered if he'd even be able to walk tomorrow. Grumbling to himself, Isaac pressed a hand to his forehead, scanning the room. Felix was nowhere in sight, and the en suite bathroom remained silent. With another groan, Isaac collapsed back onto the soft bed. His body felt sticky, unclean, and uncomfortable, but his greater concern was whether he could even manage to stand.

I told you not to overdo it, he thought, though he should have known better. Expecting restraint from Felix was asking the impossible.

Isaac draped an arm over his eyes, taking slow, steady breaths as he tried to ignore the sticky sensation of semen trickling down his thighs. Felix had overdone it this time. Drowsiness was already pulling him under.

"Are you falling asleep?" a low voice broke the quiet just as Isaac was about to drift off.

Startled, Isaac jolted upright, yanking his arm away from his face. The sudden motion caused Felix, perched on the edge of the bed with a glass of water, to spill it. A cold splash soaked his pants.

"Well, damn," Felix muttered, looking down at the mess. "This is the second time today you've ruined my pants."

"Ah…" Isaac blinked, waking from his slumber, still trying to grasp the situation. He must have broken into a cold sweat during his brief nap; his black hair clung to his forehead and cheeks.

"Did you have a nightmare or something? Why are you so surprised?" Felix asked, shaking off his damp pants. He looked clean and fresh, like he'd just taken another shower; his hair was still slightly wet. He appeared ready for bed and dressed in a white t-shirt and pajama pants. Taking in his appearance, Isaac finally relaxed his shoulders and released a long breath.

"…I'm used to sleeping alone. If someone talks to me while I'm asleep, I get startled," Isaac explained, wiping the cold sweat from his forehead.

Felix extended a half-empty cup of water to him. "Drink some water first."

His throat felt hoarse, so Isaac accepted the cup and drank it in one go. The sensation of the cool water sliding down his throat was refreshing, clearing his head a little. Still holding the empty cup, Isaac said suddenly, "I have a question,"

Felix had slipped next to him on the bed, propping his head on one arm against a pillow.

"What is it?" He asked.

Isaac stared at Felix's elongated form and took a fortifying breath, "Omegas. Why do you hate them so much?"

Felix's brow crinkled instantly at the question, as if he was recalling something he didn't want to.

Thinking he had asked a needless question, Isaac tried to wave it away. "If it's difficult for you to answer, you don't have to—"

However, Felix cut off Isaac's embarrassment and elaborated, "I didn't like them before, but I didn't hate them either. Some omegas threw themselves at me, which I hated because their pheromones smelled tacky. Sometimes, though, they could be enjoyable."

"But?"

"Four years ago, I met this insolent, impudent omega." Felix's voice became bitter as he glared at the empty air. Suddenly, his eyes turned violent, and the mere thought of this person made him grind his teeth, squeezing his fists until the veins popped out. Isaac fidgeted with his empty cup. "I found this omega suffering from his heat cycle in an unexpected location. I spent the entire night helping the poor sap through his heat like a gentleman."

"Did…you?"

"But then that cheeky omega bastard tied me up while I was asleep. The gall of him." Felix's voice darkened further, and Isaac turned away, wishing he could stop listening. But he couldn't seem to halt once Felix started until he finished. "And you know what that bastard said?"

The sound of grinding teeth was visceral. Isaac swallowed dryly, bracing himself. "'The only reason I didn't break your neck is that your plowing was decent.' He fucking said that! That impudent shit! To me! And not only that. After the fucking omega wagged his tongue, he went and broke my left arm! He fucking stomped on it! So I wouldn't be able to come after him!"

Enraged, Felix punched the mattress, indenting the thick bedding and sending dust into the air. "I went out of my way to help that bastard through his heat, and that's how he repays me? Fuck! And then he acts like he did me a huge favor by telling me he intentionally avoided my right arm."

Reaching the end of his tether, Felix erupted from the bed, his face flushed with rage. Isaac hunched his shoulders, realizing he had indeed asked a needless question.

"You know what's funny? The fucker thought he was letting

me off easy by breaking only my left arm—" Felix exuded a murderous aura, his eyes shining with a madness that sent shivers down Isaac's spine. "I'm left-handed."

"Oh dear."

Felix curled his lips into a snarl, his expression promising that if the omega appeared right then, he would snap his neck. It was a hair-raising sight, an incomparably sinister smile.

Isaac couldn't help the chill running down his spine as he rubbed at the dry corners of his mouth. His palms were soaked with sweat when a lethal voice reached his ear.

"If I ever catch that bastard, I'll break both his arms and his neck."

Chapter 11

A shapely nose, angular jaw, and full lips peeking from behind dark sunglasses captured everyone's attention. Glossy blond hair, a tall stature, and a sturdy frame dressed in high-end fashion only heightened his allure. There was not a single part of him that wasn't glamorous. He could have easily turned heads on Hollywood Boulevard, yet here he was at a birthday party for a three-year-old. It was no wonder the parents were wide-eyed in astonishment.

As Felix surveyed the chaotic backyard teeming with children, he clicked his tongue. "Look at all these brats."

The party area was already a disaster zone. Toys were being tossed around, fingers poked into the cake, and the air was filled with screams and laughter, punctuated by the occasional wail of a child who had stumbled and fallen.

Felix grimaced at the pandemonium. Behind him, Isaac shook his head, regretting his decision to bring Felix along. Why had he insisted on this?

Earlier that morning, Isaac had rushed off the boat as soon as it docked, stealing glances at Felix, who followed him with casual indifference.

"How long are you going to follow me?" Isaac finally asked, turning around and unable to hold back any longer.

"Hmm? You mentioned a birthday party, so I thought I'd join you," Felix replied, feigning innocence.

Why? He thought, struggling to voice his discomfort and making a face instead, "You really don't have to come…"

"I know I don't have to, but I want to." Issac didn't respond, so Felix asked coolly, "Why? Is there a reason I can't?"

Of course, there was no reason to stop him from joining. The more, the merrier when celebrating a child's birthday. Besides, Felix was the one tasked with protecting Benjamin, so his presence was warranted.

Still, Isaac couldn't shake his growing discomfort and scratched his chin. He knew that no matter how many hints he dropped about his reluctance, they would fall on deaf ears, and nothing would get through Felix's head. He couldn't keep refusing Felix's stubbornness as it outright felt impossible. Ultimately, he found himself hitching a ride in Felix's car to La Jolla, sighing inwardly and questioning his choices the entire way.

Isaac couldn't understand why Felix insisted on tagging along to a child's birthday party. His unease grew as the car picked up speed, the passing scenery blurring into a dull haze. In stark contrast, Felix appeared to be in high spirits, tapping away on his tablet and humming a cheerful tune. Anyone who saw him would think he was off to a picnic rather than a chaotic birthday celebration.

Upon arriving, Felix glanced at the sprawling backyard where the party was unfolding and grimaced. He seemed worlds away from anything related to children, clearly unprepared for the frenzy of a birthday bash.

Isaac stood behind him, wearing dark sunglasses to conceal his discomfort. He masked his anxious expression by rubbing the sides of his mouth. With Felix sticking out like a sore thumb, Isaac felt a surge of embarrassment wash over him.

But Isaac's worries didn't linger long. In one corner of the yard, a balloon artist was crafting animals, flowers, and swords for the kids. Benjamin, standing in line, spotted Isaac and erupted with joy. All of Isaac's doubts evaporated.

"Daddy!" the child called, waving enthusiastically and calling for his dad. He longed to run to Isaac, whom he hadn't seen in a while, but he also wanted to claim his balloon. Torn between the two desires, he jumped up and down, unable to contain his

excitement.

Watching Benjamin bounce with delight, Isaac couldn't help but laugh silently. Covering his mouth, he raised his free hand in a small wave. How precious it was that the child recognized him and was so thrilled to see him. A wide smile broke across his face, covered by his hand.

"Oh? Benjamin recognizes me!" Felix, one step ahead, waved thoughtlessly to the child. "Benjamin!"

Isaac stiffened and shot a sideways glance at Felix. Benjamin continued jumping up and down, calling for his "dad," but Felix seemed to think he was the one being called. He waved back with a bright smile, utterly oblivious to the commotion around them.

All eyes were on them, especially on Felix, who bore a striking resemblance to Benjamin. As Felix waved excitedly, whispers spread through the crowd, suggesting he must be Benjamin's father.

Isaac froze, completely caught off guard by the unexpected turn of events, leaving him at a loss for words.

"Hey, I think Benjamin likes me, doesn't he?" Felix said, looking back at Isaac with a triumphant grin, oblivious to Isaac's turmoil. Isaac struggled to respond, yet again unable to voice the truth. The words were lodged in his throat.

"I think so," he muttered, his tone weary as he averted his gaze.

Felix beamed, basking in the warm reception. As if talking to himself, he said, "Great! It was worth getting the squash presents."

Isaac glanced up in surprise, though his eyes remained hidden behind his sunglasses. "Presents? Squash?"

Felix realized he had let something slip and shrugged. "Ah, I arranged for them after I heard it was his birthday. It was supposed to be a surprise, but I guess the cat's out of the bag."

"No, before that…Did you just call Benjamin a squash?"

"Yeah," Felix replied, proud of his comment and completely unaware of the distress it caused. He couldn't be any more obnoxious.

Isaac's eyebrows shot up behind his sunglasses. "Why would you call someone's child a squash?"

"What's wrong with squashes? His hair is yellow like a ripe squash."

Most people would think of chicks when they saw something yellow, not squashes. Isaac was scandalized. Who went around calling someone else's precious child a "squash"?

"It'd be nice if he grew round like a squash," Felix added, unfazed.

It would be nicer if he'd stop talking, Isaac thought, staring speechless at Felix's self-assured interpretation. In response, Felix arched an eyebrow, looking reproachful.

"Why are you looking at me like that? You're making me want to kiss you," Felix muttered, pouting as if he could sense Isaac's gaze through the sunglasses.

"I think you've received enough payment already."

"It doesn't have to be that day for me to kiss you."

"I would prefer it to be that day."

"You're no fun." Felix pouted like a child this time, his lips jutting out further. Isaac didn't react; he kept his focus on Benjamin.

In the meantime, Benjamin temporarily forgot about Isaac, his attention captured by the balloon artist skillfully twisting balloons into a dog and then a flower. With adorably plump red cheeks and parted lips, Benjamin peered between his friends' heads, captivated by the balloon creations. At that moment, he was the center of Isaac's world.

Benjamin was Isaac's pride and joy.

Isaac gazed at him, wanting to etch the scene into his memory. After today, he wouldn't see the child for a few more days, and unlike the other parents, he wasn't free to take pictures…

"So, what did you get him?" Isaac asked, pushing his emotions aside in an attempt to distract himself.

"You'll see," Felix said with a playful grin, shrugging exaggeratedly.

Felix's confident reply suggested he had given the birthday present considerable thought. Still, Isaac was surprised he had prepared a gift in less than a day. Grateful yet burdened, he regarded Felix with mixed emotions.

For a moment, he regretted bringing up Benjamin's birthday party. However, if he had tried to avoid the topic, Felix would have pressed for an answer until he got it, making the situation inevitable.

"Benjamin will love it."

"How can you be sure when you don't even know what he likes?"

"Because I heard every kid would love one. I know I did when I was young."

Isaac didn't know what the present was, but Felix curled his lips in self-satisfaction. He crossed his arms haughtily and fixed his gaze on Benjamin, looking every bit the proud father. The thought flickered through Isaac's mind, and he quickly averted his gaze.

Finally, after a long wait in line, Benjamin received a balloon shaped like a fire truck from the artist. Beaming with joy, he ran over to Isaac, bubbling with excitement.

"Daddy, look! Fire truck!" he exclaimed, waving the balloon in the air. But in the blink of an eye, Benjamin tripped, slipping on the grass and landing flat on his face. Struggling to get up, he burst into tears.

"Wahhh! Daddy, I'm bleeding!" he wailed.

Crying echoed around them as Isaac quickly dashed over, scooping Benjamin into his arms.

The child's tender knees were scratched and red from the fall, but thankfully, he had landed on grass, and there was no blood. Benjamin, in his shock, equated being hurt with bleeding and burst into tears. Isaac's heart ached at the sight of his son's distress, even over such a minor wound.

"It's okay. It's not bleeding. See? It's not bleeding," Isaac reassured Benjamin while gently patting his back. Just then, Isaac's mother hurried over, her face etched with worry, holding ointment ready to tend to Benjamin's scraped knees.

But upon seeing her, Benjamin's cries intensified, "Grandma, I'm bleeding…"

"Don't cry, sweetheart. It'll be alright once we put on the medicine and a band-aid," she comforted him.

At that moment, as Isaac's mother was comforting the child, a shadow fell over them, and a baritone voice interrupted. "What's the fuss?"

Isaac looked up reflexively to find Felix gazing down at him, hands in his pockets. Isaac's mother noticed Felix and stared, her eyes widening in surprise before she turned to Isaac.

Who wouldn't be surprised to see a man who looked exactly like Benjamin standing imposingly over them?

She kept glancing back and forth between Felix and Benjamin, confusion etched on her face. Isaac quietly shook his head. Taking a deep breath, she helped Benjamin to his feet. "See, Benjamin? It's not bleeding, and you can't even see it now that you have a band-aid on!"

The child nodded bravely at his grandmother's gentle words, though his runny tears and short breaths betrayed his distress. Soon enough, as if intimidated by Felix's presence, Benjamin hiccuped and wiped his eyes with his sleeve.

"Now you look a bit tough," Felix said, watching Benjamin intently. "Hey, if you stop crying, I'll give you your present."

"Present?" Benjamin said, his tears vanishing in an instant as he turned eagerly to Felix as if he hadn't been crying at all. Still wiping his son's nose, Isaac glanced up at Felix, too.

"Sure. It's your birthday party, so of course, I brought a birthday present," Felix replied matter-of-factly, fully aware he had captured the child's undivided attention.

Benjamin's blue eyes sparkled with anticipation. "Present!"

"You want to see it?" Felix asked.

"Yes, please!"

Felix stood imposingly, holding Benjamin's gaze before suddenly offering him his hand. Benjamin, trusting and unguarded, took it without hesitation. In one swift motion, Felix lifted him onto his shoulders. The child squealed with excitement, seemingly forgetting his earlier tears.

Felix joked, "If you cry and then laugh, you'll grow hair on your butt!"

"Not true!" Benjamin shouted back, giggling.

"No? Then let's bet on it! How old will you be when you grow hair on your—"

"Mr. Felice!" Isaac leaped to his feet, glaring at Felix, unable to tolerate the remarks any longer. Felix arched an eyebrow at Isaac's outburst. Only then did Isaac remember who he was dealing with, and he let out a sound as he cleared his throat: "Please behave yourself."

Though he had suppressed his emotions and phrased it carefully, Felix pouted as if he were wronged. "What did I do?"

"He's only three. What's with the butt hair?"

"What about it? It's true," Felix insisted, still clueless about what he was being chastised for.

Isaac sighed, realizing that even if he explained how Felix should watch his language around children, it wouldn't register.

"Never mind," he said, giving up and shaking his head.

Felix snorted in response, then began striding across the garden with Benjamin perched on his shoulders. The way he walked off, back turned and visibly offended, only added to Isaac's frustration.

"Where are you going?" Isaac called after him.

"To give him his present," Felix replied, heading toward the back gate with Benjamin in tow.

Isaac watched them go, pressing a hand to his throbbing head. Seeing a small child stacked on top of a larger, identical man-child was almost too much to bear.

Just as Felix passed through the back gate, Isaac heard a small voice beside him. "Could he be…Benjamin's father?"

Isaac turned to his mother, a middle-aged woman of small stature with graying hair and a prim face. Looking into her familiar features, he felt a wave of apprehension and rubbed his mouth thoughtfully.

"No." Isaac struggled to keep his expression neutral, but his voice trembled. His mother gestured for him to follow her elsewhere, and he followed her into the shade of a nearby tree. It was a cheerful afternoon; the sun streamed down, and children laughed and ran around.

Standing a foot apart from his mother, Isaac surveyed the peaceful scene, but his chest felt heavy despite the joyful atmosphere and the bubbling childish laughter.

"They look the same—Benjamin and that man." his mother remarked. Isaac ignored her comment, but she pressed on. "If you're going to deny it, you should've brought someone with a different face."

"Mother—" Isaac interrupted, anxiously rubbing his forehead. He knew his mother could see through his lies; she always had a keen eye for the truth.

Ever since he was a child, his mother knew whenever he was being dishonest. A poker face was useless against her; she could read him like a book. When he was younger, he wondered how she could tell exactly what he was thinking. Now, as a father, he understood all too well.

Isaac noticed everything about Benjamin—his expressions, speech, and actions. He could instinctively grasp the child's feelings based on his every word and gesture. He was always vigilant and concerned about him. His mother must have felt the same way about him, so she could see through all his childhood lies, even now, as an adult.

"I won't pry into your situation, but it didn't seem like he knows Benjamin is his son. Isn't that cruel?" He remained silent as his mother lectured him, "Of course, some people might not want to know or refuse to accept they have a child somewhere. But he came all the way here and treated Benjamin well. Surely, you can't hide the truth from him forever. It's cruel to deny a man the chance to recognize his own child—and it's cruel to Benjamin, too."

At her admonition, Isaac closed his eyes briefly before opening them again. "Mother, he is not Benjamin's father." His firm tone startled her, and she looked at him wide-eyed. Isaac pushed up his sunglasses and clenched his jaw. "He's a man who has never wanted a child and shouldn't have one. Benjamin isn't his."

"Really?" His mother asked again, still not understanding.

This time, Isaac met her gaze directly. "I'm Benjamin's father. No one else," he stated with finality.

Only then did she fall silent. An uncomfortable pause lingered between them, both lost in their thoughts.

A high-pitched voice cut through the air, "Benjamin's grandma! That man just now must have been Benjamin's father, right? They look exactly alike!"

Isaac glanced around and spotted a slim-built man approaching his mother with an air of familiarity. He was the omega mother of one of Benjamin's preschool friends, with a delicate bone structure that embodied the typical image of a male omega.

Without meaning to, Isaac's gaze drifted to the omega's neck, which displayed a pale mating bite—a mark most married alphas and omegas bore on their partners. It was an exclusive symbol of their bond, something a beta couldn't claim. Despite being a recessive omega, Isaac did not intend to conform to such norms.

He wanted nothing to do with it.

"Is that blond man your son?" the omega asked plainly.

Though the other parents had been watching them with keen interest, this was the first time someone had asked outright. Isaac's mother forced a strained smile. "It's not like that."

"Aha! If he's not your son, then he must be your son-in-law! We wondered where Benjamin got his looks from—it must be from his father!" The omega declared, much to his mother's dismay. She waved her hand to halt the omega's chatter, but he continued unabated. "What does he do? He looks so handsome and has such an aura about him!"

Listening to the omega's relentless questions, Isaac was about to step forward, figuring enough was enough, and intervene when a sudden cheer erupted from the children, stopping him in his tracks. The rest of the parents, who had been chatting in clusters, shifted their focus to a single point. Even the omega, who had been interrogating his mother, squealed, "Oh my goodness!"

Isaac turned around, his heart sinking at the sight before him. "Oh God," he groaned, his jaw dropping in disbelief.

Benjamin and Felix were entering through the back gate side by side. More specifically, Benjamin was riding a real, living pony—a fancy-looking white one—while Felix held the reins, walking leisurely. Isaac could hardly believe his eyes.

Benjamin sat in a child's saddle, complete with a belt and a cowboy hat on his head. He gripped the saddle horn tightly, his flushed cheeks glowing with excitement. His laughter rang out, pure joy echoing across the garden.

"A pony…" Isaac muttered, still in shock.

Felix looked positively beaming as he guided the pony around

the garden. Despite being Benjamin's first time riding a horse, the child was perched on the pony's back like a natural, relishing the experience.

As the shiny white pony made its entrance, the children's cheers grew louder. Some shrieked and ran to their parents in fright, while others cried, but most stood wide-eyed, eagerly begging for a turn.

In an instant, the garden erupted into chaos. Felix had been right—Benjamin truly loved his present. Yet Isaac found himself grappling with a swirl of complicated emotions.

Where had he even found a pony like that overnight? What was he thinking?

Isaac watched as the small white pony trotted around the garden. It was the kind of gift any child would be thrilled to receive, but it was more than they could manage—financially or practically. The expenses alone—from stabling to caring for a pony—were overwhelming.

He rubbed his throbbing temples, glancing back and forth between Felix and Benjamin, who was perched happily on the pony's back. They waved at him, matching smiles of triumph on their faces.

Isaac hadn't expected Felix to go this far.

"Can you really call yourself Benjamin's only father after this?" his mother murmured beside him, her expression troubled as she watched the scene unfold. Isaac couldn't respond. A heavy weight settled in his chest, dragging his heart down.

Chapter 12

Tony hadn't stopped thinking about that pony since yesterday afternoon. Felix had called him, demanding a white, purebred pony with the grace and pedigree of a champion, and Tony hadn't slept since. Dark circles shadowed his eyes.

If Felix had asked for a limited-edition luxury car, Tony could've handled that easily. But a pure white pony? He'd spent the night and the following day scouring every source he knew, desperate to pull off the impossible.

But this was Tony. Felix's right-hand man. The guy who could do anything Felix asked—even find a white pony on zero sleep. His nerves only eased a little when he finally laid eyes on the pony. He wouldn't rest until it was in Benjamin's backyard. He spent the night with bated breath and weary, baggy eyes, but at last, word came that they had it.

On the day of the party, Tony waited near the garden, tense, drenched in a cold sweat from pacing. When the pony arrived, he and his team sighed in relief. Some had their knees give out from under them, and everyone's faces were haggard.

Felix was informed that the pony had arrived and casually walked through the back gate with Benjamin perched on his shoulders like a mini version of himself. Whether he was aware of Tony and his team's sleepless search for the pony, Felix maintained a calm and relaxed demeanor.

Tony, however, knew his explosive nature could ignite at any moment, so as soon as he saw Felix, he squeezed his fists and braced himself. They had worked hard to achieve the impossible, he wouldn't start shooting just because he was dissatisfied—not with Benjamin here…

Tony was anxiously studying his face when a soft, satisfied

smile graced Felix's lips upon glimpsing the pony in the distance. From his expression, he could rest assured that the matter of the impossible birthday present was finally over.

Then…

"Who's in charge of security here?" The sharp words flew at them from Felix's shapely lips like a knife's edge, causing Tony to tense up again. He could tell something was wrong just by his voice.

"Head of security, come out," the low voice echoed again as he gulped.

Tony glanced nervously over his shoulder.

The security team assigned to protect Benjamin and the small estate in La Jolla consisted of their top men. They were highly trained, not prone to mistakes, and as far as Tony knew, no issues had arisen.

Whatever had set Felix off, he hadn't even gone through Tony first—he'd called for the head of security directly. The chill in the air made Tony's skin prickle.

"You called, boss!" The head of security, who had been standing by, quickly stepped forward, visibly tense.

The man looked even more exhausted than Tony and his team, who'd spent the night scouring every source they could to locate a "white, elegant, pedigree"pony. He had no idea why he'd been singled out and was clearly anxious.

"You fu—" Felix began, then stopped abruptly, glancing up at Benjamin. Clearing his throat, Felix visibly reined himself in, managing an awkward smile for the child's sake before returning his narrowed gaze to the head of security.

Tony's eyes widened at Felix's uncharacteristic show of concern for Benjamin. It wasn't like him at all. But Felix didn't seem to notice Tony's surprise; his gaze was now fixed sharply on the head of security, his expression dark.

"You're the head of security here?" Felix asked, his voice cold.

"Yes, boss!" the man replied, his tone loud but shaky.

Without warning, Felix nudged Benjamin's leg and pointed toward the sky. "Wow, Benjamin! Look—there's a bird up there!"

"A birdie? Where?" Benjamin twisted around to look, and everyone's attention shifted in the direction Felix was pointing, momentarily breaking the tension.

Crack.

The brutal sound of bone meeting bone sliced through the air, followed by a muffled gasp. At the sudden, grim noise, the men flinched and quickly looked forward again, shoulders tense.

The head of security, now clutching his shin, bit back his groans, his face reddening. Felix had kicked him sharply, and everyone around froze as they registered the ruthless blow.

The head of security swallowed back his groans of pain and straightened, standing before Felix like a convict. Felix's harsh gaze fell on his head.

"You're head of security? And you can't even manage to keep the grass safe? Felix's voice grew harsher. "The kid fell while he was running—look at his knee here. See that scrape? He needed cream and a band-aid. He's like this because he fell! Is this the best you can do? You call this security?"

"The grass, boss?"

"Are your ears clogged? Didn't you hear what I just said?"

"N-No, I heard! I apologize! I'll take care of the grass," the man stammered, almost in tears, as he stood at attention. The rest of the men, Tony included, looked increasingly pale.

Dear lord, Tony thought, pressing a hand to his throbbing head. All this trouble over the grass? It wasn't even their job to mow the lawn…

"Your job," Felix said slowly, "is to keep him from getting hurt. Isn't that right? You're his guard, right?"

"Y-Yes, sir."

"Then watch him more carefully and do your job. If the kid gets hurt one more time, I'll have your head—Ahem—I'll have you sleeping with the fishies!"

...Fishies.

An awkward silence fell over the group as they processed Felix's words, eyes widening in shock. It was such an undignified twist on "I'll kill you.'

"Are there fishies?" Benjamin asked from atop Felix's shoulders, eyes round with curiosity.

"Yeah, there are," Felix replied, humoring him with a slight smile.

"Fishies?" the child repeated, giggling. Despite the cold, tense atmosphere, his sunny disposition remained unaffected.

"Make sure he doesn't get a single scratch on him. That's why I pay you all so well. Understand?" Felix's voice was a low growl laced with barely restrained menace. Tony swallowed hard, reminded of the deadly side to Felix—even when he used words like "fishies."

Something still didn't sit right with Tony, though.

Sure, their job was to protect the child, but were they really expected to monitor the state of the lawn, too? Tony stifled a sigh, deciding it was best to stay silent. He could only keep his mouth shut and hope he wouldn't get caught in the crossfire. Maybe he'd buy the head of security a drink later as an apology.

"There's no birdie. Where's the present?" Benjamin's small voice interrupted, his feet swinging as he perched on Felix's shoulders. The excitement over the "fishies" had already faded, and he looked a bit disappointed.

"Oh dear, I guess you missed it."

"Yeah…" Benjamin pouted, tugging at a strand of Felix's golden hair, then letting it fall as he grew bored with it, too.

"Too bad," Felix said, a smile creeping into his tone. "How

about we go see your real birthday present?"

"Yes, please!"

Felix's tone had softened noticeably since he'd first met Benjamin. His quick adaptability was impressive, but Tony could only manage a restrained sigh. Without glancing back, Felix motioned with a finger.

"Bring it here," he ordered in a deep, commanding voice.

If anything went wrong now, someone would indeed be sleeping with the "fishies." Dabbing his sweaty forehead, Tony shot a look at his men, signaling them to hurry. One quickly returned, leading the pony that had been waiting nearby.

"Benjamin, do you like ponies?" Felix asked.

"Waaah!" Benjamin's response was a gleeful shout as the pony approached, hooves clopping on the garden path. "Wow! Pony! Pony!"

His face flushed with delight as he clapped his hands. Felix lifted him and placed him on the child-sized saddle, fastening the belt securely. With a finishing touch, he set a small cowboy hat on Benjamin's head. The child beamed, brimming with excitement, so happy he didn't know what to do with himself.

Seeing Benjamin so ecstatic, Felix looked on with pride, holding the reins as he led the pony toward the back gate. Tony quickly stepped up beside him, "I'll—"

"No need, go away." Felix dismissed Tony without a glance, strolling forward with the reins in hand. The pony followed obediently, its hooves clopping steadily, while Benjamin sat atop, cheering and swinging his feet with carefree delight.

"You did well on such short notice." Felix's unexpected words drifted back.

Tony froze, dumbfounded, watching Felix guide the pony through the garden gate. As they passed through, children's excited cheers filled the air, but Tony remained rooted, too stunned to move or even process the sounds around him.

This wasn't the Felix Felice he knew. This Felix had demanded a pony within a day just to please a child, broke the head of security's leg over a scraped knee, censored himself to spare the child's ears—and now, he'd even given Tony a rare word of praise.

"Is he dying or something? Or did he eat something funny?" Tony muttered with a deep sigh. It was so out of character that he felt his head spin. Shaking his head, he tried to process the whirlwind of the past day and a half.

The surprises just kept coming.

Chapter 13

The children eagerly lined up for their turn on the pony. Benjamin, reluctant to dismount after circling the garden, had to be coaxed off as the other children clamored for their ride. Eventually, he relented, and one of Felix's men, rough around the edges but unexpectedly willing, stepped in to guide the children on their rides. His rugged appearance hinted at a life spent around weapons, yet he seemed to genuinely enjoy escorting the kids around the garden.

There were more men like Jack among Felix's ranks who were unexpectedly fond of children, adding to the garden's cheerful chaos. With laughter and soap bubbles floating around, the scene resembled a small amusement park.

Benjamin, who had been sulking about giving up his seat on the pony, was now engrossed in blowing bubbles with the other kids, his complaints forgotten.

Isaac felt a faint smile tug at his lips as he watched them.

But after a moment, Isaac turned quietly away from the tree's shade, where he'd been observing. He slipped out of the garden, the weight of his family's presence and his lingering resentment pressing on him. Felix had stepped out for a moment, and Isaac didn't know how to face him when he returned. His mother's words echoed in his mind, throwing his thoughts into turmoil.

Can you still say you're Benjamin's only father after this?

Isaac hadn't been able to answer her. As far as he was concerned, he was Benjamin's only father—there could be no one else. If there were someone else, it would mean revealing his secret as an omega.

All his efforts to live as a beta would be wasted, a thought that sent a shudder through him. He couldn't bear the way alphas looked at him or treated him as if he were an omega.

He wanted nothing more than to pretend he was a beta, running a flower shop, living with his mother and Benjamin. That was his only wish. Yet, he sensed the roots of this dream beginning to waver, challenged by Felix's presence.

But Isaac knew he couldn't reject Felix's helping hand or the contract being thrust upon him. He didn't have the strength to push Felix away, especially when he was being so persistent. Besides, he still needed Felix's skills for the time being.

Isaac had extended his hand first, and he understood better than anyone that he had stepped into a quagmire. Feeling pulled in every direction, he couldn't shake the sense of helplessness that threatened to overwhelm him. Adding to everything else, the uncertainty of Benjamin's paternity left him reeling.

He shook his head, trying to banish the tumult of thoughts, and vowed not to waver. He couldn't afford to waver now. He had come too far to give up. Layering his resolve, he gritted his teeth and quickened his pace.

He froze mid-step at the sight of Jack's hulking figure scanning the surroundings before slipping quietly through the garden's back gate.

Something felt off.

Instinctively, Isaac followed, holding his breath, and watched as Jack disappeared outside, his footsteps muffled. Isaac felt a twinge of suspicion. Why was a tough guy like Jack being so cautious and sneaking out? *What was going on?*

Anxiously, he opened and closed his fists as he approached the back gate. Peering through the slats, he spotted Jack moving silently toward someone waiting for him. The faint scent of tobacco hung in the air. Someone was smoking a cigarette.

"Did you bring it?" asked a figure, half-hidden in the shadows behind Jack.

"Do you have any idea how hard it was to get this?" Jack whispered, his tone a mix of secrecy and arrogance.

The other figure snorted dismissively. "You realize you can't screw this up, right?"

"Relax," Jack replied, holding something up to the faint light. "Look at this color. You, of all people, should know this isn't your average shade."

The man, partially obscured by Jack's bulk, seemed to receive something from him, followed by a brief rustling sound. Isaac narrowed his eyes, unable to see what Jack had handed over, but an ominous feeling settled in his gut.

Surely, they weren't dealing drugs or illegal arms right in front of his house, beside a garden where children played, were they?

His suspicions intensified. The two men, oblivious to Isaac's presence, leaned closer, inspecting something. It must have been what the man sought as he pocketed the item inside his jacket.

"What about the guys?" Jack asked.

"Done."

"Right, since he spent the night. Must've made things easier."

"The boss can't know. Watch your mouth."

"I know…damn. Anyway, now, if we just have the test results—"

Test results?

Isaac's suspicions deepened as he leaned closer to listen. The man hidden behind Jack turned his head slightly, and Isaac quickly pressed himself against the wall to muffle his presence.

The man glanced in Isaac's direction momentarily, a questioning look crossing his face, before nudging Jack's shoulder, signaling him to move. They soon headed away from Isaac's hiding spot and disappeared.

Isaac felt a wave of relief wash over him, grateful they hadn't noticed him. They probably assumed he was just one of the kids from the party. But along with that relief, an unsettling anxiety churned in his chest.

He couldn't shake Jack's suspicious behavior or the mysterious item he had handed over. It dawned on him that the man Jack had been speaking to must have been Tony.

Inside the house, Isaac sank into the plush sofa in the reception room, pressing his throbbing temples. The conversation between Jack and Tony replayed endlessly in his mind, stuck on a loop.

What had they exchanged? What were those test results about? And what was Tony scheming that prompted him to warn Jack not to tell Felix? Isaac drummed his fingers anxiously on the sofa's armrest.

Should he inform Felix that those two were up to something? He debated the idea but ultimately shook his head. Jack and Tony were Felix's closest subordinates. If he brought it up without concrete evidence and they played dumb, he would end up being the one in trouble.

Maybe it had nothing to do with him; perhaps it was just an internal matter. Yet, the more Isaac thought about it, the more it gnawed at him. Something in his gut urged him to uncover what they were discussing.

Rather than alert Felix, he should…

Isaac buried his face in the sofa, closing his eyes as if surrendering to exhaustion. For now, it would be better to set aside thoughts of Jack and Tony. He couldn't solve the problem alone.

As he relaxed, fatigue washed over him. He hadn't taken a break since yesterday, and his nerves frayed, making his stress palpable. It was always this way with Felix, but yesterday had been especially taxing, dragging him to the middle of the ocean. The lingering discomfort in his stomach and inability to eat spoke

volumes.

His limbs felt heavy, dropping below the sofa as if they weighed a ton. He had momentarily forgotten the strain while watching Benjamin, but now a dull ache reverberated through his overworked hips. At this rate, meeting with Felix once a week might break his back.

A leisurely voice interrupted him as he tried to ignore the stiffness and pain and take a quick nap. "What are you thinking so hard about?"

Isaac's eyes snapped open to the sight of a striking man with blond hair leaning against the half-open door, staring intently at him. Where had he come from? The haughty way Felix crossed his arms over his tall, well-built frame stirred something in Isaac's heart.

Felix...

"I was dozing off," Isaac admitted, meeting Felix's gaze.

As Felix closed in on him, he snickered, his lips stretching into a playful grin. The soft crinkle of his eyes and the curve of his smile were captivating, prompting Isaac to turn away.

"What did you think of my present?" Felix asked confidently, taking another step closer.

Isaac recalled the "birthday present" and made a noncommittal noise. Yes, there was that. Just thinking about it deepened his discomfort.

"Benjamin likes it," Isaac muttered, scratching his cheek, unsure what else to say.

"Of course! What did I tell you? Kids love it."

"Some of the children were scared."

"Most of them loved it." Felix pressed on, and Isaac shrugged, yielding to his stubbornness. It was true—most of the children had enjoyed it, and Benjamin had been ecstatic. But...

"It's too much," Isaac finally blurted, wanting to voice his concerns since he first saw the pony. Felix tilted his head, hands tucked into his pockets, his expression revealing confusion.

"What's too much? A gift reflects the giver's heart. If it's given to you, you should accept it—"

"It's too much to handle. I'm not wealthy like you, and taking care of a horse is difficult—"

"Do you think I'd give a pony as a gift just to say, 'Here, take it, that's all?'" Isaac's hesitant explanation was cut off by Felix, whose tone made it clear he didn't want to hear it. He looked somewhat sullen, causing Isaac to blink in surprise. "I've prepared a stable near here, and they'll take care of the horse. You don't have to worry about anything—just take Benjamin there whenever he wants a ride. It'll be a great opportunity for him to learn to ride properly."

Isaac's mouth fell open at Felix's revelation. It was shocking enough that he had found a horse to give as a present overnight, but a stable and a caretaker on top of that? He couldn't believe it. Still, his heart grew heavier. The gift felt so extravagant that accepting it seemed overwhelming. He stood up, Felix's steady gaze, slightly higher than his, holding his attention.

"No. This is too much, no matter how I look at it. I can't accept such an extravagant gift."

"Then what if I attach a condition?"

"A condition?" Isaac eyed him warily.

Felix's lips curled into a smirk as he moved closer. "A kiss."

The word was spoken so flatly that, at first, Isaac didn't quite grasp it. His vision blurred from the thickening alpha pheromones and Felix's mesmerizing smile. Felix lifted his hand, brushing his finger against Isaac's lips; the touch was warm and intense, like simmering heat.

"I'll take care of everything related to the horse Benjamin loves so much…" A pause, then, "In return, let me kiss you all the time."

Oh god.

Isaac stared up at Felix, who was studying his lips with greedy eyes. He had stopped Felix from kissing him earlier, citing that Monday was their agreed day. Was this his way of getting back at him? Was Felix trying to conquer every part of him, tightening a noose around him bit by bit to rob him of everything?

Isaac couldn't decide whether to feel angry or to laugh at the absurdity of it all. "Are you serious?"

"Do I ever joke?" Felix furrowed his brow as he caressed Isaac's lips.

"You're acting like you're trying to buy everything from me." Isaac felt a mix of anger and confusion as he scrutinized Felix's behavior.

Felix didn't flinch. "Shouldn't I? Honestly, my hands are itching to claim you completely. But I'm holding back, exercising patience…because you might run if I don't." He paused for a moment before adding nonchalantly, "You didn't know that?"

Isaac was left momentarily speechless, his emotions swirling as he lifted his gaze. "Why? Just because you enjoy having sex with me? Just because of that?"

Felix's expression flickered with discomfort at his directness. "Yeah. You're the first since that bastard," he replied readily, which only raised more questions.

"Who do you mean?"

"That insolent omega." The words sent a shiver down Isaac's spine. Surely not…"You're the first since that bastard to occupy my thoughts. You really get me going. You get my dick going all day like I'm some clueless virgin. You tick all the boxes when it comes to my tastes—I want to take you apart and devour you, and even then, that still wouldn't be enough."

Alpha pheromones surged from Felix, his eyes burning with lust. The scent overwhelmed Isaac's senses, informing him just how aroused Felix truly was. He could only feign ignorance, knowing a beta wouldn't experience pheromones this intensely. No matter what, he had to maintain a straight face.

"And yet, I'm holding myself back. Aren't I the perfect gentleman?"

"Felix."

It was becoming suffocating. Isaac wanted to yell at Felix to stop. Although he had been exposed to alpha pheromones countless times, it had never felt as unbearable as this. Isaac braced his legs, gritting his teeth to keep himself from breaking down.

Felix's low voice washed over Isaac, his bleary eyes struggling to focus, "So, come quietly before I lose my mind and go on a rampage. I'll meet you halfway…with just one kiss."

Isaac expelled a heavy breath. He was terrified by how effortlessly Felix alternated between threats and conciliatory words. Isaac could not escape the grip of his power.

Felix held Isaac's chin in a light yet unyielding grip, sweeping his intense blue eyes over every inch of him. Isaac's hips quaked under that dark gaze, which seemed poised to rip his clothes off and pull his legs apart at any moment.

"Besides, you can't disappoint Benjamin, right? No reason to take away something he loves so much when I've said I'd take care of it, don't you think?"

Once again, this insidious man used Benjamin as a pawn to force Isaac to submit to his whims. Isaac clenched his jaw, knowing better than anyone that he couldn't hold out for long. He felt utterly lost.

"Isaac," Felix called his name again, his voice low and rough. Isaac squeezed his eyes shut when that scratchy baritone brushed against his ears. Felix's hot breath warmed his lips. "Open your mouth."

It was an undeniable order. Isaac's trembling lips parted slightly before he even realized it.

"Hmph—" In an instant, Felix snatched up Isaac's lips and

swallowed him whole as if he were being devoured. Isaac couldn't make a sound; Felix greedily stole both his cry and his breath.

Felix forced his way between Isaac's slightly parted lips, exploring every crevice of his mouth. Their tongues wrapped together as Felix sucked at Isaac's until it throbbed. Isaac instinctively held his mouth wide open, saliva dribbling down his chin.

His legs buckled, and his vision blurred with white spots. His mind was spiraling into a complete mess. Whether Felix was aware of Isaac's spiraling thoughts, he seized the nape of Isaac's neck with one hand while wrapping the other around his waist, dragging him to his feet.

Immobile in his clutches, Isaac stumbled backward until his back hit the wall. Felix had thrown him against it, and a flash of dull pain shot through him before Felix seized his jaw, urgently guiding their lips back together.

"Mmhm—"

Felix kissed him even more violently than before. Isaac was trapped between the wall and Felix, left with no choice but to accept the brutal kiss that scoured the inside of his wide-open mouth. The previous kiss felt light compared to the intensity with which Felix held him now.

Felix's thick tongue rubbed against Isaac's soft tissues like he was marking his territory, suddenly invading deep inside as if it sought to reach his esophagus. Isaac choked on his breath, desperate to escape, but Felix tightened his grip on the back of his neck, holding him firmly in place.

The harsh movement of Felix's tongue felt akin to deep-throating, leaving Isaac gasping and coughing. Finally, Felix detached his wet lips with difficulty, clicking his tongue in disapproval. He then inserted his knee between Isaac's legs, pressing against his crotch with a heated urgency.

"Isaac, you have to do better," Felix whispered, lapping up the saliva trickling down Isaac's jaw. Isaac stared at him blearily, his chest heaving with breaths. Felix traced his swollen lips with the tip of his finger before pressing even deeper against Isaac's body.

Issac moaned. Already aroused from the kiss, the direct stimulation sent a rush of blood straight to his groin, leaving Isaac feeling helpless. Even now, half of the blood had already rushed down. Felix licked Isaac's lips like sweet candy, narrowing his eyes in satisfaction.

He looked like he was smiling, but the blue eyes behind that smile were bone-chillingly savage, barely reining in a rampaging desire.

"Why does one kiss have to be so damn hard? How much do I have to suck for you to beg me to take you?" Felix bent over again, lowering his lips until they almost brushed against Isaac's, whispering, "If you beg me to fuck you…anytime…regardless of the contract, I'll gladly oblige."

"Not likely," Isaac retorted, expelling a ragged breath as he fought against the mounting heat. He intended to sound indifferent, but his husky voice trembled.

"Yeah, I figured you would say that." Felix didn't seem upset; instead, he smiled with amusement, looking relaxed compared to Isaac, who felt helpless in the raging fire of desire.

"Open your mouth again so we can finish what we're doing." Felix swept a hand over Isaac's chin and neck, pressing his body even closer. "I'm going to suck you. Tongue out."

The rough baritone of his voice caressed Isaac's ears, making him feel faint. As if possessed, Isaac closed his eyes and parted his lips. Slowly, he stuck out his tongue, and Felix swallowed it in one gulp.

The relentless plunging of their tongues between flushed lips was wildly obscene. Felix sensually rubbed, licked, and nibbled the tip of Isaac's tongue as if giving a blowjob.

Felix's tongue snaked around Isaac's with practiced skill, and Isaac's vision blurred. Saliva leaked in rivulets down his chin, but he was oblivious to it. His breaths came in ragged gasps, his chest heaving, and his buckling knees threatened to give way at any moment.

Dear God, was every kiss meant to feel like this? The sensation, unlike anything he had ever experienced, nearly frightened him.

Isaac moaned despite himself, feeling as if his lips and mouth's soft tissues were about to melt. The ridiculous thought that he might completely disappear, absorbed by Felix, floated through his mind. Precum leaked from his cock, wetting his underwear without any direct stimulation. His rear was in an even worse state, his insides feeling soft and sticky, damp with slick.

But he wasn't the only one caught in a haze of desire. The alpha pheromones surged like a tide, assailing his senses and invading his lungs deeply. The seductive, carnal scent made the room spin, overwhelming him until he sank to his knees.

"Hmph—" If Felix hadn't been quick to loop an arm around Isaac's waist and catch him, he would have collapsed to the floor. At that moment, without warning, Felix raised his lust-hazed eyes, then buried his nose into Isaac's drooping neck, baring his teeth.

"Isaac, what's this scent of yours? What kind of scent is this? What perfume do you use?" Felix muttered, voice thick like a drunken man, as he gnawed at Isaac's neck, pushing the boundaries of pleasure and pain. He nosed Isaac's skin as if trying to drink him in or detect the omega pheromones seeping from him.

Isaac jolted back to reality, wrenching his body to escape his grasp. But breaking free from a hyper-dominant alpha's unyielding hold wasn't easy. Before he knew it, his body was steeped in Felix's overwhelming alpha pheromones, his limbs shaking in response.

"What a strange scent. Every time I smell it, I feel like I'm going blind…No, I feel like my cock will explode."

Alarm bells blared in Isaac's mind. His omega pheromones had leaked. There was no other possibility. It was sheer luck that Felix hadn't identified them yet. They had been together since yesterday, their bodies intertwined, leaving Isaac's insides saturated with

Felix's essence. It was only natural he would respond to it.

Shame washed over him for being so careless. He shouldn't have been sitting here taking a break; he should have taken his suppressants immediately. The realization felt like a bucket of ice water poured over his head. Isaac squared his jaw, steeling himself.

"Get away from me." His voice trembled as he shoved Felix off him.

At Isaac's sudden reluctance—after moments of clinging to Felix as if he would melt into his arms—Felix cocked his head, and the aura around him shifted, growing frigid. "What?"

"I already paid my share yesterday, and you can't lay a hand on me until next Monday. That's the agreement." Isaac's words cut through the haze, and with each one, Felix's glazed blue eyes, which were drunkenly glazed over, became clearer and clearer, until they flashed dangerously.

Isaac forced his trembling legs to move, stepping back, but the wall blocked any escape. He had to avoid being caught. If he succumbed now, it would be over.

"Daddy!" The door swung open just as Felix reached for Isaac, his fingers poised to grip his neck. The child's bright, innocent voice sliced through the tension.

Chapter 14

The tension shattered as Benjamin appeared. Isaac glanced up, instinctively pulling back from Felix's hand. Unaware of the unspoken standoff between the adults, Benjamin ran straight toward Isaac with a radiant smile.

Isaac, who had been attempting to retreat from Felix's overpowering presence, instantly brightened. It felt as if the anxiety had never cast a shadow over his face. He knelt, opening his arms wide to catch Benjamin in a tender embrace, the familiar scent of baby powder enveloping him and calming his frayed nerves.

Burying his face in Benjamin's hair, Isaac sighed, savoring the moment. It was always hard to keep his emotions in check around Felix.

The child fidgeted slightly before whispering, "Daddy, Daddy, let's go ride the pony."

Normally, Isaac would have leaped at any chance to indulge Benjamin's adorable requests, but his heart sank at the mention of the pony. Glancing around, he found Felix still standing like a statue, hands in his pockets, his gaze fixed coldly on them. Felix's eyes had no hint of warmth or desire—only an icy detachment.

"Go on…I need to cool off…" Felix's voice was as frigid as his stare.

Isaac avoided looking at Felix's lower half as he stood. "Are you planning to bring another contract for the pony and its care?"

"If you want," Felix replied with a tone so apathetic it grated on Isaac's nerves. He gripped Benjamin's hand and straightened, deliberately turning his back on Felix.

"It's fine. Do as you like," Isaac said firmly, walking away without waiting for Felix's response.

The only sounds that filled the room were Benjamin's cheerful chatter and the soft tread of Isaac's footsteps. He could feel Felix's gaze lingering, a silent weight pressing against his back, making the silence feel endless.

Isaac paused just before reaching the hallway. "Thank you for the gift," he murmured.

Felix didn't respond, but his eyes burned with intensity, following them as they left.

Holding Benjamin's hand as they approached the pony, Isaac's thoughts drifted back to Felix. The way he spoke, his kiss, the slip of omega pheromones despite the suppressants—Isaac's mind spun, caught in the tangled aftermath of their encounter.

"Pony!"

Benjamin's excited shout jolted Isaac from his thoughts. The party had ended, leaving the garden nearly empty except for Isaac's mother and a few of Felix's men cleaning up. Isaac clucked his tongue at the sight. Of course, Felix would enlist his men for this too—always orchestrating things without consulting him. Isaac looked back at them, feeling a pang of discomfort.

He wanted to tell them to leave it, but Benjamin was tugging insistently on his hand, practically dragging him toward the pony. The boy was already bouncing with uncontainable excitement.

"Benjamin, do you really like the pony that much?"

"Yeah! I love it!"

Looking down at Benjamin's flushed cheeks and bright, eager blue eyes, Isaac managed a bittersweet smile. Felix knew how to create a stir. How had he managed to find exactly what would light up the boy's world?

"That's wonderful. Did you thank the mister who gave it to you?"

Benjamin turned and shouted into the air, "Thank you, Uncle!"

Uncle? What…

“Who said he was your uncle?”

“The mister. He said he was ‘Uncle Felix.’”

“Really?” Isaac was caught between laughing and scowling, finally settling for biting his lip. Uncle? When they weren’t even related? What game was Felix playing now? Shaking his head, Isaac followed Benjamin to the pony, his steps heavy with skepticism.

The pony stood calmly, clearly well-trained, and perfectly suited for children. Impressive. Isaac couldn’t help but wonder where Felix had found such a gentle animal on such short notice. Though, knowing Felix, he’d probably given the order and left the logistics to his subordinates—especially Tony, who had a knack for delivering precisely what Felix wanted.

Isaac was fastening Benjamin’s belt onto the pony when the man helping beside him gave him an odd look, then let out a low groan. Isaac paused, glancing up with a questioning look. Realizing Isaac was watching, the man cleared his throat awkwardly.

“Ah, sorry. You might not be aware since you’re a beta, but… you’re giving off a strong scent of the boss’s alpha pheromones. He must have marked you, but as an alpha, it’s…a bit much for me.”

Isaac froze, his hands still on the belt. He remembered Felix’s overpowering wave of alpha pheromones during their kiss, intensifying as he nipped at Isaac’s neck. He’d thought the suffocating effect was just Felix’s excitement—but marking him?

Momentarily stunned, Isaac met the man’s gaze. Alphas were notoriously sensitive to each other’s pheromones; higher-grade alphas could even instill a sense of dread in those of lower rank. Dominant or hyper-dominant alphas like Felix often used their pheromones to impose control or intimidate, intentionally or not.

If Felix, a hyper-dominant alpha, had marked him, Isaac realized, it would make being near him difficult for most other alphas.

"I'm sorry. I didn't realize," Isaac murmured, trying to ignore the flush creeping over his cheeks.

"No, it's fine." The man, visibly sheepish, quickly untied the pony and took hold of the reins, clearly eager to put some distance between himself and Isaac.

Isaac, meanwhile, stepped back, rubbing his cheek absently—then he noticed the dagger tucked into the man's belt. "Wait."

At his call, the man, who was about to walk the pony out, stopped in his tracks and turned around. He appeared distressed to be called over when he wanted to leave as soon as possible.

"Hand over that dagger, please," Isaac said, holding out his hand as the air around him seemed to chill.

"Why?" the man said, blinking in confusion. "This dagger is essential for my job as a security guard and the one I'm used to. I can't give it to you."

His tone was defensive, sharper than before.

Without answering, Isaac extended his hand again. The man instinctively tried to fend him off, but Isaac moved faster. He struck the man's wrist with a swift chop, twisting it aside, and deftly removed the dagger from his belt.

The man gaped, rubbing his sore wrist, disbelief etched across his face. But Isaac simply examined the dagger, his gaze narrowing.

"What's going on here?" The baritone voice sounded from behind him.

Isaac turned to see Felix approaching, his stride as confident and imposing as ever. Felix's mere presence intensified the air, adding a palpable tension to the space between them.

The man whose dagger Isaac had just confiscated stood at attention, shoulders squared in forced composure.

Felix approached casually, his eyes locking onto the dagger now in Isaac's hand. Felix asked, "What's that?"

Isaac handed the dagger over. The weapon looked ordinary

enough in its sheath, but the button on the handle was distinctly unusual. "This isn't suitable for a bodyguard around children," Isaac said quietly. "I thought ballistic knives were discontinued. Isn't that right?"

A ballistic knife—distinguished by the button on its handle—was once a weapon of choice for the Soviet special forces, the Spetsnaz. With the press of a button, the blade could launch forward like a bullet, making it a high-risk, unstable weapon. Many countries, including the United States, have long since banned their sale and possession due to instability and safety risks. Felix, an arms dealer, would undoubtedly recognize the weapon—and know that having it here was illegal.

Felix tapped the dagger against his palm, his deep blue eyes lifting to meet Isaac's. "A ballistic knife, huh?"

The man stammered, his face paling as he tried to defend himself, "I-It's one I've had for a long time—"

Felix cut him off sharply. "What's your name?"

"James," he answered.

"James? What do you think you're doing, James? Letting your weapon get taken so easily—what kind of bodyguard are you? How are you supposed to protect the kid like that?"

Felix's words hung heavily in the air, each one making James shift uncomfortably as he grasped the full weight of his error.

"That is..." the man stammered, struggling to acknowledge that his judgment was clouded by the alpha pheromones emanating from Isaac. Earlier, he had witnessed the head of security suffer a broken shin just for allowing the kid to trip on some uneven grass; the recollection visibly rattled him, leaving his face pale as a sheet.

"Not only that," Felix continued coldly, "but you're carrying an illegal weapon while working for me? That's absurd."

The irony lay in the fact that Felix had ties to the mafia and was well-accustomed to handling illegal arms, yet the man wasn't about to challenge him.

"I've had it for years without any issues. I was just…careless," James murmured, apologizing repeatedly, his face pale.

Felix hardly seemed to be listening. Casually, he slid the dagger from its sheath and pressed the button on its handle. The blade shot out in a flash, leaving his fingers and embedding itself in the grass an inch from James's foot.

A tense silence fell. James, realizing he'd barely avoided a knife in his foot, stood frozen, visibly trembling. Isaac, too, looked at the blade stuck in the ground, momentarily stunned. Only Benjamin seemed unaffected, swinging his legs and whining, "Pony…"

"Oops." Felix broke the silence with a mild tone, glancing at the man with mock innocence. "Looks like my finger slipped."

With a nonchalant shrug, Felix tossed the remaining handle back to James, who caught it in a daze, glancing up in bewilderment.

"Now, are you still going to say there's never been an accident?"

"F-Forgive me," James stammered.

"James, don't step out of line if you don't want to end up as fish food."

James's head dropped, unable to meet Felix's gaze, the threat sinking in. Nearby, Isaac's eyes narrowed. Fish food? What was that about?

But Benjamin, perched atop his pony, seemed to catch on instantly, cheering, "When are we feeding the fishies?"

James's face turned even paler, and he swallowed hard.

"Return that knife to Tony," Felix ordered.

"Understood."

"You're on probation." Felix didn't bother to glance back, and James slumped as if he'd received a death sentence—though he was fortunate it was only probation.

Isaac, growing restless, bit his lip. Felix said nothing and simply walked over to Benjamin with a bright smile, taking the pony's reins. As the pony began to move, Benjamin let out a shriek of delight. Felix guided him in a gentle loop around the garden, and Isaac watched them, his gaze tangled with emotions.

After the party was over, the garden transformed into a scene of calm, and tranquility. In the lingering late afternoon light, the space felt peaceful as the children's laughter had faded into silence.

Isaac stood in the cool shade of a tree, arms crossed, watching Felix and Benjamin. Despite his outwardly indifferent expression, he couldn't help but notice Benjamin's delight as Felix led the pony, seemingly content to let the boy ride as long as he wished. Felix hadn't told Benjamin it was enough for the day, which surprised Isaac.

Whether Felix intended to let him ride until he was exhausted or was simply guiding the pony absentmindedly, Isaac couldn't tell—but it was undeniably unlike him.

Lost in his thoughts, Isaac's gaze lingered on the two of them until a gentle voice brought him back.

"You'll stay for dinner, right?" His mother stood beside him, the lines of fatigue clear on her face after the long day of planning and hosting.

Raising a child wasn't an easy job. Isaac was acutely aware of the burden he placed on his mother by relying on her to care for Benjamin, especially now that age was beginning to slow her. He couldn't help but feel a bitter pang of guilt. Isaac's chest felt heavy thinking about how hard it must have been for her to prepare Benjamin's birthday party every year. He knew she insisted she enjoyed it, telling him not to worry—but how could he not?

Isaac had hired a nanny and did whatever he could to shoulder the responsibility, but it was never enough. Deep down, he knew Benjamin needed his parents, not just a grandmother stepping in where his father faltered. Isaac had to find a way to steady their lives and bring stability where there was only this fragile balance.

"Isaac?"

"Ah, sorry. No, I don't want to trouble you." He shook his

head, pushing the weight of his thoughts aside. As much as he wanted to stay, he thought it better to leave sooner rather than later.

"Still," his mother said, her face settling into its usual look of disappointment. She never thought of her exhaustion—she just wanted to make sure he ate. "Benjamin's so happy to see you after so long. Have dinner before you go, won't you? Felix, too, if that's all right?"

Isaac's eyes widened. He'd only briefly introduced his mother to Felix when they arrived, but now she was saying his name as if they were old friends. Had they talked while he'd been away? Or had she somehow convinced herself that Felix was Benjamin's father? There was no way to tell. Isaac exhaled, his anxiety rising, and shook his head firmly. Having Felix join them for dinner? Impossible.

"We don't have time, so you don't need to—"

"What do you mean? I'm staying for dinner."

Isaac froze. He'd been carefully choosing his words to turn his mother down without upsetting her, and then he heard that gruff voice from right behind him. How could someone as solidly built as Felix move so quietly? It always startled him.

But as he turned, Isaac was surprised for a different reason—Felix was holding a peacefully sleeping Benjamin in his arms, cradling him as if it were second nature.

"I'll take him," Isaac said, reaching for Benjamin. But Felix shook his head, saying it was fine, holding onto him a moment longer.

"He's sleeping—let him be. I'll carry him to bed," Felix said bluntly. Once again, Isaac found himself at a loss for words.

Just then, his mother joined them, gently stroking Benjamin's golden hair with a soft smile, "Poor Benjamin, he must have been exhausted. He has been so excited about his party since this morning, and it's long past his naptime."

"He started nodding off on the pony," Felix explained. "So I picked him up, and he fell asleep immediately."

"That's very thoughtful of you. Thank you," she said warmly.

"Not at all."

Felix addressed his mother, who was gazing down at Benjamin, with unexpected politeness, surprising Isaac. He'd expected Felix to be his usual arrogant self, ready to brush people off without a second thought. But here he was, acting respectful—even refined.

Isaac watched him, astonished. It was hard to believe this courteous man was an arms dealer with mafia ties. At a glance, Felix could have passed for the well-mannered son of an aristocratic family. This contrast only deepened Isaac's suspicion, yet his mother seemed enchanted. Her bright expression, her admiring gaze—it was all too clear.

Isaac seemed to be the only one immune to Felix's charm.

"Felix, if you're free, would you join us for dinner?" she asked, her face lighting up with hope.

Isaac started to raise a hand, lightly furrowing his brow. "Mother, I—"

"It would be my pleasure to accept your invitation," Felix interrupted with a warm, dazzling smile. The brightness in his expression was almost disarming, as sweet as spun sugar. Isaac scoffed inwardly, knowing full well that Felix was entirely aware of the effect his charm had.

"My, how gallant you are!" she said, looking back at him with a faint blush. "Then it's settled—we'll have dinner. I'm sure Benjamin would be delighted too. Isn't that right, Isaac?"

If Felix hadn't found success as an arms dealer, he surely would have as a Casanova, Isaac thought wryly. His throat tightened at the thought, but he didn't have the heart to argue. "If you say so, Mother…"

"It'd be a grand old time if I had your blessing too, Isaac," Felix quipped, his voice laced with audacity as he sauntered toward the house.

“Good grief,” Isaac sighed quietly, unable to hide how drawn his face had become.

His mother followed Felix, her gaze lingering on Benjamin, now fast asleep in Felix’s arms. A glimmer of hope softened her expression. She fretted aloud as she unlocked the front door, “I just don’t know what to make for dinner.”

“Mrs. Parker, don’t worry, I’m not a picky eater. A homemade meal from you—how can it be anything but delicious?” Felix, the next great Casanova, replied, flashing her a devastatingly charming smile.

“Oh, my,” she murmured, charmed.

First Benjamin, and now his mother. She was all smiles under the influence of Felix’s smooth looks and silver tongue. Isaac pressed his forehead, feeling a migraine begin to brew. He’d never thought of his mother as easily swayed, but there she was, charmed like everyone else.

His plan to watch Benjamin ride his new pony and make a quick escape had officially gone down the drain. *Please let nothing happen,* he thought, his stomach twisting.

With dread weighing heavily in his chest, Isaac watched Felix follow his mother assertively into the house. Reluctantly, he dragged his feet after them.

Isaac never talked about himself. He wasn’t the oversharing or talkative type, in fact, he was a man of very few words. Felix knew this about him all too well and didn’t bother asking personal questions anymore. Even if he did, Isaac wouldn’t answer.

So, Felix had taken matters into his own hands. A background check had revealed most of Isaac’s personal details—probably more than Isaac himself would have willingly admitted. Yet, for all the information Felix had uncovered, he found himself unexpectedly enjoying the process of discovering more about Isaac firsthand.

“Now, this is really cute,” Felix said, pausing to point at a

photograph.

The image showed a crying baby Isaac, flat on his bottom with his tiny pee-pee out, wailing hysterically.

Isaac hadn't always been the stoic, expressionless man he was now. He looked so much like Benjamin in the photo—bright-eyed, innocent, and wholly unguarded.

After dinner, Jessica Parker had eagerly brought out an old photo album, delighted to show Felix snapshots of her son's childhood. With a cup of tea, fruit on the table, and a treasure trove of childhood memories before him, Felix realized this was one of the most enjoyable evenings he'd had in a long time.

He hadn't expected this, but baby Isaac was so adorable Felix could eat him up. Even now, Isaac's beauty was undeniable, and every time Felix saw him, he felt the urge to suck, lick, or nibble at him—an indulgent thought he kept tucked away behind a calm exterior.

Isaac had been especially cute and pretty as a child, and Felix's gaze softened as he took in every picture.

Sadly, the pictures ended when Isaac was around ten years old. Felix turned the page, only to find it blank. His expression fell, disappointment flickering across his face. He'd been curious to see what Isaac looked like as a teenager, but there were no photos.

Jessica noticed his reaction and offered a faint, bitter smile as she looked at the final picture. "We divorced when Isaac was ten," she said softly. "My ex-husband wouldn't let Isaac go, so I had to leave him. After I remarried, I visited occasionally, but not long after, Isaac's father suddenly moved to Washington, D.C., and took him with him. I lived in Seattle then, so it became much harder to see him."

Her voice was low, almost wistful, as she recounted the story. Isaac wasn't in the room to hear it; Benjamin had woken up from his nap earlier, eaten dinner, and then raised a fuss. Isaac had taken him upstairs for a bath and to put him to bed, leaving Felix alone with Jessica and the photo album.

Felix, who had been enjoying the evening's stories and flipping through pictures of Isaac's childhood, now regarded Jessica with serious eyes.

"We talked on the phone sometimes," she continued, "but it became less frequent after Isaac entered middle school. By the time he finished high school, I couldn't reach him at all. I didn't hear any news about Isaac until three years ago."

Jessica sighed, her gaze lingering on the picture of young Isaac. Her black eyes shimmered with unspoken regret, the weight of time and missed moments heavy in her expression.

Felix remained silent.

"I found out Isaac's father had passed away some time ago. Even after that, Isaac never came to find me. He was living on his own by then," she said. "Later, he told me he didn't want to bother me because I was remarried."

Felix could almost picture it: the way Isaac must have looked, the tone of his voice as he explained himself to his mother. The thought left a bitter taste in Felix's mouth. He wordlessly lifted his teacup, sipping the warm liquid as Jessica continued.

"Despite his thoughtfulness," she said, "I had already resolved to find him. I went around asking about him for years."

Felix remained quiet.

"But I never found out where he was," Jessica admitted, pulling the old album closer. Her eyes lingered on the faded photos as if trying to memorize every detail, then she closed the cover quietly. Regret and guilt etched deeper lines into her face.

"You couldn't find him—then how did you meet again three years ago?" he asked, the question coming to him suddenly. Felix watched her closely, his curiosity piqued.

Jessica seemed to take a moment to collect herself. Her lips curled into a placid smile, and her composure was restored. "Isaac came looking for me, unexpectedly, with a baby in his arms," she said, her voice soft but filled with emotion. "You don't know how happy I was that he came and hadn't forgotten about me. Living with Benjamin and Isaac now is a dream come true. I couldn't wish for anything more."

"Is that why your last name is different?" Felix asked, his tone careful but probing.

Jessica's expression shifted, a flicker of discomfort crossing her face. Isaac's last name was Sinclair—Isaac Sinclair. Her name, however, was Jessica, and Benjamin had taken her last name, making him Benjamin Parker. To anyone else, the three of them would seem completely unrelated.

On paper, they were strangers. Without delving into their family history, no one would guess they were connected.

"I changed my last name when I remarried," Jessica explained. Her voice softened as she added, "Though he passed away a few years ago…Isaac still asked to give Benjamin my surname. He seemed to have his reasons, so I didn't press the issue and went along with it."

She quietly slid the album into a drawer, her movements measured. Felix rubbed his chin, unable to shake a nagging feeling. He'd known early on that Isaac and Benjamin had different last names. But now, realizing Benjamin had taken Jessica's current surname—the one she adopted after remarrying, not Benjamin's biological mother's—something felt off.

"What happened to Benjamin's mother?" he asked bluntly.

Jessica's expression subtly hardened, a flicker of unease breaking through her calm. "He never talks about it, so I don't know either."

"So, between parting from Isaac when he was ten and meeting him again three years ago, you have no idea what he was up to?"

"No. I don't know the details, but I heard he finished school and got a job."

Felix frowned slightly. The explanation felt too neat and too vague. It was the same story Tony told him before. According to the background Felix had gathered, Isaac had graduated from a school that was neither remarkable nor disreputable, worked a part-time job, secured an internship, and eventually started a modest career.

Then, three years ago, he quit his job and showed up at Jessica's doorstep with a motherless newborn in his arms. Now, Isaac—a florist running a small, unassuming flower shop in a quiet corner of Downtown San Diego—spent his days crafting unimpressive bouquets while seemingly on the run from someone.

Felix's fingers tapped against his teacup as Jessica's words replayed in his mind. The more he thought about it, the more glaring the inconsistencies became. Too many things didn't add up.

"Very suspicious," he muttered under his breath, sipping his tea as unease crept in.

Who had this much backstory? Isaac, with his calm demeanor and understated life, had a mountain of secrets—secrets even his mother didn't know. The realization churned uneasily in Felix's mind, stirring a mix of curiosity and concern.

"Isaac wasn't like that when he was little," Jessica said warmly, her voice filled with maternal pride. "He can be aloof and has trouble expressing himself. But once you get to know him, you'll find he has a big heart."

Like any mother, she only wanted to speak highly of her son. After all, even a hedgehog finds its hoglet soft.

Felix's lips curled into a subtle smile, faint amusement hidden in his expression. "I'm sure he does."

Of course, Isaac was aloof and guarded—except when he was unraveling completely in bed. Felix widened his smile slightly to mask the intrusive, decidedly inappropriate thought.

"You're the first friend Isaac has brought home since he came to San Diego," Jessica continued thoughtfully. "No, actually, you might be the first friend he's had in the last three years."

Felix said nothing as he listened.

"He's always been focused on his job and Benjamin. Not to mention, he handles so much that I hardly have to lift a finger. He really is a sweet boy."

"I know," Felix murmured.

Isaac's goodness wasn't in question—Felix had no doubt he was an upright citizen. But the glaring inconsistencies in his story, the secrets he guarded so tightly, couldn't be ignored. Felix couldn't imagine Isaac explaining to Jessica why he was on the run or revealing anything about Benjamin's mother, let alone the life he'd lived before showing up at her door.

Jessica's words confirmed what Felix had already suspected: she didn't know much about Isaac's past.

"Felix, please look after Isaac," Jessica said softly, her features echoing her son's. Her tone hinted at more she wanted to say, but she held back. Felix tilted his head slightly, curious about the odd tension in her words.

His musings were interrupted as Isaac descended the stairs, his eyes locking onto Felix. Like the night sky, those dark, unfathomable eyes betrayed nothing but suspicion at the sight of Felix and Jessica sitting together.

Felix chuckled, amused by the stark contrast between Isaac in the photos and the man before him. The carefree child was long gone, replaced by this enigmatic figure.

Isaac, how many secrets are you hiding? Felix thought. When I unravel them, one by one, what kind of face will you make?

Though the thrill of anticipation sent a chill through him, Felix masked it effortlessly. Plastering on a friendly smile, he waited patiently for Isaac to reach the bottom of the stairs.

Chapter 15

Time crawled by.

The flower shop was empty as usual, and the bright, warm weather outside only emphasized the quiet boredom inside. Felix, who had been a constant presence, was nowhere to be seen. True to his word about being away on business, he hadn't visited the shop in over a week.

There hadn't been a single call or message from him either. Monday, the day they were supposed to meet, had come and gone without a word. Though Felix had paid in advance for last week, the silence stretched uncomfortably into this week.

Isaac sighed, running a hand over his forehead. He couldn't help but recall Felix's ominous warning: *I'll get my payment somehow.* Would that mean doubling up next time? The thought sent an involuntary shudder down his spine.

Isaac's thoughts wandered back to last Saturday, after dinner at his mother's house. On the ride back to his apartment, Felix had casually tossed the question at him, unprompted and out of nowhere.

Felix's deep voice echoed in his memory, cutting through the monotony: *How did you know the bodyguard's dagger was a ballistic knife?*

Isaac had turned to glance at him, only to find Felix lounging against the car's back seat, his eyes fixed on a tablet. He looked utterly relaxed as if the question hadn't been asked.

"When I have trouble falling asleep, I turn on the TV," Isaac had replied evenly. "There are a lot of interesting programs."

"TV, you say," Felix had murmured.

"It was a program where they tested weapons, comparing and

analyzing their performance. Highly informative," Isaac replied lightly.

Felix muttered, "I suppose," before falling silent and returning his focus to the tablet. Isaac glanced at him with an unreadable expression, then turned to stare out the window. The night view slid by, dark and bleak in its reflection.

"So, you marked me?" Isaac asked suddenly, his calm voice tinged with something sharper. His gaze was fixed on the passing shadows outside.

"Oh dear. I was caught."

Isaac turned his eyes to Felix, unimpressed by the flippant tone. Felix let the tablet slip onto his lap, propping his chin on one hand as his deep blue eyes bore into Isaac's. The intensity made Isaac's heart clench, and he drew a sharp breath.

"What were you thinking?" Isaac asked.

"I was marking what's mine. Why?"

"Yours?" Isaac blinked, momentarily stunned by Felix's unapologetic response. He hadn't expected an apology, but Felix's sheer arrogance left him momentarily speechless. With a hollow sigh, Isaac shook his head, only to flinch when Felix reached out suddenly.

Felix's hand closed around Isaac's neck, his thumb stroking its nape in a playful and unnervingly possessive way. Isaac's shoulders tensed reflexively at the touch, but before he could react, Felix tightened his grip and yanked him forward.

Isaac's balance shifted, his upper body pitching dangerously close to Felix. Their faces were so near that their noses might touch if either of them moved. Isaac froze, holding his breath.

"Isaac, don't you get it?" Felix whispered, his breath brushing Isaac's lips and nose like a teasing caress.

Isaac resisted the urge to close his eyes, forcing himself to meet Felix's gaze with steady defiance. "Get what?"

"You are mine." Felix's grin was utterly sinister, a sharp contrast to the aristocratic facade he'd donned earlier in front of Isaac's mother. The man who seemed polite and well-mannered now revealed himself as entirely different. There couldn't be another fraud like him in the world.

"I'm yours? When did we come to that conclusion?" Isaac shot back.

"Since the moment you signed the contract."

Isaac opened his mouth to protest but found himself speechless at Felix's audacious assertion. A surge of indignation welled inside him, but there was no room to argue. Instead, he bit his lip, swallowing the urge to lash out.

"We're here. Your apartment," Felix said, his tone laced with amusement, all while keeping a firm grip on Isaac's neck. "Get going."

"Let go, so I can get out." Isaac managed, his voice cracking as he swallowed hard.

Felix's sharp gaze drifted downward, lingering on Isaac's lips. "Ah, yes. I should. Before that," Felix murmured, his voice dropping to a low, intimate pitch, "a goodnight kiss."

Isaac froze. Felix had been the one to say there was no need for a contract and to do whatever Isaac preferred. He remembered too late that Felix did not take no for an answer. Despite his earlier gentlemanly demeanor, Felix was as thick-skinned and audacious as ever.

At a loss, Isaac half-closed his eyes and tentatively parted his lips. But before he could draw another breath, Felix's grip on his neck tightened, yanking him forward. Felix's lips, radiating soft heat, crashed against his with unrelenting force.

The suffocating warmth overwhelmed Isaac, stealing the air from his lungs. He squeezed his eyes shut and grasped at Felix's shoulders, his trembling fingers wrinkling the fabric of Felix's shirt. Despite the small resistance, Felix relentlessly consumed him with passionate, unyielding kisses.

"Ah—" The sound escaped before Isaac could stop it, and soon, Felix's alpha pheromones thickened the air. The intoxicating scent coiled around him in the confined space, seeping into every fiber of his being. The overwhelming heat spreading through Isaac's body was unmistakable now—a slow, simmering burn ignited by Felix's presence.

Isaac's breaths grew shallow and ragged, and his lips parted wider without realizing it, welcoming Felix's probing tongue. Felix explored his mouth with an intensity that left him reeling, a relentless force claiming every inch. Isaac's vision blurred and spiraled, the world around him shrinking to nothing but Felix. His arms, as if moving on their own, wrapped around Felix's neck, pulling him closer despite the chaos in his mind.

Perhaps Isaac was getting used to Felix's kisses—how they snaked around his tongue, fierce and relentless, as if intent on devouring him whole. He hated to admit it, but the heady sensation of Felix's pheromones, wrapping around him like a vice, was becoming dangerously addictive. He wanted to deny it, to fight against the pull, but his body betrayed him with its unfiltered honesty.

"Felix—" The soft, broken moan slipped from his lips as Felix bit down, hard and deliberate, on his lower lip.

"If you're going to call me like that, with that needy face… you're not getting out of this car," Felix said, his intense gaze locking onto Isaac's. "Or, shall we move this to your apartment?"

Isaac froze, Felix's words crashing over him like cold water. "Will you be okay with that?"

The playful warning, laced with a dark, laughing undertone, snapped Isaac out of his haze. His arms, still draped around Felix's shoulders, dropped. He wiped his damp lips with the back of his hand.

Isaac stared at Felix, clearly confused.

Felix, however, wore an unhurried smile as if he found Isaac amusing. Unlike Isaac, Felix's leisurely expression was full of assurance. It told Isaac that no matter how he struggled, there was no way to escape from him.

That expression also declared he already had Isaac thoroughly in his possession. But since Isaac was melting into his kisses every time, he had nothing to say.

"Thank you for today." Settling his turbulent emotions, Isaac turned around. As Felix had said, the sedan had pulled up to his apartment.

"It'll be over a week until you see me," Felix remarked.

"I see."

"Be good and wait for me."

Isaac hurried out of the car as if fleeing from Felix's gaze, which lazily lingered on him from a propped chin.

The chilly wind outside hit him immediately, bringing him to his senses. He took a deep breath, feeling as if the thick alpha pheromones surrounding him were finally being washed off.

Felix's sedan quietly began to move away, and Isaac watched the shrinking lights with conflicting emotions. It was only much later that he finally moved his feet.

No matter how he struggled, Isaac couldn't shake the fear that he would never escape Felix's grasp. How would this situation—and this relationship—end up? It had been a long night.

Isaac tapped his fingers on the table, replaying the past events in his mind, before squeezing them into a fist. Useless thoughts consumed him, and he couldn't understand why he was sitting idly when there was work to do.

Reproaching himself, Isaac stood and entered his shop, weaving through the narrow gaps between shelves crowded with plants and flowers. This place was more densely packed than most flower shops, and he moved deliberately, tending to each plant individually. He cleaned their shiny green leaves, watered them, and pruned the plants and his tangled thoughts.

The lonely hours dragged by painfully slowly. Isaac's hands moved mechanically, keeping rhythm with the monotonous ticking of the clock as he worked.

Chapter 16

Tony's face was resolute as he closed the door behind him.

In his hand was a large envelope, its tightly sealed flap bearing only the client's name. He had ensured all other documents and materials related to this matter were destroyed; this envelope held the only remaining result.

He steadied his nerves, heart pounding with a mix of anxiety and anticipation, and made his way down the hallway. Though tempted to tear it open on the spot, he resisted, walking briskly toward the emergency exit door.

Tony had come alone, deliberately leaving his subordinates behind. This test had been conducted without Felix's knowledge and had to remain entirely secret. Fortunately, Felix was away visiting his grandfather, allowing Tony to act without raising suspicion.

Foregoing the elevator, Tony descended the emergency stairwell at a hurried pace. By the time he reached the first-floor exit, his patience had worn thin. Stopping abruptly, he tore the envelope open, hands trembling as his heart raced in anticipation.

Obtaining the necessary samples had been a delicate operation. Felix's and Isaac's hair had been easy enough to collect from the yacht after their night together, but Benjamin's had been another matter entirely. Asking a security guard would have been the most straightforward route, but Tony couldn't risk it. In the end, he'd been forced to retrieve it himself, carefully and discreetly.

But getting his hands on the child's hair had proven more difficult than expected. Benjamin's birthday party seemed like the perfect opportunity, but the boy was too busy running around with the other children, always surrounded by too many eyes.

With no other option, Tony had enlisted Jack's help. Jack, who was supervising the horseback rides with a subordinate, managed to discreetly obtain a strand of Benjamin's hair. Though initially doubtful of the plan, it had turned out to be an easy task.

No one noticed Jack taking the sample—Felix was far too engrossed in Isaac to be aware of anything, not that he was particularly observant to begin with. Meanwhile, Isaac appeared distracted, lost in thought for reasons unknown.

Tony had sent the materials to a DNA diagnostics center, and now, in his grasp, was the envelope containing the paternity test results for Felix, Isaac, and Benjamin.

The sharp sound of tearing paper echoed through the empty emergency stairwell as Tony ripped the envelope open. His palms were damp with nerves as he unfolded the document, the weight of the moment pressing heavily on him.

Then, without warning, a cold, metallic sensation touched the side of his neck.

Tony froze.

He hadn't encountered anyone on his way down from the third floor to the first. In the hollow silence of the stairwell, even the faintest sound would have echoed—indeed, he would have noticed a door opening or footsteps descending.

Yet somehow, an unknown figure had approached him silently, placing a blade against his neck without leaving a trace. It was impossible. Tony swallowed hard, frozen stock still.

"Do you know who I am? Or are you doing this because you don't?" Tony's voice was calm, his tone betraying no fear.

The man behind him said nothing. Tony turned his eyes slightly and caught sight of a gloved hand in black leather gripping the knife at his throat.

The knife was about the length of a hand—thin and sleek. Its double edges, black coating, and serrated blade told Tony it was a Gerber Mark II—a professional weapon, through and through.

"What do you want from me?" he asked softly, his voice steady. The man responded by tapping the waistband of Tony's pants.

Tony quickly understood the gesture. He reached into the back pocket of his pants and pulled out his wallet, which the man snatched from his hand without delay.

"Hey, if you're doing this without knowing who I am, you're making a big mistake."

The man stayed silent.

"If you do know," Tony said, his voice dropping and laced with thinly veiled menace, "then I'm telling you…you're playing with fire." But his opponent didn't react, didn't even acknowledge the warning. Instead, he tapped Tony's left arm.

Tony frowned but complied, removing his watch and rings and handing them over. The man took them with the same efficiency, swiping a luxury watch worth tens of thousands of dollars and a diamond ring from his hand.

Finally, the man reached for the envelope Tony had been holding tightly. Tony's expression hardened immediately. It seemed the stranger intended to take it without even knowing what it contained.

"Hey, that's not even that expensive—" Tony grumbled. In one swift motion, he whipped around to strike the wrist of the man's knife-wielding hand.

Or at least, he tried.

The man was faster. He dodged the blow effortlessly and countered by smacking Tony's wrist so violently that his hand recoiled involuntarily. Tony furrowed his brow and rubbed his stinging wrist. Then, without missing a beat, he swung his other hand in retaliation.

Even if he was older now and no longer on the front lines, Tony wasn't a man to underestimate. He'd been in this business since he was young, and no one dared to show off in front of him.

Tony might have been an old hand, but he was by no means

someone to be taken lightly. It was this tenacity that had propelled him to his current stature. His rapid succession of punches forced the robber onto the defensive, leaving the man barely able to raise his arms in time. With a stagger, he fell back.

Grinding his teeth, Tony scowled at the man. Despite holding a knife, the man didn't move to use it. He remained strictly defensive as if he'd never intended to attack. Perhaps he feared the consequences of a misstep, or maybe he didn't know how to wield the blade properly in the first place.

"Are you messing with me? Or do you carry that knife around as a bluff?" Tony snapped.

The man, holding the envelope in one hand and the knife in the other, was dressed entirely in black, from his turtleneck to his pants, gloves, boots, and mask, which concealed his face. Not a single feature was visible, not even a strand of hair.

Thorough fellow, Tony thought. *Then again, no one stupid enough to expose their identity would commit a robbery.*

Still, the layers of concealment struck him as excessive. His lip curled into a mocking snicker as he studied the pitch-black figure.

"I don't know who you are, but don't think you're getting out of this easy," Tony murmured through gritted teeth.

The man responded by rolling up the envelope carelessly and tucking it into his back pocket. Then, with a flick of his wrist, he expertly flipped the knife around.

The blade spun in his hand, its movement fluid and precise—a clear rebuke to Tony's earlier assumption that he was unskilled. The gesture revealed how practiced the man's hands were, leaving no doubt about his familiarity with the weapon.

Tony watched the knife spin deftly in the man's hand, his eyes narrowing with suspicion. He clenched his fists, adjusting his stance in preparation for whatever might come next. But to his surprise, the robber slid the knife back into its sheath at his waist.

Tony's wrinkled eyes were filled with confusion, and his

bewilderment turned into alarm at the very next moment. Without warning, the man squeezed his fists and attacked with shocking speed. The sound of air splitting brushed past Tony's ears, and he barely dodged a fist aimed at his jaw.

Tony's eyes widened in shock, realizing the man's raw power. If that punch had landed, it wouldn't have just cracked his jaw—it would have shattered it entirely. A chill ran down his spine. It was a sensation Tony hadn't felt in years—a genuine sense of danger.

Swallowing dryly, Tony squared his shoulders and retaliated with a punch of his own. The robber, however, seemed entirely unbothered. He circled Tony with slow, deliberate movements, his fists clenched and ready. The man's calm, measured stance exuded confidence.

"You bastard," Tony barked, his voice rough and laced with frustration. "Who are you?"

The man remained as silent as ever.

Tony had no clue where this guy had come from, and it was clear this wasn't an ordinary situation. Losing his wallet and watch was one thing. But the thought of losing the paternity test results—the only copy—sent a wave of dread crashing over him.

If those results, still unknown even to him, were leaked…he could already imagine Felix's icy blue eyes ablaze with fury. The mere thought sent cold sweat trickling down Tony's temples.

He couldn't let that happen. No matter what it took, he had to recover the envelope. Tony tightened his damp fists, his resolve hardening like steel.

The robber, who had been circling Tony with unhurried steps, studying him like a predator, suddenly charged forward. The movement was lightning-fast, catching Tony off guard. He instinctively raised his arms and assumed a defensive stance, but the robber crouched low and swung his right leg in a sharp arc.

The air split with a sound that echoed in the narrow stairwell. Unable to avoid the low, scythe-like sweep, Tony took the hit squarely to his calves. His balance vanished instantly, and he crashed to the ground with a heavy thud.

The impact rattled his senses, momentarily clouding his vision. He tried to scramble back to his feet, but the robber's movements were too swift and precise. Before Tony could react further, the bang of a door slamming shut resounded through the stairwell.

The man had vanished through the emergency exit.

Tony slumped back against the wall, staring blankly at the door where the robber had disappeared. He couldn't believe the absurdity of the situation.

"What the hell just happened..." he muttered hoarsely, dragging a trembling hand over his ashen mouth. His thoughts swirled chaotically, a jumbled mess.

A long, despairing sigh escaped him. Losing his wallet and watch was humiliating enough, but losing Felix's paternity test results...It felt like being struck by lightning.

He couldn't chase after the man—his skills, speed, and precision were far beyond anything Tony could handle.

Chapter 17

Tony will come get you.
Get ready.

Felix sent Isaac a text message unexpectedly on a Friday afternoon. It was the first time Felix had contacted Isaac in two weeks. Rubbing his forehead, Isaac stared at the message with a mixture of confusion and anxiety.

Get ready for what?

Lacking an answer, he tried to distract himself by making bouquets and tending to the plants as usual. But no matter how hard he focused, Felix's parting words kept echoing in his mind.

Be good and wait.

Realizing he'd been cleaning the same plant for the umpteenth time, Isaac sighed and pulled his hands away.

"Why am I like this?" he muttered, removing his gloves listlessly as he returned to his post.

The doorbell jingled, startling him. Turning his head, Isaac saw Jack—the burly, bear-like man—marching into the shop.

"I was told Tony was coming," Isaac mumbled, too caught off guard to greet him properly.

"Do you think *I* wanna be here?" Jack made a disgruntled face and shrugged. "Big Bro's bedridden, so I came instead."

"Bedridden?" Isaac repeated.

"He came back roughed up yesterday," Jack explained, his voice rising in annoyance. "They say you can't lie about your age, but who'd have thought Tony would get taken down by a robber?"

"A robber?" Isaac asked cautiously. "Is he okay?"

Jack sighed heavily. "He's got some bruises on his legs and arms, but he's fine. It's the *mental shock* that has him bedridden."

"Mental shock?"

"It's the first time something like this has happened—what do you expect? I mean, sure, he's getting older…but still, how could a *robber* best Tony Costa?" Jack spat, clearly still fuming.

Isaac remained silent, unsure how to respond, and Jack eventually noticed his muteness. He cleared his throat and dismissed the topic with an annoyed cluck of his tongue.

"Never mind Tony. We don't have time, so hurry up and get ready," Jack said gruffly, his tone making it sound more like an order than a suggestion.

Isaac blinked, coming back to his senses. "Get ready for what?"

First Felix and now Jack—why did everyone assume he just *knew* what was happening?

"What do you mean, 'what'? The boss says he wants to see you, Mr. Florist, as soon as he arrives today. I'm here to bring you to him, so let's go."

Isaac's head snapped up. "He arrives *today*?"

He never seemed to know Felix's schedule.

"Yeah," Jack replied, albeit unwillingly. "He went to see his grandfather in Italy. We've just gotten word he's landed at the airport."

He checked the time and muttered, "He'll be here soon."

Isaac glanced outside; it was already dark. Dinnertime. He frowned. *He wanted to see him right after flying in from Italy? Wasn't he tired?*

"He must be jet-lagged," Isaac mumbled to himself. "He could've waited until he got some rest."

"Jet-lagged?" Jack looked up, flabbergasted. "What do you take the boss for, saying that? This is the guy who used to travel the world every other day like he was going to the grocery store.

Sure, we were practically dying to keep up with him, but him."

Clearing his throat, Jack continued, "Anyway, you can't expect the boss to have the same routine as some ordinary guy. He's laid back for now—said he's taking a break—but he still has his natural urges to manage."

Of course. What else could you expect from a hyper-dominant alpha? Isaac rolled his eyes, nodding absentmindedly as Jack snorted.

"You're calmer than I expected," Jack remarked.

"What do you mean?"

"Think about it. Why do you think the boss wants to see you right away, *Mr. Florist*?"

Isaac said nothing.

"What else would he want other than to fuck?"

At Jack's impatient words, Isaac blinked. Then reality sank in, and he let out a terse sigh. *Of course. What else could Felix possibly want?* He thought back to the Monday that had come and gone, silently berating himself for momentarily forgetting the nature of his contractual relationship with Felix.

How could I have let it slip my mind?

What had he been expecting when Felix suddenly asked to meet him? The realization left a bitter taste in his mouth.

Isaac gripped the counter, feeling as though the air had been sucked from the room. Jack, noticing his reaction, clicked his tongue in irritation, shaking his head as if Isaac were clueless.

"I'm not one to give advice," Jack said, his guttural voice breaking Isaac's thoughts, "but you should probably prepare yourself before we leave."

"Prepare?" Isaac echoed, glancing at Jack, who gave him a look of pity.

"I don't know what the boss was up to in Italy, but considering he's looking for you before his plane even landed, doesn't that tell you he's pent up? Do yourself a favor—give yourself an enema, finger yourself, whatever works for you."

Isaac said nothing, staring at Jack blankly.

"You've done it already, so you know the boss isn't a pushover," Jack sighed. "If you knew how many people had to be carried out after he was done with them, you wouldn't be staying so calm, *Mr. Florist*."

Isaac continued to stare, his expression unreadable. *Truly, like boss, like employee,* he thought. *Saying such shameless things without a second thought.*

He suddenly felt drained and rubbed his face.

"I don't think that's necessary but hold on a moment. I need to use the bathroom," he said.

"Sure," Jack replied with a shrug, retreating to the chair by the door—the spot he always claimed while waiting for Felix.

Isaac turned away and trudged toward the bathroom. Inside the cramped space, just big enough for a sink and toilet, he locked the door and leaned heavily against it. Letting out a deep sigh, he scanned the room.

Where did I put the enema kit?

In a daze, Isaac remembered stashing it away in a drawer after signing the contract with Felix. As he moved toward the sink, his eyes caught his reflection in the mirror. His cheeks were flushed, no doubt thanks to Jack's shameless comments. The face staring back at him didn't feel like his own.

Snapping out of it, he slapped his cheeks lightly and opened a drawer. Hidden deep inside was a plain box with no text or images. Inside it lay a pile of small pills—suppressants.

Isaac picked one up, turning it over between his fingers. He had taken them religiously since presenting as an omega, never missing a single dose.

Of course, Isaac had already taken this month's pill, but the thought of dealing with Felix tonight had him panicked. In his anxiety, he grabbed two or three extra pills and swallowed them all at once, dry, without a second thought.

Isaac's hands trembled as he tore open the enema kit.

Please, don't let any omega pheromones leak like last time. No matter how thoroughly Felix drenched him in alpha pheromones, no matter how much his semen filled him up and coated his skin—*please don't let any omega pheromones escape.*

Chapter 18

When Felix arrived at the airport, he bypassed his estate and went straight to the hotel. He surveyed the fancy night view and the dark, contrasting seaside. He'd insisted Tony reserve the Hotel del Coronado on Coronado Island—the oldest hotel in San Diego and a renowned tourist destination.

The Hotel del Coronado, the largest resort on the Pacific Coast, was divided into two sections: Beach Village and the main hotel building. The moment Felix arrived, he dropped his luggage in Beach Village. Although it was one of the individually constructed buildings, its interior was as luxurious as a hotel suite.

The tidy villa featured a patio that led directly to the beach, giving it the feel of a country house or private home. The living room, extending from the patio, included a separate kitchen and sitting area, reinforcing the cozy, private atmosphere.

Felix had chosen this hotel among the countless luxury options for many reasons. One reason was childish and arrogant: the hotel, with its long-standing reputation and history of hosting famous guests—including the president—had also earned his stay.

But the real draw was the village's ambiance. From his bedroom, he had a view of the white sandy beach, which added a touch of romance. The white wooden buildings with red roofs and patios paved with fine sand looked charming in the photographs.

It didn't quite live up to expectations now that he was here, though.

"Famous? What bullshit. What is this tiny room? You claimed it was a suite." Felix's voice dripped with irritation as he scanned the villa.

In truth, Felix owned several country houses scattered across the globe, including those in Southern Italy and the Mediterranean islands. These houses offered breathtaking views of paradise and luxurious estates rivaling the grandeur of the finest manors. This so-called suite felt more like an attic in comparison. It was no surprise he felt sour.

Felix should have taken Isaac to the Mediterranean or summoned him to his estate! After two weeks apart, they had to sleep in this garrett. He was incensed.

"Why didn't you stop me? If I'd said to reserve this damn attic, you should've told me otherwise!"

The blame fell squarely on Tony.

Yesterday, after being robbed, Tony had been bedridden, reeling from the emotional shock. Wiping cold sweat from his forehead with a handkerchief, he took a quick, shaky breath.

Tony didn't dare respond.

It seemed that sending Jack to fetch Isaac instead of going himself had rubbed Felix the wrong way, prompting him to lash out at Tony. *If he had known it would end like this*, Tony thought regretfully, he would've gone himself. But what was done was done.

"Still, it's San Diego's major attraction."

"Major attraction, my ass. It's just a rinky-dink building. How old did you say it was? A hundred and twenty?"

"A hundred and thirty. It was declared a historical site. But the actual old wooden building is next door, and this village is relatively new..." Tony tried anxiously to appease Felix, but his words fell on deaf ears.

Felix fumed as he looked around some more before sinking into a cushy sofa, clearly resigned. One room wall was entirely glass, with French doors opening to a picturesque ocean and beach view. However, with darkness already falling, nothing was visible. Though the distant crashing of waves could be heard, the pitch-black sea was bleak and dreary.

"The more I see it, the worse it gets." Felix ran a hand through his tousled blond locks, grinding his teeth in frustration.

"You can't see the ocean now because it's dark, but it'll be quite a sight in the morning when the sun comes up."

"Tony, that's the Pacific. Have you ever seen the sunrise in the west?"

"Ahem. Well, even though the sun doesn't rise from the ocean, once the day breaks, the view alone will—"

"Shut up."

It wasn't until Felix shot him a glare, grinding his teeth in frustration, that Tony clamped his mouth shut. He knew better than anyone that nothing good would come from provoking the notoriously temperamental Felix when he was in one of his moods.

"For fuck's sake, it's hard to date."

At Felix's muttered words, Tony's eyes widened in shock. He even forgot the aches in his body. "What?"

"Are your ears clogged on top of the *mental shock*?"

"No, I thought you just said 'date'—"

"If it's not a one-night stand, and I keep seeing his face and having sex with him, then it's dating."

Tony's jaw dropped, stunned, but Felix only shot him a surly look, sitting haughtily with his legs crossed and chin propped. Tony was at a loss for words.

Dating. *Dating!* Did Felix think he was dating Isaac? While tying him down with a contract, taking his body by force, and calling it dating?

Tony was so flabbergasted he didn't know where to start. He always thought the man lacked self-awareness, but now he realized he lacked any sense at all. His face, which had been pale from strain, now went ashen.

"Boss..." However, Tony couldn't let it slide and reluctantly parted his mouth to speak. Before he could proceed, a knock echoed at the door. Just when he was ready to clearly explain his relationship with Isaac to Felix—knowing he might face a harsh backlash—Tony groaned and turned away.

"What are you doing? There's a visitor. Go get the door."

"No, I have something to tell you first—"

"Should I go get it?" Felix quickly tidied his hair and smoothed his clothes, glaring at Tony. Under Felix's murderous gaze, Tony reluctantly gave up on telling the truth and trudged toward the door. His footsteps felt heavier with each step.

With an automatic sigh, Tony opened the door. Isaac stood there, as expressionless as ever, his back straight. Facing him only made Tony's complicated feelings more tangled, with no clear way out.

What should I do? The boss is convinced he's dating you.

Tony tried to communicate his feelings with his eyes, but Isaac only tilted his head and asked after him. "Tony? I heard you were bedridden, but you're here? Are you all right?"

"Yes, it's nothing. I was told to suck it up and got dragged out."

Tony quietly aired his grievances about Felix, but Isaac only offered an awkward smile in return—poor guy. Seeing Isaac like that made Tony's heartache.

"Tony, Jack, leave." Felix's command was sharp, his narrowed eyes making it clear he was done with their antics. Tony had no choice but to turn and let Isaac through.

Isaac entered the villa quietly, unaware he had just stepped into Felix's trap. Tony watched Isaac's confident figure with a heavy heart, shaking his head before leaving the villa alongside Jack.

"Bro, your face looks worse than before. You okay?" Jack asked, but Tony didn't hear him.

He couldn't remember ever feeling this sorry for Isaac until today. No, maybe he should feel sorry for Felix, who learned about dating only from books and had no clue what he was doing. Either way, it was a sad situation for everyone involved.

Chapter 19

Isaac glanced at Felix awkwardly. In the two weeks since they'd last met, Felix hadn't changed at all. As Jack had pointed out, there were no signs of exhaustion despite his flight from Italy. If anything, the only noticeable difference was his usually immaculate blond hair, now slightly tousled.

"What are you staring at? If you're happy to see me, hug me," Felix teased.

Two weeks wasn't long, yet it felt strangely unreal. Isaac stood there, unsure how to respond, prompting Felix to stride forward and grab his wrist. Isaac's gaze dropped to the hand gripping him tightly.

"Are we even on hugging terms?" he asked.

Jack's words from the flower shop resurfaced in his mind. What could Felix possibly want from him other than sex?

It was a grounding thought, a reminder of where he stood. For a fleeting moment, he'd allowed himself to feel something at the news that Felix wanted to see him the moment he returned.

"We have sex, we kiss, but no hugs? Then who can hug you?" Felix countered.

Isaac furrowed his brow at the question, feeling it had missed the mark somehow. Felix might have been right—or maybe not—but Isaac couldn't come up with a counterargument.

As he wrestled with the thought, Felix tilted his head and leaned in, brushing their lips together.

Isaac froze.

The soft, lingering kiss caught him off guard, his eyes widening. His shoulders tensed instinctively, bracing for the kind of searing, mind-numbing kiss Felix had given him last time. But this one was different—gentler. Felix's lips lightly sucked and teased his lower lip, warm and deliberate.

Then, just as suddenly, Felix pulled back, straightened, and met Isaac's eyes with a satisfied look.

"Now, that's better," he said.

Isaac said nothing in reply.

"Would you believe me if I said I wanted to kiss you the entire time I was in Italy?" Felix asked.

"No."

"I figured you'd say that. That blunt personality of yours isn't going anywhere," Felix replied, his lips curling into a sly smile. His eyes crinkled in a way meant to draw Isaac in, the subtle curve both charming and deliberate. "But that just makes me want you more. If you came running to me like the others, wagging your tail, I might've snapped your neck."

Though spoken with a playful tone, the words carried a dark edge. At the same time, Felix's thumb brushed the inside of Isaac's wrist, still held tightly in his grasp.

The soft, almost sensual touch sent an unbidden shiver down Isaac's spine. Whether it was Felix's gaze or the faint pressure against the sensitive skin of his wrist, warmth began to stir within him.

Uneasy, Isaac tried to pull his hand free. The effort only tightened Felix's grip, reminding him of his strength.

"Did you eat yet?" Felix asked abruptly.

"Not yet," Isaac replied hesitantly.

"Neither have I. Let's eat first."

"Dinner?" He had braced himself for Felix to demand sex immediately—just as he had the first time they met at his apartment. But this casual, almost domestic suggestion left Isaac completely off balance.

Looking at him perplexedly, Felix tugged Isaac forward, leading him by the wrist before settling him onto the plush sofa—the same spot he'd occupied before Isaac arrived.

"Room service or dining out? This hotel's pretty well-known, and it looks like they've got a variety of restaurants," Felix muttered, flipping through a glossy booklet of options. "What are you in the mood for?"

Isaac scratched his cheek, unsure how to respond. Now that he thought about it, this was their first time having dinner alone. His constant seasickness on the yacht kept him from touching the food. At his mother's house in La Jolla, he'd been too preoccupied with her and Benjamin to eat properly.

But now, the idea of sharing a meal with Felix—just the two—tied his stomach into knots. Stress-induced gastritis seemed like a real possibility.

"Aren't you here to collect this week's and last week's payment?" he asked, hoping to shift focus and ignore the unease twisting inside him.

Felix glanced up from the booklet, his deep blue eyes locking onto Isaac's.

"Of course, I'll take them," he replied, his casual tone bordered on dismissive.

The matter-of-fact response left Isaac deflated.

Of course, he thought bitterly, dropping his shoulders in resignation.

"Then right now—"

"I'm hungry. Let's eat first," Felix interrupted, his tone almost petulant as he pursed his lips like a sulking child.

Isaac hesitated, uneasy. It seemed easier to get things over with than to endure dinner in this awkward state. But Felix's behavior threw him off—what was up with him this time? Did something upset him? Isaac rubbed his sweaty palms on his pants, unsure how to proceed.

"Isaac," Felix clicked his tongue in mock disapproval. "I didn't take you for someone so coldhearted."

"What are you talking about?"

"Aren't you? I've just flown in from Italy, haven't eaten, and you're rushing me straight into the fucking. I get it—your body's riled up after seeing me again—but I'm a person, too. Let me eat before we get to the dick down."

Isaac's face flushed instantly, the crude remark catching him completely off guard. How could Felix say something like that so shamelessly without even blinking? Embarrassed, Isaac turned his gaze away, but Felix, as always, watched him with an infuriatingly innocent expression.

"So, what's the plan? Room service or eating out?" Felix pressed, his voice casual. Tapping his finger against his knee—once, twice—he added, "I'm hungry."

The gesture, deliberate and steady, felt like a silent nudge for Isaac to make a decision. Isaac tilted his head. Wasn't Felix Felice the type to do whatever he pleased? He only needed to decide whether to call room service or go out.

So why was he giving Isaac a choice?

He stared at Felix, perplexed, but Felix simply stayed silent, patiently waiting for an answer. Well, if he wanted him to choose.

"Then, I'd like to go out and have a beer with something light."

Being in an enclosed space alone with Felix was already unnerving. The thought of sitting down for a meal like this made his stomach churn. He'd rather eat somewhere with other people—grab something simple, have a beer, and let the atmosphere diffuse some tension.

"A beer and something light. Not bad," Felix said, nodding in approval. He stood abruptly, his solid frame making the small room feel even more stifling. It wasn't just his height or build—the palpable aura of command seemed to fill the space.

"This place looks cramped," Isaac muttered, watching Felix grab his jacket.

Felix glanced over his shoulder, a sheepish expression flickering across his face. "Honestly, I didn't know the room would be this small, either. I booked it because it's supposed to be famous, but when I got here, it turned out to be a dump."

Isaac's eyes widened at Felix's grumbled complaint. "This

is the Hotel del Coronado. The most famous hotel in San Diego. What are you even talking about?"

"Huh?" Felix blinked.

Isaac had heard plenty about the Hotel del Coronado, though he'd never had the chance to visit. It was far too expensive, and he had never needed to stay at a resort like this. When Jack drove him here, he'd been confused about why Felix had chosen this place—but also a little excited.

The hotel's grandeur had momentarily lifted the weight pressing on his mind ever since Jack's pointed remarks. The elegant buildings, the white sandy beach, the breathtaking night views, and the lively atmosphere of the beachfront all felt like a welcome escape.

For once in his usually relentless life, Isaac felt like he could finally breathe. He couldn't understand why Felix was complaining.

"It's perfect," he said simply.

"Really?" Felix's sharp demeanor softened at Isaac's sincere words.

"Yes. This villa, with its patio and the view, is incredible. I've never been to a place like this, but it feels like something straight out of a movie. I'd love to see the beach and ocean during the day," Isaac said, his voice calm but genuine.

He could already imagine it: the dazzling sun overhead, the sandy beach stretching out before him, lying back in a deckchair with a cold beer while gazing at the waves. At night, lighting a fire on the patio and sipping wine in the soft glow. It was the kind of idyllic scene reserved for advertisements—but here, it felt just within reach.

Isaac smiled faintly, his mind wandering to scenes of quiet leisure that seemed perfectly suited to the resort. He liked the pitch-black sky, the endless ocean, and the rhythmic crashing of waves in the distance. For a moment, he almost forgot Felix was beside him—almost forgot that the night would likely leave him drained from Felix's relentless energy.

If only he could indulge in the smallest reprieve, he would be out on the patio, savoring dinner and a beer with the cool ocean breeze. But with Felix near, such calm felt impossible. That was as far as his thoughts went.

"If you like it, then I have nothing to say," Felix's low voice murmured into his ear, breaking the moment.

Startled, Isaac turned his gaze from the dark window—only for his lips to be swallowed in a kiss.

Felix bent his head, pressing their mouths together as his tongue invaded Isaac's without hesitation. It wasn't a kiss filled with the easygoing leisure of their earlier conversation; it was rough, fervent, and unrelenting. Isaac didn't understand why Felix was like this again, but he had no choice but to grip Felix's shoulders for balance.

The kiss grew violent, exploring every inch of his mouth, biting his lips hard enough to sting. Isaac's strength ebbed from his body, his knees threatening to buckle.

"Just, why…" he gasped, his question spilling out in fragmented breaths.

But Felix didn't stop. His lips moved hungrily, trailing over Isaac's mouth, chin, and cheeks, wet and insistent. Held in an iron grip, Isaac's chest heaved against Felix's with every labored breath.

Even if he had allowed kisses, the way Felix unleashed this kind of intensity every time they met was overwhelming—borderline frightening.

"Fuck, I was trying to take it slow, but you just won't let me. Smiling like that, looking all seductive—it's shaking me up," Felix muttered sharply, wrenching himself away. Isaac's face was left damp, as though licked by a large dog. Felix spun around brusquely, adding, "Come on. Or I'll end up eating you first, dinner be damned."

Isaac stood frozen, wiping his lips, watching Felix storm across the room in wide, angry strides. The image of his retreating figure lingered in his mind.

Felix, visibly restraining himself, threw the door open and finally glanced back. The cool night air swept in, tousling his golden-blond hair. His furrowed brows framed his piercing blue eyes, which glinted with suppressed intensity.

There was nothing to criticize about him—this striking man who filled his vision. The sight alone made Isaac's pulse quicken. The urge to rush to him, throw his arms around his neck, and drag him into another kiss flared unbidden.

"Yes," Isaac said, forcing the wild impulse down. He dragged his feet forward, his face as impassive as ever despite the turmoil churning within.

With each step, he drew closer to Felix, who stood waiting like an immovable force, exuding an aura that sent Isaac's thoughts spiraling. The pheromones thickened, wrapping around him, clouding his focus.

Really…

Isaac shut his eyes briefly, trying to steady himself, but when they reopened, they were drawn back to Felix's unwavering blue gaze. His heart pounded louder with every second.

How was he supposed to endure this long, long night?

Chapter 20

Isaac had forgotten it was Friday night when he suggested a beer. He blamed himself for underestimating the frenzy of TGIF.

The hotel bar, especially the one overlooking the beach, was chaotic beyond comparison. The thumping music, the loud chatter, the boisterous laughter—all mixed together, assaulting his eardrums. Isaac, who wasn't used to such a noisy atmosphere, stood there momentarily, wide-eyed, before taking a sip from his beer bottle.

In stark contrast, Felix seemed unfazed, acting as though the noise didn't exist. He sat quietly, drinking his beer and pushing food into his mouth with casual precision. Isaac observed him with a new sense of awe.

A beautiful man who turned heads wherever he went stood out, even in a place like this. The way he wielded his fork, chewed and swallowed his food without a word—it was all so neat, so proper. Isaac had noticed this at his mother's house before, but now it struck him again: Felix's manners were flawless from head to toe.

He was typically unrestrained with his coarse language and ruthless with his men, yet in moments like this, he appeared as if he belonged to a noble family, a well-mannered scion. What a strange man.

"What are you staring at? Not eating?" Felix's voice broke through Isaac's thoughts, not even looking at him. "I know I'm handsome, but if you keep staring at me like that, you'll wear my face out."

Isaac, feeling slightly embarrassed, finally took a sip of his beer. He spoke honestly, "I was surprised by your impeccable table manners."

Felix paused mid-bite, the fork still poised in the air with chicken on it, before looking up at Isaac with a slight, amused smile. "Well, my grandfather was strict. He was especially unforgiving when it came to table manners."

"He must have been a great man."

"Not at all. He's just an eccentric old coot who pulls the trigger every other day and snuffs people out like flies, but still insists on proper manners."

Certainly, with his grandfather being the executive of a prominent mafia in Italy, he couldn't expect the typical image of a grandfather. It sent a chill down Isaac's spine. He instinctively lowered his gaze, momentarily speechless.

"Still," Felix added, "I learned a lot from him. I'm learning now."

There was a softness in Felix's face now, something more human, a fleeting expression that made him look far less like the notorious arms dealer and more like a grandson who cared for his grandfather, despite everything.

Isaac found himself staring, unable to look away, forgetting Felix's complaint. Sitting across from Felix like this, drinking beer and sharing a moment felt oddly comforting. It's like two people casually meeting for a drink after a long week. But, of course, the reality was far from that.

"By the way," breaking the silence, Isaac asked, "should you be sitting around in public for so long?"

The question came from nowhere, but Isaac couldn't help but wonder. He glanced over the crowded bar, the hustle of people oblivious to the man across from him. Felix Felice wasn't just any ordinary guy. He was constantly under government and military scrutiny. Ordinary people might not notice, but Isaac knew it was risky for someone like Felix to be out in public for extended periods.

"Why shouldn't I?"

"You're not exactly an ordinary citizen."

"Maybe not an ordinary one, but I am an upright citizen."

Was he even capable of being an "upright" citizen without all the actual upright citizens dying? Isaac regarded him with narrowed eyes, his expression etched with the word "doubt.'

"What's with that carping look? I really am an upright citizen. I voted not long ago!" Felix stopped drinking his beer and argued, feeling wronged, but Isaac's doubt didn't dissipate so easily.

"Did you file your taxes?"

"Of course. You wouldn't know how much they taxed me, they're squeezing me dry!"

"Then when is the deadline to file a tax return?"

"April."

"The date?" Isaac interrogated him.

Felix answered triumphantly, "My CPA will take care of that."

Felix tilted his chin up, his trademark arrogance on full display, though he didn't know the answer. Isaac sighed and shrugged, conceding the moment.

"Then what about you? Do you know the deadline for your tax return?" Felix asked, arms crossed as he leaned back in his seat, exuding the confidence of a prosecutor grilling the accused.

"April 15th," Isaac replied without missing a beat.

Felix's brow lifted, looking surprised. "Oh? Not bad. Filing taxes while on the run—impressive." His smirk, crooked and sharp, carried an edge of sarcasm.

Isaac kept his expression neutral, though Felix's cheekiness grated. "Well, I am an upright citizen."

"And what exactly did this *upright citizen* do to end up on the run? Loan sharks?"

"Why do you care?"

"If it's money, I'll handle it."

"And after bailing me out? What would you ask for in return?"

Felix suddenly leaned closer, his piercing blue gaze locking onto Isaac. "You."

The single syllable hung in the air, blunt and heavy. Beneath its simplicity, the intensity in Felix's stare was sharp enough to send shivers down Isaac's spine. His throat went dry, words failing him.

How was he supposed to respond to something like that? Felix's relentless approach threw him off balance every time. He couldn't make heads or tails of it.

"If I pay your debt," Felix continued, "can I have you completely?"

Isaac's breath hitched at the unexpected question. The weight of Felix's gaze, overflowing with unspoken emotion, pinned him in place. For the first time, Isaac felt exposed, and unsettled by another person's feelings.

"Felix…" he tried to say, but the name dissolved on his tongue, leaving him mute. A strange, aching pressure swelled in his chest, emotions too tangled to unravel. His fists clenched as he fought to steady himself, bracing against the overwhelming tide.

"Oops!" With a loud crash, someone stumbled and toppled over their table. Felix caught the wobbling beer bottle just in time, but the plates clattered into a messy heap, and the glasses of water shattered on the floor.

It happened in an instant. Isaac blinked, coming to his senses, and scanned the scene. Their table was a disaster.

"Haha, I fell? Guess I'm *really* drunk!" The culprit staggered to his feet, chuckling with a slurred tongue. His unsteady swaying and bleary-eyed grin left no doubt he was thoroughly drunk. Every bar had its share of these types, but Isaac hadn't expected one to stumble into their table tonight.

"It's fine. Now leave," Isaac said coldly.

The drunkard clung to the table, squinting at Isaac before leaning in uncomfortably close. The pungent stench of alcohol hit Isaac's nose like a wave.

"Man, you nag like a bitch. I had a drink, tripped, shit happens. Whatchu you glarin' fer?" Instead of apologizing, the man raised his voice, growing belligerent.

Isaac's brow furrowed, but he didn't bother responding. He'd already spotted the bar staff hurrying over. If he waited, they'd deal with it soon enough.

"Hey, jackass, are you ignoring m—ahhck!" The man's words cut off in a strangled cry as he suddenly lurched forward, face-planting into a plate of leftover food.

Isaac's gaze snapped to Felix, who remained seated, perfectly composed, with his chin resting on his hand. His other hand gripped the drunkard's wrist, the man's pinky bent unnaturally—snapped cleanly.

Felix had broken it without mercy.

Isaac's mouth fell open, stunned by the speed and brutality of the act. The drunkard's pained screams echoed through the bar.

"Fucking squawker." Felix glared at the drunkard, his expression dark and menacing.

A staff member hurried over, glancing at the crying man in confusion. "May I ask what happened?"

"As you can see," Felix answered smoothly, "this drunk man tripped and fell on our table." He clicked his tongue, the lie flowing effortlessly, "He must've hit his hand during the fall as well."

Isaac sighed, marveling at Felix's audacity and how easily he spun a story.

"We're terribly sorry," the staff member replied.

"Hit my hand? It was you. You bas— Ack!" The drunkard's shout, his face still smeared with food, was cut short as a burly man appeared seemingly out of nowhere. The bodyguard pressed a heavy hand onto his shoulders, forcing him down onto the table with a grunt of pain.

"Lift a finger, and my bodyguard will break your arm," Felix warned. "You should've thought harder about who you were running your mouth at. What could happen if you shat just anywhere? If you can't handle your liquor, maybe don't drink at all."

The drunkard groaned, his face twisted in pain, while the staff member, now pale and visibly uneasy, apologized profusely. Felix ignored the apologies. Instead, he leaned forward, patting the drunkard's cheek with mockery before rising smoothly from his seat.

"This wouldn't have happened if you'd just apologized and scurried off. Why waste your time coveting what belongs to someone else? What cheekiness."

Belongs to someone else? The words echoed in Isaac's mind, freezing him in place.

He was blaming the drunkard for looking down on him and shouting at him. The meaning behind Felix's words, *"belong to someone else,"* was unmistakable. Isaac didn't need to ask; he already knew. And, of course, he knew precisely what Felix meant by "belonging"—it was him. That phrase brought back the memory of Felix's bold declaration in the car before leaving for Italy.

Yet, despite the blatant possessiveness, Isaac couldn't bring himself to feel angry. His throat tightened, the words catching as if a frog were lodged there, leaving him speechless. Offended wasn't the right word for what he felt—it was far more complicated, tangled in emotions he couldn't fully articulate. Conflict churned within him, but Felix, oblivious as ever, wouldn't understand his feelings even if he died and came back to life.

While Isaac grappled with his emotions, Felix casually handed the staff a thick wad of cash over the drunkard's shoulder. The man's face was still buried in the plate of leftovers, a pathetic sight. Felix's gesture was almost dismissive, the amount more than double the cost of their meal.

"Take care of the rest," Felix instructed his bodyguard before turning to Isaac and tugging him up by the arm.

Isaac, lost in thought amidst the chaotic scene, stood reluctantly. The quiet dinner they'd shared—shoulder to shoulder, almost peaceful—was now a wreck. He stared at the ruined table, an inexplicable pang of regret stirring within him.

"I've lost my appetite," Felix murmured, leaning in close. His breath grazed Isaac's ear, the low timbre of his voice sending a shiver down Isaac's spine.

"You should help me refresh. What do you say?"

Soft yet heavy with intent, the words echoed in Isaac's ears. Felix's lips brushed his earlobe as he spoke, the cool baritone spreading an involuntary chill through Isaac's body.

Isaac turned to meet Felix's gaze. Those deep blue eyes were closer than before, unwavering and sharp with meaning. Anticipation clawed at Isaac's throat, leaving him breathless and dry-mouthed.

"As you wish," Isaac managed to reply, though his voice barely rose above the pulsing rhythm of the music. He couldn't tell if Felix had even heard him.

Felix's gaze lingered on him briefly before his lips curled into that familiar, crooked smirk. Felix seized his wrist and strode out of the bar, his pace swift and unrelenting.

Isaac struggled to keep up with Felix's swift, long strides. How he moved so effortlessly across the fine, shifting sand in dress shoes was beyond him. Though Isaac wasn't short, the sinking sand and lingering effects of the alcohol made his steps unsteady, and he stumbled.

"W-wait, a bit slower—" Isaac gasped, his breath hitching as his legs tangled beneath him. He wasn't drunk, but he may as well have been, given his clumsy footing.

Felix's solid arm wrapped around Isaac's waist just in time to keep him from falling. But the closeness was overwhelming, his scent and warmth flooding Isaac's senses. Beneath the salt-laden sea breeze, the unmistakable pull of alpha pheromones, thick and heady, lingered.

Oh, God.

Blood rushed south instantly, and Isaac's body betrayed him, his mouth filling with saliva like Pavlov's dog.

On the dark beach, with the cold wind biting at his skin, he gripped Felix's shoulder, his gaze locked on him as if spellbound.

Felix's eyes, so dark they seemed black, held him captive. There was a faint smirk curling Felix's lips.

"Isaac, what should I do?" Felix's voice was low, almost lost in the crash of waves.

Isaac barely registered the words before Felix's hand slid into his windblown black hair, pulling it back with a deliberate tug. Isaac's lips parted instinctively, and a soft, involuntary moan escaped.

"I think I'm going crazy because of you," Felix murmured, his voice cracking.

The sly curve of his lips and the gleam in his eyes piercing through the dark crashed over Isaac like a tidal wave. It was too much—intense, consuming, and utterly terrifying.

Chapter 21

The shower cascaded over them, drenching Isaac to the bone as he panted heavily. Water streamed down his face as he struggled to grasp the slippery tiles. Behind him, Felix, equally drenched and fervent, his face impassioned, pounded into him relentlessly.

Felix's hands spread Isaac's wet buttocks, and with each forceful thrust of his dangerous cock, water sprayed everywhere. The lewd, wet sounds echoed in the small space, almost painful to Isaac's ears.

"Felix, please…" He bit back his moans, hoping the crashing water would mask the sounds. Isaac's body strained, caught on the brink of breaking—or shattering completely. Felix, seemingly deaf to Isaac's muffled pleas, showed no signs of relenting. The room began to blur as Isaac's vision swirled in dizzying spirals.

Isaac had already climaxed once, a sluggish release. But Felix continued, his relentless rhythm pushing Isaac to his limit. Unable to bear it any longer, Isaac twisted his hips, only to be met with a firm hand on his wet ass.

"Hck—"

"Isaac, hold those hips up. Don't even think about running." He phrased it that way, but it wasn't like he was being allowed to move. Felix gripped Isaac's round ass so tightly he couldn't shift on his own. Felix's thrusts resumed, relentless and rough, leaving Isaac gasping for air. Despite the intensity, Felix's breathing remained steady, almost unaffected, as he moved his hips with practiced ease as if it were nothing more than light exercise.

"Did I tell you?" Felix's voice, tinged with laughter and mingling with the sound of the falling water, echoed in Isaac's ear. "You look so pretty, I'm dying to bite, suck, and nibble at you."

Isaac shook his head repeatedly, unable to respond or

understand what was being said. All he could do was breathe sharply, surrendering himself entirely to Felix's relentless rhythm.

As Isaac gasped for air, trembling, Felix's rock-hard chest pressed against his wet back, leaving no space between them. The heat from his body scorched Isaac's skin. He let out a low moan, but Felix responded by suddenly bending forward and sinking his teeth into Isaac's shoulder.

"Ah!" Isaac flinched, brow furrowing at the sharp twinge of pain. But Felix didn't relent, licking up the water that trickled down Isaac's hair to the nape of his neck before biting down again and repeating the motion. Soon, Isaac's neck and shoulders were covered in teeth marks and bruises. It was as though Felix was carving his name into Isaac's body.

No matter how much Felix nibbled and sucked, it was never enough. He bit down on Isaac's back and shoulders while his hands roamed over his chest, kneading and fondling with relentless force. Isaac's chest wasn't soft like a woman's, but Felix didn't seem to care. He roughly rolled Isaac's nipples between his fingertips, sending jolts of sensation through him.

The water was warm, but Isaac's nipples stood painfully erect. A shiver ran down his spine every time Felix's fingers brushed across them. His vision blurred, the alpha pheromones leaking from the semen Felix had spilled inside him, clouding his senses further.

"How lewd. Your nipples are hardening just by touching them."

Isaac couldn't respond to Felix's words as he felt the sharp nip at his earlobe. His hands trembled against the wall, his hips weakening, close to giving out. But every time they faltered, Felix's grip tightened, lifting him and forcing his body into a relentless rhythm.

"Isaac, we're far from done yet," Felix murmured darkly. "Lift your ass properly."

His hands moved to Isaac's nipples, twisting and fondling them. The swollen, reddened flesh throbbed painfully; they stung, burned, even. Yet strangely, a shiver of anticipation coursed through Isaac's body, reaching down to his aching hips.

"Please, a little slower..." Isaac's breathless pleas were ignored as Felix continued his greedy, relentless possession. Felix's fingers, which had been torturing his nipples, now clamped down on Isaac's ass, spreading his cheeks wide. The strange mix of pain and pleasure vanished as his asscheeks were spread, and the pummeling resumed mercilessly. Isaac could only moan, lost in the moment.

Felix's thrusts were so forceful that his cock seemed to disappear and reappear as an indentation on Isaac's lower stomach. Felix himself seemed possessed, his eyes wild and feral.

"Ah, fuck!" With a rough grunt, Felix pounded into Isaac, the sound of it ringing roughly, then abruptly grabbed his chin and jerked his head back. Isaac, with his ass in the air, exhaled sharply, his mouth hanging open, moans leaving with each thrust.

It was only a brief respite. Like a predator seizing its prey, Felix snatched Isaac's swollen tongue from between his wet lips, biting and sucking it hungrily. Felix went from voraciously biting and sucking at his swollen lips to his tongue invading Isaac's mouth, filling and plundering it. Saliva spilled from the corners of their lips, joining the running water.

Combined with the water, the kiss sounded even wetter and was utterly messy. Not only were they roughly fucking, they were also ferally kissing. Isaac closed his eyes, his mouth agape, and moaned as he suckled Felix's thick tongue. Felix frowned and hummed low in his throat. He rammed his cock into Isaac's ass up to the base, fully sheathed, and then stopped moving.

Felix was so deep it felt like a large blunt instrument was lodged in Isaac's stomach. He moaned loudly, involuntarily, as a hot sensation of Felix's spilled come painted his inner walls.

Would he take a breather now?

The thought, as flimsy as hope, crossed Isaac's mind. The alpha pheromones, seeping into his system, were too intoxicating,

seeping into every cell in his body. No matter how often he experienced this, he never seemed to grow accustomed to the sensation.

A moan escaped him as dizziness overwhelmed him, causing his knees to give way. His hands slid along the wall, with Felix following closely, wrapping his arms tightly around his waist. Then, descending to all fours, Felix positioned himself over Isaac, supporting himself on one knee as he climbed onto his back.

"Isaac, if the floor is more comfortable, I'll let it slide. Lift your ass."

"Ha-hah…I can't…anymore…"

"I told you, you can't say such weak words," Felix said, his voice cold and menacing. "I'll make you hang onto me, screaming like last time. So be good, lift your ass, and spread your hole."

His lips curled into a sinister smile, his blue eyes flashing with a manic intensity. His voice was cold and menacing. With a weary sigh, Isaac summoned the last of his strength in his thighs and lifted his ass, offering himself to Felix.

The moment they entered the villa, Felix had pounced, his lust driving him wild. He attacked Isaac's lips with a savage intensity, tearing at his clothes before the door had even closed.

Isaac, stripped bare in the blink of an eye, tried to reason with Felix, suggesting a shower first. But Felix, consumed by insatiable desire, refused to yield. Dragging Isaac into the bathroom, he insisted they shower together—a suggestion that sent a ripple of dread through Isaac. This time, however, Felix was unstoppable, his determination leaving no room for protest.

Even though Felix did as he pleased, he was usually quite tender and, sometimes, minded his manners. If Isaac didn't comply with his wishes, he would become petulant and pout like a child. However, when consumed by lust, Felix transforms into a different person, becoming violent and driven by instinct. He said, "I prefer to play rough like a beast."

It was an old memory, and Felix's preference had not changed.

Isaac, resigned, lifted his ass. Felix's burning cock immediately found its mark, rubbing against the sensitive flesh and leaking milky semen. Though slightly deflated from his recent climax, a few long strokes from the perineum to the entrance quickly restored its hardness.

As Felix's cock, swelling larger with each passing moment, pressed against the sensitive flesh of Isaac's ass, Isaac tensed, a sense of injustice washing over him. His mind raced with questions—had Felix even climaxed? How could he recover so quickly? Isaac demanded an explanation, his frustration bubbling to the surface.

Oblivious to Isaac's frustration, Felix focused on the task at hand. He rubbed the tip of his cock against the slick entrance, then, with a forceful thrust, penetrated Isaac without mercy.

Isaac let out a short scream.

The forceful thrusts felt like his insides were being wrenched upward. But something had changed—perhaps the position or overwhelming influence of Felix's pheromones. With each rough thrust, Isaac's body reacted differently, his sphincter spasming around Felix's cock with each thrust as Felix lifted his hips higher. The combination of semen, water, and his slick was sticky and messy. Isaac recognized the signs of his body's response and bit his lip to stifle a moan.

Isaac's cock was leaking precum. Having already climaxed twice, he assumed he was spent. But as Felix's cock pounded into his cum-filled insides, a new wave of arousal washed over him. He couldn't believe it. His vision blurred, but this time, it was from a different kind of intoxication.

"Ah, fuck! Isaac! Just what is your hole made of?" Felix exclaimed, pressing down on Isaac's shoulders as Isaac lay prone, his body instinctively reacting like an omega.

Felix began pounding into Issac savagely, akin to a rutting dog. The sound of flesh slapping against flesh filled the bathroom.

Isaac's vision blurred, and his senses were overwhelmed. His inner walls betrayed him, and he eagerly accepted Felix's relentless thrusts. Moans spilled from his lips.

Instinctively, Isaac tightened and released around Felix's cock, his thighs trembling with pleasure. His mind, clouded with ecstasy, was a blank slate. As his eyes rolled back as if on drugs, his head lolled on the wet bathroom floor. He uttered sounds of pleasure, "More, more, uh, there…Ah, yes…"

"Hah, I'm going insane," Felix muttered in disbelief, panting heavily. "Where did a seductress like you spring from?"

He thrust deep into Isaac, who sobbed and bucked his hips in response to the overwhelming pleasure. "More, deeper, ruin me. Aah, yes…"

Isaac wiggled his ass like an experienced prostitute, prompting Felix to thrust with renewed vigor. His bones ached, and his body was on the brink of collapse. He felt like he was dying. Yet, he was helpless against the wave of pleasure. How could such ecstasy exist?

Spread wide, his thighs trembled uncontrollably, and with a final, shuddering moan, Isaac collapsed forward. Milky cum spurted from his untouched cock, a sight that left him stunned.

Oh, God.

The water quickly washed away the translucent liquid sprayed over the bathroom floor without a trace. Isaac watched with vacant eyes as the water swirled down the drain before letting out an empty sigh. He now realized that Felix's alpha pheromones were filling the small shower booth to the brim. His body was full of semen and Felix's unfiltered alpha pheromones.

A couple of pills wouldn't have made a difference. He realized that now. He was lucky he hadn't gone mad from such a concentrated dose of pheromones—or perhaps he already had. His body, completely beyond his control, clung desperately to Felix's cock

"Felix…" Isaac managed to lift himself off the floor with his forearms, his voice barely a whisper.

Felix responded with a harsh kiss, gripping Isaac's chin.

Isaac parted his lips, sucking in a breath as his tongue traced Felix's, following the ambrosia. Felix hummed low in his throat, his frenzy growing. Without thinking, he nipped at Isaac's lips, tangling their tongues together.

At last, Isaac managed to pull away from Felix's relentless advances, gasping for air. "I'll let you do whatever you want…"

Felix paused, confusion flickering in his eyes as his words came out garbled.

"Let's move…to the bed." Isaac couldn't take it anymore. The alpha pheromones thickened the air, suffocating him. His only thought was escape.

"Whatever I want." Felix's smile grew, and he extended a hand. The shower above them fell silent.

Chapter 22

Isaac's eyelids felt unbearably heavy, and it took him a long, deliberate moment to pry them open.

Once he managed, Isaac blinked against the brightness of his unfamiliar surroundings. The room was quiet, save for Felix's steady breathing as he slept face down beside him. Isaac stared at him for a while, his vision hazy, before attempting to move and get out of bed. He felt his back would stick to the sheets if he stayed much longer.

But that was wishful thinking. He barely managed to turn his head before a deep ache spread through his body as if he'd been beaten. His head throbbed relentlessly, and his limbs felt impossibly heavy, as though they'd been replaced with solid rebar.

There hadn't been any reason recently for him to exhaust himself to this extent. Isaac furrowed his brow and sighed deeply, giving up on leaving the bed. He settled back down, turning slightly away from Felix, unable to shake the growing embarrassment of lying beside him.

As he lay there, breath shallow, the previous night's events replayed in his mind like a reel. The memory was filled with endless wailing—himself, lost to all logic and reason, moaning and shivering, drenched in the alpha pheromones Felix had radiated. He was frantic with lust, begging for more, to continue fucking him.

"Ah—" The memory of his moans echoed in his ears so clearly that Isaac had to raise a hand to smother his mouth.

No, it couldn't be.

What had happened?

How?

Isaac blinked rapidly, a sigh escaping deep from his chest.

Just then, a strong arm wrapped around his waist, and he flinched instinctively at the unexpected touch.

"Why don't you give me a morning kiss if you're up?" The sleepy voice tickled his ears, leaving Isaac frozen stiff. Felix tightened his arm around him, pulling him in by the waist. Isaac's bare back pressed against Felix's chest, the heat between them almost scalding. He held his breath, his skin prickling at the contact.

"Hmm. I could get used to waking up with you next to me," Felix murmured, his voice heavy with sleep.

Isaac swallowed against the scratchiness in his throat, his body tense and rigid. Unlike Felix, who seemed utterly at ease, Isaac felt like his nerves were about to snap.

"Shouldn't you be heading back?" he asked, his hoarse voice surprising even himself. He reached up to touch his throat, suddenly aware of how raw it felt. How much had he cried and screamed for it to get this bad?

"It's fine," Felix replied. "I just got back from Italy, didn't I?"

"Wasn't that yesterday?" Isaac rasped, disoriented.

Felix's soft chuckle rumbled against his back, "Isaac, do you feel like you've been in some kind of midsummer night's dream?"

"What are you—"

"It wasn't yesterday. It's been two days now."

Isaac's eyes widened in shock, his expression betraying his disbelief. It felt like someone had struck him over the head. Not last night, but the night before? How was that possible? When did time slip away?

"I was with you…that whole time?"

"Of course."

"How…"

"Because you begged," Felix replied matter-of-factly.

Isaac blinked, struggling to process, when Felix's voice from earlier echoed in his mind: *"Isaac, a day has already gone by. What will you do? The day after tomorrow is Monday, and I'll have to collect your pay again. Will you pay now or save it for Monday?"*

Felix had said that—Isaac was certain—as he wore that relaxed smile. This implied that last night…the intimacy that began the previous evening in the bathroom had continued for an entire day. Isaac, intoxicated by alpha pheromones, had clung to Felix with desperation, unwilling to release his hold.

"Now, do it now…ah, don't—don't take it out…"

Isaac shook his head and cried for him not to stop. He wound his arms around Felix's neck and clung to him when he tried to remove the cock from his ass. *Give me more,* he'd begged. *Don't take it out, just fuck me.* He'd even pressed him to come inside him.

I was out of my mind. Isaac smothered his dry lips and let out a short sigh.

"I didn't know you enjoyed sex that much," Felix murmured, his lips brushing against the nape of Isaac's neck. His hot, humid breath scattered across Isaac's skin, sending a shiver down his spine.

Isaac flinched, his shoulders squaring as he twisted his body to escape. But, as always, Felix was impossible to shake off by will alone. Isaac struggled briefly before giving up, his arm draping over Felix's.

"I do not enjoy it," he said firmly.

It was Felix's fault for carelessly radiating his alpha pheromones. Felix believed him to be a beta and wasn't cautious about it, but last night had gone too far. That level of pheromones would have overwhelmed even a true beta.

If Isaac, an omega, hadn't taken three suppressants, his heat cycle might have been triggered—or worse, his mind might have shattered. While alpha pheromones could arouse an omega, an overdose could easily drive them to madness.

Felix wasn't just any alpha—he was a hyper-dominant, the pinnacle of his kind. The thought of how powerful his pheromones were sent a chill through Isaac.

"If you don't enjoy it, why do you cry and cling so much? Isaac, I was even thinking it'd be fine if I went into rut, you know? I don't think you'd end up in shreds like you're so worried about." He chuckled, pressing a kiss to Isaac's neck. "See? You were fucked for two days, and you're fine. Turns out you were the one begging me not to stop. It's cute."

Felix kissed Isaac's neck, then pressed his nose against his skin and inhaled deeply. A shiver coursed down Isaac's spine, making him hunch his shoulders instinctively.

"Do you know?" Felix murmured lazily, his breath warm against Isaac's skin. "Since last night, you've been smelling… different. You should reek of sweat, but instead, you smell strangely fragrant. It's driving me crazy. You're not even an omega, yet your scent is so seductive. If you *were* an omega…"

His words trailed off as he sucked lightly on the sensitive skin behind Isaac's neck.

Isaac snapped, whipping around and pulling away. Felix's face crumpled like a child denied his favorite toy. "What? I didn't bite you that hard."

"I'll get going," Isaac muttered.

The icy blue eyes watching him were sharp, unrelenting. As Isaac had feared, his omega pheromones had leaked. Panic tightened his chest as he tried to pull away, but it wasn't easy. The ache in his muscles, the lingering burn inside his channel—it all hurt. But what truly held him back was Felix's arm still wrapped securely around his waist. Isaac turned back to him with a flat stare.

"Where did the seductress who rolled around with me like dogs for two straight days go, I wonder?" Felix drawled. "Well, I suppose it's better that you're different as night and day, literally. But it still stings when you act this cold."

Felix clicked his tongue before finally unwinding his arm from Isaac. Freed, Isaac shifted to the edge of the bed but didn't stand.

His legs felt weak, as though they'd give out the moment he tried.

More than that, he was afraid—afraid of the consequences of leaving Felix behind like this.

"So, I've paid up through next Monday."

"Is that disappointment I hear?" Felix teased. "I can go another round if you want."

"No, thank you," Isaac replied curtly.

Felix pouted, as if genuinely offended. Isaac averted his gaze, unwilling to engage, though he couldn't understand why Felix would even ask when he already knew the answer.

"Yeah, that's exactly what Isaac Sinclair would say." Felix chuckled, breaking the silence.

Isaac glanced back at Felix with a peculiar expression. The way Felix said his full name felt…off. Discordant, even.

"What?" Felix prompted again.

Isaac snapped out of his thoughts. "Oh, it's nothing," he replied, shaking his head.

"What a letdown," Felix smirked. Propping himself up on one elbow, he traced a finger along Isaac's side. "By the way, what's the story behind all these scars?"

Isaac followed Felix's gaze to his own body. His lean, muscular frame was marked with a scattering of small scars.

It wasn't like he had ever tried to hide them—they couldn't be hidden. But the reason Felix was only noticing them now was apparent: every other time Isaac had undressed, they'd been too preoccupied, going at it like a pair of breeding animals, for Felix to notice such details.

"I was into sports when I was younger. Sometimes, I played rough."

"Sports? Fine. But *played rough*?" Felix's lips curved in amusement. "That's unexpected."

"It happened to be like that. It was just immaturity." Isaac's tone was clipped as he turned to leave the bed. But before he could rise, Felix's hand slid across his back. Isaac realized he wasn't letting him off just yet, and flinching, he stopped in his movements.

"What kind of sports?" Felix asked casually, his fingers brushing Isaac's spine. The slow, deliberate movement felt more like praise than curiosity.

The rough stroke traced along his back, following the ridges of muscle, then skimmed down toward his waist. The ticklish sensation made Isaac's shoulders tense. With Felix's piercing gaze burning into his skin, Isaac felt his throat tighten.

"Hmm?" Felix's voice was a low murmur as Isaac failed to respond. The teasing touch had shifted, growing increasingly intimate, lingering over his hips. It wasn't just a touch anymore—it was unmistakably sensual.

"A variety," Isaac managed in a shaky voice, just as Felix's large hand cupped his rear. The grip tightened, firm and teasing, forcing a brief moan from his throat.

"I heard you moved to Washington with your father after the divorce?" Felix asked casually as if the mood wasn't charged.

"Yes."

Felix's hand shifted, his middle finger sliding between the cleft of Isaac's buttocks. Pressing against his entrance, the finger grazed dampened skin, where remnants of their previous encounter lingered. The semen inside him, not yet expelled, leaked out, and the finger prodded his swollen flesh. The touch sent a sharp jolt up Isaac's spine, his body instinctively tensing.

"And that's where you got into sports and played rough?" Felix continued, his tone as lazy as ever.

"Yes."

"What kind of man was your father?" The question rolled off Felix's tongue lazily, as though he weren't preoccupied with anything else.

Isaac turned his head toward him, unaware that the edges of his vision had blurred with a flush of red, brought on by Felix's teasing fingers. Felix grinned, taking in the sight of Isaac's shallow, uneven breaths.

"I heard some things from your mother," Felix continued, his tone casual. "I've wondered for a while. You don't have to answer if you don't want to."

His finger lingered, taunting Isaac's entrance, poised as though to press forward at any moment.

Isaac's hand shot out, seizing Felix's wrist in a tight grip. The torment stopped instantly, the pressure against his slick skin retreating.

"So, if I don't answer," Isaac said, "you'll just run a background check?"

"Wow…you really know me well now, don't you? I like that."

What a shameless man. Isaac shot Felix a sharp glare, but when he couldn't bring himself to demand the removal of that intrusive hand, he turned his head away instead. He didn't particularly want to face Felix as he shared this part of his story anyway.

"My father was an omega," he said quietly.

"Omega?" Felix's deliberately surprised tone hung in the air, but Isaac pressed on.

"After he divorced my beta mother, he took me and remarried my alpha stepfather. We moved to Washington with him."

"So, you have two fathers."

"Yes."

"And?" Felix's curious voice nudged him to continue.

Isaac took a steadying breath. "Nothing much. Around the time I graduated from high school, my omega father died in an accident."

"Hmm."

"After that, I moved out. I didn't have a relationship with my stepfather, so…I wouldn't know." His tone was sharp, signaling the end of the discussion as he shifted to stand.

Before he could rise, Felix's other hand gripped his waist and pushed him back down firmly.

Why are you like this? The thought barely formed before it was overtaken by sensation. Felix's teasing fingers finally pressed inside—two at once, sliding in with a single, smooth motion.

Isaac's body tensed, his shoulders curling inward as a low, strained moan escaped him. The fingers moved deeper, scissoring against his soft inner walls. A thick glob of semen spilled out, forcing a strange, uncomfortable sensation that made Isaac stiffen further, his teeth clenched tight.

"Wow, look at this," Felix murmured, almost to himself. "Even I think I stuffed you too much."

He twisted his fingers inside, coaxing out more of the thick fluid. Isaac could only shudder, his face burning as he hunched his shoulders, unable to stop Felix.

For what felt like an eternity, Felix worked his fingers, the motion deliberate and unrelenting. When he finally withdrew them, Isaac exhaled a shaky sigh of relief.

The sheets beneath him were soaked, evidence of everything Felix had forced out.

"Can I…go shower now?" Isaac asked quietly, brushing a hand through his sweat-dampened hair. It had only been minutes since he woke, yet he already felt drained.

"Sure," Felix replied casually, wiping his dripping hand on the sheets without a second thought.

With effort, Isaac pushed himself upright. His legs trembled, barely supporting him as he shuffled toward the bathroom. Felix watched him silently, his serene expression unreadable, before finally calling out, "Isaac."

Isaac paused, glancing back just as he reached the bathroom door.

"I'm hungry. We should eat something, don't you think?"

The question came out of nowhere, light and unaffected as if the earlier conversation hadn't happened.

Isaac stared at him for a moment before nodding. "This time… I'd like room service."

"As you wish." Felix smiled, his eyes crinkling as he propped his head on his arms, reclining comfortably against the pillows.

His grin was brighter than the sunlight streaming over the beach, and Isaac had to force himself to look away.

His footsteps felt strangely heavy as he disappeared into the bathroom.

Listening to the water flow, Felix reached for the side table. He picked up the room service menu in one hand and his phone in the other. While his eyes surveyed the menu, he quickly unlocked his phone with his fingers and dialed a number.

The call didn't ring long.

"Have you woken up now?" came Tony's grumbling voice.

"Run a background check," Felix said without preamble.

"A check on whom, all of a sudden?"

"Isaac's father. And his stepfather." Felix's tone remained calm as he listened to the sound of water from the bathroom, casually flipping through the menu.

"His stepfather?" Tony asked.

"Isaac's biological father was an omega. His stepfather was an alpha. Find him." Felix ended the call without waiting for a reply, setting the phone back in its place. His attention returned to the menu, his fingers tapping lightly against its edge.

The sound of running water ceased moments later, and Felix raised his eyes. His Prussian blue pupils glimmered with anticipation, fixed on the bathroom door, waiting for Isaac to emerge.

By the time Issac sat down to eat, it was somewhere between brunch and lunch. Regardless, the coffee paired with his omelet was surprisingly good.

His body still felt worn out—he had barely managed to shower and had no choice but to order room service. Yet, the decision turned out to be satisfying. Just as he'd imagined when he first arrived, he now sat on the patio, gazing at the endless blue ocean and enjoying a rare moment of peace.

Felix had already cleaned his plate and was now lounging with a bottle of beer. His blond hair was still half-damp and tousled from his shower, black sunglasses perched on his sharp nose. The lazy curl of his upper lip around the bottle completed the picture of an effortlessly handsome playboy.

"You said you learned proper table manners," Isaac muttered, eyeing Felix, who sat reclined with one ankle propped over his knee.

Felix arched an eyebrow, lowering the bottle slightly. "I'm done eating."

"I'm still eating."

"You sounded exactly like my grandfather just now."

"Did I?" Isaac asked without much interest, his tone neutral.

Felix didn't press further. The chatter of people passing by the villa and the distant shouts of children blended with the steady rhythm of the waves.

Isaac sat under the shade of the parasol, slowly chewing his omelet as his gaze wandered out over the boundless ocean. A faint, bitter smile tugged at his lips.

"What's that face for? What are you unhappy about?" Felix's blunt question broke the silence, revealing he had been watching him closely.

Isaac schooled his expression and turned to him. "Nothing. I was just thinking about how much Benjamin would enjoy this place. He loves playing with sand."

"You're such a dad to think of your kid at a time like this," Felix muttered, taking another swig from his bottle. He didn't seem to care that he was drinking beer in broad daylight; anyone passing by might assume it was sparkling water.

"If Benjamin were here, you wouldn't have been able to scream for two days," Felix added with a crooked smile, his tone teasingly lewd. It was clear he was making fun of him.

Isaac paused, mid-bite of his omelet, before responding flatly, "That's true. I wouldn't have let you lay a finger on me."

Felix's brow creased at the dispassionate retort. He clicked his tongue, turned away, and took another long drink, clearly sulking. Watching him pout like a child, Isaac's lips curved into a faint smile. In moments like this, Felix really did remind him of Benjamin. But the thought lingered only briefly before Isaac shook his head. It was a useless comparison.

Isaac shifted his gaze to the blue sea."This is the first time I've spent leisure time at a resort or on a beach," Isaac said softly.

It wasn't just a change of topic—it was an honest confession.

"Is it?" For once, Isaac volunteered something about himself without Felix prying, and Felix's surprise was evident.

Though Isaac had started the conversation, he sat still, fork in hand, staring at the crashing waves, momentarily lost in thought. Felix didn't press him. He simply tilted his beer bottle and waited.

After a pause, Isaac resumed in a low, reflective tone. "When I was little, my mother might have taken me places, but I don't remember any family trips. My parents had a rocky relationship. After their divorce, there was even less time for things like this."

He spoke as though recounting someone else's story, his voice devoid of emotion. "My father was loving, but he was always busy. When he had time, he couldn't spend it with me. Once I got older, I was too busy making a living. Now I'm over thirty and haven't taken a single vacation until now."

"You and I are alike in that respect," Felix added flippantly as if it were an afterthought. "I was like that too. It's only natural. When parents are busy, their kids don't get to have time either. If you haven't had the chance yet, just aim for it in the future."

Felix spoke casually, finishing his beer and setting the empty bottle down with a thud. "And besides," he continued, "I kinda like that you haven't had the chance to go out and experience things."

"What do you mean?"

"You'll be experiencing those things with me now." Felix shrugged as if he was joking. "How grand."

Isaac stared at him. "You think I'll be with you for all the things I newly experience from now on?"

Felix had spoken lightly, but Isaac's question was serious.

"Of course." Felix tilted his head, his expression asking why Isaac would even doubt it. "Who else do you think you'd experience those things with?"

"Are you being serious?"

"When have you ever seen me joke around?" Felix shot back, his confidence unwavering.

Isaac was stunned, unable to reply. How could this man say such things so easily? "You'll be at a disadvantage."

"How so?"

"There's more things I haven't done than I have done. To do all those things with me…won't you run out of time?"

"What a funny statement. I can just make time."

Isaac's unspoken concern hung in the air. In a roundabout way, he had intended to ask if Felix would still have enough time for meetings—or for hooking up with others. But as usual, Felix remained oblivious.

Isaac worried his bottom lip, feeling uneasy. "If, by chance…"

What will happen to this between us if you find someone else? Isaac almost let the question slip, but he caught himself just in time and shut his mouth. He realized he had no right to ask something like that.

"What were you going to say?" Felix asked, twisting open a new bottle of beer.

"It's nothing."

Isaac braced for Felix to press him, but to his surprise, Felix only grinned and took a swig. "Lame."

As Felix drank, Isaac's gaze lingered on the rhythmic bob of his Adam's apple. Moments like this were possible because Felix's interest hadn't waned yet. But people's feelings changed, didn't they? Especially Felix—he'd admitted as much, that he grew bored of people easily.

Isaac's thoughts trailed off as the sea breeze tossed his hair about. He brushed it back and looked up. The parasol's shade had shifted, and the blazing sun now poured over him.

Despite the heat, the cool breeze kept him comfortable. The warmth was soothing, chasing away his unease and tangled thoughts. Leaning back in his chair, Isaac closed his eyes, letting himself sink into the light and stillness.

The room's warmth could have lulled Isaac to sleep, but the wicked man beside him refused to let that happen.

The sunlight filtering through the window abruptly vanished, replaced by a cool, wet sensation on his lips. Soft lips pressed against his, moving with deliberate intent and creating quiet, wet sounds. Isaac opened his eyes, his vision filled with Felix's sharp features—his sculpted nose and intense expression. The man kissed him like he owned him, licking and sucking at his lips with greedy abandon.

The obscene sound of it filled the room, and Felix's subtle body scent, mingled with his crisp cologne, teased Isaac's senses. A rush of warmth swelled in his chest, and without hesitation, he reached out, looping his arms around Felix's neck.

The kiss was becoming familiar. Isaac parted his lips, inviting Felix's waiting tongue to delve in, sweeping across the soft heat of his mouth. The faint bitterness of beer lingered on Felix's tongue, but the taste quickly dissolved as the kiss deepened.

Felix moved slowly at first, savoring every second before hunger overtook him. He kissed Isaac with a fierce desperation, sucking at his tongue and rubbing their lips together. Isaac was lost in it, drunk on the intensity of Felix's touch.

"Isaac, don't waste time on useless thoughts. You're mine; from now on, all your time belongs to me. I won't let anyone else even think about interfering," Felix murmured, nibbling on Isaac's lower lip. The sensation made Isaac's throat tighten.

It sounds like you're dating me.

The thought surfaced in his mind but never escaped his lips. Instead, he tightened his arms around Felix's neck, pulling him closer.

Felix smirked arrogantly but gave in to the silent demand,

capturing Isaac's lips again. The kiss was intense, like the sun warming the beach—hot, cold, sweet—all at once. It stretched on, unbroken, a moment neither of them seemed willing to end.

Chapter 23

The sun was setting by the time Isaac returned to his apartment. As he stepped out of Felix's car, he dabbed at his swollen lips with the back of his hand. They throbbed painfully, stinging from the relentless biting and sucking that hadn't ceased until the car finally came to a halt.

"How am I supposed to feel when you wipe them the moment you leave?" Felix's low, surly voice broke the silence. He was leaning out the car window, watching him.

Isaac glanced back, unamused. "You bit and sucked them raw."

"It's because your lips are just that damn tasty." Felix rested his chin on one hand, propped against the lowered window, spouting nonsense with a smirk. Isaac stared at him impassively, too irritated to reply.

"See you next Monday," Felix said with a shrug, using it as his farewell.

"Won't you come before then?" The question escaped before Isaac could stop himself. Too late, he realized how unnecessary it was, heat creeping up his neck.

"Will you miss me if I wait until Monday?" Felix teased, his grin widening. "If that's the case, I'll come running."

Isaac swallowed hard, knowing he made a mistake. He muttered, "It's just…you've come by the shop on other days before."

"Sure, all right," Felix said. "If you're that desperate to see me, I'll swing by on weekdays. It's not like it's far."

"See you next Monday."

Felix's crinkled eyes betrayed his excuse, holding onto an unspoken smugness. Isaac ended the exchange with a cold nod, turned away, and headed for the apartment gates. He could feel

Felix's cloying gaze trailing him, but he feigned ignorance, slipping through the gates without a backward glance.

Only after Isaac was safely inside did the sedan's engine rev, fading into the distance. Leaning against the gate, hidden from view, Isaac waited until silence blanketed the street before he pushed off and started moving again. An unshakable restlessness gnawed at him.

Like many in San Diego, Isaac's apartment was part of a modest two-story wooden building. He lived on the upper floor. Normally, the climb up didn't bother him, but each step felt unusually heavy tonight. The wooden stairs groaned beneath his weight, the sound grating on his nerves.

Fatigue, long ignored while Felix was around, now crashed over him. When he reached the second-floor hallway, his legs dragged, his shoulders slumped. The thought of reopening the flower shop tomorrow seemed almost laughable. He'd already kept it closed for two days…

Isaac sighed, a sharp exhale of frustration. He wasn't sure what he hoped to accomplish by shutting the shop repeatedly. The doubt tasted bitter, and he scolded himself as he rifled through his bag for his keys.

As the key slid into the lock, he froze. A presence stirred nearby, just beyond the corner. His head turned instinctively toward the faint noise.

"Kay." A deep, quiet voice called the strange name, its weight unmistakable.

Isaac's eyes snapped to the source, and he rushed toward the man without hesitation. With a loud thud, the man's large frame hit the wall. Isaac's arm pressed firmly across his chest, pinning him in place. His sharp gaze cut like knives, but the man didn't resist. Instead, he calmly raised his hands in surrender, his face expressionless despite the force against him.

"How did you—"

"Relax," the middle-aged man rasped, his voice strained as he fought for air. "If I wanted to harm you, you would've been shot and rolling on the floor by now.

He coughed, his throat convulsing against the grip. "Khhhk—You know that," he gasped, patting Isaac's arm with feigned patience. "Now, how about letting me breathe?"

His face had already begun to turn an alarming shade of blue.

After a tense moment, Isaac slowly released him and stepped back, though his eyes never left the man. The man coughed a few times, exaggerating the effort, then smoothed his neatly groomed mustache with one hand. Isaac, unconvinced, watched him warily.

"Four years, huh? You've changed a lot. I might not have recognized you if we passed on the street," the man said. Isaac remained silent. "Anyway, long time no see. Are you going to keep me standing out here?"

Unfazed by Isaac's cold glare, he gestured toward the apartment door. Isaac hesitated, his jaw tightening. Finally, he turned, unlocking the door and stepping aside.

"Come in."

The man's lips curved into a faint, self-satisfied smile at Isaac's begrudging invitation. He strode inside, his movements unhurried. Isaac lingered, scanning the empty hallway with suspicion before closing the door softly behind him.

"What's going on?" Isaac's tone was clipped, his impatience evident as the man took his time surveying the sparse apartment. Finally, the man turned, meeting Isaac's tense gaze.

"What's going on? That's what I should be asking you," the man snapped. "It's been four years since I made that request. I did everything I could to help you, and then you just disappeared without a word. Do you have any idea how much I resent you for that?"

"I apologize," Isaac said quietly, bowing his head. He had no excuses to offer.

In irritation, the man clicked his tongue, pulled out a cushionless wooden chair from the dining table, and sat uninvited.

Isaac followed suit, taking the seat across from him.

"You vanished without a trace. I thought you'd skipped the country—maybe gone to some obscure corner of the world. And yet, here you are, still on American soil. In San Diego, of all places. I guess what they say is true—things are always right under your nose."

Isaac's gaze darkened as he studied the man. "How did you find me?"

In response, the man reached into his jacket pocket and pulled out a neatly folded piece of paper. He unfolded it and slid it across the table to Isaac.

The paper contained a grainy black-and-white photo, clearly taken from a distance. It showed Felix in sharp focus, his face turned toward the camera. But behind him, slightly blurred, was Isaac, his expression tense. Further back was Tony, faint but unmistakable. The wharfside setting made it immediately clear from the day Isaac had been dragged onto the yacht.

Isaac froze, staring at the photo, his fist pressing against his mouth to keep from swearing.

"When I saw this," the man said bluntly, "I thought Felix had gotten his claws into you and was on his way to dragging you to a watery grave."

He slid another photo across the table. This one was clearer, capturing Felix and Isaac walking side by side as they disembarked the yacht. Isaac instantly recognized the moment—the morning after a heated night when they'd left the yacht to attend Benjamin's birthday party.

"I relaxed when I saw you walking out on two feet the next day, but what's all this? Are you unaware Felix is a person of interest under constant surveillance?"

"There were circumstances," Isaac murmured.

"Sure there were," the man scoffed. "But you shouldn't have assumed you wouldn't get caught, parading around with him like that."

Isaac had no rebuttal. He knew being near Felix was a gamble, but he hadn't expected to be exposed this quickly.

"Steve, does anyone else have these photos, or are they only with you?" Isaac asked, rubbing his clasped hands anxiously.

The middle-aged man named Steve let out a sigh. "For now, they're only with me. But I can't promise how long that'll last. Multiple sources monitor Felix's every move."

"So, is that why you're here? To warn me?" Isaac stared at the photos for a moment longer before lifting his gaze. His eyes were darker now, unreadable.

Steve leaned forward, resting his arm on the table. "Sure, I'm here to warn you. And to make you an offer."

Of course.

Isaac said nothing, watching Steve cut straight to the point.

"I'll clear your name. Why don't we work together?"

"What do you mean?"

"Whatever anyone says, I trust you. That's why I didn't ask questions and helped you out four years ago. Now it's your turn to trust me and help me." Steve spoke quickly, his voice hushed. Then he cleared his throat, his words tapering off.

Isaac noticed and stood, moving to the fridge. Inside, there was nothing but bottled water. He grabbed two and returned to the table, handing one to Steve before opening the other for himself. He took a long sip, only then realizing how dry his own throat had become.

"Help you with what? How?" Isaac asked after draining half the bottle.

Steve, who had barely taken a sip, gripped his bottle and raised his gaze. "I want you as a witness."

"A witness?"

"Cole Patricks. You know better than anyone about his corruption. And he's likely the reason you've been hiding all this time."

The name hit Isaac like a blow, making his shoulders tense

involuntarily. Steve stopped speaking, watching for a reaction. But Isaac sat frozen, his lips pressed tightly together.

"I know this isn't easy," Steve continued. "But we can't let him get away with it. There are already whispers about the irregularities he's covered up."

"No. I know nothing." Isaac shook his head firmly, his voice flat.

Steve didn't look surprised—he had expected this. Without a word, he took a sip of his water, his expression unreadable. Finally, he broke the silence. "Is that your answer, knowing it was Cole who set you up? What do you think he'll do when he gets a whiff of you being out and about in San Diego?"

"Are you threatening me?" Isaac asked sharply.

Steve simply shrugged. "Not at all. As I said, the news is bound to spread even without me. You're already exposed in multiple places after blatantly hanging around Felix. Luckily, here, I was able to get my hands on the photos first, but it's only a matter of time before Cole gets a whiff of it. No one has eyes on Felix more than Cole."

"Regardless, I can't do anything."

"So, you're going to just keep running until it kills you? What for?"

At the razor-sharp question, Isaac thought of Benjamin—his sweet, innocent child. For him, he knew he had to escape this precarious situation. But to be a witness…

"If you stand as a witness, we'll take charge of your protection," Steve said, his voice steady. "We can even secure a new place for you. Your name will be cleared, and you'll finally live without being hunted."

Isaac remained silent.

"After the charges are dropped, you can return to your life—or start fresh. Whatever you want, we'll support you." Steve's determined gaze made Isaac waver. The offer was tempting, a flicker of hope after years of fear. But the words stuck in his throat.

Benjamin had to come first. No matter what happened—whether it was Cole or Steve—it didn't matter as long as Benjamin was safe. If it meant silencing himself, disappearing even further, living an existence devoid of joy or light, he'd endure it. He'd endure anything if it meant Benjamin could grow up carefree, go to school, make friends, and smile like a normal child.

Freedom was tempting, yes, but stepping into this quagmire recklessly could destroy everything. If he stood against Cole, it would only provoke the man's wrath—and Isaac knew Cole would stop at nothing to obliterate what little he had left.

He'd already been living on thin ice, liable to break at any moment, but if he stood as a witness…The icy realization sent a shiver through him.

Rubbing his arms, Isaac gritted his teeth. "No, I won't do it."

Wouldn't he rather go into hiding again? Close the shop, move somewhere far away, and disappear before Cole even notices? Isaac dismissed the thought. A "safe" life mattered more than a "stable" one.

"You don't think Cole will eventually forget about you if you keep hiding, do you? Not with how persistent he is," Steve said, his voice flat. Isaac remained silent. "Everyone involved in that incident ended up dead or missing. You get it, right? You're the only one still alive, and sooner or later, Cole will find you. That's why I came running when I recognized you."

The words hung heavy in the air. Isaac couldn't meet Steve's gray eyes, so he closed his own instead.

If it weren't for Benjamin…Isaac might have considered presenting himself as a witness. But now that he had something more precious than his own life to protect, he had to lie low. He knew he was being selfish. He may have been betraying his old colleagues, those who died in agony. Still, he couldn't find the courage to step forward.

"I'm sorry. It's out of my depth." A lump formed in his throat. He couldn't ask Steve to protect the child—he couldn't risk revealing his biggest secret. The truth that he had a child, that he was an omega, was something no one could know. Not even the man who had once been his most trusted ally. The past was just that—the past. He trusted no one now. He couldn't.

Steve sighed as he sat in that silence, "I heard the rumor that you disappeared with the evidence. If that's true—"

"Steve, I don't know where that rumor started, but I can't tell you anything." Isaac cut him off, his expression turning cold at the mention of it. The 'if' in Steve's voice made it clear this wasn't worth discussing further.

Steve frowned, a trace of disapproval creeping into his expression.

"If you were hoping for me to testify about something like that, all I can keep saying is I'm sorry."

For a moment, Steve's gaze locked with Isaac's, tension tightening between them. But soon enough, Steve raised his hands in surrender.

"If that's your decision, I have no choice but to step back—for now. But you should think it through. You know Cole well. He's a force to be reckoned with and doesn't give up easily. He won't let it go, no matter how much time has passed."

Isaac didn't respond.

"We might not have much time left," Steve muttered, pulling a card from his pocket and placing it on the table. "I'll leave my card. Call me anytime you change your mind."

After everything was said, Steve stood, his expression laced with regret. Isaac pretended not to notice and stood as well. But then Steve looked at him with a hint of pity, "You know I'm the only one left who'll take your side, right?"

A heavy silence fell between them. Steve didn't wait for Isaac's reply. As he moved toward the door, his footsteps felt unusually loud in the small apartment. He grabbed the doorknob without hesitation but paused as if remembering something. He glanced back at Isaac, "By the way, how the hell did you end up with Felix

Felice? No way you went to him on purpose—did he come looking for you?"

"No. He doesn't know my past."

"Hah, well, I'll be." Steve shook his head in disbelief.

"I'm sure you have your reasons, your personal affairs, but it's wise not to get too close to Felix. Though, it's better than making an enemy of him." Isaac didn't respond. Steve's expression was complicated. "Remember, out of the frying pan, into the fire."

Isaac couldn't bring himself to speak. Maybe Steve was right. Maybe, by doing whatever it took to avoid Cole, by asking for help and taking Felix's hand, he had jumped straight into the fire. The thought weighed heavily on his chest. Isaac bit his lip.

Steve shrugged and said, "Isn't it ironic how relationships unfold? Of all people, you ended up with Felix Felice."

"Why are you saying this?" Isaac snapped, shaking himself out of his thoughts. He met Steve's eyes, uneasy. Steve had been standing by the door, ready to leave the apartment, but he stepped closer to Isaac.

"I know what it was. The last secret mission Cole gave you. " Steve said, his voice soft and steady, yet it sent a chill racing down Isaac's spine. Steve continued, his tone unchanged, "The mission meant only for you."

"Steve, stop—"

"It was Felix's assassination, wasn't it?" Steve cut through, unearthing the secret Isaac had buried deep. His eyes bore into Isaac's, a mix of warning and condemnation for such a reckless act.

Isaac couldn't breathe; the ringing in his ears drowned out everything else.

Chapter 24

Time passed placidly, flowing like a quiet river, as if nothing had changed. But beneath the calm surface, the waters were rapid and vicious underneath. He could fall under the surface with a single misstep. He stood on the precipice; one wrong move could bring everything down.

Isaac snapped a rose stem with his shears, then paused. He hadn't noticed when, but a thorn had pricked his finger, and now a bead of blood was slowly welling up. He wiped it away quietly, then resumed finishing the bouquet. Unfortunately, the customer who had been waiting wasn't pleased. Isaac felt a pang of regret as the man reluctantly paid and left, his complaints echoing in Isaac's ears.

Isaac sighed and sank into a chair. He thought again that it might be time to close the shop. Yes, it was time. Something he was running out of. Isaac stood, gathering himself.

Steve had shown up a week ago, and ever since, Isaac had quietly put his affairs in order. He'd never stayed in one place long, so there wasn't much to organize, but he had destroyed anything that might expose his privacy. That meant disposing of the drawerful of letters and cards he'd written to Benjamin—ones he'd never sent.

Steve had reached out several times last week, but Isaac's response remained the same. He had torn up Steve's business card into unsalvageable shreds, though that didn't erase the number from his memory. Isaac had recited it in his mind over and over, but he never contacted Steve first.

The real problem was Felix. He didn't know how Felix would react if he suddenly disappeared without explanation. Isaac didn't have to tell him for the reaction to play out in his mind, but he shook his head, trying to push the thought away.

The more he thought about it, the less clear the answer became. His head throbbed. Isaac massaged his temples and closed his eyes. Then, the doorbell jingled, piercing his thoughts. Reluctantly, he opened his eyes.

Isaac wasn't particularly keen on having customers at the moment, so he intentionally kept the door closed. With it shut, it was hard to tell whether the shop was open. Most people wouldn't bother checking and would simply walk past.

But the customer before, and now this one, had to open the door and barge in. Of course, he hadn't switched the sign to 'closed' so they could enter. But who was it this time…?

"The weather's nice. Why are you cooped up in here?" The man grumbled as he stepped inside.

Isaac blinked, his scattered thoughts coming to a halt. How could he not be surprised to see the very man he'd been thinking of standing right before him as if he'd read Isaac's mind?

Isaac stood frozen, watching Felix stride toward him. His grip instinctively tightened around his neck. The shop, filled with the earthy scent of trees and the fragrance of flowers, suddenly felt suffocating. It was as if Felix's alpha pheromones had flooded the air the moment he stepped inside, crashing over him in waves.

Had Felix truly let off his alpha pheromones the moment he entered? Isaac couldn't tell if it was his imagination, but his body reacted so naturally to the scent that it was impossible to ignore.

His mouth went dry. The mere act of gazing upon him caused the inside of his ass to release slick. The problems he agonized over moments ago seemed to vanish, replaced by an overwhelming, almost dizzying sensation.

Have I become this conditioned?

Isaac's eyes widened in bewilderment, the black pupils trembling. Before he could gather himself, Felix was standing at the counter, staring down at him.

"What were you up to?" Felix's eyes scanned Isaac, his tone

edged with irritation. Flustered, Isaac couldn't respond, his gaze locked on Felix. Then, without warning, Felix's rough, cool hand cupped his chin, and he bent his head, sealing their lips together.

"Ah!" Isaac barely had time to react before the kiss consumed him. Felix bit and sucked at his lower lip, then parted Isaac's mouth with ease, plunging his tongue inside to mix their saliva, exploring every soft crevice with the tip of his tongue. It was a kiss that was both harsh and greedy. Even as Isaac gasped for air, his mouth stayed open, welcoming him.

The wet sounds of their kiss filled the quiet space. Felix's face was flushed with desire, his grip on Isaac's face tightening as his tongue tangled with Isaac's. Isaac moaned low in his throat, a strange thrill rising within him at the sight of Felix so undone by the kiss.

Isaac wanted Felix to hold him tighter, to show more of his hunger, to ravage him, to lose himself in this. The thought surfaced unexpectedly, and Isaac felt a surge of longing that unsettled him.

Am I insane? The desire was new, unfamiliar. But without hesitation, he opened his mouth wider, sucking Felix's tongue, drinking in his warmth. His mind melted, the world blurring around him. His arms, gripping the counter for support, trembled.

"What were you doing?" Felix growled against his lips, pulling away just enough to speak. "What am I supposed to do when you look at me like that—dripping with sex, and you're not even in bed?"

Felix sucked at Isaac's lower lip hard enough to hurt, his hand moving urgently over Isaac's cheek as if trying to strip him of his clothing in that instant.

"Did I…look like that?"

"Yeah. My dick stood up like it would explode the moment I saw you."

"Oh dear…"

"What if some other fucker came in?" Felix's hand, gently stroking his cheek, slid down to Isaac's neck. Isaac tilted his head back, exposing the vulnerable nape of his neck, the action instinctive.

Why was Felix so frantic at the thought of someone else entering? Isaac wanted to say it wasn't anyone else—his body reacted this way because Felix had walked in. He wanted to tell him, it was because of you entering that my body is reacting as it pleases, that my hole is already dripping wet and twitching.

"Felix…" Isaac lifted his arm from the counter and draped it over Felix's shoulder, his eyes dark with arousal.

"Don't look at me like that," Felix muttered irritably, his patience thinning. "It's not Monday yet."

Isaac grinned almost feverishly. With a sudden surge of boldness, he half-climbed over the counter, wrapping his arm around Felix's neck. "It's Saturday."

"So?"

"Let's do it in advance. Right here."

Felix narrowed his eyes, disbelief washing over him. Isaac was acting completely out of character, almost ready to leap over the counter. It was unexpected, but Felix couldn't resist Isaac, especially when he looked so undone, eyes hazy with desire.

"Leave." Felix's tone lowered ominously while his piercing blue eyes locked onto Isaac. Behind him, there was a faint noise—Isaac registered it only when the door jingled softly and closed.

Jack had entered. He would stand guard outside, ensuring no one else would disturb them. The bell rang once, then fell silent. Until Felix decided otherwise, the door wouldn't open again.

In that quiet moment, Isaac couldn't help but wonder: how had things gotten to this point?

He remembered, back on the beach at Hotel del Coronado, Felix told him he thought he was going mad because of him. But in retrospect, the one who was going mad wasn't Felix, it was Isaac. It certainly was with the way he was lying face down on the counter, ass out to Felix.

He hadn't even taken off his pants. With his underwear

rolled down and pants hanging on his knees, he looked like a cheap prostitute who would strip anywhere. But Felix, who was squeezing Isaac's round ass and pounding into him, had also been unable to take off his clothes.

As soon as he undid his belt and zipper, Felix grabbed hold of Isaac and mindlessly shoved his lethal cock into his hole. His eyes were unseeing. They were filled with lust, sanity thrown to the winds. Like a dog in rut, his body refused to dislodge from him. It was meaningless to question who was more insane.

The air inside the shop was thick, filled with the sound of shallow, heated breaths. Each time Felix thrust his hips, the sodden hole responded with loud squelching noises. It was accompanied by the lewd sound of Felix's thighs slapping against Isaac's buttocks.

"Hah, hah, Felix, uh— there—" Isaac had his cheek pressed against the counter, and from his mouth leaked saliva and moans of pleasure. He couldn't get enough of how it reverberated to his fingertips.

"More, more, deeper—" Isaac moved his arms to his back and spread his asscheeks, widening the hole filled with Felix's cock and entreating him to go deeper. He turned half to the side and looked up at Felix with bleary eyes, causing a deep crease in his brow.

"Fuck! Isaac!" Felix swore, unable to hold himself back. As if he intended to shove his balls in, he rammed his engorged cock into Isaac's inner walls with all his might. His stomach ached. Isaac screamed without realizing it.

But alongside the strange, borderline painful sensation was immense pleasure that made his eyes roll back. His thighs shook visibly. Isaac threw his head back and wailed. At the same time, liquid spurted from the end of his rigid cock.

"Ahh!" The unexpected climax left Isaac gasping, a sob escaping his lips. His body felt like it might melt, a willing victim to the intoxicating cocktail of alpha pheromones and raw pleasure

Felix provided. This susceptibility to desire was a shocking revelation. Sex, a concept he'd never truly considered, now held a terrifying allure.

Four years ago, he'd experienced a similar mind-melting intensity during his first heat cycle. But that was the only time, likely fueled by the hormonal surge. Since then, his heat cycles had vanished, and giving birth to Benjamin had driven his libido into the ground. Living in hiding hadn't exactly fostered a vibrant sex life either. He'd resigned himself to a life as an asexual, devoid of desire.

Now, he didn't know what was happening.

What had changed? Perhaps it was Felix, a hyper-dominant alpha. Maybe his recessive omega nature simply couldn't handle such a potent dose of pheromones, a cocktail stronger than any he'd encountered before. After all, they said a hyper-dominant alpha's scent could melt even a beta. As an omega, even a recessive one, wasn't it only natural for his defenses to crumble?

Was this why omegas went crazy and threw themselves at alphas? Isaac wondered vaguely, his mind clouded with desire. But he had to erase that thought, letting out a scream when Felix slammed into his sensitive, puffed-up inner walls with a loud smack.

"Isaac, are you at leisure to think other thoughts?" Felix's voice was sharp, his perception uncannily accurate. Isaac moaned in response, his body trembling.

Felix gently brushed Isaac's sweat-soaked hair from his face. "That won't do. Shall I wipe your mind clean?"

His smile was menacing. Isaac gulped, anticipation and fear warring within him. As Felix leaned in, his potent pheromones washed over Isaac, further clouding his mind.

Isaac's shudders went all the way down to his toes. He was at a loss, lying there on the counter, gasping for breath. His hole twitched around Felix's cock.

"Hck, Felix, no more…" he pleaded, his voice weak.

"You're driving me mad. How can you be this sensitive? Shit, I'd believe it if you were an omega instead of a beta," Felix muttered, his low voice sending shivers down Isaac's spine. For a moment, Isaac feared Felix had discovered his secret. But it was likely just a passing thought, as Felix soon returned to the task at hand, laughing softly as he hugged Isaac's waist.

"If you were an omega, I would make you mine right this moment," he whispered, his breath warm against Isaac's ear. A strange, undefinable feeling stirred within Isaac.

"Though, that's probably why it's so tantalizing," Felix mumbled to himself before thrusting deep into Isaac's core. The surge of pheromones flooding him from the inside was overwhelming, and Isaac's body convulsed in response. He let out a scream as he reflexively shook his head.

Felix lifted Isaac from the counter, stripping him of his pants. With a gentle hand, he lifted Isaac's leg, positioning it for easy access. He thrust his hips upward rhythmically. Exhausted, Isaac slumped against Felix like a lifeless puppet. Felix, however, continued his assault with effortless ease.

The wet, slapping sounds of Felix's thrusts filled the air as he thrust into his already ejaculated semen deep inside Isaac. Milky liquid trailed down his thighs. Isaac was lost in a haze of pleasure, his mind numbed by the overwhelming sensation.

It was easy for an omega to go crazy on alpha pheromones, and become addicted to them. He knew these dangers, but the intense pleasure was too much to resist. Each thrust hit his sensitive spots with precise accuracy, driving him to the brink of insanity. Isaac let off all his thoughts and worries, moaning loudly.

"You like that? Here? It always makes you cry here, right?" Felix taunted.

"Uh uh, like it…Ah, ah, don't stop, more…" Isaac moaned, his mind entirely consumed by the pleasure. Felix chuckled deeply, his voice a low rumble in Isaac's ear.

Isaac's body shook uncontrollably, his mind a blank slate.

What could he do? He couldn't think of anything. All he could do was surrender to the pleasure, letting Felix take him to the edge as he met each thrust with his own.

Chapter 25

When Isaac opened his eyes, night had fallen. Felix sat in the chair he always occupied when he was here, and Isaac was in his lap—pants off, legs straddling Felix's naked thigh, dripping slick and cum, his head resting on Felix's shoulder.

Isaac blinked in confusion. It took him a moment to register his state, and when he did, the embarrassment made him turn away, unable to look at himself. He quickly lifted his head, but the sharp pain in his hips made him slump back down, frowning.

"I couldn't do anything since you passed out." The soft words hovered above him. "There's no space to lie down, you know?"

Felix had his arm propped on the armrest, chin resting on it, eyes fixed on Isaac, limp in his lap. Isaac couldn't stand the position with any semblance of dignity. He tried to move.

But Felix's arm tightened around his waist, halting him. Isaac turned his gaze, and when their eyes met, Felix tilted his head and creased his eyes into a sunny smile. "Did you enjoy it? Whenever you grab onto me, screaming…I keep wondering."

"Wondering what?" Isaac's voice was rough, his throat raw. He must have cried and screamed again, losing himself to it.

"Wondering how long it'll take until I snap. Lose control just a little, and my greed will be limitless."

Isaac's disbelief sharpened his words. "And until now, you haven't lost control?"

Felix's only answer was a smirk, the corner of his lips curling upward, "Of course. Or I wouldn't be waiting for you like this. Even with you unconscious, I could be fucking you as much as I want."

I would with the other guys. Felix swallowed the remainder, his deep blue gaze sweeping over Isaac. The glimmer in his eyes sent a shiver down Isaac's spine as if Felix could open his legs and thrust his deadly weapon of a cock into him without a second thought.

"Last week. Did you wait? When I passed out?"

"Yeah. Wasn't it obvious? Your body was still intact after two whole days." Felix's bold response left Isaac at a loss for words. Then, Felix gently traced his fingertips along Isaac's face, clicking his tongue. "I thought about doing whatever the fuck I wanted, unconscious or not, but there's a reason I held back."

Isaac felt his throat tighten under the weight of Felix's searching gaze. He couldn't ask what it was.

"Have you lost weight? It's only been a week. Look at your face. Have you been eating?" Felix's questions were sharp, a stark contrast to his usual indifference. Isaac couldn't bring himself to answer. Partly because of the warmth radiating from Felix's fingertips on his cheek and partly because he had been skipping meals, just as Felix had noticed. "Don't be careless with yourself after everything I've done to take care of you."

Isaac was once again rendered speechless at Felix's grumbling. *Take care of him?* He didn't remember Felix ever doing that…but the chastising expression on his face wasn't unpleasant. It made something flutter in Isaac's chest.

"You don't have to worry." Looking up at Felix, Isaac felt like his fragile composure might break under the weight of his gaze. He quickly turned away, scrambling off his lap. Felix didn't stop him.

Isaac spotted his pants and underwear crumpled on the floor. He inwardly cursed at the mess, the evidence of their rushed urgency.

"By the way, what brought you here without notice on a Saturday?" Isaac threw the question over his shoulder as he wobbled toward the pile of clothes. Ignoring the wetness dripping down his thighs and ass, he stepped into his underwear.

He could feel Felix's eyes on him, sharp and unrelenting as if memorizing every movement. Isaac tried to appear unaffected as he pulled up his underwear. The fabric clung to his skin, emphasizing the curve of his hips and the taut line of his thighs.

"When have I ever notified you before coming here?" Felix muttered after a pause, his tone dragging as if his attention was entirely fixed on Isaac getting dressed.

Isaac turned to narrow his eyes at him. "It's not like I'm giving you a strip show, so quit staring."

"Why not? I've never seen a more riveting strip show in my life."

"I'm just putting on my underwear," Isaac sighed in complaint.

Felix's gaze didn't waver, burning as it moved up Isaac's exposed thighs. He was every bit the playboy, watching as if he were at a strip show. "I know, right? Who knew watching you put on underwear while you're dripping my cum down your thighs could be so…pornographic?"

True to his words, Isaac's smooth, muscular thighs were streaked with dried cum, and the wet residue trickled down, staining the bottom of his blue underwear a deeper shade.

Isaac couldn't exactly clean himself here, so he continued getting dressed, well aware of the unsightly mess. He hadn't imagined seeing him like this would get his dick going…Isaac shot him a scandalized look. He said curtly, "Regardless, we can't do that again here."

Felix shrugged, unconcerned. Isaac bent down and grabbed his pants.

"Before I came in, I saw someone passing by with a bouquet of roses. He had a big frown on his face. Honestly, I even thought it was a pretty shitty bouquet." Felix brought up the topic suddenly, his chin propped up as he stared intently at Isaac, still looking like he was watching a strip show.

Isaac froze while zipping up his pants, then shifted his gaze toward Felix.

"I could tell it was your work with one glance. No other florist could make such an awful bouquet." Isaac stayed silent. "But today? It was especially bad. Fucking shitty."

Isaac stiffened. That customer had come in before Felix, buying a bouquet of roses. Isaac had been distracted, and the result had been worse than usual. But Felix's blunt verdict, delivered without hesitation, insulted him.

"What's up with you?" Felix asked, his sharp blue eyes darkening as he studied Isaac. "The bouquet…and the way you pounced as soon as you saw me—it's all a bit suspicious."

"Hardly." Isaac swallowed, his throat dry. He was used to maintaining an impassive expression, but he couldn't control the anxious pounding of his heart.

"Isaac, if I find out you've been hiding something from me—" Felix's smile twisted as he leaned in, his voice low. "Then I'll eat you up. From head to toe. Every part of you."

His blue eyes were as cold and sharp as a blade despite the grin pulling at his lips. Isaac stood frozen, the zipper halfway up. The suffocating pressure from Felix's gaze held him captive, and if he wasn't careful, he feared he might lose his mind to him.

"I should be careful, then, not to get caught," Isaac said bluntly, forcing down the tension rising in his throat.

Felix snickered, his gaze still on Isaac.

"Sure, do your best." He waved it off as if it were a joke, and Isaac's chest eased the weight lifting. He zipped his pants up and stood barefoot in front of Felix.

"Put these on." Isaac held out Felix's pants and underwear.

Felix remained seated arrogantly, his fair pubic hair and still-tumescent cock on display. He looked up at Isaac, amused, before taking the clothes, a smile still playing on his lips. "Isaac, do you know? You're supposed to pay me back with a whole day, but it's only been a few hours. And just now, watching you put on your underwear? It drove me wild."

"Did it?"

"So, tell me. Where should we take this next? I'm itching to soak your underwear through so you won't be able to wear them again."

Isaac sighed, looking at Felix—refusing to move an inch even after being wrung out for hours until unconscious. Yet, Felix's lewd whisper still made Isaac's stomach tighten. It was a reflex now, beyond denial.

"Then…Wherever. I don't mind."

Really. He must have gone fully insane. But his voice remained indifferent. Felix's laughter rumbled deep, and the light from outside cast sharp shadows over his sculpted features.

Isaac drank him in, trying to imprint every inch of Felix's presence onto his mind. A restless, unsettling feeling lingered in his chest, a gnawing uncertainty that refused to fade.

Chapter 26

"I miss you. Sleep well. Sweet dreams," Isaac whispered into the receiver, his voice soft. In return, he heard the cheerful sound of a child's laughter, followed by the little one's clear breath, as if he were right there beside him.

"Yes, Daddy, good night." The cheery voice made Isaac's lips curve into a soft smile.

Closing his eyes, he chuckled soundlessly. "I love you."

"I love you, too!"

"I love you lots, Benjamin. More than anything in the world."

"I do, too! I love you, Daddy." Benjamin's excited voice filled the air, followed by kisses through the phone. He eagerly declared that he would be the one to hang up this time. Before Isaac could say, 'All right,' Benjamin had already ended the call. Ever since he'd learned about the 'end call' button, he'd been eager to hang up himself.

At least this time, they'd exchanged their good-nights. There were times before when Benjamin would hang up mid-conversation. Isaac couldn't help but laugh softly. He held the payphone's receiver to his ear, unable to hide the smile that lingered on his lips. It felt like he could still hear Benjamin's boisterous voice, even now.

It was always like this when he called Benjamin, but tonight it resonated longer than usual. Eventually, realizing his shoulders were chilled, Isaac folded in his regret and lowered the receiver.

The night was cold and windy. Although the temperature fluctuated sharply between day and night in this region, it was always chilly, and tonight felt especially biting. Isaac sighed, pulling the bill of his baseball cap lower over his face.

In the quiet hours, when a few cars passed, he walked down

an empty street. His shoulders were hunched, his face obscured by the cap and hoodie, hands jammed into his pockets. He looked like a neighborhood thug—a sharp contrast to the upright, proper image he usually projected as a florist.

Yet, his disheveled appearance made him blend in, keeping him inconspicuous. That's why he found himself here, walking the desolate outskirts, where only the homeless lingered. The cold wind stirred litter along the road, and the homeless huddled under blankets against the building walls. The gleaming skyscrapers of Downtown seemed worlds away, their brilliance stark against this decaying backdrop.

Isaac glanced around, then pulled his shoulders tighter against the wind. He lowered his head and quickened his pace. There was a reason he had ventured out to the fringes of the city. He used a payphone to call his mother, never his cell. There were no phone booths near his apartment, and finding one elsewhere became increasingly rare. Everyone has mobile phones these days, so payphones are nearly extinct. Even if one were nearby, Isaac wouldn't risk using it.

He made an effort to find a payphone in a distant, isolated spot each time, always changing locations. It was his way of cutting ties, of hiding any trace of his mother. But despite his precautions, Felix had somehow discovered Benjamin's existence.

The knowledge gnawed at Isaac, feeding his anxiety. After meeting with Steve, who had come to visit, his restlessness only deepened. He couldn't sleep, couldn't eat. It felt like he was on the verge of a nervous breakdown. It had been a week since everything spiraled—how much longer could he hold on?

A few days ago, Isaac had finally called his mother. He checked on her and told her to pack up quickly. The house in La Jolla was a rental; moving wasn't difficult.

Isaac had also taken care of the apartment. His plan was simple: go into hiding, find a new home for his mother and Benjamin, and close the shop, which was under a borrowed name.

But the biggest problem—Felix—was still looming. Isaac intended to see him once a week, one way or another. He didn't know what to expect, but aside from laying low for a while, he didn't have many other options.

Isaac's chest tightened as he thought these thoughts, and he paused in his tracks. He looked up at the dark sky, where the yellowish glow of the moon fought to break through thick clouds. The scene felt as hazy and oppressive as his heart.

Though the moon was hidden, its yellowish light lingered, reminiscent of Benjamin's hair. Isaac couldn't help but smile at the thought. But the smile faded as quickly as it appeared.

It had already been too long since he last saw Benjamin. The thought that it might become even harder to see him in the future only made Isaac's longing more unbearable. He would rush to him and hold him close, never letting go if he could.

He remembered Benjamin's laughter from their phone call earlier and sighed deeply. "Hah—"

With a heavy heart, Isaac forced himself to take a step forward. He was surprised by how far the car he'd parked a block away felt when he heard it.

Footsteps echoed on the deserted street—quick and drawing nearer. Isaac tensed, instinctively pulling his hands out of his pockets. Before he could react, a sharp metallic click echoed, immediate and unmistakable.

"Put your hands up." A low voice cut through the cold air. The gun pressed to Isaac's temple left him no choice but to raise both hands slowly.

Felix tossed the report onto the desk and swirled the bourbon in his glass, the ice rattling faintly. He wasn't planning to drink it—just mindlessly swirling it in his hand.

"Real funny. They must think they're paparazzi."

The report lay open, photos pasted neatly across its pages.

They were identical to the ones Isaac had received from Steve: Felix and Isaac boarding the yacht, disembarking the next day, and walking toward the car.

"Wasting taxes to follow me around, like they've got nothing better to do. Fucking Yankees." He grumbled under his breath, finally taking a sip of the bourbon.

Tony, studying the photos, glanced up at Felix. The temptation to point out that Felix himself was a 'fucking Yankee' hovered on the tip of his tongue, but he wisely held back, merely clucking inwardly.

"They got a good shot of Isaac," Felix muttered, his tone dripping with derision as he eyed the photos.

"What should we do?" Tony asked.

"Do? Nothing. It's not like they can do anything with this." Felix drained his glass in one smooth motion, the ice having melted long ago. "They can hover all they want. They'll find nothing. Even if they did, it wouldn't matter. Fucking imbeciles."

"Indeed," Tony agreed.

Felix snapped the report shut with an irritated flick of his wrist. "Anyway, why's this season's rut so late?"

In the middle of refilling Felix's glass, Tony froze and looked up, his expression comically incredulous. "Are you *waiting* for your rut?"

"It was supposed to come, but it's late," Felix replied, grabbing the glass and downing it before the ice could even begin to chill the bourbon.

Tony's incredulity only deepened. Felix's words were the opposite of everything he'd ever said on the subject.

This was the same man who treated his rut as a curse, endlessly complaining about it. He hated how his body betrayed him, how his sanity slipped away like an animal in heat. And most of all, he despised being tethered to base instincts when he had "more important" things to do.

Felix's volatile temper worsened the closer he got to his rut, turning his subordinates into unwilling targets for his wrath. Yet, despite his fiery outbursts, he abhorred suppressants and avoided them whenever possible.

He would finally cool off after venting his frustrations on multiple unsuspecting beta men, leaving no one—not even himself—eager for his rut to arrive. But to hear him complain that it wasn't coming? Had hell frozen over? Or was Felix Felice on death's doorstep?

Dumbfounded, Tony scratched his cheek, then raised an eyebrow as a thought struck him, "Does the florist please you that much?"

"You can't tell? I'm losing my mind thinking about bringing him back here and making him cry." Felix's brusque response came as he downed his bourbon like water.

"Even though you spent the entire weekend at the hotel with him two weeks ago? Jack mentioned you were…together just the day before yesterday, too."

"You think that's enough for me?"

"I mean, you see him every Monday," Tony pointed out.

Felix wasn't the type to trust people, let alone like them. He avoided relationships beyond fleeting one-night stands. He'd usually see someone three or four times before moving on.

But his behavior with Isaac had been different from the start. Tony had wondered if Felix might be serious this time—but even then, he'd assumed the novelty would wear off soon.

Felix's following words, however, yanked the rug out from under him, "It drives me insane that I only get that perfect body once a week! I'm about to burst."

Felix drummed his fingers on the table, his impatience palpable. Tony's jaw slackened in disbelief. Who would've guessed Felix would go so far as to admit something like that? He must be serious about Isaac—there was no denying it now.

"If only my rut would come," Felix muttered bitterly. "I'd suck him dry and sink my teeth into him until I've had my fill. Fucking rut! Making me wait like this."

Even once a week must have been grueling for Isaac, yet Felix still dared to complain about his rut being late. Worse, he'd taken to releasing his pheromones indiscriminately.

It didn't matter that Isaac was a beta—no one could remain unaffected by the oppressive force of a hyper-dominant alpha's pheromones. Felix knew this all too well but leaked them anyway, utterly unapologetic.

The result was predictable. Isaac, drunk on the pheromones, clung to him as though drugged, crying out in pleasure and passion. Felix, in turn, drank him in, taking his fill precisely as intended.

But now, the image of Isaac, overwhelmed and writhing like a succubus, kept haunting him. If it could even be called a *problem*. It was as if Felix were the one intoxicated instead, trapped in the memory of Isaac's wet, trembling body beneath him, lost in ecstasy.

By Saturday, Felix couldn't hold back anymore. The second he left work, he went straight to Isaac. It was insane how much he craved him—*him*, specifically. But with Isaac clinging to him first, more worked up than usual, how could Felix hope to keep his sanity?

"Fuck, I miss him," Felix muttered, licking the rim of his bourbon glass.

Isaac might be an unflappable florist most of the time, but in Felix's arms, he became a red-eyed succubus radiating raw sex appeal. That gap drove Felix wild.

The memory of that prim and proper face twisted in lust, those trembling hips refusing to let go—it consumed him. Just thinking about Isaac sent blood rushing south, an ache blooming so intense it made him curse under his breath. Fucking hell.

No one else would do. No one else could satisfy him. His appetite was ruined. All he wanted was Isaac.

"I really am in a relationship," Felix groaned, his voice vibrating with exasperation.

Half-listening to Felix's ongoing monologues, Tony suddenly froze, his eyes widening. His slack-jawed expression made him look unwell, and Felix frowned in irritation, "Don't stand there fretting like a shitting dog. Go do your own thing."

Felix waved him off, but Tony seemed to have other priorities. Instead of leaving, he gripped the edge of Felix's desk with both hands, wearing a determined look that reminded Felix of his grandfather, eyes gleaming with resolve before proposing to crush their rivals.

"What's your problem now?" Felix asked, tipping his glass and eyeing Tony suspiciously. What was up with this guy? "If you've got something to say, spill it."

Tony took a deep, fortifying breath before blurting out, "Boss, it's clear as day now—you're way more into the florist than I thought. But, uh…a relationship can't be one-sided."

That statement was outrageous.

Felix froze, "What the fuck are you saying?"

"I'm saying," Tony pressed, "however pleased you are with him, a real relationship means *both* people agree to be together. It's about mutual feelings—you know, liking each other."

Do you understand? Tony punctuated his words with a few sharp thuds on the desk, but Felix remained unfazed, watching him with blank incomprehension as he sipped his iced bourbon.

Tony was on the verge of pounding his chest in despair when Felix finally spoke, obviously not understanding, "So, what—you're saying Isaac doesn't like me?"

"This isn't about whether he likes you," Tony said, struggling to explain.

"Why not?"

"Because—" Tony hesitated, trying to phrase it carefully. "You haven't *asked* Isaac. How would you even know if he likes you?"

"Who on earth wouldn't like me?" Felix's conceited reply, paired with his nose so high in the air it might graze the clouds, left Tony utterly speechless.

Why wouldn't there be people who didn't like him? *I, Jack, the head of security whose shin you busted over unkempt grass and countless others…*

"Do I lack looks? Money? Power? Am I bad at fucking? No. So, who doesn't like me?" The audacity. How dare anyone not like him? Felix muttered indignantly, completely wrapped up in his inflated self-image.

Tony gave up then and there. This man's view on relationships—or his lack of self-awareness—was beyond salvation. He shouldn't have wasted his breath in the first place. The only thing left to do was pity poor Isaac for having to deal with him.

"Sure, boss," Tony muttered wearily, shoulders drooping in defeat as he turned to leave, drained of all energy.

"Stop talking nonsense and tell me what happened to Isaac's stepfather." Felix's sharp tone cut through the air like a knife, making Tony flinch mid-step.

Slowly, he turned back, hesitating, "Well, it's a bit…"

"A bit *what*?" Felix's glower bore into him, leaving Tony no choice but to straighten up and deliver the report he'd been reluctant to share.

"It's strange. While it's true Eugene Sinclair moved to Washington with Isaac, there's no record of him remarrying," Tony said.

"They could've lived together without registering," Felix suggested.

Tony shook his head firmly. "There's no trace of anyone else ever living with them. It was just Eugene and Isaac—until Eugene died in an accident."

Tony had spent days digging through every lead, leaving no stone unturned, but found nothing. Though Isaac had mentioned an alpha stepfather, there wasn't a single record to support it.

The lack of evidence felt like hitting an invisible wall. The more Tony investigated, the stronger his suspicion grew. Still, he came up empty-handed. Delivering an inconclusive report left a bitter taste in his mouth—rare for him and deeply unsettling.

"Where's Noah?" Felix asked abruptly, rising from his seat.

Tony's eyes widened. "You mean *that* Noah?"

Was he seriously looking for Noah?

"Who else is named Noah here? If there were another bastard like him, this world would've gone up in flames by now," Felix grumbled, his tone dripping with reluctance.

Tony blinked, confused as to why Felix asked for Noah if he so clearly loathed him. Tony replied hesitantly, "He should be in the basement."

"The basement? Why?" Felix's sharp brow arched in reproach, though *he* was the one who'd brought it up.

"Well, I was busy with the tasks you assigned me, and…uh, Noah came by in person. Knowing you wouldn't be pleased, I quietly showed him to—"

"Great. Go downstairs," Felix interrupted, cutting off Tony's stammered explanation.

With long, purposeful strides, Felix crossed the study in seconds, his sudden urgency baffling Tony. Not only had Felix asked for Noah, but now he was actually going to see him?

Who was Noah Felice? He was the one person capable of making Felix—a man brimming with audacity—shudder. He was Felix's cousin, childhood friend, and number-one nuisance. Someone Felix would go to great lengths to avoid.

And yet, here he was, asking for Noah.

The thought was shocking. Or perhaps Felix was simply that desperate.

These days, Felix was acting increasingly out of character, leaving Tony to stare at him with growing unease. Was Felix truly about to meet his end? The fleeting thought sent a chill through him before he quickly shook it off.

Please, let this pass. Tony pushed away the creeping dread and silently prayed.

Chapter 27

The cloth was ripped from Isaac's head, and light poured in, blinding him. His eyes clenched shut instinctively, stinging from the sudden glare. He blinked a few times, trying to adjust, a low sigh escaping his lips.

His wrists ached, bound tightly behind him, and his chest strained against the rope securing him to the hard chair. His ankles throbbed, similarly tied.

Isaac took in his restrained state with another weary sigh. He hadn't expected to be caught so quickly. Maybe he'd underestimated his opponent—or perhaps he'd been too late.

He'd done everything he could: cleared out the apartment, made the final call, and was seconds from getting in the car. If they'd chased him down after that, so be it. But to be caught by a hair's breadth…it stung.

"Kay." A voice crackled from a speaker just as a rough hand gripped Isaac's hair, jerking his head upward. Isaac was forced to face a monitor, and the man on the screen sat rigid and composed, watching him.

"It's been a while, hasn't it?" The middle-aged man spoke casually as if they'd parted ways only days ago. Isaac's jaw tightened. He wasn't in the mood for small talk.

The man glanced at his wristwatch, his expression darkening as he crossed his leg over the other.

Isaac couldn't help but wonder what time it was. Unfortunately, he had no way of knowing. He'd been driven far from where he'd been captured, so hours had likely passed. As he mulled over the situation, the man on the screen spoke again.

"Has it really been four years? We finally meet again, though I regret having to see you on a screen. I simply don't have the time to visit San Diego, you see."

It was either late at night or early in the morning, but the man was dressed in a sharply pressed uniform. Isaac paused, considering. The man was probably in the East. Eastern Time was three hours ahead, meaning it was likely early morning there—or perhaps even later in another time zone.

What was certain was that he was somewhere distant, out of reach. Isaac couldn't help but feel a small sense of relief. As the man had said, it wouldn't be practical for him to travel all the way here. Isaac kept his face impassive, revealing none of his thoughts.

"It must have been difficult, running for so long," the man continued. "I'm truly curious—where have you been hiding all this time?"

Isaac didn't answer.

"A man of few words, as always. Fine. I don't have time, so let's get to the point." The man's hand dropped from his crossed legs, and his smile vanished. His gaze sharpened, turning icy. "Where did you hide the document?"

The question was a direct threat. Isaac exhaled slowly. "I don't know what you're talking about."

The man leaned forward, his face tightening with barely restrained fury. "No matter how much you struggle, enough is enough. I know you took it from my room."

"Then you should look for it yourself."

"Don't play games with me. I didn't spend four years tracking you down and dragging you here just to listen to nonsense." The man straightened, his expression hardening into an emotionless mask, though his brow furrowed in frustration. Despite the passage of time, he hadn't changed a bit—his posture, his demeanor, all of it still perfectly calculated. Well, people didn't change so easily.

"After you set me up, chased me out, destroyed my reputation, and now this is all you have to say?" Isaac's anger bubbled to the surface, his teeth clenched in frustration.

The man cocked his head slightly and responded with

cold precision, "You betrayed me first. You ran away without completing your mission, didn't you? Thanks to you, the team was decimated."

"I indeed failed your mission," Isaac replied, his voice tight, "but it's not my fault the team fell apart."

"Can you honestly say that, knowing it was because you ignored my orders and went off on your own, that the whole team was wiped out?" The man's words were like a slap, each one calculated to hit Isaac where it hurt.

Isaac fell silent, knowing there was no point in arguing further. The man had no intention of listening to him—he never had. From the moment he'd been sent on the mission to when Isaac was tasked with assassinating Felix, it had all been a setup. He was always meant to be the fall guy, the scapegoat for everything that went wrong because that was the man's plan.

But life didn't always go as planned. Isaac hadn't followed the script, and that flaw was why he was here now. Maybe that's why they called life a circus. A bitter smile tugged at his lips as he reflected on the absurdity of it all.

"Now, answer me. Where is the document?" The man's patience had worn thin, and he pressed Isaac further.

Isaac met his gaze coldly. "What reason is there for me to answer?"

"Reason? Unless you hand me the document, you won't live. Is that not reason enough?"

"Won't live…?" Isaac repeated the words, his voice heavy with a resigned sigh. Short and to the point.

"Even if you live, it'll be a fate worse than death. I just need to hear the answer I want from you. And you'll still be able to talk without your limbs."

"So, what if I give you the document? Will you let me live?" Isaac sneered, the bitter irony of the situation not lost on him. The man had already pushed him off the edge. Sparing his life just because Isaac gave him what he wanted? Ridiculous.

"Yes, I won't kill you. You have my word."

"Instead, I'll end up in a fate worse than death, like you said." Isaac's lips curled into a half-smile, his tone laced with sarcasm.

The man shrugged, unfazed, "But I said I won't kill you, didn't I?"

"You already promised worse than death, so why should I hand over the document?"

"Kay, I told you I don't have time for games." The man's brow furrowed, almost with impatience, and Isaac noticed the subtle shift. It made him eye the man deliberately, a challenge in his stare.

"You threatened me instead of reasoning with me. Now it's my turn." Isaac spoke without emotion, his voice steady. "Cole, I've been laying low all this time. If I intended to do something with the document, I would've done it by now, wouldn't I?"

"What do you mean?"

"If you had left me to disappear, I wouldn't have done anything. To be honest, I don't care about your plans anymore. I don't want to care."

The man stared at Isaac, unblinking. Though he was behind a screen, Isaac could feel the cold chill of his gaze. Yet he remained unmoved, meeting his eyes with a practiced calm.

"I'm telling you to let sleeping dogs lie. I can pretend I don't know you as long as I need to. But if you're going to threaten me like this, I'm not going to stay quiet either."

"You—"

"I have a regular contact," Isaac interrupted sharply, speaking quickly. "If I go silent, the document will be handed over to the authorities and the media."

He paused briefly, his gaze steady. "However, if you meet my demands, I'm inclined to hand it over willingly."

The man simply kept his gaze fixed on Isaac, poised in his seat. If not for the rhythmic tapping of his finger on his knee, he would have seemed like a still image on the screen.

The tension in the room was suffocating, thick enough to

constrict Isaac's throat. His throat felt dry and parched. Then, unexpectedly, the man burst into biting laughter.

"Yes, that'll do. Well done," the man said, a grin spreading across his face. "I threw out the bait to see how you'd bite, and you've certainly amused me."

He clapped his hands, the sound sharp and deliberate. "Not that I expected anything less, but if you had just sat there like a fool, I'd have been greatly displeased."

Meanwhile, Isaac's face grew paler with every second. He had no idea what this farce was about.

"Needed a reaction like that to see I didn't teach you for nothing. Wouldn't you say? But you shouldn't bite the hand that feeds you. I know you were pretending to be a good little puppy, biding your time until you could pounce on me with your teeth bared. But see, I don't go easy on mongrels like that."

The man spoke without reserve, and the mirth that had once lit his face was now gone.

Isaac narrowed his eyes in indignation. "Is that why you threw me away? You tossed me out because you thought I might turn on you one day? All this time, I did as you said—your every bidding, like a mongrel on a leash. I followed you without once thinking you'd toss me aside like trash."

He glowered at the man with wild eyes. The man, in return, met his gaze with a curl of his lips, his pupils dark with the sort of curiosity reserved for an exotic animal.

Isaac took a deep breath, then spoke through gritted teeth, "I've always wondered. Why'd you throw me away when I obeyed you without question? All these four years I've spent running for my life, I've wanted to ask."

"Kay—"

"And now that we're face to face, I finally will. Why did you cast me aside? What went wrong? Did you nip me in the bud because you thought I would rebel? Is that it?" Isaac's eyes gleamed with violence as he volleyed his questions, but the man simply scratched his chin, looking as though they were more of a nuisance than anything.

"Dear me, such cute words from you. They break my heart, you know?" The man laughed softly, then abruptly hummed, propping his chin up. "Since we've come all this way, I'll be frank, shall I?"

"About what?"

"I've never once cast you away."

Isaac frowned, confused by the man's flat statement. He didn't understand, and beyond not understanding, it seemed outrageous. Isaac glared murderously at him, the words feeling like lies spat from a serpent's tongue. Yet the man's gaze was so earnest, so steady, that a chill crept up Isaac's spine.

"I needed a loyal dog. A hound of my own, one that would always have my back. You trusted and obeyed me, and in that respect, you were satisfactory. So, I favored you quite a lot. As you well know." The man continued, seemingly indifferent to Isaac's growing contempt. "However, one day, you started to stray from my ideal. That upset me."

The man murmured the words almost with a mix of disappointment and pity. Isaac closed his eyes, trying to suppress the surge of rage building inside him. If he looked at the man any longer, he knew he wouldn't be able to control it.

"It must have been after you found out about the incident, that the glint in your eyes started to change. Am I right?"

Isaac was silent.

"You said you always obeyed me, but no. You were already rebelling against me. Watching for the chance to escape. Did you really think I wouldn't know how you truly felt?"

Isaac clenched his jaw, his teeth grinding. The question, mind-numbing in its audacity, felt like a venomous bite. The man's gleaming, snake-like eyes seemed to close in on him, and Isaac suddenly had the disturbing sensation that it wasn't the ropes that held him—rather, it was the man's overwhelming alpha pheromones.

"Cole…"

"If you thought I didn't know you were in contact with Steve, you were sorely mistaken." The languid voice slid into his ear, insidious and thick with menace. A shiver ran down Isaac's spine, despite his attempts to remain unaffected. He exhaled deeply, trying to push down the fury churning inside.

Fortunately, the suffocating presence felt through the screen didn't last for long.

The man clucked his tongue, glancing at his watch. For a moment, Isaac felt as though the suffocating grip around his neck loosened, and he finally managed to draw a full breath.

The man shrugged, as though dismissing the tension. "I was angry. Thought I'd have to teach you a lesson again. So, I pulled a little trick. After all, you should only listen to me, trust me, and see things my way. Though, I didn't expect you to hide for so long."

"Does that so-called trick involve driving me out and framing me?"

The man's expression remained unfazed as he replied with unsettling calm, "A puppy is cuter when it's whining—helpless, unable to do anything without its master, don't you think?"

Isaac's fists clenched, his teeth grinding so hard it hurt.

"Enough with the chit chat," the man continued, his voice cold. "Let's return to the main subject."

Isaac remained silent.

"Bring the document to me," the man said flatly. "Then, I'll bury the hatchet and restore you to your original place. By my side. Be a good boy and bring it back to me."

His words dripped with condescension, and his gaze bore into Isaac, relentless and sickeningly persistent.

"If you're worried that your corruption will be exposed…just kill me," Isaac snarled, his voice cutting through the tension like a knife. "It would be easier that way."

The man burst into laughter. "Good gracious! Kill you? How could I possibly do that, when I've missed you so much these last four years? Kill my cute lost-and-found puppy with my own hands? Surely you jest."

He leaned closer to the screen, his manic eyes fixed on Isaac with unsettling intensity. The way his gaze roamed, filled with dark amusement, made Isaac feel like he might suffocate under its weight. If he could, Isaac would have backed away, but instead, he held his ground, even as bile rose in his throat.

"I won't say it again," the man continued, his voice now low and menacing. "Return to me with the document. Your place is by my side, and there's nowhere else for you. That's the conclusion."

Each word he spoke seemed to crush Isaac's resolve. Isaac said nothing in response. His throat burned, and his thoughts were clouded by fury and helplessness.

"If you disobey me again, you'll pay. Don't rebel against me. You just have to follow me like an obedient puppy."

The words were an ultimatum, with no room for negotiation. He turned his attention to his watch, glancing at it as if to signal the end of the conversation. Slowly, he stood up, his body language exuding finality.

Isaac closed his eyes before opening them again. "As I've told you before, I can give you the document. But only if you agree to my terms."

The man had not come here to negotiate, but it seemed, for now, it couldn't be avoided.

"Terms. Well, what are they?" he had asked lightly as if indulging a child's mischief.

Yet Isaac had looked him in the eye and delivered his demands in a heavy voice. "I had no intention of returning to you. If you promised to consider me dead and never look for me again, I'd believe you one last time and send you the document. I don't need anything. I just want the freedom to live the life I want."

He had revealed all his cards, the demand bitter on his tongue. Would that man even pretend to listen to him? His bound hands behind his back had dampened with nerves.

Silence had fallen. Neither the man beyond the screen nor Isaac, bound to the chair, had opened their mouths. The uncomfortable silence, however, hadn't lasted long. The man had checked the time again, clucked his tongue, and looked hard at Isaac.

"Of course, I'll receive the document. Sure, getting you to talk might've roughened you up. But that wouldn't matter. I could take care of you well enough."

"Cole!"

"However, there was no reality where I let you go." On that toneless note, the man had turned away. It had meant he would no longer hear whatever Isaac had to say. The man had soon left the screen, and only an empty seat had remained. This time, Isaac had glared murderously at the frozen image on the screen.

He had wanted to smash the screen into pieces. His gut had churned as he stared at the empty seat in the wake of the man's prattle. Unfortunately, he couldn't untie the knot on the chair.

All he could do was move his fists, opening and squeezing them to alleviate his anger. However, even that had been short-lived. With a smack, an iron fist had suddenly landed in his stomach. Isaac had reflexively doubled over and had hacked a cough.

Not that he could bend his waist with it tied to the chair. His head had hung low, and Isaac had coughed long and hard. Yet, under whatever orders, the men silently watching over Isaac had now begun to throw punches without discretion.

His vision had gone dark. Bile had risen in his throat. The burly men had assaulted Isaac, tearing the skin around his eyes and lips. He had become bloody in a matter of seconds. The mixed stench of sweat and blood had pervaded the confined space.

He had been unable to gauge the length of time or how it had passed. Isaac had been forced to take the indiscriminate beating, tied up and helpless. In the end, he had lost consciousness and had gone limp. Yet their merciless violence had shown no sign of stopping.

Chapter 28

At dawn, Felix woke with a frown, unsettled by a familiar discomfort. Turning his head, he caught sight of the bluish sky outside the large window, signaling the approach of morning.

He hadn't been a morning person, and it hadn't been like him to be up so early, but he just couldn't sleep. He had absently placed a hand on his forehead. Sure enough, he had been running a higher temperature than usual. Felix had registered the slight fever with his fingertips, then had lifted the corners of his lips on his otherwise frowning face.

"Well, fuck…I'm in rut." His crackly voice had been dark and wet. However, the smile he had worn hadn't matched the cold atmosphere, and he had gotten up. Since he hadn't worn pajamas to bed, he had been naked, in only his drawers as he had roused the dawn's darkened space.

With his shoulders and chest knitted with muscles, his toned abdomen and back, his pert buttocks and firm thighs, not one part of him was out of shape. His body was honed to the point of intimidation, reminiscent of the sleek weapons he had sold.

Every time Felix stretched, his muscles moved rhythmically. He walked around the still-dark room, relaxing his muscles and turning his neck back and forth according to a routine while wearing a thoughtful expression. Then he approached the table, grabbed his phone, and quickly pressed it.

"Yes, is there something you need?"

When he pressed the speed dial, the call rang, and a voice sounded on the other end. Even that early, Tony had answered Felix's call without delay. Like always.

The moment Felix had heard the other's slightly groggy voice, he had giggled like a madman.

"Tony, I think my rut's started!"

This man in his mid-thirties, with his flawless physique, was acting completely out of character, giggling and exclaiming like a child. His expression was that of a teenage alpha experiencing his first rut—overflowing with anticipation and curiosity.

No matter how excitedly Felix shouted, Tony's reaction was lukewarm, as if he'd been hit with a shovel while asleep. "Is that so?"

"What kind of reaction is that? Get your ass moving and bring Isaac here."

"Yes, but it's too early right now. I'll have someone bring him in the morning. Why don't you get some rest, boss, and manage your condition until then—"

"Shut up and get up," Felix growled through his teeth, and moments later, the sound of rustling covers came over the line. Tony had finally gotten up—lazy bastard. Felix, who could count on one hand the number of times he'd risen early, let out a supercilious snort.

A resigned sigh followed on the phone. "I'm leaving now."

"Of course you are."

Pacing the spacious room in nothing but his underwear, Felix ended the call with a satisfied smile. His rut was beginning, signaled by a slight fever, and he knew his pheromones—and uncontrollable lust—would hit full force within the day.

Though Felix typically despised his ruts and the wild, reckless urges they unleashed, like a crazed stallion, this time, he was alight with anticipation, his blue eyes gleaming. How could he not be when it meant taking Isaac as much as he wanted for three days or possibly a week?

The thought alone brought a smug smile to his face. Despite the early hour and the absence of sunlight, Felix strode to the shower, his mood uncharacteristically buoyant.

By the time morning had nearly slipped away, Felix's giddy anticipation had been completely shattered.

At dawn, he had roused the entire household from sleep, eaten breakfast, and ordered the staff to clean the house from top to bottom—without explaining. Who knew how the two things were related, but Felix had nagged them to have everything squeaky clean before Isaac arrived.

With time to spare, Felix retreated to the fitness room, pumped iron, showered, and meticulously selected his outfit. He even styled his hair and strapped on his prized watch, looking more like he was heading to a high-end date than preparing for what was really on his mind—tumbling into bed with Isaac.

Though his preparations were unnecessary, Felix's expectations soared. But as the hours ticked by, the wait stretched longer. Tony and Jack, sent to fetch Isaac, were still nowhere to be seen.

By eleven, hunger and irritation gnawed at Felix, forcing him to sit down early for lunch. Cutting into his steak, he pressed the speed dial on his phone, only for it to ring endlessly without being answered.

"Boss!"

Felix arched an eyebrow and glared at the figure who burst through the door without knocking. He tossed his phone onto the table with a clatter, "Where the hell were you all this—"

"I think something's happened." Tony's interruption made Felix narrow his eyes.

Late and without notice, and now cutting him off? Felix's glare darkened, but Tony, disheveled and sweating, was too flustered to notice. He was gasping and wiping the beads of sweat with a handkerchief.

"Breathe. What happened? Where's Isaac?" Felix demanded, scanning the room. But Isaac was nowhere in sight. Jack followed Tony in, his face grim, while Felix, temper fraying, set his knife down with a loud clink.

"Boss, I think Isaac the Florist has scampered!" Jack's disgruntled remark cut through the room as he entered, closing the door behind him.

Tony, still deliberating on how to break the news without provoking Felix's wrath, groaned and pressed a hand to his forehead. This oaf was no help, he lamented.

As expected, Felix's gaze sharpened like a blade, his blue eyes glinting dangerously. His voice was low, cold, and bone-chilling, "What kind of bullshit is that?"

Jack froze mid-step, the weight of Felix's glare pressing on him. "Ah, well…we looked all over, but we didn't see hide nor hair of him," he muttered, beginning to retreat.

"You didn't see him?"

Tony stepped forward, swallowing hard under Felix's piercing stare. "His apartment was empty. They say he moved out two days ago."

Felix's eyes, which looked about to shoot lasers, shifted to Tony, radiating fury that made him feel faint. His rut was already in motion, and if his temper exploded, the entire household would pay the price.

The mere thought made Tony feel faint, and he wiped his mouth nervously.

"Details," Felix said, his piercing blue eyes shifting from Jack to Tony, striking fear before a word was spoken.

"They say he cleared out of his apartment two days ago," Tony speedily gave the details. "The flower shop is under another name, so it hasn't been touched, but it's been closed for two days too."

Jack cut in. "It's like he went poof, you know? We found his car near downtown, but that's it! He's disappeared into thin air like some ghost. If that's not him hightailing it, what is?"

Jack had momentarily shrunk back, but now he was cut off by Tony who was speaking with vehemence. "Jack. Don't make assumptions. Nothing's been proven yet."

He essentially complained to Felix about being forced to search Isaac's apartment, shop, and around Downtown San Diego first thing in the morning.

"He's disappeared without a peep—what's that if not flying

the coop?"

Tony groaned, glaring at Jack, whose lack of awareness was more aggravating than Felix's simmering anger. Before long, their disagreement escalated into bickering.

Felix, utterly unimpressed, turned his attention back to his steak. He cut into it with cold indifference and shoved a piece into his mouth. At a glance, he appeared to be calmly enjoying a meal. His straight posture, precise knife work, and refined movements all exuded elegance.

The only difference was the oppressive, murderous aura radiating from him. It was hard to tell if he was slicing a steak or someone's pound of flesh.

"Shut your traps," Felix spat out, as their squabble showed no sign of stopping, and threw his knife and fork down on the table.

The sound instantly silenced Tony and Jack. A heavy stillness filled the dining room. Felix ate two more bites of steak in the quiet, then pushed the plate away. His appetite had vanished. Tony watched Felix's composed yet tense movements with mounting anxiety.

"Bring me the suppressants," Felix commanded, lifting a glass of water and sipping it gracefully, his voice low and steady.

Tony and Jack's eyes went wide in unison like a rabbit's, stunned by the order. Felix avoided suppressants like poison, yet here he was, asking for them?

"You mean…rut suppressants?"

"Didn't I just say my rut has started?" Felix snapped.

"Yes, you did, but wouldn't you rather call a beta like last time—"

"Call who?" Felix cut him off sharply. "I don't want anyone but Isaac. And besides, if you call them, there'll just be bodies to dispose of."

His ruthless words, delivered with an unchanging expression, were accompanied by a thickening wave of alpha pheromones. His rut, combined with his foul mood, twisted the air into something oppressive enough to make even Tony, a beta, instinctively step back.

Tony gestured quickly to Jack, who scrambled to fetch the suppressants. Moments later, he returned, handing them over with shaky hands. Felix took the pills and chewed them dry, his jaw tightening with every bite. Then he gave a bloodthirsty smile.

"Disappear? Without a word?" His voice dropped to an icy growl, sending chills through the room. Neither Tony nor Jack dared to speak, though it seemed Felix wasn't expecting an answer. He stared into the empty air, chewing the suppressants like candy.

"In short," he began slowly, his gaze darkening, stopping his chewing to ask, "Isaac has committed a breach of contract. Am I right?"

Tony flinched under the sudden question, his shoulders shrinking.

"Isaac was supposed to take care of my ruts. And now he's gone without a word. So, this is a breach of contract, isn't it?"

"Ah…it seems so," Tony stammered.

"Wow, what'll we do? The man says it's a breach of contract."

Felix stared straight ahead and curled his lips as if Isaac was before him. "Isaac, now you're really done for."

The way he smiled, the flash of his gaze—it was like watching a man completely unhinged. It almost seemed as if he were enjoying Isaac's absence.

Tony sighed heavily. This was Felix Felice, his infamous boss. But even for someone as unpredictable as Felix, how could he be so indifferent?

"Boss, aren't you worried?" Tony ventured cautiously, unable to suppress his unease. No matter how unconventional a mind this man had, it wasn't right that he was crowing about a breach of contract when a person had gone missing.

Felix didn't so much as flinch at the subtle accusation. "Worried? About what?"

Tony hesitated, but Jack jumped in without hesitation. "What if the bastard planned to run away?"

Tony whipped around to glare at Jack, his eyes blazing, but Jack simply shrugged and looked away, feigning ignorance. Tony was about to reprimand him when Felix spoke again, his tone almost amused.

"Where would he run to? Something must've come up."

Tony blinked in surprise. Felix's calm, dismissive response was the opposite of his expected tantrum. Felix cast a disdainful glance at both of them.

"Isaac? Run away?" Felix scoffed. "When I'm the one protecting Benjamin? Do you think he'd leave his kid behind and bolt? Think again. His love for that boy runs deeper than anything; he values his kid more than his life. Even if he's hiding, he'll have to surface eventually. Just keep an eye on Benjamin."

Tony couldn't close his half-open mouth. He hadn't thought that far. But he soon shook his head at another thought that occurred to him, "Then, shouldn't we be more worried? He's not the kind to disappear without a word; doesn't that mean he's missing? Something might have happened. Shouldn't we take action?"

Tony had always seen Isaac as simple and honest—a man whose life screamed harmless and law-abiding. The kind of person who vanished without a trace was a rare sight, and if Isaac hadn't run away, something else was going on.

"What do you mean, something else?" Felix's response came in a tone of complete confusion. Tony sighed. He remembered the paparazzi shot of Felix heading to the yacht, where Isaac's face had been unmistakably visible. The photo had even circulated through intelligence agencies.

"Surely they didn't kidnap him thinking he was your lover…" Tony blurted out, suddenly consumed by the scenario he'd imagined. His face twisted into an expression of shock, but he couldn't finish the thought.

Felix shot him a sharp look, clicking his tongue in disapproval. "Do you idiots have buttonholes for eyes? You think Isaac is a pushover?"

"What?"

"What?"

Felix's question simultaneously dumbfounded Tony and Jack. Both of their faces were stunned. A flower shop guy, not a pushover? What did he mean?

"Are you kidding me? I don't even know how you idiots manage the boys, being like this."

"What do you—"

"Did you think Isaac is your run-of-the-mill guy? You didn't see? How trained is his body? His build and muscles, as well as the calluses on his hands, are of a skilled and seasoned fighter. He won't go down easily." Felix tapped his fingers on the table irritably.

Tony and Jack stared at him in disbelief. What was this about Isaac being a skilled fighter? He had only ever appeared to be an ordinary neighborhood florist.

Felix was famous for his lack of awareness and care toward people, and the two kept staring at him with blatant suspicion. With his record thus far, how could they believe his sudden display of insight? As they did, Felix crumpled his brow in irritation.

"Isaac has a lot of scars on his body. Most of them were from knives, and I saw one that was a small gunshot wound on his thigh. Of course, it'll be a cold day in hell before you see it, but just know it's there."

"Knife and gunshot wounds?"

Isaac always wore long sleeves and pants, even as the weather grew warmer. They had never seen him in anything revealing. In other words, only Felix, the one person who had the privilege to nibble and suck at Isaac's naked body, could witness the scars and wounds.

Even Felix wasn't blind enough to mistake a knife wound, so he knew he wasn't wrong. Did this mean Isaac, just as Felix had claimed, was secretly skilled? Of course, an ordinary person wouldn't have knife marks and bullet scars all over his body—so it was starting to make sense.

Tony was still processing this new information about Isaac when Felix interrupted his thoughts, his tone almost mocking as he laughed at Tony's confusion.

"Last time, you think it was because the bodyguard was an idiot and lost his knife? Wrong. Isaac was more skilled than him, so he easily took it."

Tony gulped, disbelief thick in his throat. The more he heard, the less he could believe it. Jack, too, muttered, "No way," under his breath.

It was hard to wrap his head around, especially considering the bodyguards assigned to Benjamin were touted as the best of the best. But Tony had heard the story: the bodyguard was distracted enough to let Isaac take his ballistic knife at Benjamin's birthday party.

Tony remembered how appalled he had been when the bodyguard stupidly lost his weapon, but what truly shocked him was how Felix had gone easy on the guy, only giving him a simple probation. Tony had assumed Felix let it slide out of good humor, but now this? It was nothing short of surprising.

"Then what do you think Isaac's identity is, boss? Just someone good at fighting? Or is there something else he's hiding?"

Tony recalled the first time they had unexpectedly entered Isaac's flower shop late at night. He'd caught a brief gleam of recognition in Isaac's eyes—a fleeting moment that Tony had almost been proud to notice. But Isaac had been uncomfortable when he recognized Felix.

For a moment, Tony had even suspected Isaac was some kind of federal agent tailing Felix. He had believed Isaac's claim of surprise—said he knew Felix only by reputation. Over time, Tony had written Isaac off as just another average guy. Now, that realization felt like a punch to the gut.

"A cop, probably. Or the FBI," Felix said after a moment of

thought.

Tony stared at him blankly. Now that he thought about it, Felix was the most sinister in this scenario. Had he been sleeping with Isaac while sensing something was off and pretending otherwise? It was a new low, even for a man like Felix, with all his depravities.

"You've thought that far?"

"He looks the part. He might be rough around the edges, but he's not some common thug."

Next to him, Jack let out an impressed sound. Felix's rare display of awareness struck Tony equally, but his perspective differed slightly from Jack's.

Normally, Felix's lack of awareness was enough to make others around him beat their chests in frustration. But he had an almost animalistic sense when it came to business or his well-being. Tony knew that better than anyone.

It was why Felix had managed to grow his weapons business. He had an instinct for seizing profit and a sixth sense for staying out of danger. He lacked tact when it came to people because he didn't care about them—but that wasn't the case with Isaac.

So, in essence, Felix sharpened his senses only for the things and people he deemed important. That was prideful, but it was also just *Felix*. Tony found himself at a loss for words.

"Boss, that's amazing. I didn't know you had that bastard all figured out. But why'd you pretend not to know?" Jack asked, his mouth hanging open in surprise at Felix's sudden astuteness.

Felix glanced at him apathetically. "Isaac wanted to hide it."

"Huh..." Jack stared, bewildered. Then, without warning, Felix grabbed the steak knife from the table and threw it at Jack. The knife sliced through the air with terrifying precision, grazing past Jack's neck and embedding itself with a savage thud into the door behind him.

It happened in an instant—no warning. Tony and Jack froze, wide-eyed. Jack didn't dare turn around to look at the knife quivering in the door behind him.

"B-boss…?" Jack stammered, his face pale, barely managing to move his lips.

"You piece of shit. How dare you call him bastard this, bastard that. You think Isaac's your buddy?"

"N-no, boss."

"Or do you think he's one of your boys?"

"No."

"You've got some nerve, especially when you're even younger than Isaac. Watch your tongue. Next time you speak to Isaac, you'll call him 'Mr.' When you answer him, you'll say 'Sir.'"

"M-Mr.?"

"If I ever hear a single complaint about you from Isaac, that'll be the day I wring your neck. Got it?" Felix's blue eyes flashed, a chill emanating from them that could freeze everything in its path. Jack could only nod, too terrified to speak.

"Leave. And tell Noah to hurry the fuck up."

With his wrath palpable, Felix turned back toward the table and sat with authority. He snapped at a nearby steward, ordering him to clear the cold steak and bring something else. Tony watched him for a moment before slipping away. He tugged Jack along, still frozen in fear, and they left the dining room.

Once the door shut behind them, they finally exhaled. Tony released a long sigh before giving Jack a firm smack on the back.

"Ouch! What was that for?" Jack snapped wide-eyed.

"You blind idiot, knock it off, will you?"

"Am I a damn punching bag? Why's everyone coming at me?" Jack pouted. Tony raised his hand to smack him again, but when he saw the bear-like man cower, he ended up just pounding his chest in frustration.

Felix had been on edge since his rut began, and now, with Isaac missing, his nerves were even worse. Felix hadn't blown up and torn everything apart because of his excitement that Isaac had *finally* breached their contract. Under normal circumstances, it would've been unthinkable, but this was an opportunity—a joker

Felix had been waiting for. There wouldn't be another breach like this, which meant no more strokes of luck.

Jack, however, was oblivious to all of this and acted like a fool. He should've considered himself lucky there wasn't a knife in his skull. Instead, he was still pouting, completely unaware of the gravity of the situation. Tony regarded Jack and his complaints with a weary sigh of frustration.

"Heed what the boss says. You're in for a rough ride if you keep being rude to Isaac."

"What the hell does that mean?" Jack asked, completely confused. Tony shook his head, dragging him briskly down the hallway. At the end of the day, Jack was the most clueless of them all.

"Forget it. Just know that it is what it is."

"Why? What's it?"

Tony couldn't be bothered to explain, but Jack continued to heckle him from behind. Finally, Tony shot him a glare.

"What does it mean? It means Isaac's not just some one-time fling. The boss is actually excited about being in a relationship. And you go around calling him bastard this, bastard that—you think that's gonna sit well with the boss? If it were me, I'd have stuck a knife in your neck, you damn blind idiot."

Jack's face went even paler than when the knife had flown at him, and he screeched in disbelief, "What? A relationship? The boss? With that florist? No way!"

Tony, however, pretended not to hear and didn't look back. His footsteps grew restless as he made his way toward the basement to check on Noah.

Chapter 29

The goons were well-trained, no doubt about it. They had to be private mercenaries. But they weren't perfect—more like mafia or gang henchmen. They fought well enough and knew how to handle weapons, but as Cole's men, they weren't quite the professionals they should've been. Isaac had watched them carefully, only to be disappointed.

Isaac paced indoors, standing straight as if he hadn't spent the last few days roughed up and sleep-deprived. But judging by his foggy vision, he was clearly in worse shape than he let on. His deterioration wasn't just from lack of sleep—it was from being beaten to within an inch of his life.

He took shallow breaths, trying to loosen his stiff neck with a few turns, cracking his joints. His brows furrowed as he spat out blood, and his mouth busted beyond recognition. Every time he spit, it was mixed with crimson, and his lips were torn, raw, and covered in scabs. One eye was swollen shut, leaving him nearly blind in that eye.

His wrists were numb from being bound too long, and his abdomen was bruised, dark, and swollen. His thighs and shins ached with every step. He was lucky nothing had broken. Despite everything, his face remained as cold and indifferent as ever. It would've been hard to tell how badly he was injured without a second glance.

Isaac wiped his bloody mouth with the back of his hand, forcing his heavy legs to move. He glanced down. The floor was covered in blood and shattered objects, with three unconscious men lying in a heap. They were so bloodied and mangled they were barely recognizable. These were the men who had kidnapped him, beaten him, and kept him under watch.

Isaac stared at the men coldly before marching toward the door at the far end of the container. Two days had passed since he'd been dragged here, and there was no more time to waste. He needed to get out as quickly as possible.

Fortunately, Cole was preoccupied for the moment, leaving these incompetent goons to watch him instead of handling things himself. Still, that didn't mean Isaac had time to spare. The men who had locked him in the dingy warehouse for two days had recently started moving him around.

First, they'd transported him from the warehouse to the container. Once inside, they cuffed his wrists to a chair. But they hadn't bound his legs or torso as they had in the warehouse. They must've been confident that he couldn't escape.

Fortunately, they were wrong.

Surveying the container, Isaac noticed a TV and a surveillance camera running. The situation here was probably being streamed live to Cole, who could appear on the monitor whenever he wanted—or simply send a message through the speaker.

As Isaac narrowed his eyes, taking in his surroundings, the truck began to move. Since Cole couldn't act directly, it seemed he was planning to transport him this way. There was no time to waste. Isaac knew that if he faced Cole in person, trouble would follow.

Isaac closed his eyes, thinking quickly. He squeezed the fist cuffed to the chair, gathering strength in his legs. He lifted his gaze, his eyes locking onto the man seated opposite him, who was leisurely biting into an apple. Black pupils gleamed with dangerous, murderous intent.

It had only taken a short while, but the situation was already over. Isaac nudged the unconscious man aside with the tip of his foot before moving on. The truck was parked by the roadside. The driver had been watching the chaos unfold through the monitor and had pulled over to intervene. Unfortunately for him, the driver ended up joining the three others sprawled on the floor.

Thanks to that, escaping the container was much easier. It would've been troublesome if the door had been locked. Isaac gripped the cargo door's handle with his blood-soaked hand. Just as he was about to make his move, he heard a static crackle from the speaker behind him. Instinctively, he looked around.

"Kay!" The voice called his nickname urgently. At the same moment, a man's face appeared on the previously dark monitor. It was none other than Cole—the man who had held him captive threatened him and tried to drag him away. "Where do you think you're going? I told you, there's nowhere left to flee! You don't have any other option than to come back to me!"

Isaac's muscles tensed as he heard the apoplectic shout. Without hesitation, he turned to face the monitor, where Cole's enraged face filled the screen. The man furrowed his brow as Isaac calmly retraced his steps toward him.

"You're already exposed. If you run, you'll just get caught. No matter where you go or what you do, you won't escape my grasp. So— Kay!" He shouted urgently, bending over the screen, but his voice was abruptly cut off.

Isaac had detached the speaker from the monitor and tossed it aside. The man continued shouting, his face twisted in rage, but no sound reached Isaac. Still, he could read the man's lips.

You'll regret this.

Isaac's eyes narrowed with a murderous glare. Without a word, he raised his leg and kicked the monitor with all his strength. The device crashed to the floor, and Isaac felt a sense of release. He'd been itching to do that since the first time he saw Cole, and now, having done it, he felt significantly lighter.

The monitor's screen flickered as it lay on the floor, and Isaac watched the jagged lines run up, indicating the image was distorted. Without hesitation, he raised his foot again.

He crushed the camera atop the monitor, then stomped twice more onto Cole's distorted face on the screen. With one final violent kick, the monitor shattered into pieces. No more images of the man, no more words. Only silence.

Isaac paused, his chest heaving from exertion, and glared at the broken monitor. Then, with a cold, calm composure, he turned around and walked toward the door. His bruised and bloodied face was unreadable as he stepped out of the container onto the freeway, moving with the ease of someone who had just taken control of his fate.

Early in the morning, Downtown San Diego was still deep in slumber. The bustling office buildings and towering skyscrapers had long since fallen silent, and the city was caught in the lull before rush hour. An almost eerie quiet settled over the streets.

A lone car sped along the empty road, a stark contrast to the usual hustle of the afternoon traffic. It screeched to a halt in front of a flower shop, its driver looking worse for wear.

Isaac stumbled out of the car, his appearance a disturbing sight. His clothes were in tatters, soaked in blood—some of it his, some of it not. His torn-up face, swollen lips, and bruised eyes were enough to make anyone who saw him second-guess their safety. Yet, despite his state, Isaac managed to keep his back straight, stumbling only slightly as he approached the storefront.

He fumbled through his pocket for the key, his hands shaking, his movements slow with exhaustion. Cold sweat clung to his temple as he struggled to insert the key into the lock. As the moment dragged on; Isaac gritted his teeth and moved his hand again.

Then, with a click, the lock finally released. Isaac let out a long, relieved sigh, pulling the metal gate up with a loud, grating noise that briefly shattered the morning's stillness.

It was then that he heard it—a faint sound behind him, barely audible over the clamor of the gate—a small sound, but one that Isaac immediately recognized: the distinct click of a gun loading.

Isaac's spine went rigid, and his hands shot up instinctively. It had only been three or four hours since he escaped the container—had they already tracked him down? His mind raced as panic set in. His throat felt thick with anxiety. He'd assumed they found out about his shop, but this was too fast.

"Isaac, where have you been? What happened to you?" The voice that rang out was deep and cold, and it came from a man Isaac least expected. Taken aback, Isaac didn't immediately lower his hands. Instead, he whipped his head around.

Sure enough, Felix stood there, his expression a mask of frustration and anger, casually spinning a Glock 18C in his hand. Isaac's initial fear dissipated as he realized that the sound he'd heard was simply Felix loading his gun. He let out a hollow breath, his heart still racing from the shock.

"Hah. There's a time and a place for surprises…"

"I told you to take care of yourself. Where in hell have you been for you to end up like this?"

The deadened voice of the man in front of him quickly cut off Isaac's expression of exasperation at Felix's over-the-top surprise. Felix's sharp gaze swept over Isaac's battered form, and with every passing second, his expression hardened. The aura of danger he emanated grew more intense, and Isaac couldn't help but gulp in response.

"Who the fuck did this to you?" Felix growled, his voice low and menacing. His hand shot out, fingers carefully lifting Isaac's blood-soaked hair, his touch almost tender but laced with fury. "Who dared to make you into this?"

The action was akin to a parent shouting, "Who hit my baby?" when their kid showed up with a lump, and Isaac couldn't help but let out a listless laugh.

"It's nothing," Isaac muttered.

"Nothing? You're all beaten up, and you're telling me it's nothing? Do you want me to scold you?" His voice cracked with indignation.

Isaac didn't flinch. Instead, he looked over his shoulder,

pretending not to hear the accusation.

The early morning street was eerily quiet, with only a few cars drifting past in the distance. The surrounding shops were all closed, the windows dark and silent. Isaac's eyes flicked to the space around them—no one else was in sight. There was no sign of Tony or Jack either, who had been like shadows.

"Surely, you didn't come out here alone?" Isaac's eyes widened as he looked at Felix, more surprised than anything.

Felix paused, his gaze still fixed on Isaac's wounds, brow furrowed, then cocked his head. "Why? Is there a law against it?"

"But you're—"

Do you know how many eyes are watching you?

The questions Isaac wanted to throw at him got stuck in his throat like a stone. He swiped a hand across his torn mouth and sighed. Then, as if something occurred to him, he grabbed Felix's arm and hurried him into the shop. He had to stay alert. There was no time to waste out on the street.

"I'm asking what happened!" Felix protested, still not understanding why he was being dragged inside. His voice was sharp. But Isaac just covered his mouth with his hand. Felix shot him a dirty look in response.

"First, I want to know why you're here at this hour," Isaac said, his tone cold. Outside, the headlights of a few passing cars briefly illuminated his bruised, torn face, and then the darkness swallowed it again, only for it to repeat. With each brief flash, his expression grew colder.

Felix stood like a statue for a moment, glaring silently at Isaac. Finally, he sighed in resignation and muttered something ridiculous. "Are you aware you broke your contract?"

"What?"

"My rut started yesterday, right at dawn. But you disappeared, didn't you? Because of you, I had to take those damn suppressants. Since you were supposed to take responsibility for my rut, but disappeared without a word, what's that if not a breach of contract?"

Isaac gaped at Felix's swagger before letting out a long sigh. After being unexpectedly captured by Cole and barely managing to escape in two days—nearly three—he never imagined Felix would start lecturing him about a breach of contract. He had assumed things would be fine as long as they met on Mondays. But a rut? This felt more like an ambush.

"So, were you waiting for me? At this hour, in front of a closed shop, all alone?" Isaac muttered, his hand pressing against his aching head. Felix simply crossed his arms and looked at Isaac with an air of arrogance.

"Yeah, how could I sleep with you gone missing? I was tossing and turning, then figured I'd catch you eventually if I stood here watching this place."

Isaac stared at him, completely at a loss. It was clear now: where Felix lacked awareness, he made up for it with unnerving intuition. "Even so, how could you be so reckless, waiting here alone? Who knows what could've happened?"

"Oh? You're worried about me, looking like that?" Felix raised an eyebrow, his smile crooked. "Be still, my beating heart."

Isaac sighed again, watching Felix's sarcastic grin. It seemed this narrow-minded man was more irritated than he let on. Still, Isaac found himself speechless.

There were many things Isaac wanted to say, but he didn't know where to start. His lips moved restlessly, uncertain when Felix raised a hand to brush over the corner of Isaac's lips. Despite his scathing tone, the touch on the torn flesh—where blood still oozed—was careful.

"Now, tell me. What were you doing to end up like this? Who did this to you?" Felix's voice had dropped an octave, carrying the weight of a command. "Tell me."

He looked like he could dial a number and order a kill the moment Isaac spoke a name. A chill ran down Isaac's spine, and he held his breath.

Out of the frying pan, into the fire. Steve's words perfectly described the situation and echoed in Isaac's mind.

"It's a private matter. There's no need to concern yourself."

"A private matter? No need for concern? What do you take me for?" Felix's expression turned savage as he stepped closer, growling.

Isaac instinctively averted his gaze and took a step back, feeling like a rabbit caught in the jaws of a predator. In the dimly lit shop, the only illumination coming from the street outside, the temperature seemed to drop.

"Felix…" Isaac worried at his battered lips. He needed to say something and make an excuse, but the words wouldn't come. He rubbed his burning throat. That's when it happened.

Outside, on the quiet early morning road, the screeching of tires cut through the air. Isaac snapped back to attention and lifted his eyes, narrowing his gaze at the shop's glass door. Behind the car he had parked on the roadside in front of the shop, an SUV sped toward them, its bright headlights cutting through the dark.

Hitting the brakes did no good. The tires screeched, but the SUV showed no signs of slowing. As expected, the crazed vehicle plowed straight into Isaac's car. With a crash, the bumper shattered, and Isaac's car lurched forward. Only then did the SUV finally brake—right where Isaac had parked initially, in front of the shop.

"Hah, what kind of crazy asshole is that? Fucking drunk couldn't even call for a replacement—" Felix was about to storm toward the door in a fury. But Isaac was quicker, grabbing his arm and sprinting behind the counter.

"What?"

"Keep your head down and sit!" Isaac shoved Felix's head down and dropped beside him, squatting behind the counter. A deafening roar shook the air at that moment, and the glass doors and windows shattered. These men were faster and more reckless than Isaac had anticipated.

They weren't using handguns; automatic rifles blazed as they sprayed the shop with bullets, intent on turning it into Swiss cheese.

The ricochet of bullets bounced off walls, sending glass shards flying and scattering dirt, plants, and flowers in all directions. It was pure chaos.

"Who the fuck are they?" Felix swore, flabbergasted. Without hesitation, he drew a Glock from his back pocket and started firing. The Glock 18C was a semi-automatic, and sparks flew from its muzzle in rapid succession, the deafening noise filling the air.

As Felix returned fire, Isaac dropped lower and crawled deeper into the shop, maneuvering through the clutter of large flower pots. Felix shouted at him from behind the counter, but Isaac couldn't hear it over the madness.

The gunfire was relentless, filling the air like a warzone. The sound echoed in Isaac's skull, burning through his thoughts, and his expression tightened his focus hardening.

Swiftly crawling deeper into the shop, Isaac began digging through a flowerpot's soil. Weapons were hidden between the plastic wrapping, the tree's base, and the larger pot that held it. It wasn't just one pot—almost all of them were rigged. Isaac even pulled out a bag to stash the weapons.

He retrieved a handgun, a knife, and several magazines, shoving them into his pants, then stuffed the rest into the bag. Finally, he pulled out a large case and opened it. Inside was a submachine gun affixed with a silencer.

"Hah, you had an MP5SD too?" Felix, who had been covering Isaac as he worked, recognized the weapon and let out a terse groan. Isaac didn't spare him a glance; he simply moved faster.

Within seconds, Isaac had the submachine gun loaded and prepared. He aimed it in the blink of an eye, his fingers fluid and precise. The final click of the safety echoed ominously.

Felix watched, transfixed, as Isaac handled the anti-riot, anti-terrorism weapon with the ease of someone born with it in their hands. Then, without warning, a Beretta was flung at his face. He caught it momentarily stunned as Isaac yelled, "Cover me!" without looking back. Felix realized, frighteningly, that Isaac had noticed the Glock was empty.

Felix didn't respond but swiftly released the safety, gripping the Beretta. At the exact moment, Isaac's MP5SD began to fire, the silenced weapon producing a sharp, controlled burst. The sound was muffled compared to the chaos outside, where the real noise was coming from.

The screams of the men echoed through the shop. They had been firing recklessly from the SUV, but now their limbs were being blasted off one by one. Isaac's aim was deadly accurate, his focus unshakable, his fingers steady on the trigger.

Felix grumbled about his grandfather killing people like flies, but as he watched, he realized that was nothing. There was no disturbance, no flicker of emotion on Isaac's face as he watched them collapse into blood and gore.

It was as if he were mechanically shooting targets, not people. No matter how many blood curdling screams rang out, Isaac didn't flinch. His brow furrowed slightly in concentration, but aside from that, he appeared unaffected, even unbothered.

Felix had fired countless rounds himself and watched men die beside him, but he'd never seen anyone pull the trigger with such cold detachment as if wearing a mask. Even armed fanatics, screaming with rage, seemed more human in comparison.

All Felix could do was watch Isaac, his grip tight on the Beretta Isaac had tossed him. In truth, Isaac didn't need any cover. He'd shredded the SUV with ruthless precision, annihilating the thugs inside before they even had a chance to fight back.

Soon enough, there was no more retaliation, and the dust settled. Isaac stood, his gaze still fixed on the MP5S. He was on edge, poised to fire at the slightest movement. Felix felt a cold chill run through his body, emanating from Isaac as if the very air around him had frozen.

Isaac took a slow step forward, moving to where Felix sat frozen and gripped his arm. Over his shoulder hung a bag already bulging with weapons.

"There's no time. Run."

Glass crunched beneath their feet as Isaac hurried Felix out of the shop. The car had become scrap, ruined beyond recognition. Inside, there was no sound, no moans, no survivors.

Beyond the silent street, the faint wail of sirens grew closer. Given the gunfire they'd unleashed, it was a miracle the cops hadn't shown up sooner. Isaac glanced at his car, half-destroyed after the thugs' SUV had slammed into it, then turned to Felix. "Your car. Where is it?"

"This way," Felix answered, already running ahead, pulling Isaac along. A black sedan appeared a few feet in front of the wrecked car. Isaac instantly recognized it as Felix's—luxury sedans like that were rare in this area.

Upon seeing the sedan, Isaac made a beeline for the driver's seat. "I'll drive."

"Hey!"

"Trust me, for now."

Felix grumbled, but it didn't faze Isaac, who yanked open the driver's door. It unlocked automatically as Felix approached with the key, allowing Isaac to slip inside without a hitch.

Reluctantly, Felix took the passenger seat, his displeasure evident, but Isaac paid him no mind. He pushed the start button, and the engine purred to life, the dashboard lighting up. Isaac, however, immediately turned off the lights and pressed the accelerator.

The high-performance car surged forward. Without his seatbelt fastened, Felix was thrown back into his seat as the car raced through the eerily quiet city. Though the streets appeared peaceful, the night had left a heavy, tense silence in its wake, as if the entire city were holding its breath, waiting for the dawn.

Chapter 30

The tires screeched as the sedan drifted to a stop in front of Felix's estate. Isaac had driven the exact route without navigation, even though the last time he'd been here was when Felix had unknowingly kidnapped Benjamin. That was the first and only time.

Felix had stayed silent the entire ride; his eyes fixed on Isaac's skilled yet reckless driving. He released a sigh only when the car stopped, turning toward Isaac with visible exhaustion.

Under the dim glow of the yellow lamp, Isaac's battered face came into sharp relief—swollen eyes and lips, dried blood streaked across his forehead, and small, angry bruises dotting his skin. His expression was bleak.

"I didn't realize they'd messed you up this badly…" Felix muttered, his blue eyes darkening as they swept over Isaac's injuries.

Isaac gripped the door handle tightly, his mouth firmly shut.

Felix exhaled heavily. "Who were those fuckers? Who did this to you? No, actually—what are you? SWAT? You handled that submachine gun like a pro, way better than a flower bouquet."

The question was pointed, but Isaac didn't respond, his gaze fixed elsewhere. His expression remained impassive, only slightly softer than when he'd gunned down the thugs earlier.

Felix didn't let up, his stare relentless. Finally, Isaac turned to meet his eyes. His voice was heavy with weariness. "I'll tell you later."

The exhaustion on his face was undeniable. The messy, bloody wounds were bad enough, but the hollow eyes and rough stubble spoke of days without sleep or food.

Felix didn't like Isaac's answer one bit, but he sighed low as if resigned to it. He didn't want to interrogate Isaac—he wasn't in any state to be interrogated, either. What Isaac needed was treatment and stability.

"Fine. I won't pry. Just get out of the car. Let's see to your wounds first." Felix reached for the passenger door.

"No." Isaac's voice was calm from the driver's seat. "Once I drop you off, I'm leaving. I'm sorry, but I'll have to take your car. Leave the key."

Felix froze, mid-motion, eyes narrowing as he shot Isaac a disbelieving look. Isaac was talking about stealing his car with such calm dignity that it almost made Felix laugh—except for the sheer gall of Isaac insisting on leaving like that.

Felix couldn't reconcile the image of Isaac now—battered, barely holding it together—with the man who had wiped out a group of thugs with a submachine gun and then driven all the way here. He was obviously on the verge of collapsing, holding it all together by sheer force of will, and still, he refused to leave the car. Was this stubbornness or insanity?

Felix stared at him, his blue eyes dark with frustration, then squeezed them shut. He swallowed his anger, trying to hold it back.

"Are you insane?" Felix's voice rose despite his best efforts to stay calm. "Where do you think you're going, looking like that? Get out, now. Or I'll drag you out."

He couldn't keep his temper in check anymore. No matter what Isaac said, he couldn't let this go. It wasn't just that he didn't know where Isaac would go—it was that Isaac might pass out before he made it even a few miles.

Felix sighed deeply, rubbed his brow, and then reined himself in. With a resigned look, he turned away, resolved not to argue further. In truth, if Isaac did get out, it was over. Felix had the key, and the car would lock itself once the key was far enough away.

"Leave the key," Isaac said.

Felix froze again. The familiar click of a semi-automatic handgun being racked back rang clearly in his ear. Slowly, he turned his head.

"You..." Felix couldn't believe it. He'd suspected, but now he saw it for himself—Isaac had the Beretta in his hand. His face remained the same cold mask he'd worn during the shooting, the muzzle pointed directly at Felix. Felix's gaze flicked between Isaac and the gun, his eyes narrowing dangerously.

"What do you think you're doing?" Felix's voice came out flat, emotionless.

"Leave. I'll go on my own."

"Isaac. Do you know who you're pointing that gun at?"

"Of course I do. I know better than anyone." Isaac met Felix's gaze, his eyes deep and unfathomable. "So, leave. If you don't, I'll shoot."

Felix didn't back down. He couldn't. "Isaac, I won't let you run off like this."

"Listen to me now."

"I promised I won't pry! Just get yourself treated!" Felix burst out, his desperation raw. He feared that if he let go of Isaac now, he might never see or hold him again. Whether Isaac realized this or not, he simply stared at him, unyielding.

"I have something I need to prepare. Besides, nothing good can come from you getting involved. Not for you, and not for me."

"Tell me what you've gotten yourself into. I'll take care of it." Felix's voice was a low growl, filled with an edge that could chill anyone's spine. His blue eyes flashed in the dim light, ruthless and unrelenting.

"No. This is a personal matter, and you shouldn't be involved. I'll pay my part of the contract however I can. Just give me time. Please, until it's resolved." Isaac's resolve was unshakable. He refused to let Felix into his personal matter, and Felix's frustration grew. Why was Isaac shutting him out like this? He couldn't understand it.

"Isaac—"

"I won't say more." Isaac's voice was cold, final. "I assure you, I'll shoot you in a way that won't cripple you but will be excruciating. If you don't want to be laid up in bed for days, leave the key and get out now."

The words had barely left Isaac's lips when he aimed the gun at the inside of Felix's thigh. He was going to shoot next to the femur—just as he'd said, it wouldn't cripple Felix, but the pain would be prolonged, a constant reminder of the injury.

Felix's lips thinned, but he didn't move. A drop of cold sweat trickled down his spine. Without hesitation, Isaac pulled the trigger.

The gunshot was deafening. Felix's head rang with the sound. His leg was still intact, though—the bullet missed by a hair, embedding itself in the car door. Felix stared at the ruined door, expression unreadable, when Isaac swiftly aimed the muzzle at his leg again, this time more accurately.

"I gave you a demonstration since you seemed to think I couldn't do it. I won't miss the second time."

"Stop this."

"Get out."

In the end, Felix could only throw up his hands in defeat. The glint in Isaac's eyes was unmistakable. He would aim for his leg this time. He would pull the trigger without hesitation, without remorse.

Felix opened the passenger door. The cold morning air rushed in, and only then did the acrid smell of gunpowder start to dissipate. He didn't bother fixing his disheveled hair as he retrieved the key, tossing it onto the seat he'd just vacated.

"Happy now?" Felix shot Isaac a furious glare before slamming the door shut.

"I'm sorry. I'm ashamed to say this, but please take care of Benjamin." Isaac's voice was soft, unwavering as he met Felix's murderous gaze, finally letting the Beretta drop beside the car key. A hollow laugh escaped Felix's lips. Even now, Isaac was thinking about Benjamin. It never ceased to amaze him.

"You owe me big time," Felix muttered.

"I know."

"I'll make you pay everything with interest."

"Very well." Isaac's reply was quick, his tone indifferent, as if he didn't care what Felix did.

Felix gave a crooked smile. "Go."

With a dismissive flick of his hand, Felix shoved his hands into his pockets and muttered under his breath. Isaac, blood still staining his hand, shifted the sedan into gear and drove off, headlights off. The car disappeared into the darkness.

Felix stood rooted to the spot, watching the fading image of the sedan like a mirage until it was gone. The breeze tugged at his gold-spun hair, and his eyes gleamed with dangerous, violent greed in the spaces between the strands.

"Isaac, to pay off your debt with interest, you'll have to give me everything. Every last piece of you, down to a single strand of your hair. And I'll be taking it all. Thoroughly."

The words came out in a low whisper, colder and darker than the early morning wind. Felix stared murderously into the darkness, his fists clenched. Finally, he turned and walked away, his mood as heavy as the night. He could safely say it had been the worst few hours of dawn he'd ever had the misfortune of experiencing.

As soon as Felix stepped inside, the commotion hit him. The sun hadn't risen yet, but the shouts of "Boss!" and the thunder of footsteps on wooden floors reverberated through the entire estate.

Felix didn't bother to pull himself together as he watched the men rush toward him. Tony, Jack, the steward, and several lackeys were all pale, their faces a mix of concern and panic. Unsurprisingly, he'd slipped out of the house late at night without a word.

"For heaven's sake! How could you disappear like that?"

"If you have something to do, take someone with you, or we'll lose our minds!"

"We nearly reported you missing. Where on earth have you been?"

The noise swirled around him, threatening to split his head in two. He couldn't take it anymore.

"Shut up." Felix's voice cut through the chaos, laced with murderous intent. The men immediately fell silent. The heavy stillness that followed was thick with tension. Tony, Jack, the steward, and the lackeys exchanged wary glances, realizing their overreaction.

"Has something happened?" Tony ventured cautiously, following Felix down the hallway without a second glance. Felix's silence was as cold as the air around them. Whatever had gone wrong, Felix wasn't sharing.

The quiet stretched on. Tony scratched his cheek, feeling uncomfortable. What now?

Halfway down the hallway, Felix finally spoke. "Noah. Where is he?"

"In the basement, I think."

"So, no progress." Felix's gaze flicked over his shoulder, eyes narrowed in a way that made him look like a demon.

Tony hunched his shoulders, clearly uncomfortable, "He says there's no trace."

Noah had been throwing fits about his inability to find anything, and Felix had vanished. It had been a chaotic morning.

"Trace? Since when does he need a trace? Wasn't he the one who stuck his nose in the air and claimed he was the best hacker in the world?" Felix's voice dripped with disdain.

"Yes, he was…" Tony trailed off, unsure of how to respond.

Felix's patience snapped. "Lead the way. I'm going to Noah."

Felix undid a couple of buttons on his shirt, cracking his neck from side to side. It was clear he wasn't going to see Noah for a calm discussion; he was going to thrash the man.

"Boss, even so, it might be best not to press him too hard," Tony suggested cautiously, prompting Felix to turn a sharp eye on

him.

"Don't press him? How many days has it been? Do you even know what I've just been through?"

"So, you've been through something? I don't know unless you tell me." Tony thumped his chest, just as frustrated.

"That something is Isaac—" Felix paused in his stride toward the basement, raising his voice. But then he clammed up, gritting his teeth. Anger flared inside him again, the irritation he'd barely kept at bay reigniting as he recalled what had happened with Isaac at his flower shop. The more he thought about it, the harder his teeth ground.

You dare aim a gun at me? He seethed. *Do you know how long I've been waiting for this rut? You disappear, breach our contract, get yourself hurt, and then tell me I'm not involved—just leave the key?*

Then there was the unthinkable: being thrown out of his car—only for it to be stolen. His blood boiled. He was lucky he wasn't keeling over from high blood pressure. Yet, something else gnawed at him, threatening to rupture his veins.

Isaac may have stolen his car and run off, but Felix's heart churned. Where was Isaac now? What was he doing in that state? Did he collapse along the way? Would he even get his wounds treated? Felix felt wronged, having to worry about him.

"Is something wrong with Mr. Isaac?" Tony inquired cautiously, observing Felix's expression change as he struggled to suppress his anger, anxiety over Isaac intensifying.

"There's a problem, alright." Felix's cold blue eyes flashed with an unsettling intensity. Tony instinctively stepped back, feeling the tension in the air, goosebumps rising on his skin. "Thanks to Isaac, someone's about to learn a tough lesson."

"Pardon?" Tony tilted his head, confused by Felix's cryptic words. What was he saying…

Felix's lips curled into a crooked smile.

"A lesson that'll grind them down to the bone." His voice was low, his words heavy with menace. As he reached the basement door, he flung it open with a sharp motion. A string of curses and a deep sigh echoed from inside as though the air itself might sink under the weight of his frustration.

The basement was Felix's secret lair. Countless monitors and computer systems dominated the space, their blinking lights humming with activity like the nerve center of an intelligence agency. In front of the screens, a few people were working swiftly, their hands moving in practiced motions.

Information was one of the things Felix prioritized most as an arms dealer. His motto was to be the first to obtain any information. It was no surprise that he had equipped himself with such a facility.

The basement gathered reports from research centers, factories, and distributors scattered worldwide and served as a hub for Felix's operations. The company's headquarters were in another region, and its CEO handled general affairs externally. However, the information managed within Felix's private residence was far more classified.

What made it different was its level of secrecy—most of it was military-related. The facility was the heart of Felix's business, secretly established and operated beneath his private estate.

To outsiders, Felix, living in his oceanfront mansion in recreational San Diego, seemed like someone taking a break from his arms dealings. But they would be mistaken.

He maintained the playboy facade, but behind the scenes, he was deep in the grind—digging up intelligence, receiving reports, and issuing orders—leaving him hardly any time for leisure. Though he didn't often need to visit the basement in person, the workload in his office was overwhelming.

He had expanded and remodeled the entire basement, turning it into a base of operations for acquiring government intelligence and running his arms trade. That, in itself, could be problematic. However, the real issue lies in the occasional necessity for illegal hacking. And the basement? It was the home base for that.

The world-renowned hacker led these illegal operations and was currently hunched over his desk. His long hair spilled around him like a madman's mane, punctuated by swearing and frustrated sighs as he worked under Felix's watchful gaze.

"Did you finally lose your mind?"

No, the word "finally" was misleading. That bastard had been insane from the start.

Felix didn't bother with a greeting and strode in with a frown. The man lying face down in front of the keyboard was Noah Felice—Felix's cousin, a man obsessed with computers and machines, the world's best hacker, a pervert who got off digging up dangerous information, the only associate unafraid of Felix, and a hyper-dominant omega lunatic.

As Felix approached, Noah lifted his long, messy hair from his face, though it did little to change the fact that his waist-length strawberry blond locks were a tangled mess.

"You fucking bastard…" Noah muttered, still face-down. Dressed in an old, oversized t-shirt and loose pants hanging from his bony frame, he cursed when he saw Felix. But the expletive flopped out weakly, like an octopus caught in a net, as lackluster as his appearance. His olive green eyes were dull—he was out of it.

"I told you to look into Isaac's stepfather. Is that so hard? Or are you advertising you're a has-been now?" Felix taunted, his voice mocking as he flicked his nose toward Noah.

Noah shot up, his eyes flashing despite his otherwise sluggish demeanor. "You bastard, are you seeing a ghost? There's nothing! I've never come across a case this strange in my life! Isaac Sinclair and his father, Eugene Sinclair. Spick and span. So clean it's strange. There's no record of his father being involved with anyone after his divorce."

"Tony found those results when he investigated. That's why I called you. Because it's strange."

"But it's the same on my end! That's all I can find! Tony even sent men to Washington for a background check and came up empty! Are you sure this Isaac guy isn't lying to throw you off? Or maybe the records are false?"

At Noah's suggestion, Felix narrowed his eyes. He knew better than anyone that Isaac wouldn't lie. Isaac would stay silent if anything—he'd never fabricate a story.

Isaac had said he had a stepfather, an alpha. Which meant he did, indeed, have one. Felix recalled Isaac's impassive face, and he was certain. But nothing turned up in the records. Noah had tried, too, and found the same results—an ordinary school life and a run-of-the-mill job. It was bizarre.

"Falsified, most likely," Felix said casually.

Noah raised an eyebrow in response, and behind Felix, Tony let out a low sound as if mulling over the possibility.

"You said he was just an ordinary florist. How are you sure?" Noah's doubtful look seemed to stem from knowing Felix's lack of awareness or having heard the rumors.

Felix scowled, clicking his tongue in annoyance. "Because, despite Isaac's records, he can't have lived a spotless life. He went to an ordinary school, got an ordinary job, and then happened to open a flower shop? Don't make me laugh. Just now, I saw him take out an MP5SD."

"An MP5SD? That submachine gun with the integral silencer? Just now?" Noah gaped at Felix. "What the fuck were you doing? Grandpa told you not to stir up trouble!"

"Shut your trap. Who're you to bring up Grandpa?" Felix shot back, irritated. "And it wasn't me who stirred up trouble. It was the assholes after Isaac."

Oh?

Noah blinked in response to Felix's annoyed tone, letting out an idiotic noise.

"Noah, you like hacking government institutions, right?" Felix asked abruptly, ignoring Noah's reaction.

Noah nodded absently. "Like? I'm crazy about it. But I've already hit most of them, so it's no longer fun."

"Try the police department." Felix tapped the monitor in front of Noah.

"The police department?"

"A few hours ago, there was a shooting in Downtown San Diego. Some rabid dogs opened fire with automatic rifles and turned Isaac's flower shop into Swiss cheese. Can you believe that?"

"Huh?" Noah and Tony both made identical confused noises, their faces matching disbelief.

"Thanks to those assholes, his shop's a wreck. Isaac and I nearly became target practice. It would've ended that way if Isaac hadn't grabbed a submachine gun and wiped them out."

The more Felix spoke, the more the mood darkened. Neither Noah nor Tony could respond. A shooting in the peaceful, quiet city—Isaac returned fire with a submachine gun? It was hard to believe.

But judging by Felix's flinty eyes and murderous aura, it was clear he wasn't joking. His expression was deadly, as though he would strangle the perpetrators the instant he saw them.

"Find out where they're from. I'll crush their bones." His eyes flashed maniacally as he stood, arms crossed, ready for action. "They dare to shoot up Isaac's shop with rifles? In front of me? I won't let them get away with this. Noah, identify them. Now. Tony, get the boys ready. We're moving as soon as Noah locates them."

Noah sighed, watching Felix fire off orders. "Felix, if what you're saying is true, this won't just fall to the police department. It'll probably be handed to the FBI. I'll dig into it, but…what kind of person have you gotten involved with?"

Noah asked pointedly, giving Felix a once-over. He mumbled something about "birds of a feather" and how Felix must have found someone just like him. Where did he even find someone like that? His mutters were loud enough for everyone to hear.

"No matter how deep I dive, there's nothing. And now you're

telling me he used a weapon like that? What the fuck? Are you sure he's not a ghost?"

Felix shot Noah a glare, his eyes darkening with irritation.

"We're on the same wavelength for once," he said, his tone biting. "I was wondering the same thing. Who knew an 'ordinary' florist had such a suspicious backstory? I expected he wasn't average, but I didn't think he was a skilled shooter, either."

Felix's frustration was palpable, and Noah shrugged nonchalantly. "Still your fault for choosing him," he muttered.

"One thing's certain," Felix continued, his voice cold. "I don't know about ghosts, but I know he's no civilian. There aren't many civilians who can grab a submachine gun, load it, and kill a man on the spot."

Noah scratched his cheek, thinking it over. "Sure, there's a small number, but he could just be one of those gun nuts. That might explain his spotless record. Maybe he's too clean to be true."

The world was full of weapon aficionados—those who collected firearms, testing them out without concern for legality, acquiring them however they pleased.

"Maybe," Noah said, tapping his fingers on the desk. "There's always a nut obsessed with weapons. But there's a big difference between someone who's tested them a few times and an experienced professional. I mean, sure, but…"

"As I said, Isaac didn't hesitate when a group of thugs opened fire with automatic rifles on a city street. He just held his ground, no fear, no second thoughts. What kind of civilian can calmly retaliate when bullets are flying? And it didn't look like it was his first time killing someone. It looked like he had quite a tally."

Felix's eyes were distant as he recalled the unbelievable scene from just hours ago. It was hard to reconcile what he'd seen, let alone make anyone else believe it.

"It was like nothing to him. He blew their heads off like they were target dummies." Felix's voice had dropped to a rough whisper. As Noah had suggested, the more he thought about it, the more it felt like he'd encountered a ghost. The man he knew seemed so foreign now.

"Dear Lord..." Tony whispered, still stunned by Felix's account.

"Wow. What an amazing guy," Noah muttered, his eyes narrowing thoughtfully. He tilted his head, considering the possibilities. "No chance he's in the mafia or a gang, right? Gangs can be pretty crazy these days. They could be in a turf war or something."

Felix's eyes flicked down to Noah. His mind reeled at the suggestion. He knew a thing or two about organized crime, especially with his grandfather, a mafia executive, and his work as an arms dealer. Weapons were part of his everyday life, and he was accustomed to being around dangerous people who wielded them. But Isaac? Isaac didn't fit that mold.

Felix was more businessman than mafioso. Despite his deep knowledge of them, he never had the same opportunity to wield weapons as others. Yet, even among his grandfather's subordinates, he had never encountered someone like Isaac—someone with that unique, unsettling calm in the face of danger.

"They weren't some puny gangsters," Felix said.

Noah sighed, clearly disappointed by the answer. He slithered back into his chair, looking like an octopus trying to blend into the background.

"Find out where the shooters who got themselves killed today are from. The SDPD, the FBI—shake them down. We need to know who ordered the attack, first and foremost."

"This is getting really complicated," Noah grumbled, his fingers typing halfheartedly on the keyboard.

"Afterward, look into Isaac again. I won't let this slide. Something's up. Investigate everything—who he is, who his stepfather is, how his father died. All of it."

"Fuck, that's easy for you to say."

"You always bragged about being the world's best hacker.

Now show your stuff."

"I've shown you plenty! I'm a hacker, not a private investigator," Noah shot back, as though personally offended, but Felix ignored him.

"Search everything. I don't care where."

Noah sighed dramatically, mussing his hair and glaring at the screen as if it were personally responsible for his predicament. He muttered curses under his breath, but Felix was already turning to leave when he saw the exaggerated pout on Noah's face.

Felix clucked his tongue, "If you pull this off, I'll get you something good. So get to work."

Felix's voice wasn't enthusiastic, but Noah's olive-green eyes immediately lit up, "Like what? What are you going to get me?"

"That mega dildo with all those add-ons you kept pestering me about."

"Oh…That sounds delicious."

Felix snorted in disbelief, but Noah was already salivating, eyes shining. Despite Felix's half-hearted offer, Noah always quickly seized any opportunity.

Noah, a hyper-dominant omega with an aversion to alpha pheromones, had never liked the scent of others—particularly alphas. That didn't mean he preferred betas, though; he simply preferred machines, dildos, and sex toys to people. His sex drive was off the charts, and more often than not, he had something up his ass. Maybe even now, Felix mused, crinkling his brow. He was a pervert among perverts.

Felix, of course, knew this well. A big part of why he disliked omegas was an unpleasant encounter four years ago where an omega broke his arm. And Noah, as an example of a hyper-dominant omega, certainly didn't help matters. Still, Felix had gotten used to Noah's peculiarities over the years.

Noah, who had previously been flopping like an octopus, was now waving his hand enthusiastically, "Don't forget to buy it, alright? It has to be one the size of your forearm."

"Just do your job." Felix, clearly done with the conversation, turned coldly to leave. Tony, walking behind him, quickly typed a message on his phone, relaying orders to look into the thugs who shot up Isaac's shop and to prepare to strike.

They left the cluttered basement and headed up the stairs.

"Double the guards around Benjamin," Felix spat out suddenly, his tone testy.

Tony raised an eyebrow in surprise at the unexpected order. He asked back, despite himself, "Boss?"

But then Felix said something even more surprising, "No, actually, better to bring him here. Benjamin and Isaac's mother both. Show them here and be cordial about it. Having them stay here will be the 'safest.'"

Tony blinked in confusion. "How did you come to that conclusion?"

Felix stopped and turned around, flashing a cool smile that sent a chill down Tony's spine. "Isaac asked me to 'take care of Benjamin.' And where would be safer than my house?"

Tony was silent for a beat.

"Besides, to catch Isaac again, I need a lure. And the best lure is none other than his mother and Benjamin."

The way Felix's lips curled into a twisted smile made him look almost sinister. Tony couldn't argue with that logic, but it only left him with more questions. What had Isaac done to provoke this cold, calculating side of Felix? The kind that made Tony afraid to say the wrong thing.

Felix's voice cut through the silence. "Let's see how long he lasts."

With that ominous remark, Felix turned and continued up the stairs, his footsteps ringing in Tony's ears. Tony had no choice but to mask his unease, his mind racing, and follow after him.

Chapter 31

Isaac's eyes cracked open under the blinding sunlight. His eyelids felt swollen, and his head throbbed in protest. With a grunt, he tried to adjust to the brightness, squinting as his blurred vision tried to make sense of his surroundings. A heavy sigh escaped his lips. He must have passed out.

He was slouched in the driver's seat of the sedan he'd stolen from Felix, his head resting against the handle. The hours must have slipped by unnoticed. Regret washed over him as he straightened his spine, the dull ache in his body reminding him of the recklessness of the last night.

He glanced around the interior of the car with a frown. The key and a Beretta lay on the passenger seat—the items Felix had left behind. The bag full of weapons he'd taken from the shop was in the backseat. Seeing the evidence of everything that had unfolded made his stomach churn. If only it had been a bad dream. But the reality of it all sat heavy, undeniable.

Isaac released a deep, weary sigh and climbed out of the car. The sun beat down relentlessly, but the morning breeze was uncomfortably cold, carrying the scent of dry earth with it. The gas station on the freeway east of San Diego was deserted, the wind swirling around in mournful gusts.

This part of the state felt like an endless stretch of nothing beyond the cities. The freeway connected urban centers with nothing more than rocky hills and vast expanses of wilderness, which grew more barren the farther one got from the coast.

It was the same with the gas stations: sparse, isolated, with only a parking lot, restrooms, and occasionally a few vending machines for company. Some didn't even have those. They existed simply as pitstops—places to rest, stretch, and move on.

Isaac walked through the empty gas station lot, his footsteps echoing in the quiet morning. Inside the restroom, he relieved himself and washed his face, scrubbing away the dried blood and grime. But it didn't do much. He still looked as bad as before, if not worse. The mirror, a dull sheet of stainless steel marred with graffiti, reflected a man he barely recognized. His face was drawn, eyes hollow.

He clucked his tongue, irritated with himself, but instead of tending to his wounds, he fished out the phone he'd grabbed from the shop. He checked the map. His destination was still a bit further—an hour, maybe two, to a small town. There, at a nameless community bank, he grabbed something he had planted there earlier.

His plan wasn't fully fleshed out, but he couldn't afford to waste time. Isaac rewashed his hands, wiped his face, and walked back outside. The dry desert air sucked the moisture from his skin, leaving him feeling even more parched. The silence of the barren landscape was deafening.

San Diego might have been a beach city, but the desert further inland was blistering and oppressive. Yet, Isaac moved forward as though he couldn't feel the heat or the weight of the world pressing down on him. His face remained as dry as the wasteland around him.

As he neared the sedan, he heard the distinct click of the door opening. The sound caught his attention, and suddenly, Felix flashed in his mind. The memory of Felix glaring at him—furious, yet strangely concerned—clung to his thoughts. The way those blue eyes had drilled into him, full of anger and worry. Isaac instinctively clutched his chest, a sharp, unfamiliar pain spreading through him.

He stood frozen for a moment, trying to understand the ache in his heart. By remembering he was the one who pushed Felix away and ran, a dry wasteland of emotions originated from his heart. It cracked, like his heart had turned into an entire desert.

"Felix…" he murmured, the name like a weight he couldn't lift from his chest.

The sun blazed overhead, relentless and scorching as if trying to sear him alive. It was nothing like the warmth he'd once enjoyed with Felix at that distant resort. Felix, who always reminded him of the cool, endless ocean, had been by his side back then. Now, in Felix's absence, the heat seemed unbearable.

He missed him. A deep, unshakable thirst gnawed at Isaac, leaving him wanting—always wanting.

Isaac jolted awake, gasping for air. His chest rose and fell with ragged breaths as his wide, trembling eyes scanned the room. He lay sprawled on the bed in a dingy motel, the kind of place he'd never imagined staying. Slowly, it came back to him—he'd dragged himself here the night before, collapsing the moment he hit the mattress.

A long sigh escaped him. The dream had slipped away the instant he opened his eyes, but the lingering unease left his heart pounding. He'd been too tense, too wound up from running.

With a groan, Isaac forced his aching body upright. His eyes burned as he blinked at the clock on the battered nightstand. Two days had passed since his flower shop was riddled with bullets since he'd fled in Felix's car. He'd been teetering on the edge of consciousness ever since.

Shoving the clock aside, he glanced down at himself. His shirt clung to him, damp with sweat and smeared with blood. He hadn't changed since the day Cole abducted him. The filthy, stained fabric was a revolting reminder of everything he'd endured.

He stared at the shirt for a moment before yanking it off and tossing it into the trash. His pants and underwear followed. Without hesitation, he stepped into the shower, the thought of cleanliness a small comfort in the chaos.

Isaac stood under the hot stream for what felt like an eternity. The stinging pain from his still-healing wounds barely registered. His mind wandered, caught in the haze of exhaustion and fractured memories.

By the time he emerged, the heat of the water had eased his tension, washing away some of the dream's unsettling grip. He dried off, applied medicine to his wounds with careless precision, and wrapped them haphazardly. As he moved, a sharp growl from his stomach broke the silence.

He needed to eat.

Isaac put on a clean white T-shirt and the plain pants he'd bought from the shop next door. After gathering his belongings, he stepped outside.

The town lay about two hundred miles from San Diego, but the dry, punishing heat felt no different than it had on the freeway. The sun's relentless glare beat down on him, unchanged, as though mocking the chaos that had upended his life. The world carried on, indifferent to his suffering. He let out a bitter smile.

Could he ever reclaim the brief, fragile peace he'd known in San Diego? The question lingered unanswered, heavy in his mind.

Isaac began to walk, aimless and unsteady, like a shadow of himself—just another lost soul.

After forcing down a meal he could barely swallow after days of starvation, he made his way to the bank. In his grasp was the document Steve and Cole had both been desperate to take from him. He stared at the envelope in his hand.

"All that for this."

He recalled the conflicted emotions and emptiness he'd felt when he first obtained it long ago. Part of him had taken it out of necessity, just to survive. Another part had acted out of sheer desperation, overwhelmed by the chaos of his circumstances and thoughts. He'd grabbed what was within reach without considering the consequences.

But now, everything was different. He no longer cared who

ended up with it—he just wanted it out of his life. He wanted to scream at them to leave him alone.

He didn't care about clearing his name or reclaiming the status and position they dangled before him. He was not interested in risking his life for the greater good. The only thing he would protect with his life was Benjamin. Nothing else mattered.

But Cole wouldn't listen. He didn't care about Isaac's terms. He wanted both Isaac and the document—or neither. Shooting up the flower shop had made that abundantly clear. Cole's men had fired indiscriminately, knowing that Isaac could have been inside.

Or perhaps Cole had always intended to kill him. Maybe the document was just an excuse, and Cole had been waiting for the chance. Isaac didn't know then, and he still didn't know now. Cole's thoughts were an impenetrable maze.

Isaac's gaze lingered on the thick envelope before shoving it into his bag, resigned. He stepped out onto the street, his mind a storm of disorganized thoughts. But amidst the chaos, one path stood out.

He had to contact *him*.

Isaac bit his lip and kept walking, determination flickering to life beneath his exhaustion.

The situation was spiraling out of control. Cole was relentless, a formidable opponent, but Isaac couldn't afford to remain paralyzed. If he wanted to end this quickly, he needed help—just like Steve had suggested.

Though he wanted nothing more than to avoid this, Isaac sighed quietly, his expression conflicted as he glanced around. Down the street, a worn blue phone booth caught his eye. He stared at it with unease before dragging himself toward it, each step feeling heavier than the last.

His chest tightened as the booth grew closer, his heart hammering. *Please, let this be over without anything happening to Benjamin.* That was his only wish.

His face remained taut, his jaw clenched as he walked. The

booth, which had seemed impossibly distant, finally loomed before him. Isaac snatched up the receiver without hesitation. His fingers moved instinctively, slipping a coin into the slot and dialing a number he'd envisioned calling countless times before.

His pocket vibrated as he punched in the last digit of the area code. The timing was so precise it felt surreal, almost as if the number he was dialing on the payphone was calling him back.

Isaac froze, his breath catching. A cold dread slithered up his spine. No one had this number. The phone wasn't even registered under his name, and he hadn't used it once. It was meant for emergencies only, yet here it was, ringing.

With a pale face as though he were seeing a ghost, Isaac pulled the phone from his pocket. His other hand gripped the payphone receiver, which rang faintly in his ear. His ear concentrated on the faraway ringing as his eyes dropped to the mobile. His eyes darted between the mobile and the receiver. The caller ID flashed "Unknown."

Isaac's brow furrowed as his grip tightened. His mind raced. He hesitated, debating whether to hang up or answer.

Isaac's heart pounded erratically. He stared at the screen, frozen. Then, his thumb hovered before pressing the accept button as if hypnotized. He couldn't bring himself to speak. The phone was pressed against his ear, his breath shallow as he waited for the other side to break the silence.

"Cat got your tongue? You should say something when you answer the phone." The voice, low and annoyed, sent his chest plummeting. Isaac's vision blurred, a stark white haze overtaking him. His throat constricted painfully, choking him into silence. "Kay, I told you, didn't I? I know everything about you. I might have let you slip away these past four years when I didn't know where you were hiding, but now that I do, did you think I'd just sit back and watch?"

Isaac's fingers felt numb, and his palms were slick with cold sweat as he gripped the phone. His breaths came in shallow, panicked gasps.

"Even before I gave the order to grab you, I was busy watching, gathering information, and preparing. I had to be ready to catch you properly. But look at you—still running. What a troublesome child."

A click of the tongue crackled through the speaker, and Isaac shuddered, goosebumps rising across his skin. His body remained frozen, unable to breathe as his heart thundered in his chest, threatening to burst from his throat.

Watched for days? Isaac's mind reeled. He hadn't noticed anything. Not a single sign. *Dear God.* Had he been so careless, or were Cole's men that skilled? How much had they uncovered? His thoughts spun, a chaotic storm he couldn't calm.

"Hah…" A shaky, defeated sigh escaped his lips.

From the payphone receiver still in his opposite hand came a distant, sharp "Hello?"

It was Steve. The very person Isaac had resolved to contact for help, to whom he planned to hand over the documents just moments ago.

Isaac snapped back to reality at Steve's voice, his gaze falling to the payphone receiver in his trembling hand. He swallowed hard, one hand gripping the mobile, the other clutching the receiver. His shaking eyes betrayed the storm inside him.

"Kay, or should I say, Isaac?" Cole's flat, unyielding tone crackled through the mobile. Isaac's shoulders tensed at the sound of his real name, his mind grinding to a halt.

If Cole's words were true, if he had been watching and piecing everything together, then finding out his identity would have been easy. Hearing his name spoken aloud was confirmation. Isaac bit down hard on his lip.

"Isaac Sinclair," Cole mused. "I didn't know you went by that name. Well, we'll talk about it later—it's not that shocking."

Isaac remained frozen, unable to process the fact that everything about him had been laid bare. Meanwhile, Cole shifted topics, his tone disturbingly casual, "You've got the document, haven't you?"

Isaac's throat was parched. From the payphone, Steve's voice grew more frantic. "Kay, is that you? Answer me!"

But Isaac couldn't respond. His clammy hands clenched tighter around both phones, barely holding onto them.

"I won't waste words. Bring the document to me," Cole ordered coldly. "I already know where you're staying." Isaac's breath hitched as Cole continued, his tone laced with veiled menace, "And don't tell me you gave it to Steve. If you did, you'll need to retrieve it. That would be…troublesome."

"Why should I…" Isaac's voice cracked, barely above a whisper. The sound felt foreign, raw.

"Why should you?" Cole echoed smoothly, finishing the sentence for him. "You know the answer better than I do."

"What are you talking about?"

"My, how clueless you're being," Cole said, almost amused. "I told you—I've uncovered everything. There's no escape. Today, I learned your name. But that wasn't the most surprising thing. Oh no, there was something far more…astonishing."

Each word felt like a hammer blow, Isaac's heart pounding louder and faster. He couldn't bring himself to ask what it was, the weight of dread pressing down on him like a stone. He wanted to cover his ears.

"Soon, my men will be in San Diego," Cole continued nonchalantly. "And you'll have no choice but to come running to me."

"Cole…" Isaac whispered hoarsely.

"Oh, one last thing," Cole added lightly, as though sharing a joke. "While I was working on all this, I came up with a code name for you. Thought it might be fitting."

Cole's flippant tone felt like a knife twisting in Isaac's gut. The payphone crackled as Steve's voice repeated his other name, but it sounded distant and muffled, like a faint buzz in the back of his mind.

"Aren't you curious to know what I named it?" Cole's smiling, sinister voice grew clearer and clearer. Isaac squeezed his eyes shut and tightened his grip on the phone.

"Stop joking around." Isaac's voice snapped, sharp and desperate.

But Cole's whisper came, low and menacing, "The code name is—"

"Cole!"

"Dear Benjamin."

An icy chill crawled up Isaac's spine, freezing him to the core. He couldn't blink, couldn't look away. The hand holding the phone trembled violently. He couldn't breathe, as though someone was choking him.

Isaac's teeth clenched, his resolve breaking. With a sharp motion, he slammed the payphone's receiver down, the clang echoing in the empty street. His chest heaved, ragged breaths tearing at his cracked lips.

"This is the surprising piece of information I received this morning."

"Don't you dare lay a hand on him. I'll make you pay." His voice shook, darkened with fury. Cole's laughter echoed on the other end of the line, twisting Isaac's insides.

The sound was a blade in his chest, but Isaac couldn't stop himself. He started moving, stumbling at first, but his steps quickened. His eyes lifted, and he was running now, dust clouds billowing beneath his feet.

"I don't intend to make you angry. You should stop making me angry, too—fair's fair. By the way, I was shocked to learn you had a child. Who's the mother?"

"Don't touch him. Don't you dare touch him!" Isaac's voice was raw and desperate, his face turning blue with the effort.

"It's not like you to get worked up. We'll have that conversation when we meet, shall we? You'd better hurry with the document. My patience has worn thin after waiting four years. Don't waste any more of my time."

With that, Cole hung up.

Isaac stood there momentarily, the phone still clutched in his hand, silent now. Then he bolted down the empty street, his steps frantic. When he reached his car—a black sedan now coated in dust—he threw himself into the driver's seat, slamming the door behind him.

He started the engine, the tires screeching as he hit the road. His vision blurred, and nothing in front of him was registering. With a trembling hand, he dialed his mother, but she didn't answer for some reason.

There was no time to wait. He had no choice but to retrace his steps, heading back up the same freeway he'd driven just two days ago, his foot pressing the accelerator to the floor.

Chapter 32

Felix tossed the tablet onto the table and looked up. "She agreed?"

"Yes, Mrs. Parker has accepted."

"Ah, finally."

At Tony's succinct report, Felix drummed his fingers on the table. The faint twist of his lips made him look devilish—like a villain savoring the capture of a hostage. Still, it was an improvement. Ever since Isaac had threatened him at gunpoint and "stolen" the car, nothing had managed to pull Felix out of his foul mood.

Tensions simmered across the estate. Felix prowled around like a lit fuse—one wrong move, and heads were sure to roll. Everyone tread carefully, not wanting to be the one to set him off.

"Treat her with respect. If you offend her, I'll break your bones," Felix said coldly.

"Understood." Tony nodded, gauging Felix's mood. It seemed to have calmed slightly, though the glint in his icy blue eyes remained unsettling.

Three days earlier, on the morning Isaac left, Felix had ordered Tony to bring Isaac's mother and Benjamin to the estate. Tony had gone at sunrise to make the request. But, unaware of the situation, Jessica responded with confusion and hesitation, saying she'd think it over.

It was no surprise. Who would uproot their life based on the word of a stranger they'd met only once? Her suspicions were natural, especially with Isaac being unreachable. Felix hadn't been disappointed by her initial refusal, nor had Tony. They'd chosen patience, making polite, persistent requests and emphasizing the supposed safety of the move.

Today, at last, Jessica had agreed. Her decision came faster than expected—perhaps out of concern for Benjamin after Isaac's disappearance or possibly because Felix's persistence had worn her down. Whatever the reason, as soon as she gave her answer, Tony sent a team to La Jolla to pack her belongings. Now, he was reporting back to Felix.

After issuing his warning to handle her carefully, Felix turned his gaze to the window, his expression indifferent. Tony exhaled quietly in relief. He was grateful Jessica hadn't resisted further. If she had, Felix might have remained locked in this icy, volatile state until the day he caught Isaac.

"Shall I proceed with the others as planned?" Tony asked cautiously.

Felix didn't respond. Propping his chin on his hand, he simply stared out the window, lost in thought. Tony followed his gaze.

Felix's private residence was perched atop a high hill, offering an unbroken view of the vast, open sea. The study's glass wall frames the breathtaking scene, creating a perfect panorama of serenity.

It was the kind of view that could soothe chaos—quiet, endless, and peaceful. Felix needed it now. Anger still simmered beneath the surface, but the calm of the horizon worked to tether him, piece by piece.

Staring quietly beyond the sea, Felix spoke as if the thought had just struck him. "Call the maid and nanny we hired for Mrs. Parker. Tell them to come in immediately."

Tony snapped out of his thoughts. "Understood."

"Has she made any requests?" Felix turned away from the window, fixing his sharp gaze on Tony.

"She mentioned that Benjamin gets anxious when they move and has trouble sleeping alone. She asked us to put his bed in her room."

"See to it. And you told her there's no need to bring her furniture?"

Tony nodded. "Of course. The move will be straightforward."

Even before Jessica agreed to come, Felix had prepared two rooms with the best views, furnishing them with a new bed, a child's bed, and a variety of high-end furniture. He'd claimed it would be inconvenient for her to move any of her own. The child's room, in particular, was so lavish it bordered on excessive.

True to Felix's impulsive nature, all preparations had been completed in just two days—despite Jessica's initial refusal. Luckily, her agreement came just as everything was set. Perfect timing.

She would bring only a few personal items: clothes, Benjamin's toys, and essentials. Anything else would be discarded or stored in a Public Storage unit. The move was intentionally kept simple.

Felix mentally reviewed the arrangements before abruptly rising. The chair scraped loudly against the floor. Tony glanced at him, puzzled by the sudden movement, especially with Jessica and Benjamin due to arrive shortly.

"Lead the way. I'm going to check on things," Felix said gruffly, shrugging on his jacket.

Tony blinked in surprise, stepping aside. "You're going to meet Benjamin yourself?"

"Yeah. I invited them; I should receive them."

"But you don't have to—"

"Just make sure this place is spotless. Clean the rooms again before they get here. And prepare a meal—something comforting, so they'll feel at ease in a new place." Felix cut off Tony's protests and strode out of the study without another word.

Tony stared blankly at the broad expanse of Felix's shoulders before shaking his head and following. Predicting Felix's next move had become impossible. The man's uncharacteristic behavior threw Tony off balance, and it didn't look like that would change anytime soon.

As the sedan glided into the La Jolla suburbs, Felix lowered the window and scanned the neighborhood. Everything looked just as it had during Benjamin's last birthday party. If anything had changed, the house near the entrance was now draped in colorful tarps like a circus tent—a clear sign of termite fumigation.

It hadn't been long, so perhaps it was unlikely for anything to have changed, yet these little things stood out in such a quiet and cozy neighborhood.

Felix's sharp eyes lingered on the tarped house before his frown deepened. With a sharp click of his tongue, he launched into a tirade. "Seriously? That house has termites? How can anyone raise a kid in an environment like this? Don't they know fumigants are toxic? It's terrible for children!"

Tony squinted at him, bewildered. Felix, undeterred, continued. "They *have* to move. No question about it. Do you know how clean the air is at my place? Ocean views, fresh air, complete security—no one could even dream of breaking in. There's no better place to raise a child."

Arms crossed and chin jutting out, Felix surveyed the neighborhood with his usual air of arrogance. He looked thoroughly satisfied with his conclusion as if the past few days of brooding and bad temper had never happened.

Tony, however, sighed beside him. "What does it matter? Any house around here could tarp up for fumigation. Even if the wind carries the fumes, they're too far away to cause any harm."

Felix turned, his eyes narrowing into a glare. "What? Toxic fumes blowing around, and you're saying they won't affect the kid? Are you serious?"

"You don't have to overreact like this. It won't harm him at all—"

"Tony."

The tone of Felix's voice dropped an octave, freezing Tony mid-sentence. He glanced up to find Felix's piercing blue eyes burning into him. Pressing his fingers to his lips, Tony sighed and turned away. It was time to hold his tongue.

"You're just complaining because Benjamin and Mrs. Parker

will live somewhere better than this," Felix accused.

"Certainly not..." Tony muttered.

"Then why won't you use your brain, huh?" Felix patted Tony on the shoulder, a crooked grin spreading across his face as he radiated a wild, dangerous aura. "I need Benjamin and Mrs. Parker to *enjoy* living in my house so Isaac stays put when I finally catch him. Don't you think?"

Tony's eyes widened as he stared at Felix. "Dear Lord. Were you really thinking that far ahead?"

"What? About catching Isaac?"

"No, I mean...you just said you'd have him *stay*..."

"And? Leave him out there to get beat up by those vulgar bastards? Here I am, holding myself back, savoring him, and they dare lay a hand on him? Motherfuckers," Felix growled, his scowl deepening as he worked himself into a fury.

Tony's jaw dropped. "So, you're planning to live with him?"

Felix shot him a glare that screamed stupidity. Tony sighed, realizing how idiotic his question sounded.

Felix clicked his tongue in irritation. "Of course. That way, I'll have peace of mind. It's good for Isaac, too—living with Benjamin like he's always dreamed of. Huh, I don't know why I didn't think of this sooner."

Felix rubbed his chin, a self-satisfied grin spreading across his face. Tony, meanwhile, looked completely aghast.

"You'd better just marry him." The words escaped before Tony could stop them.

"What kind of nonsense is that?" Felix snapped, glaring at Tony out of the corner of his eye.

Before the conversation could escalate, the rough roar of a car engine cut through the air. Both men turned toward the sound. Tony's eyes narrowed as a black sedan sped through the residential street, well over the 25 mph limit, pushing 50.

Tony creased his brow. Felix also turned his gaze suspiciously. At the same time, the black car overtook Felix's leisurely cruising sedan—the car passed by Felix's window, a dark blur.

"What kind of crazy bastard..." Felix muttered, irritation clear in his tone.

"Hey!" Tony suddenly shouted, cutting him off, prompting Felix to ask him what the fuck he was thinking.

The speeding car wasn't just any car—it was familiar. And the driver...

"Floor it!" Tony barked at their driver.

"What the fuck are you talking about?" Felix snapped, his annoyance growing.

"Isaac! That was Isaac!"

"What?"

"That car—it's the sedan Isaac took!" Tony shouted, slapping the back of the driver's seat. The driver scrambled to accelerate, but Isaac's car had already disappeared from view.

"Was that really him?" Felix asked.

"I'm *telling* you it was him!" Tony squawked, fumbling for his phone as it began to ring. He answered it sharply, not taking his eyes off the road. "What?"

"We're in deep shit, bro! Real deep shit!" Jack's panicked voice crackled through the line. "Some freaks in black masks broke in and took Benjamin— Fuck, no, don't lose them!"

Shouting and chaos erupted in the background, punctuated by blood-curdling screams. Tony tried to respond, but the line went dead before Jack could explain further.

Tony stared at his silent phone, gripping it tightly as his brow furrowed.

"What on earth..." Tony muttered, disbelief etched on his face. He hadn't expected a call like this from Jack, who had gone ahead to help Benjamin and Jessica with the move. But it didn't take long to piece things together—the thugs who had tried to kill Isaac must have broken in and kidnapped Benjamin and Jessica. A chill ran down his spine.

If Jack had called, the situation was dire. There was a high chance he'd been injured. Usually, Jack would have handled things himself, and if he were in combat, he'd be too busy protecting Benjamin and Jessica to make a call.

Tony bit his lip, gripping the phone tightly as his mind raced. Isaac's sudden appearance and Jack's ominous call jumbled together in his head, leaving him disoriented.

"What are you waiting for?" Felix's dark baritone cut through the chaos, sharp and commanding. "Floor it."

Chapter 33

Tires screeched, deafeningly loud. The car screeched to a halt next to the sidewalk, and Isaac leaped out without hesitation. He didn't see anything else—his focus was on the house. Though he'd made a three- or four-hour trip in under two, something already felt off.

Sweat dripped down his temple as he wiped it away with the back of his hand, gripping his Beretta tightly. He tugged his baseball cap lower, masking his face.

The garden was eerily undisturbed, but chaos erupted from inside the house. Breaking glass shouted curses, panicked screams, and sporadic gunfire shattered the quiet of the neighborhood.

Isaac's palms were slick as he clenched and unclenched them, his nerves wound tight. He stayed hidden, scanning the house. The racket meant one thing: they hadn't gotten away with Benjamin and his mother yet. If they had, there would've been silence. Felix's men, touted as highly skilled, were putting up a fight.

Isaac exhaled shakily, relief flickering through him—at least they hadn't taken his mother and Benjamin yet. There was still a chance to stop them. He couldn't let them be taken. But he knew all too well that hope alone wasn't enough.

Steeling his nerves, Isaac willed his racing heart to steady and scanned the surroundings again, sharp and focused. How long would he have to wait for them to come out? Should he enter the fray? Isaac gritted his teeth, his anxiety rising as he assessed the situation.

Suddenly, the second-floor window shattered, and a dark figure flew through it. The man was hurled out, crashing to the lawn with a massive thud, shards of glass scattering around him. But instead of focusing on the unconscious figure, Isaac's attention was drawn to the chaotic noise spilling from the broken window.

No one would believe this happened in a peaceful neighborhood in La Jolla. Amid the clamor, faint cries of a child pierced the air. Isaac's eyes widened at the sound, his heart skipping a beat.

At that moment, a figure whipped past the broken window—his mother, pale and trembling, clutching Benjamin in her arms. Someone appeared to pull her along; she stumbled as if shoved, then disappeared from view. But the child's cries still pierced the air, cutting through the brutal chaos.

Unable to stand the chill crawling down his spine any longer, Isaac threw caution to the wind and ran toward the house; Beretta in hand, he muffled his footsteps as he pushed the door open, only to be met with complete mayhem inside.

The house was beyond salvage. Broken furniture and debris littered the floor as Benjamin's bodyguards fought off the assailants. Blood was splattered across the room, and knives gleamed as they were brandished in the fray. Men lay scattered, some moaning in pain, others motionless—likely dead.

Isaac entered through the open door, Beretta in hand, and concealed himself behind the first-floor bathroom door. In the chaos of the fight, no one seemed to notice his arrival. They were all too focused on the battle at hand.

Though the first floor was a gruesome scene, Isaac's attention remained fixed on the second floor, where his mother and Benjamin were. He barely registered anything else; the child's cries echoed in his ears. If he had his way, he'd rush upstairs immediately, but the stairs were positioned right in the middle of the living room, where the brawl was raging.

Isaac pressed the gun tightly against his chest, swallowing dryly before taking a deep breath. Just as he was about to make his move, a group of men descended from the second floor—it seemed the fight upstairs had ended with one side utterly wiped out. The silence that followed was proof enough.

All of them wore black masks and clothes, each armed with

a gun—except for the slim, middle-aged woman in their midst, holding a child.

Benjamin was sobbing, burying his head in his grandmother's chest. His bright blond hair looked pitiful against the chaos around him. Jessica, clutching him as tightly as she could, was dragged down the stairs by the masked assailants. Her face was pale, her legs trembling so violently it was almost palpable from a distance. The only thing keeping her from stumbling was the thug gripping her arm with brutal force.

Isaac shut his eyes, then opened them again. The next sound was the muffled crack of gunfire. It wasn't his. The shots came from the group descending the stairs, firing at Benjamin's bodyguards, still locked in combat on the first floor.

Terrible screams echoed through the room, followed by the unmistakable sound of gunfire. The assailants seemed determined to leave none of Felix's men alive. In the relentless barrage of bullets, the bodyguards fell one by one. Within seconds, the room was silent.

The child's cries cut through the stillness. Jessica was doing her best to shield Benjamin's head, trying to protect him from the gunshots and prevent him from seeing the bloody aftermath of the fallen men.

"Don't dawdle, move!" One of the thugs barked, jabbing the muzzle of his gun into Jessica's shoulder as she hesitated, taking her time descending the stairs. Behind the door, Isaac aimed his Beretta, gritting his teeth. He longed to charge at the thug and punch him in the jaw, but the harsh reality was that he couldn't make his anger boil over.

Isaac took a deep breath, forcing the rage in his chest to subside, and moved only his eyes to assess the situation. Five men were surrounding his mother and Benjamin.

With the bodyguards on the first floor wiped out, the three remaining assailants cautiously approached the group. One was limping, another was bleeding from a wound in his arm, but they were still in relatively good condition. To make matters worse, they all were alert, clutching their guns and knives.

Eight in total. If there were no hostages, Isaac might have attempted a preemptive strike, but with the situation as it was, it seemed nearly impossible. One wrong move, and he could hit Benjamin or his mother, or the thugs might use the hostages as shields, putting them at even greater risk.

Fuck. Isaac swallowed back a curse. But just then, one of the men in the lead glanced down at his chest and muttered in confusion, “Huh?” Isaac’s eyes followed his gaze, and he immediately recognized a laser’s unmistakable red spot.

As soon as he registered what it was, blood burst from the thug’s chest with a sickening, pulpy sound, and he fell backward. The crash echoed across the floor. Isaac’s breath caught in his throat. The shot was quick and clean, ringing out before he could even process a single thought.

What?

There was no time to think. The red laser sight, aimed from outside the window, shifted to the next target. Less than a second after the dot zeroed in, another thug’s chest erupted in blood.

No hesitation, no error. The third shot followed with terrifying speed, and now three men lay with ruptured chests. The remaining thugs went pale, scrambling to move as fast as they could.

Isaac, equally tense, gripped his Beretta tightly. The sniper fire had come completely out of nowhere. He couldn’t understand it—his mind was flooded with questions.

Who was the sniper outside? Were there still some of Felix’s men around? Did Felix have a sniper? There was a slim chance the sniper was part of the security team. A bodyguard’s job was to protect the client’s immediate vicinity, not to carry a sniper rifle. Besides, it was rare for a sniper to be that skilled.

The moment of doubt was brief. Isaac gritted his teeth and lifted his eyes. Whatever the case, this was fortunate. It was his only chance. With three men down, the room erupted into chaos

once more.

The men, who had thought wiping out the bodyguards and leaving with Jessica and Benjamin would be simple, were now shouting in panic over the unexpected sniper fire.

"What the hell? Get away from the window! Tell the car to wait at the back door, now!"

With the shots ringing through the window, the men quickly shifted from heading toward the front door to the back, clearly on edge. Their mission had been within reach, only to be on the brink of failure.

Where they had once moved as a unified wall around Jessica, they now broke formation, scrambling to evade the incoming fire. Two of the thugs stayed close, flanking her. Isaac seized the opportunity and pulled the trigger.

The semi-automatic Beretta fired twice. The bullets struck one thug—a bit apart from the group, peering out the window—hitting him in the stomach and shoulder. He collapsed forward, limp.

"The fuck? There's still someone inside!"

Now that bullets were coming from both inside and outside, the thugs erupted in fury, raising their guns and firing toward Isaac's hiding spot. The shots ricocheted off the walls, and Jessica screamed, collapsing to the floor, Benjamin still in her arms.

After the loud gunshots and his grandmother's collapse, Benjamin, who had been hiccupping in her arms, began to wail hysterically. "Wahhh! Grandma!"

Isaac grimaced, his teeth grinding together.

How strange. Shots were flying all around him, rattling his skull, but he couldn't hear any of it. All he could hear was Benjamin's cries. The child's sobbing ripped Isaac's mind to pieces. His pulse thudded in his eardrums. His impatience and anxiety shot up his spine, settling in his head.

Benjamin... Benjamin...

Isaac's hand trembled around the Beretta's grip. He had never been this tense; his heart had never raced so fast. He was always confident in his shooting, always more level-headed and unaffected than anyone else. But right now, with nothing but the sound of the child's desperate wails filling his ears, it was impossible to stay calm.

Isaac shut his eyes, then opened them again, clenching his teeth. With a swift motion, he turned his body and pulled the trigger. Two shots rang out, and the assailant closest to him went down with a scream.

"Near the entrance, behind the door!"

After firing, Isaac ducked behind the wall, narrowly dodging the return fire. He pressed his back against the wall, taking deep breaths as he strained his ears to hear Jessica comforting Benjamin. The three remaining men continued to fire, indiscriminately spraying bullets.

While Isaac remained pinned behind the wall, the men hauled Jessica to her feet and sprinted toward the opposite end of the house. As they'd mentioned earlier, they were heading for the back door.

Amidst the returning fire, Isaac listened intently to their footsteps, counting the seconds until they reached the kitchen. The moment they disappeared around the corner, he surged forward. But it was harder than he anticipated to catch up. Benjamin's cries were growing fainter, slipping farther away. The hand gripping the Beretta grew slick with cold sweat.

Crossing the living room and entering the kitchen, Isaac spotted the disappeared men. A van sat waiting in front of the kitchen door leading to the backyard; its front end rammed through the wooden fence to get inside.

The men were forcing Jessica into the open doors of the van. Benjamin clung to his grandmother's clothes, sobbing with fear. The men shouted at him to shut up, only making him cry harder.

"Benjamin… Benjamin!" Isaac's mind snapped at the sight. He ran, his vision tunneling in on Benjamin and nothing else. The thought of losing him like this made his heart pound so violently that it felt as though it might burst.

"Daddy? Daddy, wahhh, Daddy!" Benjamin's tear-filled eyes locked onto Isaac's voice, and he wailed even more desperately. He flailed his little hands as if trying to run to him.

His mother looked up, her face etched with surprise, "Stop! Benjamin!"

But the men shoved her into the van, paying no attention to her cries. Thrown into the van with Benjamin in her arms, Jessica moaned in pain. Benjamin's cries grew louder, more frantic.

Don't cry, Benjamin. Don't cry. I'm coming. Isaac shouted in his heart, his chest tight with anguish, the pain nearly suffocating him.

Isaac fired as he ran, but his gun shook. His aim missed the men scrambling into the van. They slammed the accelerator, and as the van lurched forward, they raised their guns at Isaac. But all he saw was his mother, holding Benjamin, her face blurred with the desperation to reach them. He didn't notice the barrels pointed at him. Through the doors not yet fully closed, Benjamin's tear-streaked face appeared.

Benjamin…

Isaac's heart twisted. He needed to wipe away the tears and snot, to tell him everything would be okay. He needed to pull him close, reassure him, and kiss his soft, golden hair. Instead, he cursed the widening distance between him and the van as it rolled out of the yard. Isaac ran after it, his steps driven by a frantic, mindless need to reach Benjamin.

"Isaac!"

The voice rang through the chaos, a distant echo amid Benjamin's cries. Isaac thought faintly that it sounded almost like Felix. Then, someone tackled him to the ground.

A long, drawn-out gunshot followed. His body was thrown to the ground, his head hitting hard, the impact ringing in his skull. He heard the person who had tackled him yelp, but Isaac didn't look back. His eyes remained fixed on the van, watching it pull away with Benjamin inside.

"Ah, no…Benjamin…Mother…!" he mumbled like a madman, struggling to rise. But the dizziness in his head kept his limbs paralyzed, leaving him to flounder on the pavement, helpless. The thugs slammed the van doors shut, and he lost sight of Benjamin's tear-streaked face. His own eyes filled with tears.

He fumbled for the Beretta, gripping it in shaking hands, but the van was already gone. His whole body trembled—his hands, arms, legs—as if he were a leaf in the wind. His jaw quivered, teeth chattering uncontrollably.

"Benjamin! Benjamin! No!" Isaac screamed as though the words could tear him apart. His vision blurred to black, and his body gave in. He collapsed forward.

"Shit!" A voice cursed, but strong arms caught him before Isaac could process it. There was no strength left to stay awake. His eyelids closed heavily, but his tears continued to flow, unrelenting.

Chapter 34

Felix sat motionless, his chin propped up in his hand. Beside him, his doctor struggled to dress the wound on his shoulder from the near-miss bullet.

Felix, lost in thought, felt nothing.

"Isaac?" It was the first thing Felix had said in what felt like ages.

Having sewn up the wound and now gathering his things, the doctor paused. "He's still asleep."

"He's not seriously injured?"

"He has several wounds but no broken bones." The doctor answered carefully. "Due to the concussion, he might experience dizziness when he gets up. He's had a rough few days. He should be careful with what he eats and take time to rest."

Felix waved him off. The doctor nodded, quickly packed his bag, and left. Felix slipped his arms into his sleeves and stood.

Standing watch with a drawn expression, Tony rushed to his side, "Boss, are you alright?"

"No need to make a fuss over a flesh wound like this. How are Jack and the others?" Felix didn't bother buttoning his shirt as he walked to the minibar in his study and poured himself a glass of straight bourbon. The sound of the liquid filling the glass broke the heavy silence.

"Jack was shot in the side and thigh, but they said he'll recover soon enough. The others—three survived."

"The rest are dead?"

"Yes." Tony's reply was short and heavy with meaning.

Felix tossed back the bourbon and turned. "Who were those fuckers?"

"Mercenaries, according to Noah."

"Hired by whom?"

"Noah said he'd tell you himself."

"Oh?" Felix had been planning to see Noah anyway. He marched across the study and into the hall, his quick strides smooth as he buttoned his shirt. He looked unbothered, as if the bandage around his recently shot shoulder didn't exist.

A moment later, Felix stormed down the stairs to the basement and flung open the door.

Noah turned his head toward him, his mood markedly different from before. "Welcome back. Heard you got shot?"

"I'm not in the mood for jokes. Get to the point." Felix bared his teeth at Noah's comment and advanced.

Noah took in his expression—not one for humor—and shrugged. He knew the situation at the estate was serious and wasn't in the mood for jokes either. "I'm not joking. Just surprised to hear you tried to save Isaac and took the shot for him."

"Get to the damn point." Felix loomed over Noah, his voice edged with a razor-sharp tension. No matter the words, it was clear he wasn't in a good mood. Fifteen of his men were dead, Benjamin and Jessica Parker were kidnapped, Isaac had fainted from shock and wasn't waking up.

"I don't know if showing you this will make you feel better or worse. I, myself, was pretty turned on. Only managed to calm down because of your situation." Noah, attempting to tread lightly, opened his mouth, conscious of Felix's mood.

Felix narrowed his eyes, sensing something was off. "Let's hear it."

At his curt reply, Noah tapped his keyboard. "First off, the ones who shot up Isaac's shop the other day were mercenaries from an outsourcing company called Shadow. The ones who decimated your men today are probably from the same group."

"Shadow mercenaries? Who hired them?"

"Isn't that the million-dollar question? Who would hire mercenaries to go after your precious Isaac? So I went and unearthed their entire system." Noah spun a pen around his fingers, his eyes beginning to gleam disturbingly. He must have found something important. "And it all came to light, piece by piece…" Instead of immediately revealing what he'd uncovered, Noah posed a question, his face slightly flushed. "Do you know where I just hacked into?"

"How should I know?" Felix shot back, refusing to play games. "Get to the point."

Noah seemed to forget he was supposed to be gauging Felix's mood and stared at his monitor, his olive-green eyes glittering. Something flashed across the multiple screens in front of him. "The JSOC! Fuck! Can you believe it? Jesus Christ, the JSOC…! If I end up in prison, you're taking responsibility, got it?"

Noah's fingers danced over the keyboard as he ranted about landing in jail for hacking the Joint Special Operations Command.

"Are you trying to give me a headache, too? JSOC? Why the hell would you hack them and expect me to take responsibility?"

If Noah were caught hacking the JSOC and thrown behind bars, Felix would be right there with him or, at the very least, have to answer to many people. They were engaging in something they should never be caught doing. But the truth was, neither of them were truly worried about it.

"Oh, never mind. Why don't you sit down? Your legs might give out when you hear the info I've got for you." Noah shrugged.

Felix regarded him with cold amusement at the arrogant remark. "Fuck off with your unnecessary concern."

"I'm just looking out for you. But if you insist…"

"What are you so pompous about? It's not like a JSOC commander hired mercenaries." Felix commented casually, frowning at the screen.

"Ding, ding, ding!" Noah nodded, confirming Felix's suspicion. Felix's face twisted at his flippant tone.

"What the fuck are you—" Felix started, but Noah shrugged and tapped the keyboard. A large photo of a man in uniform appeared. As soon as Felix recognized him, his brow furrowed deeply. "That bastard…"

"Commander Cole Patricks of the Navy. You know him well, right?"

"Are you asking if I know this bastard of a bastard?" Was Noah trying to dredge up his past? Why was he showing Felix this creepy bastard's face? Felix gritted his teeth at the resurfacing memories, then shook it off and looked back at Noah. Felix muttered the thought aloud, "You're not telling me he's the one who hired mercs to kill Isaac and kidnap Benjamin, are you?"

Noah smirked. "You're quicker on the uptake than before."

"How is he connected to Isaac—"

"He's the guy you've been looking for all along."

Felix felt like he was holding a puzzle with no matching pieces. Noah snickered at the confusion flashing across Felix's face before throwing him a lifeline. "Your darling Isaac's stepfather is none other than this bastard. Cole Patricks."

"What?" For a moment, Felix went deaf to everything around him. He couldn't believe what he was hearing, even going so far as to scrub his ear with a finger. The identity of this person was dropped on him without warning, and it was impossible to process it any faster.

"Say that again. Isaac's stepfather is who?"

"Cole Patricks."

"This mad dog?"

Noah didn't answer Felix's disbelieving question. Instead, he flipped the pen between his fingers and pressed the keyboard again. The screen switched to a new face. A young man in the same uniform as Cole Patricks. Unfortunately, Felix recognized him all too well.

"Who do you think this is?" Noah asked, his lips curling into a smirk. Felix couldn't respond. He stood frozen, swallowing dryly. Noah continued, "Lieutenant Kaysid Patricks of the Navy. Cole's son. More accurately, his adopted son."

The man filling the screen looked no different from the one who had ordered Felix out of the car a few days ago, pointing a Beretta at him. If anything, his hair was long enough now to cover his forehead and sweep over his eyes, while the man on the screen had a military crew cut. The man on the screen was also more solidly built than the thinner figure before him.

And, of course, he looked younger. But aside from that, the same poker face, the unreadable black eyes, and the tightly pressed lips were all Isaac. Ah, but that same poker face had been shattered just hours ago…

Felix pushed the bitter thought aside and stared unblinkingly at the uniformed Isaac on the screen, who seemed to stare back at him. Isaac, so familiar that Felix could draw his face blindfolded, now seemed like a stranger.

If he were dealing with the police, the FBI, or even a SWAT team, Felix could have let it slide. But a Navy lieutenant? He was dumbfounded. And Cole Patricks' adopted son? It felt like he'd been hit with a sledgehammer.

"You were right. He can't be just an ordinary florist." Noah continued, unbothered by Felix's stunned silence as he stared at the screen. "But why couldn't I or your men find anything on him? Why do you know him as Isaac Sinclair, and he's registered as just a regular guy?"

Felix remained silent. Noah slapped his knee. "Because Isaac Sinclair and Kaysid Patricks are registered as completely different people! And it's not that one is fake—they're both legit. In other words, he has a dual identity for a pretty interesting reason."

With a tap, a photo of an unfamiliar man appeared on the screen. His androgynous face left little impression.

"Eugene Sinclair. Isaac Sinclair's biological father and Jessica Parker's ex-husband. Pretty normal, right? That's what we all know. But it turns out Eugene had a different name and career. Can you guess?"

Felix hesitated. Noah's eyes gleamed triumphantly, "A CIA

agent. His name as a CIA agent was Keith Benjamin Lee, Cole Patricks' partner."

"Preposterous."

"Right? I had to dig around the CIA for this! They had it locked up so tight, and if it weren't for me, no one would have gotten near it." Noah stuck his nose in the air while Felix rubbed his dry lips with the palm of his hand. Words failed him. His blue eyes trembled, revealing just how shaken he was.

Noah leaned back in his chair, a smirk tugging at the corners of his lips. He wasn't done yet. "Since Eugene had two different identities, his son ended up with two as well—Isaac Sinclair and Kaysid Lee. But when Kaysid Lee became Cole's son, he became Kaysid Patricks. Complicated, right?"

"Unbelievably," Felix muttered in annoyance, which Noah pretended not to hear.

Noah continued, "Isaac—well, Kaysid Lee—became Cole's adopted son when he was ten. After that, I think Cole purposely raised him to be a soldier. Probably wanted a son to succeed him? Anyway, Kaysid trained in all sorts of martial arts and combat. After high school, he went to the Naval Academy. His grades were stellar. As soon as he graduated, he moved up quickly and became a lieutenant at an unusually young age."

Watching Noah recite the profile of someone completely different from the Isaac Sinclair Felix had known, Felix made a sound in his throat and finally collapsed into an empty chair beside him. As Noah suggested earlier, his legs had gone out, and he could no longer stand.

"Isaac, a Navy lieutenant? How does that make sense? He gets seasick!" Felix felt an indescribable sense of wrongness, palming his forehead and raising his voice. It didn't help that Noah had never met Isaac and snorted in response.

"What do I care? I'm just telling you, it says Navy lieutenant on the record." Noah shrugged, then chugged a glass of water from the table.

Felix's throat was equally parched. Out of energy, he mumbled for water. Behind him, Tony—who had been listening to the conversation, equally stunned—hastened to hand him a bottle.

Felix twisted it open and drank. The cold, crisp water traveled down his throat, and he felt a bit saner for a moment. It was as if he'd been falling into the abyss for days because of Isaac, only now pulling himself back up. No, he was still trapped, flailing. Everything was a convoluted mess.

"Then what does he have to be on the run for?" Felix muttered. What kind of personal matter would cause a Navy lieutenant to run an unsuccessful flower shop and hide his identity? And why would his stepfather—Cole Patricks, of all people—be desperate enough to kill him and kidnap his son, Benjamin? The more Felix learned, the more lost he became.

He glared at the screen, his sense of futility growing. Just then, Noah slapped the glass of water down on the table. Tucking a fist under his chin, he eyed Felix intently, his pupils wide with excitement.

"Good question, Felix. The fun part's just starting." Noah grinned, his smile so wide it bordered on obscene, "Listen closely."

Felix froze mid-gulp, turning his icy gaze toward him. "What else is there? Isaac, who gets seasick, is a Navy lieutenant. His omega father was a CIA agent, and his stepfather is Cole fucking Patricks. What shocking piece of news is left?"

Noah's smile grew, but this time, it was too bright, too manic. It was the kind of excitement Felix only saw when Noah was in a rut, desperate for some twisted thrill. He dragged his chair closer to Felix as if savoring the moment. The whole purpose of Noah's hacking was to gather new information, especially sordid gossip, and get high on it. Felix didn't have to ask to know he was getting himself off on this.

"Noah, I'm already at my limit," Felix snapped. "My head is about to explode trying to process Isaac's ridiculous identity. If there's more—"

Noah cut him off with relish, his voice dropping to a conspiratorial whisper. “Kaysid Patricks is currently discharged from and wanted by the Navy.”

“What?” Felix’s eyes widened in disbelief.

Noah shushed him with a gesture and shook his head, signaling Felix to stay quiet and listen until he was done. “And you know who made that happen?”

“Don’t say fucking Cole Patricks,” Felix growled, his teeth clenched in frustration.

Noah flicked his finger dismissively. “Bingo. Cole. He dragged down his adoptive son and made him a wanted man.”

Felix let out a hollow laugh, his disgust palpable.

“With a laundry list of charges. Violation of duty, breach of confidentiality, desertion…and the biggest one—corruption.”

“Corruption? The pot calling the kettle black?” Felix scoffed.

“My words exactly. Whatever Kaysid did, it wouldn’t even make a dent in Cole’s bucket,” Noah added.

Felix rubbed his forehead, the headache intensifying. None of it made sense, and knowing Cole Patricks as he did, it felt like a sick joke.

“Unfortunately, that’s not all. The fun’s just beginning, remember?” Noah smirked.

“Noah…just spit it out.”

“Do you know where exactly Kaysid Patricks works?” Noah asked.

“The Navy?” Felix shot back.

“We’ve already established he’s in the Navy, you dunce,” Noah sneered, clearly unimpressed by Felix’s answer.

Felix hesitated, his brow furrowing. “Not the Navy SEALs, surely?”

Noah’s smile widened, and he chuckled darkly. “A notch above the Navy SEALs. Precisely, he was a member of the Naval Special Warfare Development Group—DEVGRU.”

“Fuck, stop with all this nonsense. DEVGRU…” Felix

muttered despondently, rubbing his forehead as if trying to ward off the crushing weight in his chest. It felt like a boulder had dropped onto him. Sure, his shooting skills were out of the ordinary, but this? This was too much. Isaac, a special ops agent dealing in counterterrorism? Who could have ever imagined?

There were plenty of bloodthirsty, inhuman lunatics in special forces—men who would mutilate corpses for sport. The stories surrounding them were dark, filled with trouble and horror. Of course, some of them had to be sane, but even psychiatrists said it was difficult for anyone who spent their life killing to maintain a normal mental state. Many soldiers in special ops had to commit to therapy after leaving the field.

Isaac, with his calm demeanor and innocent appearance, a DEVGRU agent? It was impossible to reconcile. But then, Felix's mind flashed back to Isaac handling that submachine gun like it was an extension of his own body. No hesitation. No fear. He shot with precision and coldness, which Felix could never have imagined.

Noah's voice slid into his ear, filled with amusement. "And there, he was in the Red Squadron. He was a team leader." Felix remained staring at the screen with shaky eyes, gripping his forehead. "Becoming a lieutenant at such a young age and leading a DEVGRU team? Yeah, he's not ordinary."

"It means there won't be bones left to pick once he's done with you," Felix murmured absently.

Noah's laughter deepened. "Who cares about bones at this rate? You're just fucked. He's practically a walking murder weapon—DEVGRU special ops agent!"

Noah mimicked the motion of cutting his throat with a line drawn across his neck. Unlike Felix, who sank deeper into disbelief, Noah seemed to enjoy himself more with each passing moment. Felix clenched his jaw, saying nothing for a long while. His face grew drawn.

It was more bizarre and complicated than he could have ever

guessed. How was he supposed to have known that the seemingly ordinary florist had a hidden past—that he was an ex-Navy lieutenant, a DEVGRU operative, and now on the run from Cole Patricks?

His head spun. It was all too much, too convoluted. He couldn't think straight. Noah watched him silently for a moment before tossing the pen he'd been absentmindedly spinning onto the table, a sigh escaping his lips. The gleeful look from before had vanished entirely.

"Felix," Noah began, his tone far more serious than before. "I'm saying this from the bottom of my heart, but I think it'll be best for you if you wash your hands of Isaac before things go to shit."

Felix blinked, taken aback. His brows furrowed in response.

"His personal matters are more complicated than I expected, but not so much that I need to wash my hands clean," Felix's voice darkened, his tone sharp with warning. He didn't want Noah to interfere.

Noah shook his head slowly. "I'm not just saying this because Kaysid's situation is shitty. I'm saying this because yours might get a whole lot worse."

Felix's eyes narrowed, his voice cutting through the tension. "What does that mean?"

Noah sighed, "You remember the incident four years ago, right? The government tried to destroy your island base, claiming you were aiding terrorism."

Felix lost his temper with Noah's unnecessary reminder. "Remember? I'm still licking my wounds from that fiasco."

Noah leaned forward and tutted at Felix. "On the surface, it was an operation carried out by the CIA and the FBI. They intervened, but the mastermind behind the whole plan to get rid of you was Cole Patricks."

Felix's patience snapped. "I know. I know it very well. That's why I'm calling him a motherfucking bastard."

Noah threw him the bait almost pityingly, "But what you didn't know was that the forces Cole sent after you…were DEVGRU."

Felix's jaw dropped, his mind spinning as the words hung in the air. The truth dawned on him slowly, like a chilling revelation he could barely process. The truth…it couldn't be…

"I can tell by your expression you've guessed it."

"Don't you dare say Isaac was involved."

"I wouldn't, except, unfortunately, you're right. Four years ago, the DEVGRU team sent to your island was led by Kaysid, and that team was annihilated." Felix sighed at Noah's words. "The team you wiped out— the one you used all your fancy new weapons on to teach them a lesson—was Kaysid's."

God. A faint groan escaped his throat. His head spun. He wanted to stop hearing this. It was easier when he knew nothing. Yet Noah voiced the conclusion, "The only survivor of the DEVGRU team that attacked your base was Isaac."

Felix's eyes fluttered shut of their own accord. His breath caught like someone was choking him. Noah watched him, then sighed. "Now, do you understand why you're fucked?"

Chapter 35

The second-floor hallway was quiet. Although the estate was mourning, the air on the second floor felt incredibly still and heavy. Felix listened to the echo of his footsteps as he opened the bedroom door.

Isaac, whom he'd left sleeping in the room, had been deep in slumber with no signs of waking before Felix went to see Noah. But now, the bed was empty, and Isaac was nowhere to be seen. The mattress was exposed, the rumpled, lukewarm sheets proof that someone had been there only moments ago.

Felix brushed his fingers over the sheets before turning around. He walked a few steps down the hallway until a low voice stopped him. It was familiar. Felix strained his ears toward the soft, elegant tone, his feet moving as if drawn by an invisible force.

The door was half-open. The golden light of the setting sun filled the neat little room, creating a serene mood. Beyond the large window, the blue ocean stretched over the hills below, a picture-perfect view. One wall was painted with Mickey Mouse and his friends, and a bed shaped like Mickey's car was beneath it. The bedspread matched, also Mickey-themed. Another wall had rows of bookcases full of children's books and toys.

It was the room Felix had prepared for Benjamin. In the center, Isaac stood like a shadow, his back to Felix, speaking softly into the phone, "I'll do anything you ask of me."

Felix didn't need to ask to know who he was speaking to. Isaac's voice, however, was calmer than he'd expected. There was no trace of temper, no hint of killing intent. He was simply having a conversation as if it were any other day.

"When should I be there? Understood. Promise me one thing: Don't touch Benjamin or my mother."

Felix felt a chill from Isaac's indifferent tone. This was a situation where his mother and the child he valued more than his life had been kidnapped. Just that morning, Isaac had been crying and screaming before passing out. But now, awake, he was answering the phone calmly as any other day. His unnervingly calm demeanor raised questions even considering he'd been asleep until late afternoon.

How many people could maintain such composure in a situation like this? Would Felix be able to stay so collected if he were in Isaac's shoes? No, he would not. He would be consumed by rage, ablaze with wrath.

Felix clicked his tongue inwardly, watching Isaac's shadow. As he did, the call ended. Isaac tucked the phone into his pocket as if it were just another mundane conversation and slowly turned to face Felix.

In that instant, Felix instinctively hunched his shoulders at the eerie chill radiating from Isaac. His expression was strange. Like on the phone, there was no hint of murderous intent or anger. And yet, his cold, deadened black eyes were bloodcurdling. The pupils were sharpened to a knife's edge as if a single touch would slice Felix's hand.

When Felix remained silent, his tension palpable as he simply stared at Isaac, the latter turned toward the Mickey Mouse on the wall and asked, "This room…did you decorate it for Benjamin?"

Felix snapped out of his daze and answered, "Yes. I was going to have your mother and Benjamin move in here. I thought it would be safest if they lived in my house."

It was a bit too late for that now, though. Felix whispered the words like an apology, even though Isaac hadn't said anything. Isaac looked around slowly and nodded.

"It's a pretty room," he said, his tone emotionless.

Felix remembered Isaac once telling him that Benjamin liked Mickey Mouse. The memory resurfaced of Isaac holding a cute Mickey Mouse card in his hand, quite unlike himself, wearing a dreamy expression of joy.

That image lingered stubbornly in Felix's mind, like a fading aftereffect. This is why he had the room decorated with Mickey Mouse themes and personally chose the bed shaped like Mickey's red car. He had hoped to see Benjamin's eyes light up with happiness and Isaac's soft smile as he watched the joyful child.

But instead of that wish, he was granted this…fuckery. His insides burned with a bitterness that felt like acid.

"I never made a room like this for Benjamin. We could never stay in one place for long. We always had to move." Isaac spoke in a tone far different from when he'd opened the Mickey Mouse card and held a pen. The once-dreamy expression was now gone, replaced by emptiness, devoid of emotion.

Felix couldn't find the words to respond. Bitterness coated his tongue.

"I never had the chance to decorate a room for him like this or even play with him." There was guilt in Isaac's toneless voice. "I couldn't do anything for him—except involve him in something terrible."

Felix exhaled slowly. *It's not your fault*, he wanted to say, but the words didn't come easily, stuck in his throat.

Instead, he listened to Isaac's confession, "Before I came to San Diego, I moved around overseas a lot. It was rough. Then I came here and finally had a few months of peace. I think that's what made me forget my place."

"Isaac."

"I got used to this peaceful life and became careless. And as a result, I endangered my mother and Benjamin. You got hurt because of me. I know many of your men are dead or injured, too." Isaac's gaze fell to Felix's shoulder, and he sighed. He seemed to be looking right through his shirt, exactly at the bandaged wound beneath it.

Felix lifted his perplexed gaze. Back then, Isaac hadn't been aware that Felix was chasing after him at all—after all, he had been completely consumed by the search for his kidnapped mother and Benjamin. He had lost sight of the van, watched it disappear, and then, unable to maintain his indifferent mask, had broken down in sobs. How was it, then, that Isaac was now so calm and composed, taking everything in?

"I'm sorry. Thank you. If not for you, I'd be dead right now."

"It's nothing." Felix tutted, finding Isaac's apology misplaced. He didn't need it—not the apology or the thanks. Hearing Isaac say these unexpected things only made his chest tighten.

"You must have been the one who sniped them from outside, right?" Isaac asked again, his tone indifferent, but the question cutting through the air. "Thinking about it, only you would have the skills to fire a rifle in that situation."

"I simply happened to have a new weapon I wanted to try out. Don't worry about it." Felix shrugged, brushing it off. He didn't want Isaac to waste energy on such trivial matters. Isaac had enough to deal with as it was.

"I've been receiving an excessive amount of help from you all along."

"It was a fair contract. And I know I'm to blame for not perfectly protecting your mother and Benjamin. So tell me, what do you need? How can I help you?"

Isaac looked up at Felix's firm reply. The edge in his gaze had dulled slightly, but his pupils were still bone-chillingly cold. Felix stifled a sigh when their eyes met and waited for Isaac to speak first, "I know I'm being audacious saying this to you, but…I need your help."

"Of course." *I'll give you anything you want,* Felix answered silently, watching as Isaac hesitated, biting his torn, chapped lips. Then Isaac spoke.

"What are you capable of?" His voice dropped as if sharing a secret.

Felix tilted his head, frowning in confusion. Parrying the demand with one of his own, he replied, "Capable? If you're asking about my position and wealth, I need to know how you plan to use it first."

Isaac stared at him, his expression unreadable. Slowly, he responded with a question Felix hadn't expected, causing his eyes to narrow.

"Hypothetically speaking, if I wanted to…kill someone in a high position, could you help?"

z

To be continued in
Dear Benjamin
Volume 2

Dear Benjamin